The Critic's Choice—*Angel Fire*

"*Angel Fire* is Ron Franscell's debut novel and documents him as an author with an immense ability for language and storytelling. Highly recommended."—Midwest Book Review

"Franscell transcends the temptation to be trite and formulaic. His themes—hard to describe without giving away the ending—are not only of loss and restoration, or of a serach for self. They also involve a fresh measuring of popular plot vehicle in our national fiction—early rural roots as a font for the elusive American spirit. Finishing *Angel Fire* leaves the reader with that feeling characteristic of many great reads—a sort of pleasing intellectual exhaustion, a feeling that one has literally climbed back to real life from the pages themselves. It's a brief mood that finds the reader reflecting on not only the fate of the characters, but on the human condition. It doesn't happen very often. It happened with this novel."   —John Hanchette, *USA Today*

"Franscell has a wonderful command of the English language and a writing style that cannot fail to capture the reader's imagination. Recommended."   —*Library Journal*

"...undeniable proof that not all stellar literary works come from big publishing houses ... Laughing Owl Publishing was smart to recognize Franscell's brilliance. Readers should ... follow suit."
                                                    —*The Denver Post*

"The most powerful novel I've read this year ... destined to become a classic."   —Greg Bean

"...deep insights and understanding of the human condition rarely seen in contemporary novels."—Warren Adler, *War of the Roses.*

"*Angel Fire* is an imaginative, riveting book. Lets's hope we see more of his work soon."   —*San Bernardino County Sun*

"Like Ray Bradbury's *Dandelion Wine*, though in a much harder and less sentimental vein, Franscell's book has a dreamy, intoxicating quality, full of wistful nostalgia and melancholy. The book gives a glimpse through the gauze of memory of a place and time."

—*The Boulder Camera*

THE DEADLINE

A Mystery
by
Ron Franscell

A Write Way Publishing Book

This is a work of fiction. Names, characters, locales and incidents are either the product of the author's imagination or are used fictitiously, and any resemblance to actual persons, living or dead, is entirely coincidental.

To ASHLEY and MATTHEW
Who never set any deadline
for my becoming a good father

"This is the Hour of Lead—
Remembered, if outlived,
As freezing persons recollect the snow—
First chill—then stupor—then the letting go."

—Emily Dickinson

"In the earnest struggle to influence men's minds
... you must alienate some."

Bruce Kennedy
Weekly newspaperman

THE BRIDGE:
August, 1948

In the sunlight, the child's blood was brilliant red and smelled like wet, musty earth. His frightened hands were sticky with it.

He wished for her to wake up, nearly spoke it out loud, but she was pale and dead. He was sure of it, even before he brushed a fly from her lifeless lips with his bloody finger.

A nervous sweat prickled on his back. Her tiny body was heavier than before. She was only nine years old, with only ten feet between the car and the abyss, but he could barely lift her out of the back seat.

His rapid breathing suddenly stopped.

His heart thundered inside his chest, choking him. He froze.

A plume of dust rose from the road, two or three miles back. The dry air scratched his unblinking eyes as he watched the dust curl toward heaven, then disappear.

A dust devil.

He wasted no more time. He wormed his arms beneath her body, clutching her to his aching chest. As he staggered away from the car, he felt her blood seeping into his shirt. He draped her over the railing like a rag doll on a fence wire while he caught his breath.

For a moment, death seemed a soothing thought. He never wanted to hurt her. He looked down into the dizzying canyon and the railing dissolved under him. In his mind, he plummeted through his shame, toward the water. She would open her eyes and go for help, and the whole awful mess would be finished.

Tears streamed down his face. He stood in a puddle of his own piss.

And before he let her corpse drop, he looked over the edge to make sure she would hit the water, not hang up on a canyon outcrop or a steel rod. The only sounds he heard were the prairie winds whistling across the gaping maw of the gorge and the thundering brown water far below. It boiled and growled, waiting to be fed.

The solitary witness was a red-tailed hawk that drifted in wide circles in the cloud-shredded blue sky over the gorge. He spotted it only because he'd looked up when he let her body slip over the railing; he couldn't watch her fall, so he looked at the sky.

The bird's presence unnerved him. He filled his mind with crazy thoughts so he wouldn't hear her splash. For a moment, he even imagined she had transformed into the hawk, that her soul had taken wing as she plunged toward the water. But he knew better. It was just a carrion-eater in search of dead flesh to eat.

Maybe hers.

By the time he finished vomiting in the road, she had been swallowed by the river and was being slowly digested in its icy bowels.

A drunken fisherman named Pick Sandefur found her bloated body wedged between some jagged rocks in the Black Thunder River. He smelled putrefying flesh long before he stumbled upon it. Water-logged meat floated in the backwash like a fringe of pale lace around her fishbelly-white corpse.

Sandefur scrambled out of the canyon and floored his pickup over twelve miles of bad road back to Winchester, mumbling to himself all the way. He was still so shaken when he arrived, he bounced his truck onto the courthouse lawn and left it to catch its breath while he ran inside to tell the sheriff.

Though it was no longer recognizable to the deputies who fished it out of the water, they knew what it was: Aimee Little Spotted Horse, a nine-year-old girl, had been missing for ten days.

***

The day Aimee disappeared, in the fallow time between midsummer haying and fall roundup, her mother and father were riding the Sun-Seven Ranch's fence, a barbed-wire boundary that encircled more than seventy-thousand acres of prime prairie grasslands. They'd left her alone that morning, as they often did, while they tended to ranch chores for their boss, Jack Madigan.

The last time they saw their daughter she was still asleep in a tangle of handmade quilts on a wooden pallet in their abandoned homesteader's shack on Poison Creek.

It was dark when they returned, and Aimee was gone.

An unfinished garland of yellow tickseed flowers was scattered on the rough-hewn porch, a little girl's idle project in pieces. The door was standing open and her only pair of shoes was still in the cabin. Nothing else was missing, except Aimee.

Search parties combed the north-county for a week, but their numbers dwindled as swiftly as their hope that she was still alive. When Pick Sandefur, the fisherman, found Aimee's body in the river, she was more than twenty-eight miles from the Poison Creek homestead. She didn't get there alone.

Derealous McWayne, the only mortician within eighty miles, had been elected eight times as the county coroner because nobody else in Perry County felt so comfortable in the company of death. So it was McWayne's official duty to ease his lumbering Oldsmobile hearse up the rutted road to a narrow turn-out below the Iron Mountain Bridge. A renowned eater whose prodigious appetite was never quelled by his work, the corpulent mortician waited on the road for the deputies to carry Aimee Little Spotted Horse's body up the steep talus slope. They stumbled all the way, like drunken pall-bearers, her water-logged body slung between them on a tarp.

Just standing there in the afternoon heat, letting his protruding eyes scan the precipitous canyon and the rumbling water below, the fat coroner sweated profusely.

A photograph in Winchester's weekly *Bullet* showed a fleshy-faced Derealous McWayne, his short-sleeved white shirt stained with sweat beneath the arms, sliding a metal gurney into the back of his fat, black hearse. On it was a bloated heap hidden by a wet sheet. She'd been in the water too long for there to be any recognizable shape to her tiny body in death.

Within a few hours, a deputy found a scrap of Aimee's thin cotton blouse fluttering from a bolt on the guardrail of the Iron Mountain Bridge, a mile upstream from where her tattered, pulpous body was lodged. A day later, bloodhounds found more of her shredded cotton blouse and bloody denim trousers washed up on a sand bar.

A small-town coroner who had no experience in forensic pathology, McWayne could not officially determine the direct cause of Aimee's death. Her body was too damaged by the violent river even to know for sure if any of her wounds were inflicted before she went into the water. And in some places, her mushy flesh had been nibbled by fish. Her hands were shriveled from soaking in the river, and the skin slipped easily off in his hands. Her body's advanced decay suggested she'd died around the same time she disappeared. He'd seen "floaters" like this before, clumsy fishermen whose gassy bodies were fished out of the voracious Black Thunder River every other summer. But they died accidentally; Aimee was something different altogether.

The next day, Dr. Henry Gwinnett, for three decades the only doctor in Winchester and, at 74, dying slowly from diabetes, performed a superficial autopsy.

Despite his training, the soft-spoken Dr. Gwinnett had always been disturbed by the sight of a child's body in the morgue. He prayed briefly before he cut a wide incision from her neck to her groin. A rancid stench belched out as mossy, brown water spilled onto the floor of Derealous McWayne's usually immaculate embalming-room floor and splashed the old doctor's scuffed wingtips. The scummy fluid had seeped in through numerous tears and gashes in her frail skin.

Her internal organs were decomposing. Gwinnett examined and weighed her heart and liver, opened her stomach and bowels but found nothing unusual. He respectfully waited until McWayne was called out of the room to inspect the girl's vagina and rectum. He finished in a few minutes and made some notes to himself before the coroner returned.

Gwinnett found enough water in Aimee's lungs to leave open the possibility that she had drowned, but not enough to say it definitely caused her death. No diagnosis of drowning was ever certain, but usually the result of eliminating all other possible causes of death. Aimee Little Spotted Horse was not shot and did not appear to have any stab wounds, but beyond that, the condition of her body made it impossible for him to determine if she'd been strangled, poisoned or beaten.

"My best guess," he told the sheriff later, "is she was alive when she went over the rail, and died in the water. I pray to God she never knew what happened."

Perry County Sheriff Deuce Kerrigan further surmised Aimee was thrown into the water at least partially clothed, but the violently raging waters had swept her little body toward oblivion and ripped her clothing off. He had no stomach for lurid details, real or imagined; the job of notifying the next of kin was difficult enough without the odd horrors that accompany death.

In the end, the coroner simply wrote on the death certificate what Kerrigan told him to write: "Homicide." How it happened that Aimee Little Spotted Horse turned up dead so far from home, he couldn't say. He couldn't even guess. He left the guessing to the sheriff and went home to dinner.

The whole town of Winchester, Wyoming, was gossiping about the murder of Aimee Little Spotted Horse. The stories had their own lives, suffused with secret spites and shades of fancy. Her father was a heathen drunkard and probably beat the little girl to death in one of his boozy rages, they said.

He'd beaten her before, they knew from the court blotter in
The Bullet, so it was a good theory for lawyerly housewives
trying the case over the back fence.

Or the girl's mother did it, they said, because squaws' savage breeding robbed them of the proper instinct. Like killing a
litter of unwanted kittens by tying them in a burlap sack and
tossing them in the irrigation canal, which was a sorry task that
fell to any farm wife, but that was very different. Civilized
mothers would never do that to a child, but Indian mothers
would, the proper white ladies said over their laundry and bridge
tables, as if the raw genetics of self-survival had flooded out the
native mother's instincts to protect her children.

Two weeks after the quiet funeral in the Madigan family
cemetery, an out-of-work sawmill hand named Neeley Gilmartin
was arrested for the murder of Aimee Little Spotted Horse.

Gilmartin had been fingered by a couple of the pool-hall
regulars. They claimed Gilmartin was dead drunk when he
lost a stud poker game a few months before in the back room
at the Cozy Club out Highway 57. He picked a fight with
Charlie Little Spotted Horse, who'd finally had a bellyful of
being called "a cheatin' mother-fuckin' prairie nigger."

Gilmartin threw the first punch, they told the sheriff, a
blow that flattened the Indian's nose and spattered blood on
the other players. Charlie flew across the table. The two men
tumbled in the sawdust until he got his hand on a beer bottle
and smashed it across Gilmartin's skull.

And they were fairly certain that the enraged Neeley
Gilmartin, blood spattered in a red web across his face, promised "to make that dirty fuckin' squaw-nigger sorry he ever
was fuckin' born."

That was enough for Deuce Kerrigan. Just after sunrise on
a dewy September morning, Deuce himself arrested Gilmartin.
He found him still asleep in the arms of a prostitute at a
brothel down on the railroad tracks. The sheriff had his Colt

cocked and ready when a startled Gilmartin leaped straight up in the bed and stood there on the mattress confused and naked, his penis semi-erect.

His only possessions were a bottle of bootleg whiskey he'd bought at the front desk, a pile of smoky clothes, a couple of torn ticket stubs from the Biograph Movie Theater, and a black leather wallet containing eighty-five dollars.

The authorities of Perry County knew Gilmartin well enough. The former sailor had spent a month of Sundays in the drunk tank, and two six-month sentences in the past four years for assault and battery. He couldn't stay out of bar fights and he couldn't tell the truth to save his life. In one, he'd bitten a man's ear clean off and denied he was even in the bar. Once he dried out, he got on well with his jailers, but he was such a violent drunk, deputies regularly beat him with the thick oak truncheons hidden in a jail broom closet.

Gilmartin was a tough son of a bitch. Short and sturdy, he was barely twenty-five years old and well suited to the heavy work in the mill, when he was sober. His arms were smooth and well muscled, with a malevolent tattoo on his left biceps: TERROR. His chest was thick and hairy, tapering down his flat stomach to narrow hips.

Gilmartin's black hair was shaved close on the sides, but tumbled in uncombed, greasy curls across his forehead. A swollen red welt kept his left eye almost closed, and his thick upper lip was split by a fresh gash.

Perry County Judge Darby Hand appointed the unluckiest lawyer in Winchester to defend him. Not that he had much of a choice. Simeon Fenwick, who had the pretentious habit of signing "Esq." after his name, even on his personal checks, was one of only four lawyers in town. And to be fair, none of them had ever defended a capital case.

The choice of Sim Fenwick was defensible, if only because he had as good a shot as any of them to get his client acquit-

ted, and that chance was zero. Zero because the public sentiment against Gilmartin was already simmering, and because
the lackluster, bookish Sim Fenwick had never tried a criminal case before.

When Sim Fenwick, just six years out of law school, first
visited his new client in the courthouse's basement jail, a deputy
sat nearby and later reported every word to Sheriff Kerrigan.
But it didn't matter. A defensive, nervous Gilmartin told his
lawyer what he'd told the sheriff and the two deputies who'd
roughed him up that first morning: He didn't know anything
about anything.

"Where were you on the day she disappeared?"

"What day was that?"

"The second."

"Fuck if I know," Gilmartin growled, taking a long drag
on a cigarette. The smoke curled toward the open barred
jailhouse window high above them. It was the only ventila-
tion they had.

"Did you ever threaten the girl's father?" the lawyer asked
him.

Gilmartin shrugged, staring at the floor.

"Can you help me at all?" Fenwick said.

Gilmartin rocked silently with his head bent forward above
his knees. His powerful forearms rippled as he laced his calloused hands behind his head, covering his ears.

Gilmartin was headed straight to Hell and he knew it.

County Attorney Calvin Davis, a stuffed shirt whose ran-
cor for criminals was rivaled only by his political savvy, was
on his way up. Playing matchmaker to the child-killer Gilmartin
and "Big Sparky"—the pet name of the Wyoming State
Penitentiary's electric chair—would only enhance his guberna-
torial prospects.

Gilmartin's lawyer was a nervous little mouse, the public
was growing more antagonistic as each day passed, and the

judge was known among the county's criminal class as severe and unmerciful. Without saying as much, a photograph in the local paper made him out to be a child-killing monster. Worst of all, he had no alibi and his mind was too muddled to lie convincingly.

Gilmartin saw no forgiveness in his abbreviated future.

He pressed a lighted cigarette against the inside of his wrist and tried to imagine what it would feel like to have a lightning bolt rip through his body, cooking his guts and frying his brain. After dark, demons visited his sleep. One night, he shit his pants there in the dark and awoke crying like a baby.

Gilmartin heard voices in the dark. Some were real voices, driving by on the street outside the courthouse. Although most the basement jail was submerged beneath ground-level, its narrow, grated windows were placed high on the interior wall and opened onto the courthouse lawn. He could hear them, jeering and throwing beer bottles and revving their engines: *Burn in hell, you son of a bitch!* they yelled as they passed. *Fry, you fuckin' baby-killer!*

The guards made no effort to quell the slow, deliberate parade of hateful kids who circled the courthouse most of the night. To them, it seemed fair enough.

Other voices came from inside him. Voices from the past, long dead.

Would he feel the heat flash through him before he died? Did they?

As much as any living man, he knew what it was like to die by fire. Sometimes he held his forearm tight against his nostrils, blocking some odor that only he could smell. The memory of charred flesh seared his brain, its unearthly smell haunting him still. He was frightened.

For three nights after that first meeting with Sim Fenwick, he dreamed not just about dying, but about being cooked alive in Big Sparky, a killing contraption he imagined to be part iron maiden and part torture-fire wired directly to Hell.

The nights were endless, the horror of his memories unrelenting. *The fire* ...

On the fourth morning, he scribbled an anxious note to his lawyer, summoning him to the jail immediately.

Gilmartin, boiling with fear, proposed a deal. Begged for it. He'd plead guilty to Aimee Little Spotted Horse's murder if his life would be spared.

"Are you sure about this?" Fenwick asked him.

"Don't fuck with me now," he said. "They'll pay you just the same. Just take this to the man."

Half relieved, Sim Fenwick trudged up two flights through empty, echoing stairwells, and knocked meekly at the prosecutor's door. For two days, Calvin Davis let Gilmartin's hasty note sit under his green desk blotter, allowing the prisoner's raw nerves to stew a little longer. He felt in no particular hurry to offer a child-killer solace. Privately, he had his doubts about winning a death sentence anyway, because the evidence was weak.

Gilmartin couldn't fight off the death dreams. He sat awake, his gut knotted around him like a noose, waiting for word from the prosecutor. He vomited so much, the deputies stopped bringing food.

Barely three weeks after he'd been arrested, the county prosecutor accepted his plea. Gilmartin was hideously relieved. He'd spend the rest of his life in prison, but he wouldn't die. Not by fire anyway.

The sheriff made him sign some papers he couldn't read, then left him alone in his cell. He smoked a cigarette and slept for the first time in two days. The next morning, two deputies shackled him and stuffed him in the back seat of Deuce Kerrigan's black Buick for the five-hour drive to the Wyoming State Penitentiary.

CHAPTER ONE
Late July, 1996

Time passed in Winchester, Wyoming, at more or less the same rate as any other forgotten town on the edge of the high plains, but *The Bullet*'s newsroom clock appeared to be running backward.

The last time Jefferson Morgan had looked at the clock, just a few minutes before, it was almost eleven. Indeed, his wristwatch said it was eleven. Deadline.

But the clock on the wall now read ten-fifty. And four front-page stories were still unwritten.

Morgan thumped his watch. He had no way of knowing his two smart-ass reporters cranked the big hand back ten minutes at deadline time almost every Wednesday, stealing just a little more time to write stories that were, for the most part, already a week old.

Morgan watched as his impatient printer, Cal Nussbaum, whose own ink-smudged backshop clock was set *forward* ten minutes, prowled the jumbled newsroom. Anger stretched his long face even longer.

"Nobody gives a good goddamn about deadlines anymore," he mumbled.

The press was ready, if the news was not. The ink fountains filled, Cal rubbed his massive hands in a greasy black rag. He faced Morgan in the narrow space between the newsroom's prehistoric oak desks, dragging a vapor trail of oily ink, solvent and body odor.

Cal had worked for *The Bullet* since he was a kid back in the Forties, when he made fifty cents a day as a printer's devil.

Cal's veins ran inky black. He hated reporters. Their only virtue, in his mind, was their egotistic ambition to do less work for more pay: Few of them stayed more than a year.

The more Cal knew about young reporters, the more he preferred the company of pressroom rats. And for the reporters who dared trespass in his space, he displayed on his backshop wall several years worth of girlie calendars left by newsprint salesmen. It was a trifling rebellion, except that it asserted the sovereignty of Cal's borders.

Nonetheless, until the newsroom clock ticked past the eleven AM deadline, Cal restrained himself, barely.

"Wouldn'ta happened when Old Bell was around," he complained.

"Old Bell"—Belleau Wood Cockins—had been the editor of *The Bullet* for more than fifty years. When he sold out to Jefferson Morgan a month before, he just cleaned out the deep drawers of his desk, packed up the only two reference books he ever needed—an annotated Shakespeare and a King James version of the Bible—and handed Morgan the keys. He never came back.

Since that day four weeks before, Morgan hadn't met a single deadline, and it pissed him off. The damned paper wouldn't even have been delivered on time if Cal Nussbaum hadn't bribed the boys at the post office with a twelve-pack of Coors every week.

In almost eighteen years at the *Chicago Tribune*, where the massive machinery of journalism churned every minute of every day in a near-perfect synchronicity, Morgan had never known anyone to challenge the consecrated institution of The Deadline. It existed as a kind of covenant between newspapermen and their deluded gods, and punishment would be swift and painful if it were ever violated. It was somehow sacrilegious that here, *in the very newsroom where Old Bell Cockins gave him his first byline,* the sin of missing a deadline could be atoned with twelve beers.

Morgan hovered over his two reporters, a pair of $250-a-week community college grads who'd been at *The Bullet* for less than a year. They bent their heads toward their ancient Macintoshes, pecking away at their late stories, always keeping the editor in the periphery of their sight.

The tiny brass bell above the front door jingled.

Morgan glanced up. Crystal Sandoval, the counter girl who took classified ads, renewed subscriptions, answered the phone and calmed all but the angriest readers with her friendly smile, was away from her chair.

The frail old man who shuffled through *The Bullet*'s door looked lost. He slouched across the foyer's checkered tile, as if gravity itself threatened to drag him under. His sharp face was hollow, almost cadaverous. A ragged thatch of white hair tangled at the sides of his bald head like dead weeds flattened under a weathered fence. The long sleeves of a stiff blue shirt hung past his wrists; the collar was buttoned at his skinny throat, and his canvas belt was cinched so tight around his thin hips that the waistband of his brown trousers folded in a thick pleat at the front.

The old man looked around. His dark, sunken eyes were as sharp and serious as a worn sawtooth.

"Sorry. The paper's not out yet," Morgan apologized. Readers often visited *The Bullet* before noon on Wednesdays to snatch one of the first papers off the press. Over tuna melts and iced tea down at The Griddle, every word—from the police blotter to the Little League results to the editor's weekly column—would be cussed and discussed.

"Ain't here for no paper. You the editor?" the old man asked Morgan. His voice was a coarse scrape.

"That's me. What can I do for you?" Morgan asked, circling around the reporters' desks to the waist-high, swinging wooden gate that separated the tiny waiting area from the newsroom. He held a piece of copy paper with some scribbled notes in his left hand, as he extended his right courteously across the gate.

The old man's hand was knobby and dry, his wan grip as cold and blue as the paper-thin skin stretched across his arthritic knuckles. The insides of his knotted index and middle fingers were stained brown, and his fingernails were cracked and yellow. Shaking his hand, Morgan smelled stale cigarettes and aging flesh.

"You don't know me," the old man said, lowering his voice to almost a whisper. "My name's Gilmartin. Neeley Gilmartin."

He waited for some recognition from Morgan, but Gilmartin wasn't a name he knew.

"Glad to meet you, Mr. Gilmartin. I'm Jeff Morgan. I've only got a minute. We're just finishing up the paper and I was just ..."

An impatient glower settled on Gilmartin's brow.

"I ain't got no time for fuckin' around here either," he rasped, suddenly less brittle than he'd first appeared.

"Mr. Gilmartin, I understand, but this is a bad time for me. Can you come back in an hour or two, after we put out the paper? Then we can talk."

The old man waved him off, as if he were brushing away a fly. The cracked corners of his mouth turned down in disgust.

"I'll wait right here. No place else I gotta be. Go sell your goddam papers," Gilmartin said, shuffling toward the three spindle-backed Windsor chairs lining one wall of the cramped foyer. He eased his bony hips into the farthest from the window.

"And don't make me wait all fuckin' day," Gilmartin sniped. His face twinged in discomfort as he fished a crumpled

pack of Camels from his shirt pocket. He knocked one out of
the squarish package and wedged it between his thin, crooked
lips. Then he took it out again, stiffening momentarily, his
eyes closed so tight his face seemed to fold at the middle.

There was pain in this old man.

The stories were an hour late.

Cal Nussbaum was so angry he wouldn't even speak as he
sliced long slicks of type into precise blocks, carving off wasted
margins of white paper like a butcher cuts fat off a good steak.
The pages fell together under Cal's knife, and he finished his
work long past the time he'd normally go to lunch. The old
four-unit Goss Community press waited, its hungry black belly
rumbling.

Morgan was angry, too. He jammed a pica pole in his
back pocket and felt his jaw tighten as he left the backshop,
preparing to reprimand his reporters for their insouciance
about deadlines. He composed his come-to-Jesus sermon in
his head as he threaded his way down the narrow hallway, past
the pungent bathroom that doubled as a darkroom, toward
the newsroom.

But the reporters were gone. They'd sneaked out to lunch
like scared, hungry fugitives. The newsroom was quiet except
for the metallic ticking of the ceiling fan that droned inces-
santly all summer, occasionally sailing a stray sheet of paper
off the litter-strewn archipelago of desks.

But Gilmartin hadn't left.

For two hours, he'd squirmed his aching hips in the hardpan wooden chair, chain-smoking and watching townfolk pass
The Bullet's gold-lettered front window. If a passerby looked
in, Gilmartin turned away.

From time to time, he'd get up and read the yellowing
front-pages Old Bell had hung on the foyer wall. Five decades
worth of the town's biggest stories, banner headlines tall and
thick, lined up across the wall in earnest black frames. "SLURRY

BOMBER DOUSES THEATER FIRE," said one. "BASEBALL
PARK NAMED FOR BIG-LEAGUER," said another.

The old man lingered in front of one in particular: "GIRL'S
KILLER CONFESSES."

The swinging gate into the front foyer squealed as Morgan
stepped through. The checkered floor around the old man's
shoes was dusted with cigarette ashes.

"Mr. Gilmartin, I'm very sorry it took me so long. I guess
we're going to have to get better at this newspaper stuff," he
said. He smiled but wasn't in the mood to make excuses for
his indolent reporters. "Anyway, can I get you anything? Coffee? Water?"

The old man turned around and glared at him. If his
body was slowly decaying, the fire in his eyes was not. He
ignored Morgan's offer.

"Where's the old guy who used to be here?" Gilmartin
asked.

"Bell Cockins? He retired about a month ago. You know
him?"

"Yeah, a long time ago. I been away."

"Things change pretty quick, even here, I guess," Morgan
said.

Gilmartin pointed at the newspaper on the wall.

"You read this shit?"

"Some of it," Morgan said. "There's a lot of local history
up there."

"Fuck that," Gilmartin scoffed. "Some of it is bullshit."

Morgan was a little surprised.

"How's that?"

Gilmartin put his finger on one of the front-page photos,
the one he'd studied so long. In it, a young man, an accused
killer, glared banefully at the camera over his tattooed shoulder. The look was malignant and cold.

"That's me," Gilmartin said.

Morgan didn't believe it, or couldn't. *This old man, a killer?*

He studied the photo and looked at the old man. The body had wasted away, but the eyes were the same. The old man wasn't lying.

Gilmartin patted down a pack of Camels, searching for one more. It was empty.

"You got a smoke?" he asked. Morgan shook his head. Exasperated, Gilmartin tossed the crumpled pack on the pile of unfiltered butts in the ashtray beside him.

"I need a smoke bad," the old man said, scowling. He sidled stiffly past Morgan to the front door. Hot air boiled off the sidewalk as he held it open.

"I gotta get outta here. The place stinks," he said impatiently. "You comin' or just breathin' hard?"

Morgan looked around the empty newsroom. Cal Nussbaum leaned against a doorway, watching them. When Morgan caught his eye, Cal shook his head in disgust and disappeared into the back.

They walked a block down Main Street to the Conoco, the nearest cigarette machine. It was midday in late July, hot enough to curdle the asphalt were the street met the gutter. Gilmartin shuffled along, sweating. Morgan could hear him breathing hard before they'd taken a dozen steps, but he persisted.

"I ain't got no silver," the old man said, patting his pockets. Morgan had just enough change for two packs. Gilmartin hastily stripped off the cellophane, peeled back the top of one pack and whacked it against the heel of his palm. He clamped his lips around the cigarette that stuck out farthest, then lit up.

Gilmartin took a long drag and exhaled slowly, letting the smoke seep out of him in devilish blue curls. He stuffed both packs safely in his breast pocket, which now bulged against his cratered chest.

"I been smokin' all my life and it ain't killed me yet. Ain't gonna get a chance to kill me neither," Gilmartin said, then paused while he took another long draw at his cigarette. "You ever come close to dyin'?"

"Maybe once," Morgan answered. He shoved his hands deep in the empty pockets of his khaki slacks and studied Gilmartin's face. He was reluctant to share personal information with the old man, but it sounded to him as if a door might be opened.

"I was just a kid, maybe seven or eight. I was playing alone on an inflatable raft out at Rochelle Lake. The wind came up and blew me out farther and farther into the deep water. Nobody heard me screaming. I was afraid the raft would spring a leak or tip over and I'd drown. I held on for dear life until a fisherman came by and pulled me out."

Gilmartin looked even paler and more pinched in the harsh sunlight. He avoided looking at Morgan as he spoke, just peered down into the gutter, where a thin drool of muddy water trickled almost imperceptibly toward the storm drain. He flipped an ash into the tiny stream, where it floated a few feet then dissolved.

"You make any deals when you was out there? You promise your god that you'd be a good little boy if he'd just blow your scared little ass back to shore? Did you lie to Him just to save yourself?"

The sun was hot and the smell of gasoline overpowering as they stood there on the corner by the gas station. Morgan scuffed the sole of his worn leather Oxford across the sidewalk as if he were trying to scrape something off, but he was trying to remember what it felt like to encounter death. The skin on his back prickled in the heat as he imagined, all over again, cold water spilling into his lungs, weighing him down, clamping his throat closed.

"Not any I remember. I was just scared. I didn't want to die."

"You do dumb shit when you think you might die," the old man said, smoking and watching the empty street in front of them.

The air was dead calm. Smoke hovered around Gilmartin.

He tilted his head back and breathed deeply through the cigarette, his cheeks sucking slowly inward. His hand trembled. Then from nowhere, a cough wracked his whole body, distorting his face as it erupted from deep inside.

"Let's find someplace cool to sit, Mr. Gilmartin," Morgan suggested, touching the old man's elbow.

"Yeah, sure, paper boy."

Across the street and up past a few storefronts was Winchester Park, a patch of sprinkled green near the center of town. They sat on a concrete bench in the cool shade beneath the towering cottonwoods. Birds bickered unseen in the branches above them. The playground thirty yards away was crawling with children on summer vacation.

"I'm not sure what you need from me, Mr. Gilmartin," Morgan said, his leg bent across the park bench as he faced the old man.

"I need your help to do something I can't do for myself. I'm seventy-three fuckin' years old and I can hardly wipe my ass without help. If I could do this thing on my own, I would," Gilmartin said. He fumbled in his lumpy shirt pocket for another cigarette. "I hate reporters, but I ain't got no other choice. I need *you*."

Morgan learned one good lesson on the cop beat: Don't waste time being indignant. Only the amateurs stay mad, his city editor once told him.

"Okay, fair enough. But let's cut to the chase here. Why me and what for?" Morgan asked coolly.

Gilmartin scratched his skeletal fingers through the thin mat of his white hair and stared between his knees at the thick grass. His trousers draped across his emaciated thighs and the muscles at the back of his bent neck bowed out like the slack cords on a marionette. He sat unmoving for a while, elbows on his knees, cupping a lighted cigarette in his palm.

"I ain't proud of what I am, but I ain't no killer," Gilmartin said. "I been almost fifty years in prison for a crime I never done. That's the fuckin' truth. When I was your age, I already done thirteen years of hard time and I was lookin' at a life-time still to go. It was like dyin' real slow. Back then, I made some choices to save my life, and maybe they was the wrong choices. Now I'm seventy-three and I'm dyin' fast. Got cancer all through me. Hurts like a motherfucker and I'd just as soon be six feet under where it don't hurt no more. But I don't wanna go without clearin' up my name."

Morgan's lips thinned. It was all just a con. He'd heard crooks deny their crimes since his first day on the beat at the *Chicago Tribune*. After a while, he stopped believing prisoners altogether. Reporters were easy marks for sociopathic inmates who were always screwing with the system, exploiting every soft spot. Young reporters, hungry for a big story or in a hurry to change the world, yearned to believe they could fer-ret out injustice, tip the scales back into equilibrium, and clear an innocent man's name. Even Jefferson Morgan had that crusading spirit once, but he soon found out it never really happened that way. Cons had too much time to think up new ways to manipulate honest people.

Gilmartin was lying, too. Morgan didn't know why, but it didn't matter.

Except the cancer.

Only that part seemed true. Gilmartin's body was decay-ing in front of his eyes. Morgan recognized the surrender that follows every jolt of pain. He'd seen how it consumed the flesh, then snuffed out the light inside.

Bridger's face flickered across Morgan's memory. His only child was just eight years old when he died of leukemia, two years before. Morgan found no comfort in death except that his little boy's pain had finally ended.

The old man tossed his cigarette on the grass and smoth-ered it with a cheap shoe. Then Gilmartin turned to Morgan and looked deep into him. The severe old man, rough as a cob, had tears in his eyes.

"The state docs said I only got another few weeks, a month maybe, before I die. They just opened the gate and turned me out like a sick animal they didn't have no guts to shoot. That was a couple weeks ago. I'll be feedin' worms long before the first snow, but ... you're the only guy what can save my name. You gotta believe me."

But Morgan didn't.

The high Wyoming sky was the color of worn denim, rendering Gilmartin's pale features more sickly, more desperate. Morgan said nothing, but the old man must have seen misgiving in his eyes.

Children giggled as they teetered and tottered, and Gilmartin's gaze drifted toward them. A pain from somewhere deep inside him crawled across his brow like a poisonous black bug. His jaw tightened and his bottom lip quavered.

When he finally spoke, the old man's voice had softened, the words almost stuck in his raspy craw.

"I never done killed that little girl ..."

CHAPTER TWO

The sun was almost down.

Claire Morgan gracefully balanced an open bottle of sauvignon blanc, a bowl of fresh strawberries and an empty glass as she glided across the back lawn.

Her husband, still in his button-down shirt and work tie, loosened at the collar, lay in an Adirondack chair beside the immense lilac hedge, one bare foot in the cool grass. His eyes were closed.

Through the screen door behind her bounded T.J., their new dog. He was a border collie, just eight months old, a housewarming gift from Morgan's mother. She still lived in his childhood home outside Winchester's town limits, where good sheep dogs are prized more than blue ribbons at the county fair. Upon making her gift, she'd told them a border collie was the smartest breed of dog. So after a few glasses of wine, they named the pup "T.J." because Thomas Jefferson was the thinker most admired by Jefferson Morgan, a tired, journeyman newspaper reporter who had been named after the great man, too.

T.J. nudged Morgan's hand, begging with his deep brown eyes to be scratched under his furry jowls, where woolly puppy hair grew like sideburns. Morgan obliged.

Claire stood over them, reading the wine label. A white tank top set off her tanned skin.

"This is what we should call our little estate," she said, handing him the bottle and glass. He sat up and read the label, too.

"Annie Green Springs?"

Claire cocked her head and gave him *that* look, the one that she gave him at cocktail parties when he wasn't being as funny as he thought he was.

"Stone Creek," she corrected him, sitting down on the lawn beside his chair. Ever the artist, she drew pictures in the air for him. "It has a romantic feel, doesn't it? A little brook murmuring beside a big house made of gray fieldstone, a meadow of blue lupine, some statuesque pine trees and maybe a mountainside where you see deer in the evening. Don't you think?"

Claire's eyes were closed as she imagined it, painted it across the canvas of her mind.

Morgan smiled and sipped his wine. Sauvignon blanc had been Claire's favorite since they'd met at the *Chicago Tribune*, where she worked as a clerk in the newspaper's morgue. On their first date fifteen years before, he took her to dinner at a stylish restaurant called Printer's Row, among the reborn lofts and gracious old apartment buildings on Dearborn Street. He ordered sauvignon blanc blindly because it sounded French and elegant; Claire ordered Rocky Mountain trout, and he knew immediately he could love her.

Later, filled with the new wine, he told her it reminded him of her hair: Soft, smooth and the color of yellow sand. She'd given him *that* look back then, too, for the first time. But he'd meant it.

"Let's see ... how much advertising would I have to sell at four dollars a column inch to buy your dreams?" he said.

"Dreams are cheap," she said, her eyes bright. "Mortgages are expensive."

Claire popped a whole strawberry in her mouth. With a gentle roll of her neck, she swept her long blond hair over her shoulder.

"I don't know, Claire. Your dreams always seem to have hidden costs," Morgan said, tucking a wispy, errant strand of blond hair behind her ear. His fingers settled on her brown shoulder.

"Hey, it wasn't me who had this dream of running his own newspaper," she teased. "I wasn't the one who had the brilliant idea of selling a four-bedroom house in Oak Park to move West."

Morgan knew his wife felt uprooted by their move, but they had isolated themselves in their separate cocoons of grief after Bridger died. Things hadn't gone well for them in the past two years, together or alone.

"You're right, as usual," he admitted, avoiding another argument. "I guess my dreams have hidden costs, too."

Morgan gulped his wine and lay back in his chair. The canopy of cottonwoods above him reflected the last light of the day, framing a circle of oyster-shell sky. T.J. lay flat in the grass under his chair, asleep. Morgan smelled steaks barbecuing somewhere down the block and saw the smoke drift overhead. He closed his eyes again. He wasn't hungry.

Claire slipped her hand between his ink-smudged fingers and rested her head on his khakied hip. The ink wouldn't wash off, an indelible mark of his trade.

"Another bad Wednesday for my country editor?"

Morgan groaned softly.

"Want to talk about it?"

Morgan parodied a smile.

"We missed deadline again, more than an hour. If we get any later we'll be a monthly paper. My reporters disappeared after lunch. Three readers cancelled their subscriptions because I haven't gone to church yet. The press broke down while I was out this afternoon. And the Post Office guys are starting to ask for a better brand of beer. Golly, things are just great. And how was your day, dear?"

"I'm sorry, Jeff. Really I am," Claire said, threading her

fingers in his. Better than anyone else in his life, she under-stood why he was doing this. "Oh, well, maybe you can write off the beer."

Even in the bad times, she could always make him smile. Morgan rolled the cool wine glass across his frustrated fore-head. The missed deadlines, indignant readers, malingering re-porters, a fickle press, low-grade bribery of federal officials ... none of that bothered him as much as the visit from Neeley Gilmartin. The old man was dying, that was certain. Almost as certainly, Morgan believed, Gilmartin was lying. His instincts told him so, but the old man and his crime haunted him.

"Where did you go this afternoon?" Claire asked.

"Huh?" Morgan opened his eyes and looked at her, dis-turbed from a distant thought.

"You said the press broke down while you were out. Did that used-car guy call and pull all of his advertising again?"

"Not yet," he said. "But the week's not over."

Morgan traced his finger around the rim of his wine glass, thinking. After a moment's silence, he told his wife about his extraordinary visit from the convicted killer Neeley Gilmartin, how the abrasive old man had sought Morgan's help to exoner-ate himself. He told her how Gilmartin had served almost fifty years in prison for killing a little girl, a crime he now says he didn't commit. And he told her how the old man was probably dying, alone in his rented trailer behind the Teepee Motor Lodge, his ebbing life suspended between the grating hum of a spas-modic air conditioner and a black-and-white television that got only three indistinct channels, visited only by a Mexican maid who wouldn't understand him even if he spoke.

"Is he telling the truth?" she asked.

"I doubt it," Morgan said. "These guys lie more often than they tell the truth. He couldn't give me any hard evi-dence to prove he *didn't* do it. I promised him I'd look into the story, that's all. After I got back to the office, I went up to the attic to look at some of the old papers, to check it out. I mean, we're talking about a murder almost fifty years ago. Never was a trial, so there's not much to know for sure."

"But something about it still bothers you, I can tell."

"I've heard a million sob stories from these assholes. Bad guys never do the crime."

"So why worry?"

"Maybe I'm getting too cynical. It's eating me up. What good would it all be if I ignored the one truly innocent person who needed my help?"

"Oh Jesus, Jeff, it's not like your life's been wasted. You didn't get into journalism because you thought you could write a few words and make the world perfect. You're more pragmatic than that."

"True, but I got into this business for something else. What the hell would it all mean if I missed that chance just because I got too numb?"

The trees rustled above them. A breeze passed over them like a cool blessing.

"What happened with this guy?" Claire sat up and swiveled in the grass to face her husband attentively.

As Morgan retold the peculiar story in the fresh air of a waning summer night, he could almost smell the musty, yellowing *Bullets*, all hidden away in the vacant second floor of the newspaper's ancient brick building.

The cumbersome, hardbound books of old papers were stacked in a dark closet in a windowless room where the roof joists narrowed to a sharp corner at one end. Each was embossed on its rigid spine with the year covered by the newspapers inside, going back to 1904.

The stories weren't hard to find: A murder and its aftermath were always front-page news in a small town.

"Did you know anything about this case when you were growing up here?" Claire asked her husband.

"No, but everybody always told us to stay off the Iron Mountain Bridge because it was haunted. We just figured the adults were trying to scare us into being careful. I never really knew why, until now. Trey Kerrigan was my best friend, and he used to tell me a little girl died there but, hell, he was just a kid, too. I thought he was pulling my leg. But I guess he would have known."

"Why's that?"

"His daddy was the sheriff of Perry County back then. Ol' Deuce Kerrigan," Morgan reminisced. "This was Ol' Deuce's first big case after he became sheriff. The biggest one he ever had, I imagine."

"A family thing, huh?"

"His real name was Kelton Kerrigan Jr., but everybody in town called him Deuce because he hated to be called Junior almost as much as he hated to be called Kelton," Morgan told her. "Damned if I know why he named his own kid Kelton Kerrigan the Third, but it wasn't long before everybody just called him 'Trey.'"

"Perfect," Claire laughed. "After Deuce comes a Trey."

"I remember going over to Trey's house all the time when we were little and he'd show me his dad's gun and his black leather holster hanging behind the door. I can still smell the leather and the gun oil. I was mildly impressed, but Trey, he was obsessed. He only wanted to be a sheriff like his old man. When we were in high school, he even joined the posse, like a cadet or something. I guess he got his wish."

"He became a cop?"

"Got himself elected sheriff of Perry County, just like his daddy," Morgan said. "I bumped into him down at The Griddle not long after we got here. He's still the same. Still wants to be just like his daddy, a good ol' boy who'd rather give a drunk a ride home than slap him in the drunk tank. You'd like him, I think."

Claire was always thinking of ways to ferret out hidden information. It was a gift that made her one of the most intuitive librarians the *Chicago Tribune* ever had. All the reporters sought her out, the way Morgan had first sought her out to help him on the Blue Island serial murders, the biggest story he'd ever covered. She might have made a good reporter, but she was content to sort through the old clippings in the morgue, deep inside the *Tribune* Tower. She understood what good reporters had to do, she just didn't have the stomach for it.

She worked at the *Tribune* until Bridger was diagnosed with leukemia. Suddenly, her vast world shriveled to the size of an eight-year-old boy's bedroom, and then later, to the confining, sanitized space of a hospital room. In many ways, she remained trapped there in that empty room, alone, without light to warm her. Morgan's grief had gone its own way. Day by day, Claire pushed her invisible walls back ever so slightly until now, two years later, she might have room to dance, if not to dream again, like before. The grief never left her, just gave her room to breathe.

"Could he help you?" she asked now. "It's almost fifty years later. The old files should be open by now. There might be all kinds of evidence and investigatory stuff that would never have been printed in the paper. Maybe it would prove the old man's story one way or the other."

"That's a good idea," he said. "But first I want to talk to the reporter who covered the killing."

Claire, apparently surprised by the possibility, held a strawberry in midair between the bowl and her soft lips.

"He's still around?"

Morgan poured himself another glass of wine, then looked in the grass for Claire's glass.

"Old Bell's byline was on every one of the stories I saw. And they were great stories. He talked to everybody, and they talked to him. He wrote with this extraordinary eye for emotional detail, like nothing we do today. Bell would tell me straight. He's a newspaperman and he was there. How's that for a primary source?"

Morgan looked over the arm of his chair into the lawn,

holding the wine bottle aloft, still searching for a vessel to fill. Claire sat with the bowl of strawberries between her legs. She plucked a fat red one from the bowl and studied it.

"So why'd they bust this Gilmartin guy anyway? What evidence did they have?"

"There was no physical evidence. The body was badly decomposed. The sharp rocks in the river had torn her up pretty bad. Ol' Deuce wasn't even sure what killed her. He just knew she was dead and too far from home to get there herself."

"Yeah, but what led them to this particular guy?"

"A couple snitches said they witnessed Gilmartin threatening the girl's father after a fight over a card game. It came out later that Gilmartin owed them some money."

"They didn't have much, did they?" Claire remarked, holding a strawberry at her husband's lips. "The say-so of a couple shady characters who had an axe to grind. Nothing to physically link him to the crime. Only circumstantial evidence that a crime was committed at all. No murder weapon. No idea if this guy ever had any opportunity to kill the girl. It's all pretty flimsy."

Morgan opened his mouth and closed it quickly around Claire's finger. She pulled it away, almost embarrassed.

"Well, I only know what I read in the paper," he said, wiping strawberry juice from his lips. "If Ol' Deuce had more evidence, he didn't share it with Bell Cockins. But remember, this was fifty years ago, this was a small town, and when it came to busting criminals, cops could do more with less. If Gilmartin made such a threat and Aimee turned up dead, that was enough to lock him up while they made a better case."

"So much for civil rights," Claire huffed.

"Who's going to stand up for some low-life, unemployed punk who might have killed a little girl? Not here, baby, not here. And look around, Claire, because it hasn't changed all that much."

Winchester hadn't changed much, it was true. They lived in

a sixty-year-old California bungalow, built from plans sold in the Sears and Roebuck catalog with pre-cut lumber and hardware shipped by train from the Midwest. It was functional, a house reduced to its simplest form. Its low, broad proportions rooted it amid the giant cottonwoods that lined Rockwood Street. Two bedrooms, a living room that spilled into the dining room, exposed beams of natural oak that suggested the strength of character that comes with simplicity. And, finally, there was the small room with sloping eaves at the top of the stairs, big enough for Morgan's books and a small desk.

It was, in all ways, a simple house to meet their simple needs, if not their dreams. No pretentions, no dark corners, no hidden spaces.

Crickets chirped in the tall grass beside the fence. The sun was weakening, moving on. High clouds, lined in red, scudded across the evening sky. Claire sat silently, caressing T.J.'s head in her lap. His long, happy tail drooped in the damp grass and his eyes lolled as if he were dreaming about a heaven with endless meadows of wildflowers where a million butterflies begged for a puppy to chase them.

Morgan poured his third glass of wine and held the near-empty bottle out to his wife.

"Where's your glass?"

"I'm not drinking tonight," she said, drawing light circles on T.J.'s twitching snout with a blade of grass.

"Finally hopped on the wagon, eh?" he teased her.

In fact, Claire never drank much. Two glasses of wine usually made her a little silly. Three made her laugh at her husband's jokes. "What finally pushed you over the edge? An afternoon giggle bender?"

Claire demurred as Morgan caressed her sun-tanned shoulder. There was something more, he quickly realized. He stopped teasing when she didn't answer.

"Claire ... what is it?"

"Well, you know how you missed your deadline again

today? I guess ... I mean, I kind of missed a deadline, too, a few weeks ago."

She choked back a sob and spoke too fast.

"You were busy trying to get the paper off the ground and we were trying to settle in, and I wasn't sure, and I wanted things to be better between us, and I didn't want you to worry about me, too ..."

Morgan touched his wife's cheek, confounded by her sudden burst of emotion. His first thought: He'd broken the promise he made when they left Chicago, to work less and leave more of his work in the newsroom.

"What deadline? Claire, sorry if I messed up ..."

She wiped a tear from her cheek with the back of her hand. Suddenly, she was impatient and angry with her husband, a normally resourceful observer who nonetheless seemed to miss every subtlety in her communication.

"Jesus, Jeff, I missed my period. Okay? It's been almost two months since my last one. I went down to the corner drug today and got one of those home tests, and now I think I ... the goddam dot turned blue and I just sat and cried all afternoon. Oh, God, I don't know if I'm ready for this again."

He knew what she meant.

It wasn't just that Claire was thirty-eight years old, or that she hadn't dreamed about having another child in an awfully long time. No, she still had nightmares about Bridger. After all this time, she would wake up crying every few nights. She'd asked Morgan to bring strawberries from their backyard garden to the hospital on the morning Bridger was born, and she held Bridger's hand on the rainy Chicago night when he died in that same hospital. And she never wanted to let him go.

She never would.

Morgan knew she was scared. He was, too. He wasn't sure himself if he could ever love so fully and lose so completely again. In the two years since he died, they couldn't bring themselves to scatter their little boy's ashes. They were still sealed in a small cardboard box in the top drawer of Claire's mahogany armoire, a beloved heirloom passed down through four generations of her Midwestern family. The fifth generation was entombed in it, for now, while Claire and Jefferson Morgan mourned in their incomplete way. For them, no place had ever seemed a proper place for Bridger, except with them.

He let the wine bottle slip from his fingers. It spilled into the grass as he put his arms around his frightened, pregnant wife.

She smelled faintly of sweet strawberries.

CHAPTER THREE

A low stone wall marked the way to Mount Eden. It began
where the blacktop ended and shadowed more than a mile of
the winding South Road.

Jefferson Morgan bumped along, dust billowing behind
him in a choking cloud in the late-afternoon light. Few Perry
County roads were well marked. Unconsciously, he turned
down the volume on his car's hoarse speakers, "Sweet Home
Alabama" fading out as he slowed down to watch for landmarks.

Finally, up ahead, he saw the legion of Lombardy poplars
that guarded the shaded lane to Belleau Wood Cockins's country retreat.

Mount Eden occupied twenty thousand rolling acres against
the foothills of the Powder River Mountains, five miles south
of Winchester. Although it was a fair spread, even by the standards of Wyoming's unbounded ranges, Old Bell wasn't a
true rancher. A gentleman farmer, at best, he ran a few nomi-
nal head of cattle and had started grazing buffalo in recent
years, but much of Mount Eden was leased out for grazing to
families that needed the land worse than he did. Other than
that, it was a ranch in almost every way except its name and
its brand: A fig leaf.

Like *The Bullet*, Mount Eden was more a place for Old
Bell's soul than his sustenance.

Morgan turned off the county road beneath an iron gate bearing Mount Eden's name. He maneuvered his gutless 1984 Ford Escort, an afflicted heap dying an undignified death, around a few muddy sumps on the lane, uncertain if their tranquil surface hid a darker, deeper rut. Gravel crunched under his tires. It reminded him that he'd need a four-wheel drive truck soon, maybe this fall, as soon as he could scrape together enough cash or credit to buy one. The purchase of *The Bullet* and the house took all they had, cash and credit. Not much was left anyway after paying all the expenses of Bridger's illness that the insurance didn't cover.

They'd paid well over six hundred thousand dollars for the newspaper, its building and presses. Most of the income in the first month were payments on old ads and didn't belong to Morgan. He paid his workers' wages with some cash sales, subscription payments and the small rainy-day account he'd set up at the bank. Now, toward the end of his first month, every day was rain. Reporters never had to worry where the money came from; publishers did. Morgan hadn't even written his own first paycheck yet and his first payment on *The Bullet*'s bank note was due in a few days. Claire estimated they could survive another week or so on the last of their savings.

The lane forked one way to an enormous garage and workshed, the other way to a semicircular drive in front of a long, arcaded portico. It wrapped around the front half of the three-story white house, which rose before a thick forest of ancient poplar, spruce and box elder trees, like a white jewel wrapped in green velvet.

The house's architecture was a pleasing if peculiar blend of Italianate and Southern revival: the tall, round-headed windows of Tuscan villas, ornate green shutters, fancy hand-carved brackets beneath elegantly sloped eaves that seemed to lift up like wings at the corners, two towering chimneys, and a porch swing for summer nights. Bright marigolds and geraniums spilled over the sides of large clay urns set at regular intervals down the long porch.

But there was something more.

The house at Mount Eden was octagonal. It was almost like a carousel at rest, topped with a lantern-like cupola of windowed walls that provided eight views of the surrounding countryside.

Jefferson Morgan unfolded his six-foot-two frame from the cramped car, looking over the marvelous house as he stretched his legs. The Escort continued to sputter, even after he'd turned off the key, gotten out and closed the door.

Mount Eden's main house was built by Bell's father in 1920, the year after he was born. A gift to his war-bride mother, it was the only home the old editor had ever known. Over the years, he'd bought more land, here and there, from neighbors who were destitute or had lost their passion for working the hardscrabble, until Mount Eden had grown to its present size. To Old Bell Cockins, an eight-sided house was no more remarkable than a heated henhouse.

An arthritic Irish setter, graying around the muzzle, lay on the porch, too sleepy to bark. Morgan opened the squeaky screen door and knocked a few times, but nobody answered. He'd called ahead from the newspaper office that morning, and he was surprised nobody seemed to be expecting him.

The warm breeze was fresh. Morgan had spent his day in the stale air of the newspaper office, trying to get ahead of the next deadline. Although he'd cooled off significantly since the day before, he still chided his two reporters about their slowness, while they glanced sideways at one another, annoyed at his insensitivity to their needs. In the end, they just shrugged and went back to shuffling papers on their desks.

Morgan rubbed the dog behind its ear. Feeling like he had landed on a serene prairie island, Morgan stepped off the porch and found a flagstone path toward the back.

It led him across an unmowed expanse of lawn, into an

acre-wide windbreak of ancient trees behind the main house, so thick he couldn't see through. The stones soon gave way to a wide trail of chipped wood and bark. Morgan came upon another rock wall beside the meandering path, then a small creek no more than a foot wide where someone had recently crossed with a small cart or wheelbarrow. Its water trickled musically down the gentle slope to join the chorus of some unknown river.

Morgan crossed the brook and followed the path through the grove. Suddenly, the man-made forest gave way to a man-made meadow, a luminous garden like Morgan had seen in photographs of old English estates, except wilder. Colors drifted like bright snow, embracing the light, reflecting the warmth of the day, and melting into deep pools beside the path.

The garden easily covered two acres. The silence beckoned him into it, to walk among the flowers and ornamental grasses that overflowed their appointed but irregular spaces, all girdled by low stone walls no more than a foot high.

It was Eden in the middle of the wilderness.

"Can you grab that shovel, over there by the bench?" someone called. Old Bell stood up, just beyond a tall spray of fine, lavender-colored flowers. The knees of his loose cotton trousers were soiled. Fresh earth clung to his hands.

Morgan looked around. Old Bell pointed farther along the path. He found it, a rough-hewn wooden pew in a nave of daisies and iris flags. He picked up the shovel and followed the path to the spot where his old editor stood.

"Damned meadow rue," he said, passing his hand through the slender, airy stems that grew to his shoulder. "Another Japanese import that ain't worth a shit except to look at."

Morgan stooped to smell the rue's delicate lavender flowers. Bees flitted among them.

Old Bell had been using a small hand spade to dig a narrow space just inside the wall for some new irises. Now that he had a proper shovel, he thrust it into the moist, black soil and turned it. A fat earthworm wriggled then disappeared back into the loose clump.

"Thanks for inviting me up," Morgan said. "All the time I lived here, I'd never seen this place."

Bell didn't look up from his digging.

"My mother called it her 'pleasance.' Very English. She came from a poor district of London and always dreamed of working the earth of a beautiful garden. My father thought she wanted a big house, but all she wanted was a garden. This was hers."

"She must have felt as though she were in heaven."

Bell Cockins broke up a clod of dirt with his spade.

"She died here in 'fifty-two," he said. "She wanted to be buried here, too, at the first sunset after her death. So after my father found her here that day, we carried her inside and my father washed the black soil from her hands and her feet, combed her hair and dressed her in her wedding dress. He built a fine casket that night from lumber left over from the house. All night, I heard him out in the shed, sawing, hammering and crying."

The old editor shaded his eyes against the sun and pointed to a small spot in the center of the garden, enclosed by a black, wrought-iron fence. Three headstones rose from a fresh green blanket.

"We buried her among the sweet woodruff, right over there," he said. "It's a crappy little European herb with tiny white flowers. My mother occasionally made wine in the root cellar and used it for flavoring. God-awful tasting stuff. But it bloomed in June, almost always for my mother's birthday. She picked the spot herself."

"Not too many of us get to choose where we'll end up for eternity," Morgan said. "She was very lucky."

"So she was," Bell said, moving down the row. He changed the subject and he tilled the dirt, a spadeful at a time. "Now it's Thursday and you got the paper out—a little late, from

what I hear—and you've come to me with questions about ol'
Neeley Gilmartin. Sad story, it is, but it made damned fine
copy. We don't get too many like it. It wasn't about buildings
or politics, it was about people. Good and bad people. So
what do you want to know about that moldy old story?"

"He came to see me yesterday," Morgan said.

Old Bell stopped digging, his shovel stuck halfway in the
ground. He was clearly surprised.

"Well, I'll be goddamned," he gusted, flipping back the
sweaty bill of his ballcap. His thick white hair pooched out
over his damp, incredulous brow. "The son of a bitch finally
got out. And he's here?"

"He's dying," Morgan said. "He wants me to help clear
his name, to prove he didn't kill the girl."

Bell Cockins shook his head and snorted cynically, stomp-
ing his shovel deeper into the soft soil.

"Yeah, and I never took the Lord's name in vain," Bell
seethed, his jowly face flushing redder. "Fuck him, that lying
son of a bitch. I wouldn't give him the sweat off my balls if he
was dying of thirst."

Neither Old Bell nor his colorful language had faded in
retirement.

Old Bell was a legend around Winchester, mostly because
he'd run the weekly *Bullet* for fifty years.

And nobody on Main Street had outlasted him. At sev-
enty-seven, he'd already lived long enough to fulfill his sol-
emn promise to just about all the self-important big shots
who ever challenged or impugned his integrity: He'd survive
to write their obituaries.

Hardly anything escaped his notice, even now in retirement, whether it was printable or not.

Morgan knew most of the stories about Bell Cockins's
pluck. Some he'd even witnessed. He'd grown up in Winchester and even worked after school for Old Bell back in high

school, writing local chicken-dinner fluff and sports stories for forty bucks a week. That was twenty years before.

In the autumn of 1917, Old Bell's father was a seventeen-year-old railroad hand on the old Union Pacific when he volunteered to fight the Germans. The Marines sent him to boot camp at Parris Island, where he survived an outbreak of influenza only to be sent to the bloody trenches in Europe. By the next June, the Marine Brigade of the U.S. Second Division—Lance Corporal Ray Cockins among them—found itself in a woodland hunting preserve the maps called *Bois de Belleau*, Belleau Wood.

Hours stretched to days, then to weeks as they fought inside that square-mile grove, which had been stripped of limbs and leaves in the first frantic flashes of fighting.

The gas came toward the end. It seared Ray Cockins's lungs before he could get his gas mask on. And when his squad ran from the deadly cloud, a Maxim machine-gunner's bullet ripped through his upper thigh, dropping him face-down into blood-soaked mud. His wound, though serious, was his salvation in the end, for the others were soon cut down in a crossfire farther down the path. By the time the sun settled, the broken branches and torn leaves of Belleau Wood covered his unconscious body, hiding him from sharpshooters. He was the only survivor among them that day, embraced by the dark safety of Belleau Wood.

An ambulance driver who was lost in the dark found Ray Cockins later that night. He was sent to a hospital in London, where his first days and nights were spent in a morphine haze. But as his leg and lungs healed, he was attended by a warm-centered Cockney nurse, Brigid Lindsey, who changed the dressings on his groin almost every day. No woman had ever touched him there, and it aroused in him more than just a feeling of extraordinary intimacy.

Before he was shipped home three months later, Ray Cockins asked Brigid to marry him and she accepted. He promised himself, secretly, their first son would be named after the place that would haunt him for the rest of his life.

His son was born late in 1919 in the small town of Winchester, Wyoming. And when he had recovered sufficiently from his wounds, he laid the foundation of Mount Eden. Beside it, he planted a circular grove of trees as a sort of shrine to the tiny forest that saved his life and loaned its name to his only son.

Belleau Wood Cockins grew up in Winchester, or more accurately, in the backshop of *The Bullet*, a staunchly Republican paper that fought off all comers in a day when weekly papers came and went on the wind. He ran copy, set type, mucked out ink wells and sold a few ads. Before he could shave, he was writing stories, and before he could vote, he was writing biting editorials about politics. Bell Cockins was only twenty-five years old and the paper's soberest employee in 1945 when he bought *The Bullet*, lock, stock and barrel, from his drunkard boss. He took hold of the place and never let go for more than fifty years, scattering legends as he went.

The blood never settled deep in Old Bell, but instead simmered below his collar, ready to boil up into his head at the first sign of either indignance or indignity. In that moment of silence before his tempest, he'd run his craggy knuckles through his wavy cloud-white hair, then let loose like a summer cloudburst, always in a torrent of profanity.

Morgan himself had been caught in Old Bell Cockins's storms. Once, assigned to get a comment from the mayor about some local boondoggle, he came back with a few quotes scribbled in the notebook he carried in his shirtpocket, a habit he picked up from Old Bell. The old editor thumbed through them and his brow clouded up like the anvil of a red nimbus.

"This is all horseshit, kid," he said sharply, if not loudly. He never had to yell. "The mayor's a lying sack of shit."

"But that's what he said, word for word," Morgan defended himself, feeling his face flush hot. He'd taken special care to get the words down right.

"Kid, if your mother says she loves you, check it out," Cockins said derisively. He tossed young Morgan's ragged notebook back to him and walked away.

But Morgan suspected Old Bell Cockins was neither as tempestuous nor as implacable as his scattered storms suggested. The old man simply knew that complexity of character was considered an imperfection in a small town, so he seldom allowed any other side of himself to shine through.

Proof of his gentleness existed all around Winchester, but nobody knew it for certain. Morgan's father ran the only hardware store in town, so he heard all the gossip about local folks by day, and repeated it over the dinner table at night.

Unlike much of what he heard, the stories about Old Bell Cockins rang true.

Many years before, Old Bell secretly paid for the construction of Winchester's first lighted Little League ballfield. It was naturally named for Hug Clancy, a strapping ranch boy who was the only Winchester boy ever to play in the majors.

Hug Clancy's celebrity, however, lasted much longer than his big-league career. In 1912, he pinch-hit in one at-bat in one game for the Brooklyn Dodgers.

That was all.

Facing the great New York Giant right-hander Rube Marquard, then pitching the best season of his career, Hug Clancy had two strikes against him when he slapped a fly to shallow right field, where it was caught.

But it was said that he grinned his gap-toothed grin all the way back to the dugout, because what he feared most was striking out. And he hadn't struck out in his first major league appearance—and, as it turned out, his last.

The season ended a few games later. Hug Clancy came home to help his ailing father run the family's dried-up cattle ranch and never played again, except in some town games on the fourth of July when the opposing outfielders would backpedal nervously toward the fence every time he came to the plate.

When the Winchester town fathers dedicated Hug Clancy Field in 1965—eight-year-old Jefferson Morgan was there on Opening Day and saw the withered old ballplayer rolled out to the pitcher's mound in his wheelchair, hardly the heroic figure that was the stuff of local legend—a sign-painter summarized his life's work on the gateway sign: *He never struck out.*

For a long time, young Jefferson Morgan wasn't quite sure if that was the highest achievement in any boy's life or merely the minimum expectation.

At any rate, nobody knew for a long time that Bell Cockins was the real benefactor of the new ballpark, nor that he had personally implored the elderly Rube Marquard to write a letter to Hug Clancy a few months before he died in the dark fog of his dementia in 1968.

Hug couldn't remember his own name most of the time, but when he read the letter from Rube Marquard, he wept.

So when Morgan went off to college at Northwestern University in Chicago in the fall of 1975, he hauled one suitcase and a dream to become a newspaperman, just like Old Bell. His father had wished he'd pursue a more practical career, so Morgan took a few architecture classes to please his father. But at the time, after the fall of Nixon and Vietnam, changing the world seemed like a reasonable design, even for a kid from an end-of-the-road Wyoming town where nothing, including the architecture, had changed in a hundred years. Still, the study of building design had added an abstract element to his perceptive skills: Morgan saw human frailties and virtues reflected in the walls that surrounded the lives he covered.

Morgan's mother sent him a clipping when Old Bell's wife, Leah, died of a stroke, sometime back in the early 'eighties. The old man must have written her obituary himself. Hers was the third headstone in Mount Eden's heavenly garden, Morgan surmised now, beside Old Bell's mother and father.

Old Bell and Leah never had any children of their own, but it was said the crusty old man helped put some of

Winchester's best and brightest kids through college, even though he'd never gone himself and was known to verbally savage the "god-damnable sissy, clock-watchin', good for nothin' college boys" he hired. He made some of them cry and some just ran away. Old Bell himself told those stories; his washouts would never be so kind.

Like the house his father built, Old Bell had many sides. And most of them were hidden from view.

The sun had dropped behind the softly murmuring trees, casting long shadows across Old Bell's resplendent garden. The encircling woodland grew darker, more protective.

They'd walked down every foot-weary path. Old Bell told stories about his flowers and yanked the occasional weed that dared take root among them. He told how his father had run underground tiles from the foothills to the "pleasance" and how the springwater was diverted to the roots through a complex system of hidden aqueducts, manipulated by leaky valves hidden among the bog-loving, purple lythrum.

Morgan sat alone on a weathered garden bench, and told Old Bell about Gilmartin's peculiar visit to the newspaper office the day before. The old editor listened, his jaw clenched.

"I never talked to the man, directly. Just saw him in the jail after he was arrested," Old Bell said, pulling a dandelion hidden in a clump of pungent catmint that draped over the stone wall.

"Back then, nobody I talked to had much good to say about him. And I talked to everybody. Gilmartin was a violent drunk and he was drunk most of the time. Couldn't hold a job to save his sorry ass. He came back from the war pissed at the world."

"He fought in the war?"

"Navy. A damn swabby. It's the one part of his life he never lied about because he never talked about it to anybody."

"What happened after he got back?"

"He fell in with the back-room boys and his world was dark, let me tell you. Women, booze, cards. Trouble all around. He's bad news, I tell you."

"Maybe so," Morgan admitted.

"No maybe about it," Old Bell grumbled. "This guy wouldn't tell the truth if it would help him. He's congenitally unable to be honest. He's jacking you around. Hold these gloves, would you?"

Old Bell stripped his creased leather workgloves off and dug in his trouser pockets. He flipped open the blade of a Swiss Army knife and neatly clipped a four-foot-tall cluster of pink and carmine flowers that looked like a hundred delicate bells suspended on a slender rope.

"Foxglove," Old Bell said, handing the brightly colored stem to Morgan. "In another week, all these blossoms will be gone. End of the season. Pretty little flowers, but the leaves will kill you. Goes to show, you can't always tell by looking."

Morgan wasn't sure just how lethal the foxglove's foliage might be, so he handled the flowers gingerly. But he grasped Old Bell's metaphor: He was talking about Neeley Gilmartin.

"So you think he's lying now?" Morgan asked, uncertain if he wanted reassurance or a challenge. "You think he did it and is just playing out this one last con?"

"Jesus, kid, I'm talking about a goddam flower and you're off in some other dimension," Old Bell needled him. "You covered the cops and robbers in Chicago? Jesus Christ. If you're gonna turn out to be a good reporter, you gotta keep your eye on the damn ball. But, hell, if he didn't kill that little girl, who did?"

Nearly twenty years covering one of the most savage news beats in America, Morgan thought, and suddenly he felt like a high school kid blowing his first assignment on the local paper. He'd covered John Wayne Gacy, even crept through the serial child-killer's crawl space as investigators dug for more bodies. And by blending several computer databases from dozens of government agencies, he proved another psycho had been killing truck-stop prostitutes along Interstate 90, from Chicago to Spokane, but never in the same place, for eighteen years.

The hunt had been a dark one. After compiling leads from a public news database, he made a simple list of all the killings, cross-indexed with the grisly details in every case: cause of death, the estimated time of the killing, whether there had been a sexual assault, the nature of the wounds, the condition of the victim's body, the color of her eyes and hair, even weather conditions at the time of the murder.

In that case, Morgan had acted on a hunch. He believed the killer traveled for a living, a salesman or a trucker. So he fleshed out his results with data from the FBI's minutely detailed VICAP database of unsolved crimes, from road maps and, eventually, interstate trucking records from Chicago to Seattle. Each successive layer of data eliminated suspects until there was only one.

When the FBI finally arrested the killer, a long-haul gypsy trucker who lived in a trailer in Blue Island, Illinois, they credited Morgan's stories with ending the deadly wanderings of one of America's most prolific death angels.

Now he felt as if that was another life, and he was starting all over, green as ever. Old Bell had always been his highest standard, and now the old man made him feel a little sheepish. But that's how the stormy Belleau Wood Cockins showed affection.

Old Bell stuffed his gloves in his back pocket. He wiped his knife blade against his trouser leg and folded it back into his pocket. Without a word, he strode off toward the trees, favoring a stiff knee. He stopped on the way to pick three plump, fresh tomatoes from his free-flowing vines.

Morgan followed him back through the darkening woods to the main house, a few steps behind. As he walked, he contemplated the foxglove, alluring and deadly.

They stopped at the back door and scraped the mud off their shoes against a metal grate.

Old Bell's house smelled like wet earth after a rain. It was first a gardener's house, second a widower's. The large, country kitchen was festooned with pots and pans hanging from the ceiling, colanders and jars cluttering the countertops, the sink overflowing with undone dishes. Clumps of drying flowers and herbs hung from a warped traverse rod in a dark corner of the unused dining room. A police scanner, a remnant of the editor's journalistic habits, scrolled through its channels silently inside an empty breadbox.

The breakfast table had four chairs, three of them stacked with old newspapers. A bowl of shiny apples sat amid a clutter of botanical books and seed catalogs, many of them opened to certain pages and set aside, as if their reader might return at any moment. Other books were heaped up in the window sill and on chairs. A field guide to wildflowers, garnished with little scraps of paper bearing handwritten notes, was left inexplicably on one of the burners of Old Bell's gas range.

The last light of day slanted through the western window, dappling the unswept floor and illuminating motes of dust that migrated on unseen currents.

Old Bell dumped some dead flowers out of a thin pewter vase and filled it with water for the foxglove.

Then he banged some dirty pots out of his way and came up with a long, serious knife, which he used to carve the unwashed tomatoes into thin slices on a plate. He poured a little olive oil over them and sprinkled some herbs and parmesan cheese, then fished two clean forks from the drying rack on the sink.

Handing the seasoned tomatoes to Morgan, he yanked open a drawer full of kitchen utensils and pawed around until he found a corkscrew. The aroma of basil tantalized Morgan as Old Bell chose a good red wine from the pantry shelf.

"Let's go see the world," Old Bell said, leading the way out of the kitchen into a large, open den. Last week's *Bullet*—and maybe a few previous weeks—was scattered in sections on the rumpled sofa, where a colorful hand-knitted afghan lay in a comfortable heap. Old Bell's reading glasses were on the edge of a water-stained coffee table, where he might have laid them while he napped. More books lay strewn over the table top like leftover puzzle pieces waiting for their proper place to be found.

"This way," he said from the bottom step of a circular wood-and-iron staircase. It rose through the ceiling to the cupola Morgan had seen from outside.

The view was magnificent. It stretched for twenty miles all around Mount Eden. A high-powered spotting scope was set up in the southern window, pointed toward the distant mountain where Old Bell could watch wildlife and gathering storms.

Morgan paused at the tall north window. His eye settled upon Winchester in the distance, a timid little stopping place amid the vast expanse of wind-burnished flatlands beyond. Bathed in the salmon light of the day's end, he could pick out the Presbyterian Church's white steeple and the four-story brick facade of the elementary school. The houses of Winchester huddled around the trees near the center of town, then spread in diminishing order toward the emptiness of the surrounding plains. A low hill shyly interrupted the flatness around Winchester; its most prominent feature was a large white "W" and because of the physical hardships each autumn's tradition-plagued freshman football players endured to whitewash it, the little prairie lump was known locally as Puke Hill.

A thunderhead was building far to the north of the town, reflecting the sunset somewhere over Montana. Once, Montana had seemed to be another world to Morgan, now it fit under his own big sky.

Old Bell handed him a glass of wine and bid him to sit in the soft leather chair that swiveled for the full view from his glass lookout. A hardbound copy of James Joyce's *Ulysses* was butterflied face down on the armrest. Morgan imagined the old man sitting here, alone, on summer nights, missing the ones who'd passed on. Lonely. For all his crustiness, Old Bell's heart must have been able to see as far as his eyes from this place.

The old editor had sagged into an antique loveseat that took up most of the rest of the tiny, round room. He pushed a few scattered magazines to the side. One had been separated from its cover, which lay partially crumpled under the sofa, looking as if it had been torn off purposely: Teddy Kennedy had been on the cover. Old Bell's politics were transparent.

His plate of sliced tomatoes sat atop a round coffee table that was inlaid with old wooden type from newspapering's hot-type days. Old Bell cut into one and ate it, washing it down with a gulp of wine.

All around him lay unshelved books in disordered piles. From what Morgan had seen, the old editor's house looked like a madman's library, a kind of paradise for an obsessive reader who moved from tale to tale the way a junkie moves from fix to fix.

"What do you think?" Old Bell asked, his wine glass tucked between his legs.

"I've never seen it like this," Morgan said. "It's better than looking down from the Sears Tower. This is the most remarkable house I've ever been in."

"Goddammit, there you go again," the old editor said. "Keep your eye on the ball. I meant this case. What do you think about Gilmartin's story? You don't really think he's innocent, do you?"

Morgan sipped his wine and thought for a moment.

"I don't know. I think he's a helluva good suspect, but there wasn't much evidence beyond his threat against Charlie Little Spotted Horse. I mean, this isn't some cheap mystery where a clever killer outwits the cops. That never happens in real life. Ninety-nine out of a hundred guys who get busted are guilty—and that's from the best *defense* lawyer in Chicago. Who else could have done it—and why? Could there have been anything else I didn't see?"

Old Bell looked offended.

"If there was, I'd have goddam well printed it," he said.

"I didn't mean it that way," Morgan apologized. "I just wonder if there was evidence to the contrary that got swept under the rug? Did Gilmartin get railroaded?"

"Railroaded? Shit, kid, let me tell you a story. I got a call in the middle of the night, maybe a week after they arrested him. Somebody on the line said they were going to give him the 'long drop' from the Iron Mountain Bridge, just like he did to that little girl. By the time I got to town, there was a helluva ruckus on the courthouse lawn, looked like hundreds of drunkards with ball bats and deer rifles. Only one man stood between those hooligans and Gilmartin."

"Deuce Kerrigan?"

"Damn straight. If Deuce had a mind to railroad anybody, he'd have let 'em walk right in and stretch that boy's neck longer than a horse pecker. But he wasn't that kind of man."

"Did he ever suspect the parents?"

Old Bell waved him off.

"You're pissin' up a rope, kid. I never saw the sheriff's file, but Deuce Kerrigan was as honest as he was tough. Sure, he knew the father belted the kid a few times, whole damn town did, but he told me later their story checked out. He wouldn't have put a noose around a man's neck if he wasn't sure. That bastard had a damned good head on his shoulders, but he had an even better gut for solving crimes, and his gut told him it wasn't the parents. It was Neeley Gilmartin."

"How 'bout your gut, Bell? Were you sure?"

"Right after they busted him, a deputy let me in to take a picture for the paper. Gilmartin just flipped me off and turned his face away. I asked him a few questions, but he just told me to fuck off."

"So how'd you get his picture?"

"I stuck one flashbulb in my old Speed-Graphic four-by-five and one in my mouth. I kept the shutter closed, but popped the flash into his cell. Faster'n hell, I stuck that new bulb in the camera and hollered for the deputy to let me out. The dumb fucker Gilmartin turned toward me, 'cause he was sure he'd snookered the newspaperman. And that's how I got my picture."

The jeering face of Neeley Gilmartin, cocked wickedly over his bare, muscular shoulder, was printed three columns wide in the next week's edition of *The Bullet*. Old Bell had cropped the photo so the word TERROR, tattooed on his arm, could be seen clearly.

"He must have been pissed," Morgan said.

"He had that look, you know? His eyes were dead. He had this evil air about him. You've sensed it, a kind of evil electricity. Like bolts of anger. That tattoo has stuck with me all these years. He chose terror more than it chose him. My gut? Yeah, he did it."

Disappointment nudged Morgan. Maybe he'd hoped to hear that Old Bell had doubted the case against Gilmartin. Or that some vital piece of evidence had turned up in the intervening years that proved his guilt. But if even a feeble flame of his old passionate idealism still burned in Morgan's heart, it now flickered as if a cold draft had blown through his chest.

The two newspapermen sat without talking, watching the sun go down all around them. Morgan swirled the wine in his glass, absorbed in thought.

Old Bell interrupted the silence.

"Some nights, a red-tailed hawk circles around the place and you can watch him while he watches you, three-hundred-and-sixty degrees as he swings around this little perch. The Crows say the hawk is a spirit, if you believe that shamanistic Indian crap. But I think he's looking for dinner. Damn rabbits are thicker than spinsters in the front pew. But it's a sight no city folks ever see," he said.

Old Bell raised his glass.

"Welcome home, kid," he said. He sounded genuinely pleased.

Morgan clinked his glass and turned to watch the darkening sky. Old Bell pointed toward the setting sun.

"I pay taxes on all you can see to the west, for better or worse," he said, sweeping his arm in a slow circle. "The town's to the north over there, and the damned Forest Service has most of the mountain out back. To the east there, that's Malachi Pierce's land. Runs all the way to the Black Thunder River. He's one scary son of a bitch, that Pierce. All that anti-government, racist crap. Some nights, I watch the stars from the garden and I hear automatic weapons fire over there. He sure as hell isn't hunting goddam deer, I'll tell you."

"I remember him from when I was a kid," Morgan said. "Didn't have much use for local folks, I recall, but an assault weapon goes beyond being unsociable. Is it some kind of militia?"

"Malachi Pierce has been bent all his miserable life. First he got God, then he got mad. At everybody. Must have been thirty years ago when he started writing these crazy goddam letters to the paper every week. At first, they were just long, rambling diatribes about how folks didn't obey the Bible anymore. Sticking it to the 'godless' ones, he'd say, all those goddam liberals who didn't believe America was a white man's sanctuary. There was always a racist stink to those letters."

Morgan knew Old Bell and Pierce had clashed more than once, in print and at least once physically in the parking lot behind the Elks Lodge. They were enemies in spirit as well as body, one as inclement as the other.

"He just got older and meaner. Then he had that girl, the retarded one," Old Bell continued. His points grew vigorous, so his wine nearly sloshed out of its glass. "He's past eighty now, but he'd married late in his life to some teen-age girl, fourteen or fifteen. There he was, a twisted old man in his fifties, squirting out more wrong-headed children. That little daughter of his must be near thirty now. She was still pretty young, maybe eight, when he tried to have her put away, but they wouldn't let him. He's kept her out there at Wormwood Camp ever since."

"Wormwood Camp?"

"That's what he calls that god-forsaken ranch now," Old Bell said. "Go back and read your Revelations, where some angry angel hurls a star called Wormwood into the Earth and it poisons the sea. A third of the men who drink from it are embittered. Pierce believes it was the sea that covered these parts at Creation, and that Wormwood smashed into the pisspot he now calls home. That bastard knows his Bible and he uses it like a deadly weapon."

Morgan looked into the distance and saw a hawk swoop steeply toward the ground, like a falling star. For a new editor trying to get his feet firmly planted in the community, he knew Pierce could be a problem.

"A lot of these militia guys are all wind and no water," Morgan said. "Is there anything going on at Pierce's ranch beyond target practice?"

"I guess you might call it a compound now, with all its fences and locked gates. Makes you wonder, doesn't it? He's gathered a few of his crazy sympathizers, mostly drifters and other invisible people. They all live out there in cheap trailers and shacks. They put up their own church and even run their own candidates for county offices. Scariest goddam people you'll ever want to meet. Loonies who carry guns."

"Have they made any trouble?" Morgan asked.

"Not yet," Old Bell said, looking down into his glass. "But they're fixing to. I feel it in these old bones."

"Something to worry about?"

Old Bell just stared out toward the east, toward Pierce.

"I hear the gunfire more nights now, sometimes explosions. Trey Kerrigan gives them a wide berth, that chickenshit tinhorn. And Pierce has gotten bolder since the Oklahoma City bomb. A few months back, he sent a letter to the paper making some vague threats against the Fish and Game wardens around here. He and his fellow wingnuts even started one of those goddam computer whatzits on the Internet ..."

"A web site?"

"Yeah, that's it. They're wired up to the whole goddam world. They spread their vicious gospel, inciting folks to hate the government, the media, immigrants, Indians, Negroes, environmentalists, you name it. They hate just about any damned group in the, quote, New World Order that twists their tail. Won't be long before your name finds its way onto his enemies list. You're like goddam fresh meat to those coyotes."

"It's nice to know it's nothing personal," Morgan joked.

"Oh, it'll be personal. Count on it. And he's got some folks around here believing his crap. Hard to believe, isn't it? Some uneducated sodbuster becomes the goddam Messiah? When it comes to Malachi Pierce, watch your step."

Malachi Pierce.

Neeley Gilmartin.

The bank.

His reporters.

His own printing press.

Claire and a new baby, so soon after Bridger went away.

Even time itself seemed to be conspiring against him.

Morgan leaned against the cool window casement and counted the pitfalls that awaited him. He wasn't the kind to be paranoid, but neither did he like leaving control of his fate in other people's hands.

In the distance, the hawk still circled, looking for prey.

"What next?" he asked himself out loud, exasperated.

Old Bell's answer wasn't what Morgan expected. He spoke softly, his faded blue eyes focused on the horizon beyond Mount Eden. If he doubted Gilmartin's innocence, or himself, this was the closest he'd come to admitting it.

"Gilmartin is next. It's like a goddamned quest, kid. If he didn't do it, you're the only one who can help him now."

CHAPTER FOUR

Morgan arrived at the sheriff's office before eight AM Friday morning, but Trey Kerrigan was down in the basement jail, serving breakfast to its lone occupant. Arly Bucknell had been face down in his own vomit when a deputy lifted him out of the gutter the night before.

The sheriff's secretary, a large but pretty woman whose chin unfolded in thick pleats down her neck, was expecting Morgan. She fetched him a Styrofoam cup of coffee from a drip coffeemaker behind her desk. After he'd swizzled two packets of sweetener into it, she led him into a comfortable office to wait.

Sheriff Trey Kerrigan's walls were a shrine to his late father.

Plaques, framed letters, mounted heads and several dozen photographs were hung in a mosaic so dense that barely a half inch of the dark maple-paneled wall behind showed around each one. Almost all of them were engraved or addressed to Deuce Kerrigan, or pictured the broad-shouldered, barrel-chested sheriff posing with one of his trophy game animals, shoulder to beefy shoulder with a famous politician or, occasionally, escorting one of his "customers" from his black squad car.

And in some, a familiar little face appeared, sometimes in the margins of the image. A devoted son who wanted only to be a lawman like his father. He appeared like a smiling little shadow to the bigger-than-life Deuce Kerrigan.

It was Trey.

The same little kid who'd bedecked the walls of his courthouse office with these remembrances of his father.

Deuce was never given to such narcissism. In Perry County, conceit was a flaw almost as intolerable as having reason to be conceited. Small towns had a way of keeping their citizens' feet on level ground.

The door opened and Sheriff Trey Kerrigan walked across the room in long, loping strides, his secretary in tow. He was drying his hands on a paper towel.

"Carol, get Tommy on the radio and have him run back over to the Four Aces," he instructed while she took a few notes. "Arly lost his false teeth and I reckon he puked 'em up in the gutter last night. Poor old boozer can't eat without 'em."

Carol smiled wanly at Morgan and left the room. As soon as the door closed behind her, Trey tossed the wadded paper towel in an elegant arc toward his trash can, sinking the shot like the natural, hot-handed forward he'd been in high school.

"You never lose the touch," he said, his wrist still cocked downward a few seconds after his flat-footed jump-shot hit its mark. His eyes gleamed.

"Well, for once, I can't claim the assist," Morgan joked.

Morgan had been a starting guard for the Perry County High School Wolves back in 1975, their senior year. He fed Trey Kerrigan the ball for most of the 323 baskets he sunk that season. The future sheriff was named to the All-State team; the future editor, whose passes were more accurate than his jumpers, barely got mentioned in the yearbook.

Trey's smile was obscured by his prodigious mustache, which curled around the sides of his mouth nearly to his chin, like Wild Bill Hickok's. Except for that, he was the spit and image of his father: wide shoulders and a thick chest that narrowed to strong hips, with only a hint of a belly showing beneath his starched brown uniform. A hand-tooled belt with a buckle half the size of a manhole cover held up his tight

Wranglers, still a fresh blue. He needed no gun and he seldom wore a hat, except in election years. It was just for show. Folks around Winchester liked to think their sheriff always wore a cowboy hat and a six gun, just like in the movies.

Trey Kerrigan had been Morgan's best friend when they were growing up, but lost touch after Morgan went off to Northwestern. Kerrigan took a basketball scholarship at a junior college in Montana, studied law enforcement for a year, then came home to take a job as a town cop.

Sometimes they'd bump into each other when Morgan came home for visits during and after college. Kerrigan's wife, Debbie, had brought two pies out to the house when Morgan's father died seven years ago. But Trey's own father, Deuce, had died only a few months before—barely a year after he retired from law enforcement—and he couldn't bear to attend Gray Morgan's funeral himself. Morgan understood, then and now.

Morgan sat down in one of two chairs in front of the sheriff's antique oak desk. Trey Kerrigan settled into his cracked leather swivel chair and held up a campaign poster for Morgan to see. RE-ELECT KERRIGAN is all it said, the dot on the "i" a white star against a red and blue background.

"What do you think? Pretty damn snazzy, huh?" he asked.

"You mean you have to campaign? I thought the name Kerrigan was carved in stone over the courthouse door. Who'd waste their money running against you?" Morgan asked, only half teasing.

"Ain't it a bitch, Jeff? Dad was the sheriff of Perry County for forty years, and I've been here for almost eight," he said proudly. "Now this town marshal who's hardly had time to wash his dirty socks from the police academy wants to be sheriff. That just sucks."

The election was around the corner. Trey Kerrigan was pitted against Winchester's town marshal, Highlander Goldsmith, who supervised the town's three-man police force. The primary was in August, just a few weeks away, but there were so few Democrats in Perry County, almost every race was decided in the Republican primary.

Goldsmith's main campaign plank was simple, straightforward and appealing: After forty-eight years of Kerrigans in the sheriff's office, almost half a century, it was time for a change.

Morgan prayed his old friend wouldn't ask for *The Bullet*'s endorsement. Even though he hoped Trey Kerrigan would keep the office he'd dreamed of holding all his life, he worried that his journalistic roots weren't yet deep enough in Winchester's political soil to make such pronouncements. And he knew Kerrigan wouldn't understand.

"You gonna endorse me, old buddy?" Kerrigan blurted out.

Morgan's answer came slowly. Too slowly for his old friend.

"Trey, I don't know if I'm even going to do endorsements. It's not you, because you know how I feel about you. It's just that I haven't been back here long enough ..."

Trey Kerrigan gave a disappointed little smile and looked down at the neat piles of paper on his desk. He made Morgan feel as if he'd let his childhood pal down.

"It'd sure help me if you did," Kerrigan said. "Old Bell stood behind my dad all the way, and behind me, too, even if it was only because of my dad. I'd sure like to have somebody support me because of me, and you know me better than anybody except my wife and my mother. We were like brothers."

That last little bit stung Morgan. They *had* been like brothers. Neither one had siblings at home. They'd defended one another on the playground like brothers, and fought each other like brothers. But Morgan sensed there was something distinctly political about Kerrigan's bringing it up now.

"Give me some time, Trey," Morgan said. "I've got to worry about the paper right now. Nothing personal, but people have to trust me before it means anything. I hope you understand."

"Sure enough," he said, far from satisfied. He tipped back in his creaky, overstuffed chair, propping one of his shiny brown cowboy boots on an open desk drawer. "But you didn't come here to talk politics with your ol' buddy, did you?"

The secretary waddled in. She carried Arly Bucknell's false teeth between her outstretched thumb and forefinger, as if she were delivering a dead mouse. Certainly, the look on her face couldn't have been more disgusted if it *had* been a dead mouse. She dropped Arly's teeth on the sheriff's desk and left the room without speaking.

"Now poor Arly's got to eat jail food," Kerrigan chuckled. "I ain't sure the punishment fits the crime."

Morgan took advantage of the comic relief Arly's false teeth provided in a tense moment. He leaned forward in his chair, his elbows on his knees.

"Trey, I need some help on an old murder case," he said. "If you've got it, I'd like to see your file on Neeley Gilmartin, back in 'forty-eight."

Kerrigan stretched a rubber band between his fingers. He didn't look up, nor did he look particularly surprised by the request.

"The parole board called me a few weeks back and told me he was out of the Big House, so I looked him up. He killed a little Indian girl a long time ago. Big case back then, but I reckon most folks have forgot about it by now. What's your interest?"

"I'm just curious. There are a few things I'd like to know. That's all."

"Personal or for the paper?"

"Does it matter?"

The sheriff tossed his well-worked rubber band on the desk and eased back farther in his chair, rocking slightly and looking at the ceiling.

"A life sentence is a joke," he said. "This old boy kills a little girl, pleads guilty and now he's out on the streets. It's a fuckin' joke. Everybody whines about crime, but nobody's got the balls to stick an admitted baby-killer in the chair and fry his ass."

"Forty-seven years in prison is still a long time," Morgan said. "It's a lifetime."

"If he ain't dead, it ain't life," Kerrigan said, thwacking his index finger angrily against his desk.

"No, it isn't," Morgan agreed, but to no avail. Kerrigan wasn't going to be any help. "But what's done is done. I just want to see the file on the case, if I could. No harm in that, is there?"

"Maybe. Why?"

Legally, a citizen wasn't required to say why he wanted to see a public document, but Morgan was reluctant to get lawyerly.

"Gilmartin says he didn't do it. He wants me to check it out."

"And you believe him? Jesus, he pleaded guilty and spent most of his sorry-assed life in prison. Everybody in town knew he was a goddam liar. Now he's conning you. Take off those rose-colored glasses, my friend. I did a long time ago, and now I can see you just want to sell a few papers."

"I don't know if I believe him." Morgan thought it over. "No, to be honest, I don't think I believe him at all. But what can it hurt to check it out?"

"Nobody gives a shit. Let this dog sleep, Jeff. There ain't nobody—nobody—wants to see this skank get off the hook for killing that girl. Ask anybody. He's the most evil son of a bitch this town ever saw and he'll be lucky if somebody doesn't whack him in the middle of the night. Folks have long memories."

"But you wouldn't let that happen, would you, Sheriff?" Morgan asked sarcastically.

"I just might," Kerrigan said.

Morgan shook his head as Kerrigan continued his diatribe.

"I don't understand you media guys," Kerrigan chafed. "Always looking to stir things up and sell papers. You don't believe this lyin' baby-killer, but you're gonna make a big stink of it. That's a fuckin' hoot."

Morgan's face flushed hot. The two of them might have been close once as children, but as adults they'd become natural enemies: a lawman and a reporter.

"I never said I was going to do a story, Trey. Dammit, I just want to know what happened. You've got the file. Just let me take a look at it. That's all. It can't hurt. For my own peace of mind."

"How about this town's peace of mind? The boogey-man is back and you want to scratch open this bloody scab? You'll get somebody hurt. There's still people alive who wanted to string this fucker up and they'd love another shot at him."

"And your dad didn't let them do it," Morgan said.

Kerrigan winced.

"That was a long time ago," the sheriff glowered. "It's old news, Jeff. Leave it alone. You run out of stories already? Why don't you go do something positive for this town. We don't need this kind of sensational tabloid crap right now."

"You mean *you* don't need it right now," Morgan said, pushing back his chair. "If there's anything to Gilmartin's claims, you don't want it out before the election. You want it to look like everything's under control. That's it, isn't it?"

Kerrigan twisted the drooping ends of his mustache, forming a response and quelling his anger. Then he spoke.

"If you weren't my friend, I'd throw your ass out of here," Kerrigan seethed. His jaw muscles flexed as he stifled an outburst. "As for the file, even if I've got it, I don't think you could see it, being an investigatory record and all. I'll see what the county attorney says."

"C'mon. It's a closed case, Trey. Nearly fifty years old," Morgan argued, but he'd already lost. "It's not an ongoing investigation. It should be public, unless you're trying to hide something."

"Well, you can have your lawyer call my lawyer and hash it out, but I'm not going to let you have any files today. Maybe never. Nothing personal, but I'm not gonna help you stir up this town."

Then he added, mockingly, "I hope you understand."

On Friday mornings, only the front desk clerk came to work at *The Bullet* before nine. The newsroom was quiet. The lingering smell of ink and paper had settled overnight. The ceiling fan chirped like a cricket in the dwindling coolness of the room. The backshop lights were off because Cal Nussbaum had taken the day off. Morgan knew he needed it.

Crystal had left a pink phone message on his chair because his desk was too cluttered. It was from Neeley Gilmartin at the Teepee Motor Lodge, Room Eight. Although time now passed much more swiftly for the old man, Morgan wanted to know more before he talked to Gilmartin again.

Maybe next week.

Morgan understood why Trey Kerrigan wouldn't want an old murder case reopened just before the election. But Morgan also sensed a son's loyalty had something to do with his stubbornness. Maybe he didn't want to believe his father would send the wrong man to prison in a brutal crime. Or maybe Morgan's interest suggested some question about Deuce's integrity, or at least his investigative abilities. Either way, Trey Kerrigan would guard his father's memory with the same devotion that made his office a virtual museum to Deuce Kerrigan.

The hell of it was, Morgan remained skeptical of Gilmartin's story. He couldn't imagine any man had the capacity to endure almost fifty years in prison if he were truly innocent. If the old man was telling the truth, why would he plead guilty and say nothing more for five decades? Wouldn't he have screamed from the prison walls every day and every night he was forced to remain there? Still, the facts of the case had never been truly knitted together to prove Gilmartin's guilt. A few stitches were missing.

But the sheriff's file wasn't critical to his inquiry. In Deuce's day, cops took the unenlightened view that the less they wrote down, the less ammunition they gave defense attorneys. It was likely that Deuce Kerrigan's file on the murder of Aimee Little Spotted Horse contained a few graphic photographs, an arrest record and some informal notes handwritten after the fact. Nothing more. And it almost certainly would not contain information that obviously exonerated Neeley Gilmartin. If anything, the file was more likely to damage Gilmartin's claims than to prove them.

But even in the days before DNA analysis and complex forensic testing, the file might have contained key incriminating evidence that never came out in the newspaper, saving Morgan from a wild goose chase. Even if Old Bell Cockins had supported Deuce Kerrigan in ten straight elections, a smart old cop wouldn't have given him everything.

Alone in the silent newsroom, Morgan assessed his few options and made a list on the back of an envelope. He also made a note to himself to invite Trey and Debbie Kerrigan to supper sometime next week, after the sheriff had time to cool off.

Almost no state agency enjoyed as much official secrecy as the Wyoming Parole Board. Its purpose was to decide which prisoners could be safely returned to society, but society didn't want them. So the Parole Board succumbed to a kind of siege mentality and hid in a fortress of bureaucracy.

A receptionist answered the phone, then transferred him to a secretary who quizzed Morgan, then put him on hold. Country music twanged in his ear for two or three minutes.

Finally, a man's voice came on the line.

"How may I help you?" he asked curtly without identifying himself.

"Hi. My name is Jefferson Morgan, and I'm the editor of the newspaper up in Winchester. I was calling about an inmate who was recently paroled. His name is Neeley Gilmartin."

After a short silence on the other end, the man spoke again. His deep voice was deliberate, his tone official.

"I'm sure you understand we can't discuss specific cases. State law. Our inmates have lost many of their rights, but they are still deemed to have a right to their privacy."

"Yes, I understand, but this particular parolee has come to me seeking help. I'm quite sure he wouldn't mind if you chatted with me about his case. Again, his name is ..."

"Gilmartin. I know. I have his file here, but I'll be honest with you, Mr. Morgan. There's really very little I'm going to be able to discuss with you or anyone else. I can tell you that Mr. Gilmartin was paroled June thirtieth, almost three weeks ago. That's about all I can say under state law."

Morgan knew there was more, if he was careful. Bureaucrats were like cops and lawyers who made a big show of their antipathy toward reporters—and secretly wanted to tell everything.

"Okay, let me just ask a few very general questions about process and policy. Just in general terms, how does an inmate get paroled from a life sentence, Mister ... I'm sorry, I didn't catch your name."

"Barron. Allan Barron. And in general, the governor must commute his sentence. In this particular case, it's a public record that he did so, on the recommendation of the entire Parole Board."

"The Parole Board sought a commutation?"

"Yes."

"Why?"

"That's privileged information. I really don't believe we can discuss that."

"In general terms, then, Mr. Barron. Why would the Parole Board seek a commutation for a convicted murderer?"

The officious Allan Barron paused, then answered in a bureaucrat's monotone.

"Speaking in general terms, and not about any specific case, mind you, the Parole Board sometimes finds it necessary to release prisoners who are no longer a threat to society to make room for more violent offenders. Also, an inmate can be freed to seek outside treatment for severe medical conditions. This can be done for any prisoner who isn't on Death Row, but in the case of a lifer, the board needs a governor's commutation."

"Medical conditions, like cancer?"

"Yes, but only if the inmate can adequately provide for his own care. If not, we believe it would be cruel and inhumane to dump him into a society that has no inclination to help him recover."

"Are murderers routinely paroled, Mr. Barron?"

"Don't be naive, Mr. Morgan. It's a reality of the system. It's highly irregular for an inmate to stay in prison for forty-seven years. In fact, I personally know of no other offender who has been in Wyoming's correctional system that long."

Morgan had connected. Barron was adhering to the letter of his law, but bending its spirit by talking indirectly about Neeley Gilmartin.

"Really? Why's that?"

"Prison is an inhospitable place, Mr. Morgan. A prisoner will survive there only by steering clear of unhealthy behavior. He must not put himself in harm's way, so to speak. Drugs, gambling, or any other risky liaisons, if you catch my meaning. He must be mentally tough. He must stay physically healthy, too. If he keeps his nose clean, he lives. He also earns a chance at parole. So, in general terms, good inmates tend to go free, bad inmates tend to die. Either way, nobody stays long."

"Hypothetically, Mr. Barron, why might an otherwise well-behaved prisoner find himself confined for almost fifty years if it's so unusual?"

"Many reasons. He might have enemies who have the governor's ear. Or he might not be so well-behaved as you think. Under Wyoming law, for instance, an escape attempt renders an inmate ineligible for parole at any time during his original sentence. For a lifer, that's forever."

"Did Neeley Gilmartin attempt to escape?" Morgan asked.

"Now, I really cannot comment on that, Mr. Morgan. In fact, I believe I've spoken far too candidly with you already," Barron said firmly. His sonorous voice carried no hint of apology.

"One last thing, then, Mr. Barron. You said a seriously ill inmate can be paroled only if he can pay for his own medical care. Mr. Gilmartin was unemployed and had eighty-five dollars when he was arrested. Even with a generous interest rate, he couldn't have had much money when he got out. Hypothetically speaking, how could a convicted killer make enough money to pay for his own cancer treatment on the outside?"

"Inmates can earn money inside. It's assigned to an account which they can use for personal items, but they never actually get their hands on the money. I believe Mr. Gilmartin, for instance, tied fishing flies and wholesaled them to a local sporting goods shop. Conceivably, an inmate could accumulate a sizeable sum in his prison account. Will there be anything else?"

Morgan pressed one last question.

"Hypothetically, Mr. Barron, how much money must accumulate before a convicted killer with terminal cancer would be released after almost fifty years in prison?"

Morgan heard pages rustling over the phone as Barron contemplated the question. Morgan was certain he was thumbing through Neeley Gilmartin's prison files.

"*Hypothetically*, Mr. Morgan," he replied, "in excess of seventy thousand dollars."

That afternoon, Morgan wrote the next week's editorial about the town council's expensive new dog pound and sent one of his phlegmatic reporters to a Little League game, the other to interview a farm-wife poet who'd been published in a Denver literary magazine. But he couldn't get Neeley Gilmartin out of his skull.

Seventy thousand dollars. How could a con start with almost nothing and end up with that kind of cash?

Just after four o'clock, he ventured back out into the parching July heat. He loosened his tie as he walked back toward the courthouse and felt sweat trickle down the middle of his back.

The district court clerk's office was on the third floor opposite the dark state courtroom. The door was a frame of brown wood around a panel of frosted glass, the office name handpainted in discreet Roman lettering.

A small bell tinkled when Morgan came through the door. The counter was empty and a few women worked quietly at computer terminals beneath fluorescent lights. One of them looked up briefly, but quickly resumed her muted tapping at the keyboard.

A teen-age girl who looked like a summer employee came out of a small room at one end of the office and walked directly to the counter.

"Can I help you?" she asked.

She had braces on her teeth and her limp, dark hair hung straight down, except for two strands that were pulled back across her temples and clipped in back. The syrupy scent of strawberry perfume was so strong, Morgan could almost see a pink haze around her.

"I'd like to see a court file," he said.

"Come on back here," she said, lifting a hinged piece of the counter to let him pass through.

She led him into the dead air of the vault. She showed him a bank of dented card-files, some labeled with letters of the alphabet, some with six-digit numbers. The whole cabinet was thick with dust.

"These are by name of the parties in the case," she said, touching the first several rows of drawers, "and those are by case number."

"Thanks," he said, hoping she'd leave him in unscented peace.

"Is there a specific case you're looking for?" she asked, more curious than helpful.

"I think I can find it, thanks."

Morgan opened drawer "G-H" and thumbed through yellowing index cards until he found the State of Wyoming v.

Neeley Gilmartin, Criminal Case No. 48-0237. He scribbled the number in his notebook and closed the drawer, sending a small cloud of dust into the stagnant air of the government vault.

The young clerk helped him find the conspicuously thin file. He'd seen some capital murder cases take up four or five thick folders in Cook County's Hall of Records; Gacy's alone filled a shelf. Gilmartin's folder had a few affidavits signed by Deuce Kerrigan, Judge Darby Hand's order assigning Simeon Fenwick to the case, a brief confession and a few other perfunctory court records.

The sheriff's affidavits outlined the flimsy case against Gilmartin, relying largely upon statements by the two witnesses to his drunken threat against Charlie Little Spotted Horse. While authorities could not account for Gilmartin's whereabouts on the day Aimee disappeared, a fact omitted from the sheriff's affidavit, Deuce Kerrigan took pains to point out that the suspect himself offered no alibi.

The tragic part to Morgan was that the prosecution's case was so weak, it likely would have been thrown out at the preliminary hearing—if Gilmartin's lawyer were tough and the judge fair. Perhaps neither was a reasonable expectation, even for the gambler Gilmartin, but it didn't matter. He folded before the prelim.

His one-paragraph confession, typed on the county attorney's stationery, signed with an "X" and witnessed by the prosecutor, ironically offered even less proof of his guilt:

On or about August 4, 1948, the undersigned did willfully and maliciously murder by undetermined means one Aimee Little Spotted Horse, nine years of age, approximately at a site known as the Iron Mountain Bridge in Perry County, the State of Wyoming. The accused admits his crime and submits a plea of guilty to the charge of first-degree murder.

(X) Neeley Gilmartin
Witness: Calvin Davis
September 21, 1948

County Prosecutor Calvin Davis held up his end of the bargain, submitting his written recommendation to Judge Hand that Gilmartin receive a life sentence in return for his guilty plea. The judge accepted it and the case was neatly closed less than a month after Aimee was killed.

But in their haste to dispose of Neeley Gilmartin, nobody ever asked him to explain how it really happened. Perhaps they didn't even care.

Claire was waiting for Morgan at *The Bullet* when he got back with copies of Gilmartin's court file. It was after five.

She'd cleared off his desk, which was now covered with a red-and-white checked tablecloth. Two white tapers flickered in sterling silver candlesticks between two complete place settings. Claire had unpacked their best china and rolled their flatware in cloth napkins.

Her long, blond hair was up, the way he liked it, just a few strands cascading around her pretty face. One curled down and touched the corner of her mouth.

"What's this? A candle-lit, Friday night dinner on the town?" Morgan asked, pleasantly surprised. The office lights were turned off, but it was still quite bright outside. Main Street was quiet, as it usually was at the bitter end of the week.

Claire bit her lower lip like a shy schoolgirl and dipped into the cooler beside his desk. She served their supper: Cold cucumber sandwiches, corn chips, guacamole, some nectarines, a beer for him and a ginger ale for her.

"I told the hired help to take the night off," she said, loosening his tie and tucking his napkin in his collar. "Tonight, it's just you and me and our humble little shop on Main Street. Isn't that romantic?"

"This is the most thoughtful thing you could have done, Claire," he said. "I had a cup of coffee for breakfast and skipped lunch. I didn't even know I was hungry until now."

Morgan wolfed down half a sandwich and took a long,

hungry swig of his beer. Claire reached across the desk and touched his hand lightly.

"I went to see the cold-fingered Doctor Grady today," Claire said. Morgan stopped chewing and raised his eyebrows expectantly. "Actually, I think his first name is Benjamin, but everybody around here just calls him Doc."

"Around here, they call anybody who wears rubber gloves 'Doc,'" Morgan corrected her. He almost sounded like a patronizing tour guide. "Veterinarians. Dentists. Hell, Doc Chandler is just an optometrist and everybody calls him 'Doc,' too."

Claire straightened her napkin across her lap demurely. Silently.

"Sorry," Morgan apologized. "What did Doc Grady tell you?"

"We're definitely pregnant," she said. She sounded resigned, but not as frightened as before. "Not quite two months, he guessed. That'd be about right."

"Is everything okay?"

"He says everything's fine. He drew some blood and got a urine sample for tests, but other than the fact I'm thirty-eight years old and married to a workaholic, he says there's not much to worry about."

Morgan raised his beer can.

"Then a toast to the new mother," he said, his eyes sparkling in the candlelight.

Claire clunked her can of ginger ale against it and smiled sweetly at her husband. Then she offered her own toast.

"To my dear editor, who once promised me he wouldn't work so hard."

Just as Claire began to drink to him, she abruptly set her soda on the desk and hurriedly wiped her mouth while it fizzed over. She searched under the desk for her purse.

"I almost forgot this," she said, handing Morgan an envelope. "Somebody slipped it under the door before you got here, then hurried away. It was a man, I think, but I just caught a glimpse of him. I don't know why he didn't come in. The door was unlocked."

The plain white envelope had no return address. The sender had scrawled "Jefferson Morgan, Letter to the Editor" on its front. Setting his beer aside, Morgan slipped his finger under the sealed flap and tore a jagged opening in it.

The letter was two pages long, single-spaced, and signed by Malachi Pierce.

CHAPTER FIVE

July 26, 1996
Dear Editor:

Many times I have seen a flock of sheep devoured by wild dogs in the darkness, because they could not see where to run and because they were not smart enough to fight back. The smell of the slaughter, like the violent blue color of their entrails strewn on the ground, stays with you always.

We are sheep. Our society is deteriorating and we cannot see in the darkness. We are the Supreme race—Supremely stupid. Homosexuality, AIDS, the explosion of so-called "knowledge," pornography and wickedness everywhere, rampant crime in the streets, the New World Order: "All these are the beginning of sorrows." (Matthew 24:8)

The remnant People have been persecuted by our government and its Deathmakers in the ATF, the IRS and the FBI. They are like dark angels who come in the night to steal our God-given liberties. They are the wild dogs of tribulation and we must shoot them dead before they take our guns, our homes and our freedom. There will be no warning. We will not hear them coming in the night.

Who will warn us then? Certainly it won't be

our liberal media. Even in our own humble town,
we now have a liberal, big-city, Jew-loving
editor. He is a journalistic Judas, a betrayer
who was once one of us but who has been indoc-
trinated to serve New Zion. And as the Jew Judas
betrayed Jesus Christ with a kiss, Jefferson
Morgan has come back to Winchester as a tool of
the New World Order to create unrest through his
so-called objective reporting and censorship of
our free speech!

What proof is there of my words? Let me quote
directly from the actual source: "'The crucial
key to our investigation was the work done not
by a law enforcement official, but by Jefferson
Morgan of the Tribune. I can't give him enough
credit,' FBI Special Agent Carlton Wickes said
at a press conference announcing the capture of
(accused serial killer Phineas Dwight) Comeaux
in Blue Island, Ill., on Monday. Based on materials found in his rural trailer home, Comeaux
is also believed to have ties to a little-known
radical Christian anti-government group known as
the Fourth Sign." (October 12, 1993, Chicago
Tribune) I can send a copy of the entire news
story to anyone who requests it so you can
discover for yourself how our new editor is
another pawn of the federal thugs and Christ-
hating propagandists who have been sent to
silence us.

They are the sons and daughters of the false
city of Edom! "They eat the bread of wickedness
and drink the wine of violence." (Proverbs 4:17)
The wild dogs are among us! We must see through
the dark! Jesus Christ said "Because thou art
lukewarm, and neither cold nor hot, I will spue
thee out of my mouth!" (Revelations 3:16) We
must be white hot as we strike out against our
oppressors. If we do not rise against them, we
will suffer the manifold curses of Yahweh
(Deuteronomy 28)

The Shepherd has come to warn us it is the
time of the end. Only the Shepherd will warn us

against the wild dogs of tribulation. He watches
over us and protects us. He speaks Truth and is
the Bringer of the Holocaust. You must follow
the Shepherd or burn in Hell for eternity. May
He direct our aim at the enemies of freedom and
guide our bullets to their heart.

A sign is coming. The Shepherd will show us
His heat burns hotter than twelve suns and He
will light the darkness so we may find our way
to paradise.

You have been warned! Prepare to meet thy
God.

Malachi Pierce

P.S. to the Editor: Do not censor this letter. These words cannot be altered anymore than
your fate can be altered.

Morgan folded the letter and put it back in its envelope.
He had no intention of publishing it. He tugged the napkin
out of his collar and tossed it on the table. The evening wasn't
so playful anymore.

"Can I see it?" Claire asked.

"Nah, it's nothing."

He forced a smile.

"I can see by the look on your face it's something," she
said. "Show me."

"Claire, it's just a letter to the editor," he said. "I'm the
editor, remember? You can't read other people's mail."

"Yeah, but I'm the editor's wife. And why would anybody
send the newspaper a letter if they didn't want other people to
read it?"

"Not tonight, Claire. Some other time. Let's go get some ice
cream. Just leave all this stuff here and we'll come back for it."

Claire persisted.

"Jeff, how can I help if you don't share things? You always do this. I'm in this thing just as far as you are. Go ahead, trouble me."

"I'll share a double scoop of rocky road. Deal?"

Claire was tough. Morgan knew it. But the moment wasn't right. He didn't want her to be afraid of this strange new place where he fit and she didn't. Tonight, he wanted her to talk about the baby growing inside her.

"Not rocky road. I've got a craving. Something with nuts and caramel," she said.

The Garvis Creamery, on a narrow sidestreet two blocks over from Main, had fewer than thirty-three flavors, but its ice cream was hand-made every day. The teen-aged girl who worked behind the counter on this Friday evening was most certainly a Garvis, too. Like most of the creamery's namesake family, she had frizzy, carrot-red hair and a galaxy of freckles strewn across her heavenly face. Her name tag simply said "Emily," and at the end of her long day, Emily Garvis summoned a frail grin.

"Hi, folks. Can I help you?" she asked, swirling her scoop in a kettle of cloudy, warm water.

"We'll have the specialty of the house, as long as it has nuts and caramel," Morgan said.

"In it or on it?" Emily asked.

"In it," Claire interjected.

Emily balanced two generous globes of Powder River Crunch on a sugar cone and passed it over the counter to Claire. She held the teetering top scoop in place with her fingertip as she slid her tongue across the cold curve of it.

Emily followed them to the door and flipped the "Open" sign to "Closed" as they left. She wiggled her fingers in a tired wave and went back to her clean-up.

It was after seven. The sun was slowly sinking as they sat on a sidewalk bench outside the creamery. The carved stone facade of the old building, one of the oldest in town, reflected the day's heat. Too soon, the ice cream began to soften, and little droplets of sweet cream trickled down Claire's fingers.

"We came down here on field trips when we were kids," Morgan told her, catching a drip with his finger before it fell in his wife's lap. "They'd show us how they bottled milk and made cheese, then every kid got a tiny little ice cream cone with about two bites of vanilla in it. You remember how exciting it was to come to class and see a film projector set up? Well, a field trip to Garvises' creamery was even better. Those were really good days."

Claire leaned against him, but focused on staunching the ice cream that dribbled down the sides of her cone. Some of it clung to the lower rim of her sunglasses after she tried to catch a hesitant trickle with her darting tongue. She wasn't licking the ice cream as much as it was licking her.

Claire, a normally dignified woman seldom at the mercy of undignified circumstances, was fighting a losing battle with an ice cream cone.

"If I eat any faster, I'm gonna get a brain freeze. You've got to help me here," she begged.

Mildly exasperated, Claire surrendered what was left of the dribbling cone to her husband and wiped her long fingers with a wadded paper napkin. Her tongue made a quick round trip around her chilled lips, which she dabbed at the corners with her napkin. Claire wasn't dainty, but whether she had just stepped out of the shower or was preparing to go grocery shopping, she had a scrupulous way of making herself look fresh without much makeup or primping.

Morgan did his best to finish the ice cream before it dissolved in the summer night, then tossed what remained of the soggy cone in a trash barrel chained to a nearby honeylocust tree.

"Come on, I'll walk you home," he offered.

He held her hand as they walked slowly, listening to children playing in the fading light. A meadowlark trilled from somewhere high in the trees until a teen-ager in a bright yellow Camaro rumbled past them on the street, his robust stereo woofers thumping like an inside-out kettle drum on mag wheels.

The pumping bass faded away and again the meadowlark sang a lilting soprano refrain.

"Listen, Claire, I'm sorry I've been so wrapped up with the paper," Morgan said. "I don't know where the time goes. It seems like we just get the paper to bed and it's deadline time again. I didn't mean for you to share so much of me with the paper."

"Things will slow down," she said. "I'm with you all the way on this, Jeff. You've got to know that. We'll do just fine. Try not to bite off more than you can chew. Just one scoop at a time, okay?"

Claire could be funny, even hilarious, but it took a good listener. Her humor was often cerebral where Morgan's was frisky.

"I've been too preoccupied to show you how happy I am about the baby, I mean, you and me and the baby. It seems like one thing after another ... the move, taking over the paper, this murder thing ..."

Finally, he heard her little joke. "One scoop. I get it. Sorry."

Claire squeezed his hand and kept the conversation moving.

"The murder thing. What's new with that?"

"Trey Kerrigan isn't going to be much help. He's pissed off because I won't endorse him."

"You won't? Why not?"

"Well, I don't know if I won't. I just told him I wasn't sure I'd be doing endorsements."

"Wimp."

"Hey, what the hell good does it do for some newcomer to start throwing his political opinions around as if he knows what the hell is going on? I just don't think it would be credible. That's no way to start off in a new job."

"That's crap, Jeff," she said. "You grew up here. You know these people. You know their politics. I just think you're afraid you might rock the boat a little. You kicked ass in Chicago where nobody knew you, and now you're chickening out just when you can make a real difference as a newspaperman. You need to loosen up and do what you do. Let the Force be with you."

"Thanks, Yoda," he said sheepishly. "I notice how effortlessly you dispatched Darth the Sugar Cone back there. Do you think you can teach me that tongue thing?"

"Watch it, Luke, or you and your light-saber will never see my tongue again."

They laughed together. Claire put her arm around his waist. She was tall enough to rest her head against his shoulder as they walked up tree-lined Lincoln Street toward home. Morgan rested his arm across her shoulder and held her close.

"I'm thinking about making the workshed out back into a studio," she said. "Someday, we could put in a bigger north window to gather light. Maybe I could offer a few art lessons in the afternoon, make a little extra money. I measured it off today and I think the room is big enough for two or three people to work comfortably. What do you think?"

Morgan was pleasantly surprised to hear his wife talk about working again. She hadn't painted in almost two years. If she wasn't escaping the confinement of her grief, she was certainly looking for a way out.

Claire grew up among the neatly trimmed lawns and shaded lanes of Winnetka, Illinois. Her father was a corporate accountant in the city. Her mother stayed at home, dabbling in sculpture and watercolors, selling occasional works for the benefit of local charities. They kept their lives safely distant from the city, hidden away in a place they called a "small" town. Their middle daughter was pretty, outgoing and far more serious about academics and life than her two sisters.

After high school, Claire majored in art at Millikin University, a small, respected and expensive liberal arts college downstate in Decatur, but she drifted naturally toward history, toward what could be known and what could be found with a little effort. In her, the disciplines of art and history— of unfettered imagination and the precise synthesis of fact— melded perfectly, as if she were the dusk between night and day. Until Bridger became ill, she painted beautiful pictures, selling a few here and there, but she had learned more than light and shadow in her home and at Millikin: She was creative, studious, persistent, explicit, beautiful and usually correct. Ideas always flickered behind her brown eyes.

"I think it would be a very good thing to do, Claire. Very good."

"It wouldn't take much. I've still got my easels and brushes somewhere in that mess of boxes in the garage. You've got the attic space for your books and writing and all that strange stuff you accumulate. This will be my space, just for me. I thought about the second bedroom for a studio, but that will be the baby's nursery ..."

Claire was making plans again, and that was good. She was happy. She was telling him, in her way, that she was better now. She was almost dancing again, twirling in delicate circles in the space she fashioned for herself, breathing in.

The house was locked when they got home and they were both a little abashed. They had relished the idea of living in a small town where they needn't lock their doors or their car, but old habits die hard. Morgan retrieved a spare key from its hiding place under a rock beside the porch and opened the door. T.J. met them at the door, so excited he squirted urine all over the foot-worn hardwood floor.

"I remember when I was that happy to see you come in the door," Morgan said, embracing his wife.

"Me, too," Claire responded, standing on her tiptoes. "But I like you much better now that you're housebroken."

They kissed. Morgan slipped his hand down the back of his wife's jeans as she unknotted his tie and unbuttoned his shirt. Without their lips parting, they edged toward the living room couch a few feet away, shedding clothing as they went. They made love there as if they were horny teen-agers again, like kids copping furtive feels on the basement sofa while mom and dad watched TV upstairs. Their lovemaking was more playful than lusty, more relaxed than deliberate.

When they finished, Morgan sat naked on the floor beside her, curling her soft, blond hair around his finger while she lay back on the couch. Her eyes were closed. He studied her body in the soft light, and decided she was perhaps even more beautiful as a mature, fully blossomed woman than the young girl he'd met fifteen years before. And it wasn't just her body. He was captivated by the strong woman inside.

He let his hand drift across her naked belly. Their child floated under his palm, safe and warm.

"That was nice," she said. "We should go out on dates more often."

"Yes. That ice cream must have had something special in it."

"I'm sure you'll go order a gallon of it to be delivered every week now, but next time it'll take more than an ice cream cone to charm me, buster. Maybe a whole sundae," she teased him.

"That's not a bad idea," he said. Quite naturally, the next thing out of his mouth was, "I love you, Claire. Did you know?"

"I know."

Morgan laid his head against her breast and drifted. He heard Claire's heart surging beneath him, bringing him back into rhythm with the world. In a few moments, maybe longer, he began to dream. Claire let her fingers skim lightly across his shoulders and he awakened with a start. He didn't know if he'd slept for seconds or hours; time had fallen out of rhythm again.

"I'm tired," he said. He rubbed his eyes and groped for his pants. "I should go back down to the paper and get the stuff. It'll only take a few minutes, then we can turn in early.

We'll go for a drive tomorrow, up to the Sun-Seven. We'll visit Aimee's grave and see the place where she lived."

Claire covered her nakedness with a small pillow and blew him a kiss.

Morgan dressed again, minus the tie, and walked back down to the paper. It was only five blocks but his legs felt heavy, his eyelids stiff. The front door was locked but the alley door was open.

He stacked the plates, silverware and leftovers in the cooler, then began to fold Claire's checkered tablecloth.

Malachi Pierce's letter fell to the floor.

Morgan picked it up and slumped into his chair, weighted down by it. He tapped the torn envelope against his knee and studied the coarse handwriting on it, but didn't open it again.

As a police reporter, he'd spent much of his professional life in close quarters with bad people who got what they wanted through intimidation. Most of their threats—menacing phone calls, hateful letters, petty vandalism, almost always anonymous—were empty. Morgan knew every crime reporter was a lightning rod for the simmering contempt of the people he covered. It came with the territory.

That's why Pierce's letter disturbed him. He'd only felt real fear once before, that Halloween night in 1993 when the phone rang at his home in Oak Park.

P.D. Comeaux was on the other end.

"Trick or treat, Jeffie. This here's your favorite boy comin' 'round to see what kind of sweets you've got at your house tonight," the unmistakably voluble voice of the serial killer drawled over the line, as clear as if he were next door.

A jolt of ice-cold adrenaline surged through Morgan's veins. It had been more than a year since Illinois extradited Comeaux to South Dakota, where he was convicted and sentenced to die at the maximum-security prison in Sioux Falls. The last time Morgan heard P.D. Comeaux's voice was at his sentencing, when the remorseless killer told the Hispanic judge to "kiss my lily-white ass."

Now Comeaux seemed to be in the same room. Had he escaped and come looking for the man who helped end his malignant life on the road?

Jesus Christ, he could hardly breathe as the fear tumbled through him, *Claire had taken Bridger trick-or-treating and hadn't returned.*

Comeaux's voice undulated smoothly through the receiver, like the ripples on warm water.

"Sweet things you got, too, Jeffie. That pretty wife of yours, so blond. I bet she's a natural blond, too, huh, Jeffie? Like that bitch I done in Sturgis. You remember her? Her pretty blond snatch was the best I ever ate. First a trick, then a treat ..."

Comeaux erupted in a squalid laugh.

Sandra Tarrant, a former high school homecoming queen who became a prostitute to maintain her $1,000-a-week cocaine habit, was one of P.D. Comeaux's fourteen known victims. In 1992, a night watchman at a used-car lot in Sturgis, South Dakota, found her naked body in an alley dumpster. She'd been strangled with her own pantyhose, just a few days after her twenty-third birthday.

At first, investigators assumed her genitals had been gnawed by vermin, until the medical examiner told them it was a human animal, not any four-legged creature, that had chewed away her clitoris and labia.

But it was her face that Morgan remembered from the crime-scene photos. Her eyes were slightly open in her deathwatch, pretty green eyes under dark swaths of mascara that made her bloodless face look like a silent movie star's. Her head was propped against a crushed cardboard box, tilting her painted face down as if she were embarrassed by her nakedness. Her angelic blond hair fell around her shoulders, almost long enough to cover the crooked, bloody bite marks on her bare breast.

Those distinctive teeth marks, the skin scrapings under the dead woman's fingernails, the semen smeared on the hosiery around her throat and the pubic hair in her mouth, all be-

longed to Phineas Dwight Comeaux. Nine prosecutors in six
states agreed South Dakota had the strongest of fourteen potential murder cases against him. Sandra Tarrant, whose short life
had once held so much promise, was their best witness.

But now Sandra Tarrant's face wasn't *her* face anymore.
That Halloween night, as Morgan stood in the hallway listening to her killer's pornographic cackle, the face he remembered was Claire's.

"Fuck you, Comeaux," Morgan blurted angrily. The words
came from a wicked place inside him. "You'll burn in hell."

"No, Jeffie," the serial killer said calmly. "Fuck you. Fuck
you, Jeffie. And fuck that pretty blond, Jew-girl wife of yours.
In the ass. And down her throat. I will, you know. Oh, yes. I
dream about it every night. Just like all the others. Yeah, I'm
gonna fuck her 'til she's dead, Jeffie."

Comeaux rattled with another hideous laugh, then hung
up abruptly. Trembling, Morgan instantly dialed the main
number for Chicago's Metro Police. While he waited for the
watch commander to come on the line, he checked his watch.
It was after nine, and a gentle snow was falling. Claire hadn't
expected to be out past eight.

The night captain, who was still working Homicide when
Morgan started on the beat, took a few notes about the startling call and promised to call the prison that night.

A few minutes after they hung up, the doorbell rang.

Still agitated, Morgan cradled a mixing bowl full of
Hershey's Kisses in his arm as he opened the door.

Nobody was there.

He stepped out on the well-lighted brick porch and saw
nothing but gleeful little footprints spattered across the skiff
of snow that was beginning to stick to the lawn.

Suddenly, his eye caught a movement in the hedge beside
the walk. Before he could raise his arm to defend himself, he
lost his footing on the slick bricks and landed on his hip,
scattering candy like big, silvery snowflakes. Claire and Bridger

fell on top of him, tickling him and laughing. Bridger's little Chicago Bears football uniform was damp from the wet night, but he giggled as he pummeled his father gently with a pillow-case half-full of goodies.

Relieved and cold, Morgan hugged both of them as if he'd never let either one of them out of his sight again. They went back inside for hot chocolate, then turned out the lights. Halloween was over.

The phone rang again just after midnight.

Morgan, who had been floating between waking and anxious sleep, groped for the receiver on his nightstand. It was the Metro captain, who reported that Comeaux was still safely in his cell in South Dakota, and except for his meals and exercise periods, hadn't been out of lockup for days. The guards in Sioux Falls couldn't explain how he might have gotten access to a telephone that night. Maybe it was just a Halloween prank, the cop theorized.

Morgan knew it wasn't. He thanked the police captain for checking it out and hung up. Before he snuggled back under covers against Claire's warmth, he opened the drawer beside the bed and reached in to finger the cold comfort of his thirty-eight.

Now, three years later, Pierce invoked the specter of Comeaux. Morgan felt sick to his stomach all over again. He sat at his desk, pondering how Claire was again the innocent pawn of an evil mind. His first instinct was to protect her as fiercely as he could, but he also felt so much was out of his control. She had no part of this, but Morgan's tormentors didn't care.

He didn't know with certainty how Pierce knew Claire was Jewish, but it wouldn't have been hard to piece it together. Morgan's own mother had asked Old Bell Cockins to print their wedding announcement in *The Bullet*. There it was for all his mostly Protestant neighbors in the homogenous village of Winchester, Wyoming, to read: He'd married the former Claire

Bergman, daughter of Aaron and Nina Bergman of Winnetka, Ill., in the Jewish Community Center in Chicago, in a ceremony performed by both a rabbi and a Presbyterian pastor.

How Comeaux knew was a more mysterious question. Morgan always assumed the killer maintained close ties to the radical religious underground and its anti-Semitic conspiracy promoters, even from prison. Using basic public records, they could discover far more about the reporter Jefferson Morgan than just his wife's faith. And they probably did.

So he'd never told Claire about Comeaux's monstrous call, and he didn't want to tell her about Pierce's letter either. Especially now, when she seemed to be regaining her equilibrium.

Morgan squinted against the gathering darkness of *The Bullet*'s newsroom. The space blurred into a sullen watercolor of steel and paper and wood, the elements of his existence as a newspaperman.

He thought about that Halloween night three years before, how he'd gone to bed with his wife that cold night without telling her. He held her close until she fell asleep in his arms.

He thought about P.D. Comeaux, the virulent killer whose appeals would keep him alive for many more years. So far he had admitted to the fourteen murders originally attributed to him, and every Christmas morning for the past four years, he'd told investigators about one more they never knew about. His grisly death toll was now eighteen, and counting.

And Morgan thought about Bridger, who died before Halloween came around again. None of the neighborhood children ventured near the house that next year, and Morgan remembered how lonely he felt to see them hurry past without stopping.

CHAPTER SIX

Buck Madigan didn't look like royalty.

He had the thin hips of a cowboy and his knees bowed at painful angles away from each other. The manure clinging to his boots was wet; the stuff that ringed the hat band of his gray felt Stetson was dry and crusted. A wad of chewing tobacco in his cheek protruded unnaturally, throwing his otherwise patrician face out of balance. His immense hands were weather-beaten and rough, and they bore the working scars of over fifty hard years.

He was doctoring a bloody gash on the flank of a buckskin stallion snubbed to a post in a round corral. He plunged his ointment-slathered fingers into the wound, then painted the yellow jelly around the torn flesh. Flies mustered on smaller cuts across the horse's thigh and rump. The taut muscles beneath his sleek tan coat twitched and his tail flickered like a frayed black bullwhip, but if flies had fear in them, the smell of blood inspired a far more powerful instinct.

But he *was* royalty. Buck Madigan, the bent-up former pro rodeo cowboy now ankle deep in horse manure, was a genuine earl with an enormous Scottish estate.

Buck Madigan was also the bachelor heir to the magnificent Sun-Seven Ranch, where Aimee Little Spotted Horse had disappeared forty-seven years before. On the phone that morning, he'd cheerfully agreed to show Morgan around, admitting there wasn't much left to see. That was okay, Morgan told him, because he didn't know what he expected to see anyway.

Buck spoke softly to the horse, his voice so low and calm that Jefferson and Claire couldn't hear what he said. He screwed a red lid back on the yellow can of antiseptic ointment and stroked the horse's sinuous neck soothingly. Then he unlooped the nylon halter and freed the stallion to run out the open gate into a sloping pasture blanketed with clover.

"Fences were a bad idea right from the get-go," he said, stepping on the middle rail of the corral gate and throwing one lanky leg over the top. The words weren't angry, but resigned. "Damn fences cost as much as the land they surround. Ain't sure anymore what the damn fences keep out. But I know a horse ain't got the good sense to know where he ain't wanted and a damn fence ain't gonna keep him from gettin' there."

Buck Madigan wiped his greasy, bloody hand against his thigh, then held it out to Morgan, who noticed Madigan's right thumb was missing. He shook it nonetheless as he introduced Claire.

"That's how you know a roper," Buck said, holding up his thumbless palm. "It's a damn painful lesson to learn, keepin' your thumb out of the loop."

Claire laughed nervously, but Buck just kept talking.

"I reckon the easiest way for you to get up to the shack and the cemetery from here is for me to take you. This place ain't much for roads and your rig there,"—he pointed dismissively at Morgan's miserable little car—"well, hell, we got piles of cow shit bigger'n that."

Madigan's sleek, diesel-powered Dodge Ram, the latest model, was parked by the corral. They all piled in, Claire in the middle.

Before they got twenty yards up the lane, Buck Madigan stopped the truck and hollered out his window.

"Murphy ... Fiona ... come!"

Before long, two tall Irish wolfhounds, stately animals with wiry coats and proud gaits, trotted up and leaped gracefully into the back of the truck.

The Sun-Seven was the biggest ranch in Perry County. It covered fully one-quarter of the county agent's map and encompassed some of the best grasslands in the basin. Just driving through the ranch on the state highway took an hour; it might take a day to cross it on the web of dirt roads that traversed its varied terrain.

They headed northeast from the big ranch house, back behind the main corral and spring house. For a few miles, the road had been graveled and graded, but it soon dwindled into little more than an erratic, eastward scratch across the rolling prairie.

Eager to make conversation on the bumpy ride, Claire asked about the history of the Sun-Seven. Buck obliged.

His great-grandfather, Graeme, the youngest of seven sons born to the eighteenth Earl of Ballantrae, was a "remittance man," a victim of British primogeniture and his own lusty behavior. To the chagrin of several of Ballantrae's ladies—and the upstairs maid at his father's estate—he was sent away from his ancestral lands on Scotland's gray, western coast with only his father's promise of a semi-annual payment of two hundred pounds—about one hundred American dollars at the time.

The charming young lordling borrowed enough to buy a herd, hire cowboys and build a magnificent house on land he promised would belong to every son he ever sired. The thought of sons left him vulnerable to the comely daughter of a powerful Tammany ward boss, to whom he was betrothed after a brief courtship. Together, they gathered twenty-thousand head of cattle, all marked with the distinctive brand of the proud seventh son of a Scottish nobleman: A sun over the numeral seven.

In 1886, Graeme and Anna Madigan's only child was born. The infant Adhamh survived his difficult birth but his mother did not. Graeme Madigan raised his son alone.

The Madigans' place in the new American aristocracy was sealed when Adhamh, at the passionate age of twenty-six, was elected to the Wyoming State Senate in 1912. He served until he died of a heart attack on the Senate floor in Cheyenne in 1945.

Adhamh's son John was called "Jack" by all who knew him. And Jack begat Robert Roy Madigan, who grew up to ride in the rodeo and came to be known simply as "Buck." The Madigan line ended there; Buck was a confirmed bachelor with no children, no heirs.

"So how did you come to have a title of nobility back in Scotland after all these years?"

Buck shrugged and splurted a brown stream of tobacco out his window. A juicy grin spilled across his thin lips. From the side, his distinctive Roman nose was almost regal.

"Damned if I know. Them Englishmen got some way to know who gets the goods. Near as I can tell, all the other branches of the family tree just petered out a few years back. Next thing I know, some fancy-soundin' English fella's on the phone and tellin' me I'm the Earl. I kept tellin' him my name was Robert Roy and some folks call me Buck."

Buck winked at Claire. Such was his nobility, borne of a kind of reverse evolution. His bloodlines ran thick with a nobleman's passion, a senator's spirit, an authentic cowboy's quiet grace, and the raw courage of a bronc rider.

"But I reckon a fancy title ain't no more useful than the curl in a pig's tail," he said.

In the distance, a dark ribbon of trees snaked down from the north and disappeared into the shallow washes toward the south. Their roots suckled from Poison Creek, just ahead. The road had all but disappeared beneath them and Buck Madigan seemed to be navigating from memory across the grassland.

He stepped off the gas for a moment, shielding his eyes against the noon sun as he searched for landmarks. The truck growled, rolling slightly forward, until Buck spun the steering wheel hard to the left and jounced off across the range.

"Not far now," he said. He squirted a brown gob of tobacco out the open window. "Somewhere right in here, up next to the crick."

Then he saw it, whatever it was. He aimed the Dodge's curved hood straight toward a broad bend of the creek and gave it a little gas. As they neared the creek, Morgan saw the bleached white bones of a tumble-down old corral and a deteriorated shack dug into the side of a shallow embankment.

"An old-timer built this place to stake a claim back in the homestead days," Buck explained as he parked beside the old corral. "Froze all his fingers off the second winter and sold out. This place has been here near a hundred years now, I reckon."

The homesteader's shack would soon seep into the prairie earth. It was the only home Aimee Little Spotted Horse ever knew, but if her ghost still wandered here, it left no sign.

The planks of the porch were rotten. One end of the eave had collapsed across the windowless façade, which listed like a leaky boat in a lagoon of thistles. Five decades of rain and melting snow had carved deep crevasses in the silty hill that surrounded it.

Morgan stepped carefully among the porch's broken boards. Weeds poked through the rotting wood. The wooden door, cobbled from two thick slabs of pine, had been wrenched from its bottom hinge by the sagging frame. Morgan stood at the threshold, beneath a broken deer horn nailed over the portal, and looked inside.

A bed frame had collapsed upon itself, its foot- and headboards fallen inward on a box spring mattress long ago stripped of its ticking by rodents. In the opposite corner stood an upright two-burner woodstove, its belly rusted through. The oven door hung open like a toothless, hungry mouth and some small animal had built a nest inside. The plank floor was carpeted with dried mud that must have trickled through the walls every spring, and the low ceiling dripped with dusty cobwebs. Hanging among them on a short piece of wire was a circlet of willow, laced with dried rawhide thongs.

"What's that hanging there?" he asked Madigan.

Madigan squinted into the dark cabin.

"That's a dream-catcher. A sort of Indian good luck token. Little Aimee used to make 'em for all her little friends. Even give me one, once, to hang by my bed, to catch dreams. Hell, I don't know about stuff like that. Can't rightly say why they left it here.

"I ain't been out here in years, but I think they had a little garden up on top," Buck said. He and Morgan clambered up the loose slope to a flat spot, now overgrown with sagebrush. A flicker of yellow caught Morgan's eye.

A small cluster of tickseed blossomed beside a clump of prairie grass. It must have re-seeded itself year after year, surviving hungry cattle and the razor-sharp wind. It was the only sign that someone had done more than seek a meager shelter in this forsaken spot, that someone had aspired to make it a home against God's better judgment. In time, Morgan thought, the Lord might reclaim the lifeless dwelling, but not the flowers, which would cast their seed on the wind and never die.

Not like Aimee.

Or Bridger.

Morgan had come to see mortality as a series of accidental events, just arrhythmic beats shared by random hearts. He'd long ago stopped looking for purpose in the mayhem he witnessed. That's when he stopped going to church. He could not believe God had a plan for the baby in Cabrini Green who was hit by a stray nine-millimeter bullet, or a former homecoming queen whose body is left to rot in the garbage, or a happy little boy poisoned by his own blood. They hadn't shared much, except living too briefly and dying too soon.

Unhappy endings weren't supposed to be God's plan. To Morgan, they weren't any more evil than they were purposeful. They were simply excruciating misfortunes carried by the wind and dropped where they might take root before anyone noticed. Like tickseed.

"Whatever happened to Charlie and Catherine? Did they stick around?" Morgan asked Buck, who was using his good left thumb and forefinger to twist a rusty nail out of a solitary weathered fence post.

"I think they went back to the rez up in Montana not long after their little girl passed. Her mama sent a few nice letters to my daddy, but those stopped after a while. Nobody knows what become of them. She was good folks, real pretty. And Charlie was a good hand when he wasn't drinkin' and beatin' on 'em."

The nail came loose and Buck sidearmed it a good thirty yards, plinking it into Poison Creek. It landed in the water with a tiny splash, as if a silvery minnow had bravely crested the surface for one shining moment.

They left the old shack to decay in peace and headed back west, the way they'd come. After a few miles, they were in broken country, where arroyos twisted through the dry soil like empty veins.

Buck Madigan gunned his powerful truck across a dry wash and up the other side. As they topped the hill, a small cemetery came into view, encircled by a crooked wrought-iron fence and a few scrubby cedar trees. Sagebrush thrived inside the tumbleweed-choked fence, which protected it from hungry cattle.

The gate's latch was rusted shut, so Buck found a softball-sized sandstone to loosen it. The hinges were so choked with rust they screamed like the angels of Hell as he horsed the gate open. The plaintive, persistent wind moaned all around them.

"Don't get up here much," Buck said, lifting some trapped tumbleweeds over the fence and watching them roll away to the west. "My great-granddaddy's original house was just down over there, but he moved it after the Twister of 'aught-two. Damn near two hundred head of cattle just disappeared. Put the fear of God in him, lemme tell you. He didn't have a goddam clue what a tornado was, and it scared the bejeezus outta him."

Graeme Madigan's grave, which he shared with his young wife, was marked by a pyramid-shaped block of granite topped with a sun. It was the most ostentatious of all the markers and sat in the center of the square plot, which was easily forty feet wide. Adhamh and Suzanne Madigan were buried together on the right side of his father. Jack and Marie Madigan, Buck's parents, were buried under plain marble headstones on the other side. Jack died in 1969, leaving the place to his only son, unmarried, unrooted and unblessed with children of his own.

How odd it was, Morgan thought, that this small empire was created by a man who was prevented from claiming his family's legacy. After Buck, there was no one left to claim it at all.

"Here she is here," Buck said.

Aimee Little Spotted Horse's final resting place was easily overlooked. The stone was a cube of granite, no bigger than a shoebox, nestled so deep in the weeds, it could not be seen.

"I was near nine years old when she died, you know," Buck said. "Her daddy come runnin' over to our house to call the sheriff that night she disappeared. He was scared to death. I knew her a little, from the summer picnics for the hired hands and from school, but we didn't mix much. She was Indian, you know, and them was different times. But I felt real sad for her. I didn't know that little kids died and I couldn't understand how somebody could just go away and never come back."

Morgan put his hand on the old cowboy's shoulder. The muscles under his hand were rigid and hard.

"Did you go to the funeral?" he asked.

"Yeah, I come up here with my daddy for the buryin'. He helped her daddy lower that little pine-wood coffin into the hole, real slow and easy, so it didn't bump on the bottom. It was like they didn't want to disturb her no more. Her mama was in pretty bad shape. The preacher said some words, but I don't recall what he said. I got to thinkin' after you called this morning, and I still get a little choked to think about that little girl."

Claire yanked some weeds and kneeled on the ground beside Buck. Beneath the thick cover of ragweed and spurge, a few wildflowers clung to life close to the ground. They held fast to the soil, soaking up what little rain was left to them, but they survived.

"I'll be goddamned," Buck said.

He reached into the thicket of sticky weeds. Morgan glimpsed a flash of silver as Buck handed something to Claire.

It was a silver vase, tarnished by weather.

It contained a half dozen dried up flowers whose wilted stalks were still slightly green. Their shriveled petals curled around the brown seed disk, still attached and undispersed.

Claire studied the raised floral pattern on its side. She rubbed away some dried dust, and as she tipped it to look at the bottom, fetid brown water spilled out.

The vase had been overturned, hidden in the tangle of weeds and buffalo grass that covered Aimee Little Spotted Horse's grave. It had likely been in the cemetery for a long time, but the desiccated flowers were newer. They hadn't been there more than a few weeks, Morgan guessed.

And he recognized them.

Tickseed.

CHAPTER SEVEN

By Monday morning, Morgan was less certain about many things.

The first payment on *The Bullet* was due, almost six thousand dollars, and he wasn't sure where he'd find the money.

The copy basket on his desk was empty. The reporters hadn't worked all weekend. Morgan was furious, but he wasn't sure he could put out the paper himself if he gave in to his seething anger and fired them on the spot.

Malachi Pierce's letter haunted him. Morgan's instincts about the criminal mind were usually keen, but he couldn't read Pierce, who was given more to allegory than actuality.

Most of all, he was conflicted about Neeley Gilmartin's guilt.

The old man had called again that morning, twice. Morgan called back, and a disdainful motel clerk said she'd take a message rather than rouse him at his trailer, which had no phone. Morgan apologized for not calling sooner, and promised to visit Thursday, after the paper was out.

"He's not doin' so good, you know," the churlish clerk said. She turned her head away from the phone and hacked something glutinous from the pit of her lungs. Morgan winced and said goodbye. He feared he was just wasting his time—time he didn't have—on Gilmartin.

Morgan had plenty of questions, but they all betrayed his

cynical suspicions. If Gilmartin didn't do it, why can't he explain where he was when Aimee disappeared? Why did he cop a plea if he wasn't guilty? And how was it possible for a virtually penniless, lifelong convict to accrue more than seventy thousand dollars if he wasn't guilty of *something*?

Morgan wished it all added up to a rock-solid case against Gilmartin, but it didn't. It wasn't what he knew that bothered him. An old city editor's warning echoed in his head: *You don't know what you don't know.*

Like the flowers at Aimee's grave. He brought the vase back from the cemetery, and left it among the papers on his desk, sealed in a plastic food bag. Even if he cajoled Sheriff Trey Kerrigan into dusting it for fingerprints, what would it prove? It wasn't against the law to decorate a child's grave.

But the vase intrigued him because it meant somebody out there still felt an intimate connection to the girl.

It had to be someone who knew the terrain, someone who felt compelled to trespass, and probably someone who was old enough to care about the death of a little Indian girl in 1948, at least fifty years old. And although the choice of a tickseed memorial might only be a coincidence, Morgan's gut said it wasn't.

Who fit? Who still cared secretly about Aimee Little Spotted Horse, forty-eight years after her death?

It probably wasn't the unpretentious Buck Madigan. He was genuinely surprised by the discovery and readily admitted his continuing sadness over the girl's death. If he'd placed the vase at her grave, he simply would have said so. End of story.

Even if the ailing Gilmartin had the physical strength and wits to find his way to the remote cemetery, it wasn't likely in his character to be so sentimental. Morgan made a mental note to ask him, but already knew the answer.

Morgan checked his watch and rubbed his tired eyes. Ten-twenty. He'd let himself be distracted too long by this mouldering case, and he needed to get back to current events. He had a paper to make.

"How many pages?" Cal Nussbaum was looming over Morgan's desk, a sour expression as indelible as printer's ink on his face.

"Sorry," Morgan said, as if he'd just been startled from an angry dream. "What?"

"How many pages you want to print this week?" the overworked printer asked again brusquely.

"How many ads do we have?"

The volume of advertisements typically determined the size of the paper. A good one was roughly half ads, half news.

"Four hundred and twenty inches," Nussbaum muttered, then added sarcastically, "good enough for a humdinger of a seven-page paper."

Winchester was a town of declining fortunes. Business had been tough since Wyoming's oil boom days went bust in 1986. When the oil went away, so did the easy money. The vagabond roughnecks and itinerant toolpushers were all gone now, and only the sons of native sons remained, plying their fathers' gentler trades up and down the proud but deteriorating Main Street.

Morgan did the math and it didn't add up. Four hundred and twenty column inches might bring twenty-one hundred dollars, if everybody paid. Newsstand sales might bring in another three hundred, thanks to the grocery coupons. He needed twice that to break even.

"Make it a ten-pager," he said, already a little uneasy with the decision. "I think we can dig up enough news to make it look like we know what the hell is going on."

Cal Nussbaum's long face rumpled in a morose smile.

"I doubt it," he mumbled, then slouched off toward the backshop.

Morgan slumped in his chair. The brass bell over the front door giggled at the pressman's sardonic remark. He swiveled to see his mother in the foyer, fishing deep in her oversized handbag. Her pragmatic approach to life tended to fill her purse with items that, ironically, seemed highly impractical for any sixty-year-old woman to haul around.

"'Morning, Mom," he said, coming through the wooden gate that separated the newsroom from the small waiting area. "What brings you into town today?"

"My glasses," Rachel Morgan said.

"Your glasses?"

"I can't find my glasses," she insisted, rummaging through the collection of candies, Kleenex, odd scraps of paper, pencils, a year's worth of grocery receipts, an unopened watermelon seed packet, keys and assorted other detritus in her bag. A yellow feather fell out of her purse and floated to the floor as she dug.

"Good God, I'm starting to feel like some old woman," Rachel said.

Her silvery gray hair had a new style, cut close and permed with tiny curls. Silver bracelets with tiny Navajo symbols jangled around her wrists as she grubbed deeper in her bag. With her denim skirt, silver concho belt and tiny howling-coyote earrings, she looked every bit a Southwestern matron, maybe even a doyenne of Pueblo artisans. She had always dreamed of retiring to Santa Fe, Flagstaff, or maybe Sedona, where she knew she would see an original Georgia O'Keeffe painting and smell piñon smoke in the autumn. Maybe, when the winters grew too rigorous for her aging bones, she'd sell the place, she always said, and move "down south."

"Mom ..." Morgan said.

It was no use. She wasn't listening. In her mind, she was already retracing her steps through that clear, hot morning. Her eyes were closed, moving as they followed invisible footsteps through her memory.

"I had them this morning when I was reading the paper at home. Then I had coffee with Claire, and she showed me some darling old photographs of Bridger. Then I was reading a magazine at the hairdresser's, and I'm sure I put them ... in here ... somewhere," she said, squinting back into the dark maw of her purse.

"Mom, they're hanging around your neck," Morgan said. He tried not to sound as if he were making fun, for she prided herself on being organized.

Rachel Morgan touched her hand to the front of her faded blue western blouse, the color of Arizona sky, then smiled gamely. A red tinge crept up her neck.

"Getting old is no fun, Jeff," she demurred.

"You're not old, Mom. I think you're just *too* organized. It does a body good to forget some things every once in a while," he teased her.

"Pshaw. I came to town to have my hair done and see Claire, and I decided to come in and renew my subscription. Is this how you treat all your customers, young man?"

"Mom, that's okay. I'll take care of it," he said. He tried to close her checkbook.

"I insist, Jeff," she said stiffly, pushing his hand aside. "Anyway, I think you are working far too much, son, and not paying enough attention to your wife. She's such a good woman. You should go home earlier at night. It's not good for you to stay up all night down in this ... this filthy place. And Claire needs your help now more than ever."

It was obvious, to Morgan at least, that Claire had told her the news about the baby.

"So you know?"

A look settled across Rachel Morgan's face that every mother's child recognizes when a secret is uncovered, a look of all-knowing grace that inspires equal parts of astonishment and guilt.

"I wouldn't know up from down if I waited for my own son to tell me. Mothers have their ways. I'm very happy for you, son, but I'm afraid you're leaving Claire alone far too much at a time she needs you desperately. She's frightened."

Rachel Morgan feared something else, too. Her husband,

Ernest, long a victim of high blood pressure, died of a brain aneurysm when he was fifty-three years old. To Rachel, who'd worked twice as hard as any man raising a son and being a loyal wife to a workaholic hardware merchant, the workplace was a death chamber. And, of course, she sympathized less now with her son than with his worried, lonely wife. She saw in Jefferson the same hard-working, serious tendencies that killed her husband.

And if she only knew how close her son was to busting a vein over his business now, she'd pinch his ear and march him straight home to save his life.

"Mom, we're just getting started in business here," he explained. "It's always tough at the beginning. Things will slow down when I get into the swing of it. Claire is a trouper. Don't worry."

With her spectacles now on her nose, Rachel Morgan was making out a check for her subscription, like the proud and dutiful mother of a newspaperman she was. She stripped off the check, then dropped the pen and checkbook back into hiding in her cluttered handbag.

"Well, just remember that it makes no sense to have a heart attack over something that sells for a quarter," she warned him. "Just make sure I get my paper. It's been late the last few weeks. I can't do anything on a Thursday 'til I get my paper. See what you can do, son. And don't be a stranger. Come visit your lonesome mother once in a while."

Rachel Morgan handed him her check and left, sweeping out the front door and up Main Street in her denim skirt.

No matter how imperiled the business got, Jefferson Morgan didn't think a mother should pay for a subscription to her own son's newspaper. He started to tear up her check, but stopped when he looked closer.

The check was for ten thousand dollars.

The paper devoured time voraciously, like a hungry animal.

For three days, Jefferson Morgan did nothing else but produce the latest edition of the Winchester *Bullet* as if it were the last. He was determined not to miss deadline for the fifth consecutive week. He postponed every task that wasn't part of making a newspaper, except one:. He called his mother and thanked her for the generous loan, promising to pay it back within the year. Her money bought him more than she knew: Time. Maybe a month.

Other than that, Morgan worked feverishly, unaware of the time for hours at a stretch. He wrote a dozen stories, answered phones, "souped" film and printed photos, sketched out dummies for a few pages, and rode herd on the reporters and ad saleswoman. He looked up once from his terminal and they were all gone. He cursed, then realized it was after seven, long past quitting time.

He came home at dawn on Tuesday, slept a few hours, then went back to the newsroom, where he fell asleep at his desk sometime after midnight. He awoke just before dawn Wednesday.

Morgan's mouth was pasty and rancid. His head ached, and his hands were thick and clumsy. After two cups of coffee, he felt human again, but hollow. He sniffed under the arms of his wrinkled shirt and decided he could safely go down to The Griddle, a favorite breakfast spot for truckers, ranchers and other working men who carried their musk with virile pride. He didn't have a choice anyway, since it was the only place in town open before sunrise.

The morning sky was like dark suede, reflecting the coming light. Winchester's only traffic light slowly blinked yellow, lending a cautious rhythm to the silent dark.

Warm light spilled through The Griddle's front window. Tiny bells tinkled as Morgan came through the front door and he took a seat at the long counter cluttered with ketchup bottles, sugar dispensers, little plastic creamers and menus crammed between stainless steel napkin holders. Too tired to look through the menu, he scanned The Griddle's Wednesday special, scrawled, misspellings and all, in yellow chalk on a blackboard over the coffee machine:. *Two eggs (any style) hashbrowns, sausauge or bacon, toast or short stack, coffe $3.95. No subsistitutions.*

The waitress, Suzie, was a petite woman in her late twenties. She was pretty, but wore too much eye makeup, giving her a raccoon-like appearance under the fluorescent lights. Her bleached blond hair was short and looked as if it was still wet when she arrived at work that morning. Her fingernails were trimmed working-woman close and painted cherry red, to match her lipstick.

She had that far-off look he'd seen in people who never went anywhere. Still, she was pretty enough to catch some cowboy's eye long before last call on a Saturday night.

Morgan ordered the breakfast special, over medium with bacon.

"Regular or unleaded?" she asked, snatching a fat glass pot of coffee from a warmer behind the counter. Comforting curls of steam rose from the opaque liquid inside.

"Better give me the hard stuff," he said.

The coffee was hot and thick, a liquid alarm clock.

Suzie leaned forward and looked down the counter. A couple of ranch hands were shoveling mashed eggs into their mouths in heaping forkfuls, washing it down with coffee. One of them, a rough-looking guy with long hair, wore a cellular phone on his wide leather belt. As she bent near Morgan, she smelled like peach soap, an unexpected scent among the odors of cooking fat, fresh black coffee and male sweat.

"What's news?" she asked as she fetched a pencil hidden beneath her hair and toted up somebody's breakfast tab.

"You tell me," Morgan said, stirring his oversweetened coffee. "You probably know better than me."

"I hear it all," she said without looking up.

"Maybe I ought to hire you as a reporter. Maybe we could get some of that good stuff in the paper."

"Maybe so," Suzie responded, "but you couldn't print half the stuff I hear in this place. Who's makin' love to who, who's got money troubles, who's got The Goat. It's, like, a family newspaper, right?"

"The Goat" was a quaint tradition in Winchester. Any married man or woman who dared commit adultery might awake any morning to find a billy goat tethered in his or her front yard, the town's unique symbol for faithlessness.

With the graceful dispatch peculiar to seasoned waitresses, Suzie hustled off to her other customers, busing tables and combining some half-empty ketchup bottles. Morgan watched her work, knowing she washed the same tables twenty times a day, poured a thousand cups of coffee, for a couple of bucks an hour plus tips. He couldn't know what her dreams were, but he knew she must have them. Some might come true, most wouldn't. In the end, he simply didn't know if there was much difference between the two of them.

She slid Morgan's ticket under his coffee saucer as she took his empty plate away.

"I'll make a deal with you. If you're gonna keep working so damn hard, I'll let you know if I hear anything you could print," she said. "Deal?"

"Sure," he said, shaking her hand, still damp from the bar rag she used to wipe down the counter on both sides of him. It never occurred that she might feel sorry for him more than he felt sorry for her. "Deal."

He left five one-dollar bills on the counter and left. The sun was just beginning to spill its orange light on Main Street's east-facing shops as he walked toward *The Bullet*.

It was the last day of July and it was already hot. It would get hotter, Morgan knew.

The paper was late again. More than an hour.

The guys at the post office hooted and jostled one another when Cal Nussbaum brought nearly four thousand papers to the back door. It was just before seven o'clock, two hours past closing.

"Six forty-eight," one of them said. "Who had six forty-eight?"

"Clem was closest," said another. "Clem, dammit. I had eight-forty."

Clement Judy, one of the front-desk mail clerks, had won the postmen's pool on how late *The Bullet* would be this week. The papers arrived thirteen minutes before he said they would, but his guess was still good enough to take the pot.

Cal Nussbaum was angry and more than a little humiliated. A butt-sprung postal worker had won sixteen bucks and two of the paper's bribery beers for betting on *The Bullet*'s tardiness. He'd always hated them because they hid behind their union rules and sniveled about working harder than they ever did. Cal had worked all his life at *The Bullet*, working twice as hard and earning half as much as any of them. Now they were laughing at him.

Without saying a word, he dropped a twelve-pack of Michelob on a mail-sorting table and cursed to himself all the way back to the delivery van.

A fuckin' postal worker, goddammit. Ain't they got nothin' better to do?

Steamed, Cal threw the van into reverse. Gravel spewed beneath the salt-corroded underbelly of the old Chevy wreck.

Things got to be pretty fuckin' piss-poor when even the psycho geeks down at the post office think you've screwed the pooch. Can't deliver the goddam mail in less than three days, but they can hoot about the paper being a couple hours late. Motherfuckers.

Cal jammed the brakes hard, spun around and horsed the wheel toward the street. A few postal workers watched him from the loading dock, drinking beer and guffawing like light-blue, stripe-legged crows. The van jolted over the curb, scraping its bottom on the sidewalk and leaving a rusty slash that pointed in the general direction of the Four Aces saloon.

Fuck 'em all, goddammit.

CHAPTER EIGHT

The Teepee Motor Lodge was a roadside relic, a cheap fleabag on the western edge of Winchester where the crumbling brown stucco looked like a peeling scab.

The neon "Vacancy" light on the tipi-shaped sign in the parking lot had long ago flamed out, probably because most of the dump's twenty dollar-a-night cubby holes had been available around the clock for a decade.

Morgan drove past the motel office, where an unnozzled hose was propped on some white-washed rocks, bubbling into a frowzy patch of crabgrass no bigger than a twin blanket. It was late morning on a summer Thursday, an hour before checkout time, but no cars were parked in the unpaved lot. Renegade ragweed poked through the hardpan and scattered gravel, and thrived beneath the rooms' blinded windows, where condensation dripped off rust-flecked air conditioners.

The place was empty.

Morgan circled behind the long row of rooms to the rear, where a jungle of thistle and quackgrass, broken hoses, unidentifiable reddish-brown machine parts and grasshoppers flourished. The body of a wrecked pickup, its tires crapped out long ago, nestled in a snarl of tumbleweeds. A faded bumper sticker was peeling off a piece of cockeyed chrome:

Lord, please grant us another boom.
We won't piss it away this time.

In those salad days of the oil boom, the trailers out back were rented to freelance hookers who, the roughnecks joked, pumped more barrels than any rig. The law generally looked the other way because the girls' presence gave oilfield workers an outlet for both their white-hot urges and wads of money that would otherwise be spent on drinking, speed and dog fights. Prostitution was the least of worries for the overworked and outnumbered deputies of Perry County.

But now, ten years later, the trailers were rented out to too-lost and too-thrifty tourist families who invariably complained about the big bugs in the tiny shower stalls and the cratered mattresses that once gave so much pleasure. Of course, the traveler paid a little more for these "deluxe" accommodations: Twenty-five dollars a night, no charge for the bug spray.

The bent aluminum screen door on Number Eight was propped open with a rusty pipe, though Morgan wondered why: The screen itself was gone and the closing spring dangled from a rusty chain. The trailer rested on four sunken piles of cinder blocks and the crawlspace underneath was partially hidden by weathered scraps of plywood cut in irregular shapes.

Morgan knocked. All the shades were drawn, but he heard creaking footsteps inside, slow and painful, the floor moaning churlishly beneath each one.

Gilmartin cracked open the door and some of the sour air inside escaped. He stood there in a soiled tee-shirt and blue, prison-issue boxer shorts. His legs were painfully emaciated, hairless and webbed with blue veins. A cigarette dangled from his pale, thin lips.

"Looky who's here," he rasped in his sandpapery, sarcastic voice. "It's the paper boy. Sorry, sonny, I canceled my subscription. You're too fuckin' late."

"Mr. Gilmartin, did you get my message? I told the clerk to tell you I was coming today."

"It's been a week, goddammit."

The old convict's abraded voice was weaker, if not gentler,

and his face was pallid. His white hair was matted to his skull. But his eyes were searing.

Morgan shoved his hands in his pockets, feeling suddenly uneasy and unwelcome.

"I'm sorry, but I told you I had to check out your story and I had other obligations at the paper. I came as soon as I could. I think we ..."

"I don't give a fuck about your other obligations. Got that? I haven't got time for your newspaper bullshit."

Gilmartin flicked his half-smoked cigarette out the door and retreated back into the trailer's foul darkness, leaving the door open. After a moment standing alone outside, watching a filament of thin blue smoke rise from the dry weeds then disappear, Morgan followed him, certain it was the only invitation he'd get.

The trailer's one long room was squalid. Flies clustered around something rotting in the sink, undaunted by the ceaseless trickle of water from the leaky tap. A dozen prescription bottles lay open on the unwashed counter, loose pills scattered among half-eaten pizza crusts and puddles of spilled water. Van Johnson was on the television in an old World War II movie, but the sound was turned down.

While Morgan surveyed the mess around him, the swamp cooler rattled to life, awakened from its algae-encrusted metallic dreams. It clacked and sputtered as if someone had started an ancient truck engine inside the trailer.

Morgan saw a few crumpled fast-food bags and unopened ketchup packets on the linoleum floor. Some empty soup cans and dirty spoons were stuck to the top of the dented electric stove. And unfiltered cigarette butts were snubbed out on plastic dinner plates on a card table in front of the TV. Gilmartin wasn't eating well.

The old man sagged into a shabby couch a few feet from the screen and lit another cigarette, a butt-clogged ashtray within easy reach. A *Hustler* magazine was draped across the sofa's armrest. The fly of Gilmartin's wrinkled boxer shorts gapped immodestly, but if he knew it, he didn't care.

Morgan took the only other seat, a steel dinette chair with no back, ornamented with smelly socks.

For an uncomfortable moment, they simply watched each other. Then Morgan spoke.

"Well, Mr. Gilmartin, I've looked into your case. I know you've been waiting to hear back from me. I don't know where to begin. There's just not much to go on. A few newspaper stories, the court file, what you've already told me ..."

"No shit, Sherlock," Gilmartin growled.

A silent war raged on the television and the old man's eyes strayed to it as he spoke, as if Morgan's presence meant less to him than Van Johnson's.

"I thought you were supposed to be some hotshot crime reporter. You're gonna have to do more than read all the fuckin' lies they told about me. They wanted to fry my ass. Do you think they're gonna give me a break? Do you think anybody was gonna tell my side of the story?"

Morgan got a notebook and pencil from his shirt pocket. He flipped the pages until he found a blank one.

"Okay, let's start there. What *is* your side of the story, Mr. Gilmartin?"

"I didn't do it," the old man said. "That's my side of the story, paper boy. Period. End of fuckin' story."

By being prickly and feigning indifference, Gilmartin made it difficult to be sympathetic. If Gilmartin was testing his limits, he'd gone far enough. Morgan suppressed his impatience, barely, and spoke a language Gilmartin understood.

"That's not good enough, and you know it. You came to me, remember? If you want my help, you're going to have to be totally honest with me, or I'm out of here. You've got to answer a lot of questions. I've got better things to do with my time than be dicked around by some asshole con man who hates the world."

Gilmartin's attention suddenly shifted away from the television. He fixed his gaze on Morgan, his eyes like black ice.

Morgan knew there was a time when he could not have talked to the former millworker like that without a thrashing. In a way, he'd be relieved now if the old man threw him out. He could get on with his life, while Gilmartin got on with his death.

"You ask the questions," Gilmartin said finally. The hatred had drained from his voice, and his eyes warmed, albeit only by a degree or two. The old con would respect him only if he demanded it. "I'll tell you what I know. And I'll tell you what I don't know. But it all starts the same: I didn't do it."

"But you pleaded guilty. That's the thing I can't get out of my mind. Forty-eight years ago, you admitted you did it. If you didn't kill Aimee, why did you plead guilty?"

"I was fucked seven ways to sundown, see?" Gilmartin said. A Camel cigarette was clamped between his fingers, a long ash ready to fall in his lap. "They gave me a faggot lawyer who couldn't find his ass with both hands. He was scared shitless. They said they had witnesses who would say I threatened that girl's daddy. The paper got everybody whipped up so I never stood a chance with a jury. I was fucked, just fucked."

"Why didn't you have an alibi? You could have helped yourself more than you did. You only had to tell them where you were when it happened."

Gilmartin turned his eyes away, back to the television. He took a long, thoughtful draw on his cigarette, then tapped his ash onto the haggard carpet.

"They busted me two weeks after that girl disappeared. How the fuck do I know where I was? I was out of work and hadn't worked in a month. I was living in the bars, whorin' around and stealin' cows to make a few bucks so I could drink and whore some more. Most of the time, I was drunk on my ass. Whacked out, you know? I don't know exactly where I was when it happened, that's the truth, but I wasn't bein' a Boy Scout, I'm pretty sure of that."

Clearly, the subject of an alibi—perhaps the single, elusive memory that meant the difference between a man's death and his freedom—had consumed Gilmartin for most of his life, but Morgan pressed him further.

"You have no idea whatsoever where you were? That's hard to believe, even now. If my life depended on it, I think I could remember what I had for breakfast on this day last year."

Sinewy muscles pulsed under the paper-thin skin that stretched across Gilmartin's jaw, but he looked squarely into Morgan's eyes when he spoke.

"You wasn't me, paper boy. And it's a good chance that wherever I was I didn't want anybody to know. Partners fuck you up every time. That's the God's honest truth. I've had near fifty years to think about it, but I'll be goddamned if I can recall. When you ain't got no point in life, and I didn't, what the fuck is there to remember? But they told me to keep my mouth shut anyhow."

"Who told you?"

"The lawyer, Fenwick. Said I was better to say I didn't remember than to risk lookin' like a liar. Said they'd have to prove their case. Innocent 'til proven guilty and all that shit. So I kept my trap closed until things looked real bad for me, and then it was too goddamned late."

For all his inexperience, Fenwick appeared to have given his client at least one good bit of advice. Morgan had once seen an enormous largemouth bass mounted on the wall of a famous criminal defense lawyer's Chicago law office, with a brass plaque beneath it that said: "He'd be free today if he'd only kept his mouth shut."

"Did Fenwick tell you to plead guilty, too?"

The wet end of Gilmartin's Camel was beginning to dissolve into soggy paper and bits of tobacco. He pursed his lips like he was blowing a trumpet, spitting a tiny brown fleck toward the TV.

"No. That was my idea. All I could think about was dyin'

in that fuckin' chair. It sort of throttled me. I couldn't breathe. Then I lost my fuckin' nerve. It was the only way I could save my own ass. No jury was gonna look at me and say I was innocent. No fuckin' way. And when I thought about dyin' in that chair ..."

Gilmartin paused for a long time, his lips stiffening as he swallowed the ache in the back of his throat.

"I made a deal to save my life. I didn't want to be cooked alive. I knew what that was like."

"How could you be so sure you'd be convicted?" Morgan asked.

"Are you fuckin' kidding me? No way I was gonna get a fair shake. The paper said I was guilty and everybody believed it."

Morgan let it ride. Most cons were congenitally incapable of taking responsibility for their actions. They always blamed somebody or something else, nurture, nature, society, grade school teachers, parents, their own lawyers, even the press. Gilmartin was no different. *The Bullet* had pursued the story aggressively, Morgan knew from reading the back issues, but short of interviewing Gilmartin himself, the coverage had been fair.

"I read the old papers, Mr. Gilmartin," he said. "But I never saw anything like that."

Gilmartin snapped back, pointing at Morgan angrily with the stubby cigarette.

"It was there, goddammit. In black and white. Said I done killed that little girl. Printed a picture to make me look like I done it, too. They come out and said I done it."

"No, I'm sorry, but it didn't say that."

In the angry silence between them, Morgan remembered the typed confession in Gilmartin's court jacket. It bore no signature, just an X where Gilmartin should have signed.

"Can you read, Mr. Gilmartin?" he asked.

"What the fuck do you mean by that?"

"You signed your own confession with an 'X.' I need to know if you can read and write."

"I can read as good as you, you arrogant prick. I read lots of books in the joint."

"So why didn't you sign your name?—Why do you think the newspaper printed something it never printed? Mr. Gilmartin, you promised me you'd be honest."

"Fuck you," Gilmartin said, relenting. "I learned to read in the joint after that, but I know what the papers said about me. They said I was a killer. I saw the fuckin' pictures. Everybody saw the fuckin' pictures. The paper didn't need to say it right out. They had it in for me."

For the first time, Morgan felt sorry for the old man. He was clearly ashamed of his inability to read or write. But he was right about one thing: Anybody who saw his jailhouse photo in *The Bullet*, with his malevolent smile and "TERROR" tattooed on his arm, would have presumed his guilt.

"Did you know Charlie Little Spotted Horse before the murder? Did you threaten him?"

"I saw him around, sometimes we played cards. Yeah, we scrapped once over some money, maybe ten bucks, but I was drunk and I don't recollect what happened. Maybe I said some stuff, but it ended there. Anyhow, I didn't know nothin' about no daughter or anything like that. I didn't give a shit about no damn Indian, not like to kill some innocent little girl over ten lousy bucks."

"But you threatened him?"

"Open your ears up, boy," Gilmartin barked, poking a bony finger in his right ear. "I said maybe so. But I said lots of shit worse in my life. Didn't make no matter if it was a Indian or a gook or a nigger or a white guy. It didn't mean nothin'. Just words."

Just then, somebody knocked on the door.

"Goddam maid," Gilmartin said. Then he yelled loud enough for her to hear outside, "*Mañana.*"

Another knock rattled the metal door, its detached chain rattling against it like a discordant chime. Whoever waited outside wasn't leaving.

"*Mañana*, goddammit!" Gilmartin cursed loudly.

Three insistent knocks followed.

Morgan got up and opened the door. A fat Mexican woman stood on the wooden step, her pudgy chestnut face shiny with sweat. She was surprised to see him in the doorway, and her wide, dark eyes looked spooked, as if she might run. She wore a maid's uniform but she had no cart or towels. A greasy lunch bag dangled from her sausage-like fingers.

"*Por señor,*" she said nervously, holding the bag out in front of her. "*Merienda. Hamburguesa.*"

"Give her ten bucks," Gilmartin yelled from the couch. "Wallet's behind the toilet tank."

Morgan squeezed into the trailer's rancid lavatory and groped behind the cool porcelain tank, which trickled constantly somewhere inside. Gilmartin's thick, leather billfold was jammed between the tank and the wall. It was stuffed with money, mostly hundreds and fifties. Morgan found a ten among them and handed it to the maid, who lingered expectantly on the porch, smiling lewdly.

He smiled back and waved at her. She wouldn't leave.

"She's still here," he said to Gilmartin. "She looks like she's expecting more."

"*Mañana, Celestina, mañana. Gracias,*" Gilmartin hollered again in his bad Mexican accent, and she waddled off toward the motel office.

Morgan handed the bag to Gilmartin, who fished inside and tore off the waxed paper that was neatly wrapped around a homemade hamburger. The mouth-watering smell of it filled the dirty little space they shared and Morgan suddenly felt hungry.

"Celestina, nice gal, for a Mex. She brings me food every day," he said, nibbling at the edges of the saucer-sized sandwich. "Her old man ran off and left her with five or six *muchachos* to feed. I give her ten bucks no matter what she brings. What the fuck else can I spend it on? Some days, she throws in a hand job for an extra ten-spot. I guess you could say I was a big tipper."

Amused by his own humor, Gilmartin cackled a hoarse laugh, then coughed violently into his hand. After the spell had passed, when he wiped his fingers across his T-shirt, Morgan saw tinges of blood in the sticky sputum.

"I was twenty-five years old the last time a woman touched my dick. Can't hardly remember what it was like to have it get hard as a rock. Shit, most of the time I can't get it up at all because of all these fuckin' pills, so she gets ten bucks for the good-faith effort. Damn Mexican gal's got real soft hands, you know?"

Morgan was a little embarrassed and a little sad for the old man, but tried not to let it show. He knew he could never understand the deprivation, sexual or otherwise, of almost fifty years in prison. Now the old man had a month, maybe less, to live, no time for the pretense of romance.

"Where does the money come from?" Morgan asked.

Gilmartin stopped eating after a bite or two. He searched Morgan's eyes for a sign that he already knew.

"I had some saved up in prison. The last five or six years, I tied fishing flies and sold 'em to a sporting goods place in town. Takes good eyes, you know, all that tiny work. Always had sharp eyes. I got good at it, made some money. Kept me out of trouble. Nothin' wrong with that, is there?"

"How much did you earn for tying flies?"

"Thirty cents on most of 'em. Sixty on the whoppers. Good days, I done maybe ten first-class flies. Money went straight to my prison account. Good money, too, for prison."

Morgan penciled out the math in his notebook.

"Best case, at six bucks a day, you'd do what, a couple thousand bucks a year? In six years, assuming you didn't spend any of it, you'd have, at most, twelve thousand bucks," Morgan said.

The old man re-wrapped his partially eaten burger in the greasy wax paper and stuffed it back in its bag. He wiped a dollop of mustard off his finger onto his shorts and scratched his testicles.

"Lost my fuckin' appetite. Yeah, it came out maybe seven or eight thousand all together, I reckon. It adds up. That kind of money goes a long way in the joint."

"Mr. Gilmartin, the parole office tells me you left prison with almost seventy thousand dollars. Where'd you get that kind of money? It wasn't from tying Royal Coachmen and Yellow Sallies."

Gilmartin sucked a piece of food from between his graying teeth, then smiled slyly.

"So, paper boy, you know your fishin' flies. And you done more research than lookin' in them old papers, didn't you?"

"Mr. Gilmartin, if you don't intend to tell me everything, there's no way I can help you. So far, you haven't been much help. Time is running out. The longer you stall, the less time I have to find out what happened. Why don't you start by telling me where you got the money?"

If he heard, he didn't show it. Gilmartin dug his finger inside an empty pack of Camels, then tossed it on the floor. His steely eyes searched all the flat spots within an arm's reach of where he sat. Nothing.

Then he spoke as he peeled back the sofa cushion beside him and looked beneath it.

"Well, if you find out, we'll both know, paper boy. I haven't got the faintest fuckin' idea. About ten years back, it just started showin' up in my account. The warden told me an envelope was left at the front gate with a lot of cash, which they put in my account. Every year at the same time, the envelope showed up. Once, there was ten thousand dollars stuffed inside, but most of the time it was less. Hey, you seen a fresh pack of smokes around here?"

"So you don't know where it came from?"

"It came from the store across the road. Camels."

Morgan was losing his patience with the old man. He leaned forward, a grave furrow rippling across his forehead as he lowered his voice one angry octave.

"The money you got in prison, not the cigarettes."

"I'm shittin' you, paper boy. You're too fuckin' serious. Jesus, get a sense of humor or you're gonna die of a stroke before I die of cancer. If there's one thing I know about life it's how to stay in it. I didn't survive no fuckin' forty-eight years in prison by gettin' steamed about every little goddam thing."

Morgan took a deep breath and let it out slowly, imperceptibly.

"The money, Mr. Gilmartin. An inheritance? A pay-off? An old investment? A lottery ticket? Help me understand how seventy thousand dollars just lands in your lap."

"My daddy died so poor they put him in one grave with six other dead folks. Lucky they was all related some way. Poor folks always are. I never had no money to start with and the interest on nothin' is nothin'. And who'd pay me off? For what?"

"Maybe to take the fall for a murder?"

Gilmartin found his pack of Camels hidden under some dirty underwear piled capriciously on the floor. He lit up and savored his first breath of its unfiltered smoke.

"Fuck you, paper boy. I didn't do it and if I knew who did, I sure wouldn't take that secret to my grave. I'd tell you right here, wouldn't I? Why would I come to you to clear my name if I could clear it myself by writing a letter to the goddam governor? What the hell would keep me from telling you now? Fear of dyin'? Don't make me laugh. It hurts to laugh."

It was the first thing Gilmartin had said that Morgan could believe. He had no reason to protect anyone if he expected to die within a few weeks. And if it had been a pay-off, why was it being paid so long after the killing? Convinced as he was that Gilmartin was telling the truth about that much, the money remained a mystery.

"Did anyone ever see this person who left the envelope?"

"Sure, but it was never the same people. Just some poor junkies hired to deliver the envelope."

"There was never any note? Nothing to help you understand where this money came from?"

"Nothing. Just cold cash in a plain envelope. Fuckin' warden wouldn't let me spend any of it, though. Just let it sit in my account. It was like them girls in the magazines, too pretty to touch. I reckon the warden wanted me to put him in my will, the fuck."

Morgan watched Gilmartin's eyes. Common liars avoided eye contact; expert liars looked right through you. Gilmartin's small, slicing eyes were now riveted on Morgan.

"You said it came about the same time every year."

"Yeah, about this time of year, first week of August. Always in August. Ten years, like clockwork. Always on the same day, too."

"Always?"

"You think I'd forget? No fuckin' way. It always came on the day that little girl disappeared, August second."

Morgan glanced at the date window on his watch.

"That's tomorrow," he said.

"No shit," the old man rolled his eyes. "You went to college to get so observant?"

So Gilmartin's mysterious windfall *was* related somehow to Aimee Little Spotted Horse's death. *One day.* It was no coincidence, but the puzzle was far from solved. And Morgan was growing intolerant of the old man's game of twenty questions.

"I asked if you had any idea why somebody would pay you seventy thousand dollars and you told me you didn't," Morgan said, boiling over. "You think it was a goddam coincidence that it was delivered on that particular day, of all days, *ten years in a row*? Are you just yanking my chain here? Goddammit, I'm this close to walking out of here right now. You can die with this on your head, for all I care."

Gilmartin swatted the air, dismissing Morgan's spurt of hostility.

"You didn't ask me *why* I got it. You asked me *where* it come from. A con learns fast to answer only the questions he's asked and keep his trap shut on everything else. Ask me better questions and I'll give you better answers."

Morgan clenched his jaw and glared back at the old man.

"Do you have any idea who, what, when, where, why or how this money was given to you? Any idea at all?" Morgan asked in a lower voice. He was back in control, but his anger was restrained by the barest thread.

"Like I said, I know nothin' about any of that," Gilmartin said. "And it ain't likely I'll be seein' any more of it now that I'm out. This should be enough to bury my sorry ass, right fine."

He raised his empty, incised palms toward Morgan as if he were surrendering. His arthritic fingers looked like gnarled sprouts from a patch of cracked earth. Morgan glowered at him.

"It came on that day every year, and fuck if I know who did it or why. There ain't no more. End of fuckin' story. I swear."

"You never asked?"

"Sure I asked, but nobody knew nothin'. Fuckin' screws. Why would The Man help a con? What the fuck did they care?"

A fly flitted around Morgan's head and he swept his hand in front of his face as it darted toward him. He studied Gilmartin, who had turned back toward the television.

The old man's body was wasting away. His arms and legs looked longer than they were, their joints bulging. Every few minutes, he flinched in pain. Holding his breath, he'd press his palm against his abdomen until the discomfort washed through him.

"Are you going to be okay, Mr. Gilmartin?"

"No," he said. "I'm gonna die."

The old man's dark humor was a morbid comfort to Morgan. Some light still burned inside him that wasn't evil.

"Can I get you something? Medicine? Water?"

Gilmartin shook his head and closed his eyes as a new surge of pain swelled in him. Morgan watched his face twist as he stopped his shallow breathing. The cigarette butt between his fingers fell onto the couch cushion. Morgan couldn't snatch it up before it burned a small, pungent hole in the threadbare cover. He dropped it into an empty mushroom soup can that lay half-submerged in the sink's dirty water.

A low, tormented groan murmured in Gilmartin's throat. After a painful moment of silence, he breathed again, but his eyes were glassy and dispirited.

"Get me two of them red caps on the counter, and one of the big-assed white ones," Gilmartin said. "They won't kill this fuckin' beast, but they'll settle it down for a while."

Morgan sorted through the multi-colored potpourri of pain-killers and empty prescription bottles strewn across the counter. Tylox, Mepergan-Fortis, Demerol, all analgesics. Only one bottle remained unopened. It was placed on the window sill above the putrid sink, safe and waiting: Morphine tabs.

Morgan rinsed a stained coffee cup under the sputtering tap and filled it with cold water.

"What kind of cancer do you have, Mr. Gilmartin?" he asked as the old man choked down his medicine.

"Lung cancer. They called it 'oat-cell' cancer, as in oatmeal mush. Fuck if I know why. The prison docs guess it's from the smokes, but how the fuck would they know? I breathed plenty of bad air in the joint. Lots had death floating in it like dust. Could be death I sucked in."

Maybe death does lurk in the air, waiting to be inhaled, Morgan thought. Gilmartin went on.

"Anyhow, the cancer's startin' to bust outta my lung and get into my guts, pancreas, up the asshole, all that. Can't do nothin' about it except take these fuckin' pain pills and wait for it to kill me, which ain't gonna be long."

Cancer could be long or short, but never merciful, Morgan knew. Bridger had suffered long with his leukemia, and the last few weeks were excruciating. Morgan prayed that death would steal him away, absolve the little boy's pain, but it didn't come quick enough. When it was over at last, a small, hidden part of Morgan was unburdened. He never told Claire, but he believed she, too, had prayed for the end to be swift. It wasn't.

"You should go to a hospital, maybe get chemotherapy," he said.

"No way. I spent most of my life locked up and I ain't gonna spend the rest of it tied down. No fuckin' way. I'm free now and I'm gonna die free. No radiation and no chemistry is gonna make me live forever. Might hurt like a motherfucker, I don't know, but I ain't dyin' closed up from the world, pukin' and glowin' in the dark. Just me, here. Alone."

"Dying could be more comfortable in a hospital," Morgan told him. "It doesn't have to be painful."

Morgan knew he was lying to the old man. He knew it would hurt, no matter what.

"I'm out now, and I'm stayin' out. Not gonna sleep through my last liberty. No fuckin' way. That's why I'm saving that morphine for the last, to keep the dyin' from hurtin'."

Gilmartin fished another cigarette out of his pack.

"Why don't you quit," Morgan said. "The smoking can't help."

"What's it gonna do, kill me? Dyin's bad enough without trying to quit smokin' at the same time. A man should die with at least one bad habit, or what the fuck was the reason for livin'?"

"Well, it might mean a few more hours, maybe days," Morgan said.

"Not my style, paper boy. Every time I got straight, seems like I fucked myself up. Why stop now? I even got to the top once, goddammit ..."

Gilmartin clouded up. His bottom lip quivered as he sucked a long draw on his cigarette.

"The top?" Morgan asked.

"Top of the joint. It had three tiers, sort of like balconies around the open middle. A hundred fuckin' years old, that place. The heat come from an old steam plant, where I worked when I first got to the joint. In the winter, when it got cold enough to freeze the evil out of a man, that old steamer would run night and day. But the heat rose up to the top tier, leavin' the bottom colder than a witch's tit. That's where the fresh meat started, down at the bottom, with all the Ice Men."

"The Ice Men?"

"The troublemakers and the baby-fuckers. The hard cases were always at the bottom, the coldest corner of that Hell. Yeah, the Ice Men. The cold only made them harder. When I first got to the joint, I was there at the bottom and in the first winter, four guys froze to death in their cells. Couldn't bury 'em in the prison graveyard because the ground was froze too solid to dig. They just parked 'em in the ice house 'til spring."

"Five more winters, I was down there in the hole. I stayed straight, mostly. Got to know the color of blue a man turns when he freezes to death, like the sky when it gets washed out by the sun reflectin' off snow, you know? Before they died, these guys would see shit that wasn't there and holler at the moon. Their minds were all fucked up. They'd strip off their clothes and die with their eyes wide open. Crazy assholes. The Ice Men would carry them out, froze in whatever position they died. Most was just sitting."

Victims of hypothermia were often found naked, Morgan knew from hundreds of police reports he'd seen in Chicago winters. A medical examiner in the city morgue once told him a freezing person suffered terminal hallucinations and, because his internal thermostat was paralyzed by the cold, actually feels warm. So he takes off his clothes.

"So the idea was to move higher, then, right?" Morgan asked.

"Get to the top," Gilmartin brooded in his memory. "Fuck, yeah. The guys at the top, they didn't die froze to their toilet. That was the Ritz. That was livin'."

"So you got to the top. You made it."

"Damn straight. They moved me to the middle six years after I got to the joint, and then to the top three years after that. Was there for ten years. It was the good life in the joint."

"What happened?"

Gilmartin rubbed an invisible blemish from his naked thigh, trying to erase a stain as indelible as time. He didn't speak for a long while.

"I got stupid. Back in 'sixty-seven, some punks on my steam crew wanted to make a run for it. Had a plan and everything. They busted some heater pipes, and then hid out in the repairman's van. He drove 'em out the front gate. Fuckin' clean getaway."

"Why didn't you go with them?"

"First, I was gonna go with them, but I got hinky. I was up for parole in a year. I stayed behind, but I kept my mouth shut. The Man caught one of 'em in a few days, but the other two was never caught, not to this day. Goddam, I coulda been with 'em. Been free."

Freedom had its cost, Morgan knew, even for a man who'd steal it.

"So how'd you get moved off the top tier?"

"The kid snitched after they caught him. The little fucker," Gilmartin spewed. "Said I was in on the escape plan all the way. Fuck, the worst thing I did was keep my trap shut. I fought like hell, but the warden busted me back to the bottom anyhow. Worse than that, I lost my chance for parole. Nineteen years, I kept my nose clean, then I'm back at the bottom with the Ice Men, frozen in my time like a dead man."

Morgan remembered what the parole director had told him, perhaps telegraphing Gilmartin's difficulty: Under Wyoming law, an escape attempt renders an inmate ineligible for parole during his natural sentence. In Gilmartin's case, that was the rest of his life.

He thought it was ironic that Neeley Gilmartin, who had avoided the lethal heat of the electric chair, was instead condemned to life in a frigid abyss. Worse, the old man's idea of freedom was dying alone in a whorehouse trailer, no needles, no tubes. His only nurse was a Mexican maid who brought him food and sometimes made him feel like a man again.

"Did you ever try to tell anybody at the prison what you've told me?"

"Shit, paper boy, nobody in the joint ever did the crime. Everybody's innocent, to hear them tell it. Sure I told some people, but nobody listens. After eight or ten years of tellin' the same story, you just stop. You don't even bother tryin' anymore. You just focus on stayin' alive."

"When they let you out, why'd you come back here?" Morgan wanted to know.

"No place else to go. Lived here most of my life, except for the war and the joint. And you were here."

"Me?"

"I saw in the paper at the prison library, before I got out. That's how I taught myself to read in the joint, readin' the newspapers. Short words and lots of pictures. I saw the story about you bein' the new editor, and I knew you would help me."

"Why me?"

"I don't know. Your picture looked honest maybe. You ain't one of them, you didn't know. Or maybe because you come back here, too. We both come back here to save ourselves, didn't we? Huh?"

Morgan was still wary. He'd been used by cons almost from the first week on the cop beat in Chicago. Gilmartin, a tough jailhouse veteran who was by turns threatening and vulnerable, now seemed genuinely desperate. But Morgan still believed they were far from kindred spirits.

The old man's pain-dulled eyes were fixed on the television's flickering screen, sometimes rolling upward as the drugs began seeping through his veins. Grenades exploded and machine guns roared noiselessly in a dissonant war. Van Johnson was still fighting his way across some Jap-infested island, making the world safe for democracy and, eventually, cheap electronics.

"Tell me about the war. Where did you serve?"

"I don't want to talk about it, paper boy. You ask too many questions."

Morgan put away his notebook.

"You mentioned it a couple times before. It sounds like you saw some action."

Gilmartin huffed. His speech began to sound sedated, soft. "Where?"

"Goddammit, you're a pesterin' son of a bitch. A fuckin' nosey reporter. Why don't you go bug somebody else to find who killed that little girl?"

Morgan shrugged. He'd encountered a lot of veterans who claimed they never told war stories, then with a little prodding, filled the air with their tales. So he clicked his ballpoint pen and slid it back into his shirt pocket, a deliberate indication that he was finished with his questions. He stood, smoothing his slacks where they'd rumpled around his hips, ready to leave.

"Hey, if you don't want to talk about it, fine. Some other time, huh?"

A war story couldn't be shut away so easily. Gilmartin's shoulders slumped, relaxed by the Demerol, but he motioned Morgan to sit back down. Morgan waited for him to begin.

"I was Navy, okay? A gunner's mate on a minelayer. Saw the fuckin' world before I was twenty, and saw too goddam much. First tour, we laid down mines in Casablanca and then we laid down women in Norfolk. Good duty, huh? By 'forty-four, we was sent to the other side of the world, to Guadalcanal, the Carolines, the Marshalls and Tarawa ..."

Gilmartin drifted with his memories, as if the story continued silently in his head. A cigarette burned down between his fingers as he sat there, slack-jawed. His speech was slow and fatigued.

"Those were some pretty hot spots," Morgan prompted him.

"Not like Iwo."

"You were at Iwo Jima?"

"Yeah. What a crap hole. We anchored in the harbor of a little island called Kerama Retto, on the south tip of Iwo. We was the flagship for the Pacific mine fleet, and we took all the wounded from other ships. My job was shootin' a forty-milli-meter gun, keepin' an eye out for kamikazes. Fuckin' Japs was everywhere. Shit, after a couple months, we seen it all: Suicide swimmers, kamikaze boats and planes. In April of 'forty-five we went to general quarters ninety-three times. Can you believe that shit? Every time you closed your eyes, some peckerhead Jap was trying to kill us. I had a good job. I shot back."

"Hit any?"

Smoke wreathed Gilmartin's squinted face.

"Sure. It was my job. Had a good eye, too. Always had good eyes. Expert shooter, and that's no shit. Daddy taught me on the rabbits. I didn't have no problems killin' them bastards. The Japs."

"Tell me about it."

"It's ancient history, paper boy."

"I'd still like to know."

A cigarette haze enveloped him as he collected his thoughts. He looked down at the floor as he spoke, transported back to another time.

"It was May Day in 'forty-five and my early-morning watch was almost over. The smoking lamp wasn't even lit, so it was before oh-four-hundred. The smoking lamp come on when you could smoke. It was my twenty-second birthday. The sun wasn't up, but the light was starting to seep through the smoke screen we laid down. Man, I was needin' some serious rack time. Dead tired. Then all of a sudden, four Jap planes come out of the smoke."

Slowly, Gilmartin's hands glided through the thick air, retracing the kamikazes' flight path. His sluggish, rheumy eyes followed them as if they were real, then he squinted as he got them in his imaginary sights again.

"It all happened so fuckin' fast I was the only gun that got off a shot. I kept my crosshairs on them and splashed that first motherfucker a hundred yards off the starboard bow.

"The next two come down from the stern, and I swung around on 'em. I musta hit the bomb on one and he lit up the sky in an orange fireball. The third one I hit and he veered off back into the smoke and I heard him hit the water somewheres out there.

"The last one, he come in on the port beam behind me, banked around the stern and come straight at me on the starboard side. It was misty gray, before dawn, but I swear I could see that fucker's slope-eyes as he flew in. Just me and him, like old-time gunfighters. I poured everything I had at that prick. If I hit him, it didn't do no good. Went through him like he was a goddam ghost.

"He slammed into the communications deck. He hit so hard his goddam engine pierced through the steel bulkheads and landed in the wardroom. Killed a bunch of guys eating breakfast. The rest of his plane sheared off and hit the fifty-two turret, and that's when his bomb exploded."

Gilmartin's right hand smacked into his left, his fingers splaying grotesquely. He drew a deep breath and hacked a couple times.

"Them boys inside never had a chance," he said, licking his dry lips. "Six of 'em in that closed-up turret. Never got off a shot. Fuckin' shielded mounts on them five-inch guns never was meant to take a direct hit. The crash crumpled it like a tin can so's the door wouldn't open, and they couldn't get out."

The old man showed Morgan a burn scar on the inside of

his arm, a long, liquefied swatch of skin from his wrist to the inside of his elbow that looked barely congealed.

"I tried to lever the steel door open, but the fire flared up and burned my arm and my hands. We could hear them screaming in there. They screamed going on fifteen minutes, then they stopped before we got the fire out and the wreckage cleared. Them boys ..."

A rattle shuddered in his collapsed chest. He cleared his constricted throat.

"... them boys cooked to death inside."

Gilmartin's hands began to shake. His brow tensed and his chin pressed his lips together hard. He closed his eyes and wiped his forearm across his mouth.

"After the fire was out, I was detailed to help clean out that gun mount. We pried open the door and found them. Their blistery faces were roasted brown and leathery, like the skin of an overcooked turkey. Where they touched the hot steel, their hands were almost melted away like wax. When we picked 'em up, their skin would just slip off the muscle. You'd be standin' there, holdin' this patch of a man's hide in your hands. And the stink of it can't ever be washed off. I smell it in my sleep."

"I'm sorry ..." Morgan started to say.

"You think I should be sorry, too, don't you? Fuck that. I done what I could for them. They was my buddies, too. I spent that night puking over the rail. I was twenty-two, a grown man compared to those dead boys. But I never saw nothin' like that in my life, these boys' meat all cooked, their eyeballs exploded, their fingers reaching out to me. Their mouths ... oh, God ... their mouths screaming but nothin' coming out."

Gilmartin was agitated now, more angry at himself and at the dead than at Morgan.

"Goddammit, I did everything I could. I tried to splash that last fuckin' Jap. I tried. I got the other three, didn't I? Why didn't they shoot, too? They gave me that fuckin' medal, didn't they? I did my part. I tried to save them. It was like they was screaming to me while they cooked. Their skin just come off ... But it wasn't my fault. Those poor fuckers could have shot." His throat suffocated his words, even as he determined to speak them. "I ... tried."

Gilmartin wept.

His memories and his cancer choked him. The fire had burned him up inside, too. It consumed his forgiveness and his spirit, and welded a hard core at the center of him. Neeley Gilmartin's war wound was deep within him where it couldn't be seen.

For one single, sad moment, Morgan pitied Gilmartin.

Maybe the old man really did kill Aimee Little Spotted Horse and only confessed to avoid the electric chair. But now there was an alternate, but equally plausible, explanation: He so feared dying that way, he'd say anything to avoid it.

Maybe even take the fall for a crime he didn't commit.

If his story was true, it could answer the question that nagged Morgan the most, why Gilmartin had pleaded guilty if he didn't kill the girl. It would also mean something that few people—perhaps even Gilmartin himself—knew: Guilty or not, the convicted child-killer Gilmartin might have been a genuine war hero.

Morgan stood and touched Gilmartin's heaving shoulder. He knew he'd still have to check out the old man's story, but he believed it because his cynical gut told him to believe it.

Gilmartin looked up with sad, red eyes. He was fighting off his narcotic haze, his hands floating out of rhythm with his words.

"I didn't kill that little girl, so help me God," he said. "You gotta help me. I don't want to die with it hanging over my head. That would be worse than dyin' in the chair."

"I'll do what I can, Mr. Gilmartin. I promise. Is there anything else I can get you for now?"

Gilmartin swiped the back of his hand across his eyes,

gamely trying to wipe away most traces of his misery. He grunted a little, breathed deeply and regained his familiar, steely composure.

"Yeah, paper boy," he said. "If you see Celestina, tell her to come see me tomorrow. I got something she needs to handle."

"I'll do that," Morgan said, smiling for the first time since he'd arrived.

He patted Gilmartin's shoulder and headed toward the door. It wouldn't take long to investigate Gilmartin's military background, if he got lucky and had the right information. Halfway out the door, one last question stopped him.

"Mr. Gilmartin, it would help me if I knew what ship you served on."

The old man hunched forward on his couch and raised his tee-shirt's short sleeve over his gaunt, left shoulder, proudly bearing his tattoo.

"The *USS Terror*," he said.

CHAPTER NINE

A plump clerk named Ellen, whose discount-store bifocals hung around her thick neck on a chain of yellowish faux pearls, led him into the county records vault. It was a sort of governmental library, four long walls lined with cumbersome, leather-bound deed books. They encircled a row of thick-legged work tables, built to bear the weight of the vast history surrounding them.

"Here they are," Ellen said, drawing her hand efficiently across the spines of four small volumes. "They're in order, from the First World War to the Gulf War, although there's not too many of those. These are all certified copies, some of the old ones made by hand. We file them for free in case the originals are ever lost. Let me know if I can help you find anything else."

Few people, even veteran courthouse reporters, know county clerks routinely register soldiers' discharge papers as a permanent record of their service. Morgan had stumbled on the documents years ago while researching a Vietnam veteran's murder case, and found them to be a wealth of biographical and military data taken directly from official records.

If Gilmartin's tattoo wasn't a symbol of an evil disposition, but of his patriotism, then Morgan's gut wasn't failsafe. He came to the courthouse to find out.

The clerk left Morgan alone in the vault's dead air. Volume Three, the thickest, contained records from World War Two. Scanning through the hand-written cross-index, he quickly found Neeley Gilmartin's discharge papers.

The pertinent, provable facts of his life were all there, in the government's orderly, detail-obsessed shorthand:

Neeley Gilmartin had been born May 1, 1923, in Sand Flats, Wyoming, a railroad enclave long gone from any map. He attended school through the eighth grade, not uncommon for rural children in the Depression. He joined the Navy in 1942 at the Naval Recruiting Station in Cheyenne, then was sent to basic training in San Diego. After a short stint in gunnery school, he was assigned to the USS Terror (CM5), a minelayer home-ported at Norfolk. A few years later, he spent some time in the U.S. Naval Hospital in Aiea Heights in Hawaii—to be treated for the severe burn on his arm after the kamikaze attack, Morgan surmised—then was discharged in February 1946 by the Navy's processing center in Bremerton, Washington. According to his discharge papers, he'd served four years, one month and twelve days in a war that would haunt him forever.

He left the service with a Good Conduct Medal, medals for serving in both the European and Pacific theaters, the World War Two Victory medal and a Purple Heart.

And the Navy Cross. It was the service's highest honor for heroism, second only to the Congressional Medal of Honor.

Morgan could hardly believe it. Gilmartin was a bona fide hero. Alone in the gathering light of dawn on his twenty-second birthday, he'd shot down three kamikazes, saving not only dozens of lives, but perhaps his ship, the *USS Terror*, itself. For that, he got a handful of precious scrap iron hung from pretty ribbons.

Perhaps more important to Gilmartin at the time, the Navy also gave him one hundred dollars for bus fare after mustering out, according to his discharge records.

In the winter of 1946, Neeley Gilmartin disembarked from the *USS Terror* for the last time. She was berthed in San Francisco for repairs when he was discharged. Within a month, he was back in Perry County, according to the filing date stamped on the document. A long bus ride or a long drunk, Morgan thought. Maybe both.

A few numbered boxes at the bottom of the faded page suggested somebody cared what he'd do after he left the service. Under two questions about his future job preferences and plans for further training, he responded "None."

The government's records reflected that Gunner's Mate Second Class Neeley Gilmartin had served his country honorably. They didn't say, however, that he left the Navy with little more than a handful of medals and scars, inside and out, that would never heal properly.

He was a hero without hope, on a bus to oblivion.

When Jefferson Morgan returned to *The Bullet* late Thursday afternoon, the mayor had already called to complain about his dog-pound editorial, someone had stolen all the papers from five of his twelve newsstands, and Bob Buck of Bob Buck Buick had refused to pay for his ad because he claimed the picture in it made him look fat.

"Do we ever do anything right?" Morgan asked Crystal as she handed him a small stack of pink phone messages. There were at least a dozen.

"If we did, they'd start to expect it every week," she said, pressing her ruby lips into a sorry smile. Morgan truly believed she was the only one of his employees making a game effort to help.

Morgan thumbed through the messages as he sat at his desk. He started with the first one and worked his way through the pile.

The mayor, a clammy, retired schoolteacher who tolerated no heat in his political kitchen, chided him for being too negative.

"You media guys are all alike, always focusing on the negative just to sell your papers," he said, then hung up abruptly.

The next four messages came from parents of 4-H kids who were convinced Morgan hated ranchers because he'd omitted the weekly club report. Morgan tried to explain calmly that he'd never received it and he had no such animosity toward ranchers, but they didn't believe him. Three of them hung up on him.

The next message was from Claire, who called to see if he'd like to come home for a late lunch. Too late. It was already after four o'clock, so he set it aside and called the car dealer Bob Buck instead.

"I pay you a lot of money to make me look good. I can't believe you'd put such a terrible picture of me in the paper and expect to get paid for it. You'd better get your act together, mister, and realize who's butterin' your bread. I won't pay a thin dime for that atrocity and I expect this will teach you a lesson to take better care of your customers."

Morgan had owned *The Bullet* for only six weeks, and Bob Buck had refused to pay for his ads—the biggest in the paper—four times. Morgan decided it was true what he'd heard from his friends on the *Tribune*'s sales staff: Car dealers are, at the same time, the best advertisers and the worst clients.

According to Crystal's other messages, three angry ex-readers only wanted him to know they had canceled their subscriptions for various reasons (one didn't like a particular letter to the editor, one believed the photographs were too dull, and the third was canceling on behalf of his Uncle Gerve, who died and wouldn't be needing his paper anymore).

The next pink slip was from an anonymous caller, who gleefully pointed out a minor typographical error in a headline.

The last message was from Hamilton Tasker, the president of the First Wyoming Bank who'd signed off on the Morgans' loan for *The Bullet*. He had been genial enough back then, a little too obsequious for Claire, but far more pleasant than one expected a banker to be.

Morgan glanced at the newsroom clock. It was after four, but he dialed anyway. A bank secretary answered.

"Hello. This is Jefferson Morgan, returning Mr. Tasker's call," he said.

"Oh, yes," she said, a note of recognition in her voice. "He's been expecting you to call all afternoon."

Ham Tasker got on the line, his deep baritone voice immediately foreshadowing serious news. It was clear this was no social call. Tasker was all business and he got directly to the point.

"Jeff, thank you for calling. I just wanted to let you know that we've had a little trouble on your payment. You have insufficient funds to cover it."

"That's impossible," Morgan said, feeling his face grow hot. "I deposited ten thousand dollars earlier this week."

"That's the other problem, Jeff. There were no funds to cover *that* check. All of your mother's accounts together have less than two thousand dollars in them. I'm sorry you had to hear it from me, but we need to clear this up rather quickly."

"Could there be some mistake? Jesus, Ham, a mother wouldn't write a bad check to her son."

"Look, Jeff, I don't know all the circumstances, but I'm sure you understand our predicament and would like to settle any little problems before they become big ones. I'd sure hate to see you get started out on the wrong foot because of a little misunderstanding. We'll need exactly five thousand, eight hundred and twenty-seven dollars by the close of business tomorrow, Jeff. Can I expect to see you here at the bank by that time?"

Morgan didn't know what to say. He had no hope of scraping together that much money in less than twenty-four hours.

"Can I have a couple days?"

Tasker got the job of collecting late debts because he was good at it. He wouldn't budge. "Really, I'd like to get this cleared up as quickly as possible."

"That'll be damn near impossible, Ham. This first month has just been a nightmare. Old Bell got all the receivables, and the cashflow just hasn't started yet."

Hamilton Tasker paused for a long, uncomfortable moment. "Yes, well, maybe it's just a little time management problem."

"Meaning what?" Morgan asked.

"Some people tell me you've been spending a lot of time picking at some old scabs that are better left alone. Maybe there are, shall we say, 'more productive' things you could be working on. I'm sure you understand. Tomorrow, then?"

"Hold on, Ham," Morgan said, suddenly confused and a little angry. "What wounds would those be?"

"We try to focus on the future, not the past. Progress is good for a town, and progress looks forward. Looking back is bad for business. Why bring up something awful and painful for no good reason? Maybe it sells a few papers, but what does it really accomplish?"

"I'm not sure I follow."

"Do I need to spell it out, Jeff? You might find it easier to do business if you saw things our way."

"Your way? What's your way?"

"At the moment, there's more of our money at risk than yours. We need to come to ... an understanding about this story you're working on. As your new partners in this newspaper, we'd prefer that you spent your time of more positive news."

"Jesus, Ham, are you suggesting I drop a story or lose my newspaper? It sure sounds like you are, and that's not a choice I'm willing to make. And I resent your implication that by loaning me money you assume some editorial privilege at my newspaper. Pardon me, but that's pure bullshit."

His message delivered, Hamilton Tasker remained cool and unruffled. "Why, I'm saying nothing of the kind, Jeff. I'm only telling you what people are saying. And some of my bank officers are watching your operation quite closely. They might be a little more understanding if you merely 're-arranged' your priorities. Right now, I need to know you'll be here tomorrow to put this little problem behind us."

"Sure, Ham," Morgan said through clenched teeth. "I'll see you tomorrow."

Incensed, he hung up.

"No money at all?"

Claire was incredulous. The corners of her mouth fell and she closed her eyes as they rocked gently on the porch swing. Children were playing in the street in front of the house, but their laughter drifted off in another direction.

"Nothing," Morgan said. "She's got nothing. A couple thousand bucks. That's it."

"Maybe she's got some stock or a retirement fund someplace," Claire said. "Maybe there's a fund transfer that's been delayed."

"Dad didn't believe in the stock market and after he died, we checked everywhere for any money he might have stashed away for retirement. There wasn't any."

"How has she been supporting herself then?"

"The house was paid off, so she doesn't need much. She leases out most of the land to a neighbor, who runs a few cows and horses on it. Mom was so eager to get out from under the hardware store, she sold it cheap. She made a little money, but not much. I guess I thought she was doing better. That's a whole different problem."

"Have you talked to her yet?"

"I don't know what I'd say. 'Mom, your check bounced and you're damn near broke'?"

"God, Jeff, she needs your help. You don't want your mom to be a bag lady, do you?"

Frustrated, Morgan raised his hands to stop the conversation about his mother's finances.

"One thing at a time, Claire. I'll take care of my mother.

She won't be homeless. Right now, I'm worried about us being homeless. I won't be much help to my mother if I'm on welfare myself."

"Okay, so we have a little problem. Let's not panic. We have exactly one hundred and fifty-two dollars in the bank, Jeff," she said. "Tomorrow you need to come up with almost six thousand dollars. No sweat. Any ideas?"

Morgan shrugged. He watched two little girls from next door drawing endless hopscotch boxes on their sidewalk with colorful chalk. They were circumscribing the entire block, earnestly working their way back home in a big circle.

"The paper's payroll account has a couple thousand, but if I raid it, I can't pay anybody next week," he said. "We could sell one of the cars, but that's only two or three thousand, at best, and we can't do it by tomorrow."

"How about your computer? Could we get anything for that?" Claire asked.

Morgan looked as if she'd suggested selling the family scrapbook. He'd used his IBM 760ED laptop, one of the most powerful portable computers on the market when he bought it, and a database search program called Paradox to help find the serial killer P.D. Comeaux. There was no way in hell he'd sell it to some pimply kid to use as a souped-up GameBoy.

"No, Claire. Not that. It wouldn't bring much either, but I wouldn't sell it."

Claire took a deep breath. "What if I called my dad and asked for a loan?" she said. "He could wire it to the bank tomorrow. He'd be happy to help."

Claire's parents, especially her father, hadn't been pleased to hear their daughter would be moving to Wyoming. To them, it was a wild place where few people except cowboys and prospectors could scratch out a living. They also hated the idea of Claire being so far away. Of course, they blamed Morgan, although they were too kind to ever say it out loud.

"Let's keep that as a last resort, Claire," he said. "The bank won't foreclose just because the first payment is a little late. They just want to be sure it's not going to be a habit. Maybe we can work something out without cutting holes in our safety net."

Claire watched some children playing kick the can in the dying light on the shaded street. She was frightened, Morgan could tell, but she tried not to let it show at times like this. She always said something hopeful just when the outlook seemed nearly hopeless.

"Someday, we'll be sitting here watching our own child play," she said. "And all this will be behind us."

Later that night, after Claire had gone to bed, Morgan sat in his attic room. He couldn't sleep, and his thoughts bounced from *The Bullet*'s financial straits to Neeley Gilmartin to Aimee Little Spotted Horse to the night's unyielding heat. They all smothered him.

After midnight, still no closer to sleep, he put on his shorts and running shoes and slipped out of the house into the impenetrable night air of August. He hated running, so he did it infrequently, when he needed to be distracted or tired.

Morgan stretched on the freshly sprinkled lawn. As he lay back in the cool grass to stretch his taut quadriceps, he tried to remember when he last ran, but couldn't.

The pulsing chirp of crickets surrounded him in the darkness. The sky was infinitely deep, its stars burning like sparks from a campfire. A ring around the moon meant rain was coming, but it wasn't here yet, just the suffocating heat.

Morgan jogged into the middle of Rockwood Street and followed the hazy, yellow hum of the streetlights toward downtown. The darkness swallowed him.

After a few blocks, his footsteps fell in rhythm with the crickets, beating flatly against the still-warm asphalt. He heard himself breathing, felt the dull ache in his chest as he passed from the sleeping sidestreets onto Main Street. He was out of shape, and already his underused muscles and aching joints were demanding his attention, stealing it away from his problems.

Except for the railyard at the end of the avenue, Main Street was deserted. Morgan ran down the middle of it, where the surface was smooth, unlike the buckled sidewalks the city had postponed fixing. The hot air filled him, pumped through his veins and seeped through his skin. Sweat dripped off his chin.

As he passed *The Bullet*, he noticed a sliver of unexpected light from the backshop. Someone had forgotten to turn it off, and the light bill came due at the end of the month. As a reporter, he'd never had to worry about leaving the lights on; as a publisher, especially a publisher on the verge of a financial debacle, he did. He circled around the next block and came up the alley behind the newspaper building, where a key had always been hidden in the drain pipe.

The key was gone. In the dark, cursing between breaths, Morgan felt around in the weeds below the spout, but without light he couldn't find it. When he jiggled the back door's knob to make sure it was locked, he was startled to find it wasn't.

There wasn't much to steal inside, maybe a few old computers and some antiquated office equipment. Certainly there was no money. No, it was likely someone had left without turning off the lights, but he'd been the last one to leave the office that night.

His heart pounded as he eased the balky door open. Just inside, the storage room was dark, no bigger than a two-car suburban garage with a rank of newsprint rolls stacked three high just inside the overhead door. He walked through the darkness with one hand ahead of him, waist-high, should he encounter an unexpected dolly handle or table edge at groin level.

As Morgan's eyes adjusted better to the pure darkness of the storage area, he saw light seeping beneath the adjacent press room's door. He crow-stepped carefully toward the paper-thin blade of light until his hand found the door's brass knob.

He pulled it gently toward him, trying not to wake its yowling hinges. The fluorescent lights on the other side hurt his eyes; all of them were on.

The press was an inky hulk. It sat in the center of the room, surrounded by four mottled walls, dripping ink barrels and stacks of imperfectly printed papers waiting to be dumped. The pungent smell of ink, a familiar odor that Morgan had forgotten until he returned to Winchester, hung in the air.

The light switch was on the opposite wall, behind the printing plate-burner. Morgan crossed the press room toward it, but even before a jolt of cold adrenaline speared through his veins, he sensed he wasn't alone.

"It's the smell," Old Bell said. "I miss it."

He was standing beneath the folder, where an unbroken sheet of flowing newsprint would course beneath razor-sharp knives and mechanical pinchers to be separated, pleated and dumped onto a conveyor. It was the critical point where steel, raw pulp, ink and words came together, at last, to make a newspaper.

"Jesus Christ, Bell, you scared the shit out of me," Morgan said, blood still pulsing in his ears. He mopped his face with his sweat-soaked gray athletic T-shirt.

"You should have knocked, kid. That would have saved us both the trouble of a surprise."

"Knocked on my own door? What the hell are you doing down here at this time of night?"

Old Bell wandered among the press's four units, touching the cold iron frame the way an old man might stroke his loyal dog. "I guess I couldn't walk away as easily as I thought. I thought I'd absorbed enough of this ink in my life to turn my bones black, but I guess not. I didn't want you to know because it's all yours now, even the smell of it. That's what I missed the most, I think. The smell. God, how I love it."

"You're welcome here, any time, and you know it," Morgan said. "I'm always glad to see you. In fact, I'd like to see you down here more often. I could use your help. Lots of it."

Old Bell traced his fingers along the edge of an ink well. He looked at the black stain it left on them, and he smiled.

"A newspaper is printed here," he said, extending his smudged fingers so Morgan could see. "Goddam if that isn't a good thing."

Morgan leaned across a roll of newsprint, feeling the perfect, smooth curve of it under him. A droplet of sweat dribbled down his forearm and soaked into what would be next week's *Bullet*.

"When I was just a kid working for you, I wanted to know everything you knew. You always saw things I couldn't see. You stood for something. You had this passion."

"A man in passion rides a mad horse, kid," Old Bell said, sidestepping the sentimentality. "Press Delahanty was the editor here and he gave me my first job, right here in this shop. You know what I had to do on my first day? I had to muck out the puke bucket he hid back there behind the old flatbed press."

Old Bell hitched his thumb toward the darkened end of the pressroom, where all the obsolete presses were heaped in a deadfall of bygone iron.

"Press was a drunken son of a bitch who watched 'em hang Tom Horn and rode with the Johnson County Invaders. He'd hit the bottle, then write these editorials full of piss and vinegar and the damnedest beautiful prose you ever read. He was a classic storyteller who knew how to put the words down just so. And a goddam drunk, to boot. Years later, when old Press seemed bigger than life to me, I'd go get that old puke bucket and put it under my desk, just in case I ever got the kind of passion old Press had."

"Did you?"

"That particular muse never called here. Not on Wednesdays, anyhow. Never missed a paper. Never. I always considered it a sort of sacred covenant with the folks. They trusted me to make a newspaper. That's all. It was a simple relationship."

Every week for fifty years, a paper. Snowstorms, floods, illness, even deaths: Nothing stopped *The Bullet*. Morgan admired Old Bell even more.

"Is there one story that you remember more than any other?" Morgan asked.

Old Bell looked down at the floor for a few moments, rubbing the bare spot that peeked through the crown of his snowy hair.

"Back in the summer of 'fifty-one, the whole damn county was burnin' up. Seemed like flames were just part of the landscape. The lakes were mud flats, the river was low, and all the wells were damn near dried out. Then the Biograph Theater went up."

The Big Fire, as it came to be known, was a flashpoint in Winchester's history, a day when the whole town pondered its mortality. Old Bell was there.

"Jesus Christ, the damn thing was roaring like some unholy animal, just three doors down from the paper. Fire trucks poured everything they had on it, but it only made it madder. Wasn't much else to do but watch it burn. Up and down Main Street, all the shopkeepers were frantically loading up their goods in the back of trucks, wheelbarrows, anything they could find."

Old Bell relished the retelling.

"Damn, it was a sight. Everybody knew the whole damn town was going to go up. I had to choose: Cover the fire or try to save what I could from this place."

Morgan had heard the stories. He'd seen the front page and its thick banner headline hanging in the newspaper's foyer.

"You covered the fire."

"Yeah, I was a dumb fucker back then. I only thought about it later. I might have had a great story with no place to print it."

"My dad told me it was the most amazing thing he ever saw."

"No, it was a miracle. A goddamned miracle. This pilot was flying a load of retardant to a forest fire when he saw smoke right here in town. He swooped down and dumped his whole load on the theater. Doused the damn fire like he was blowing out a candle. Oh Christ, it was beautiful. Saved the whole goddamned town. He came down out of the sky like some thundering angel at the most desperate moment, saved our asses and flew away. Jesus, that was a story, a once-in-a-lifetime story."

The fluorescent lights flickered and hummed. Old Bell looked up, and Morgan saw his eyes were moist, burning from the smoke of a fire deep in his memory.

"Was it ever hard for you, being the editor?" he asked.

Old Bell contemplated his blackened fingers for a moment.

"Every week was hard," he said. "Wednesdays seemed endless. But Thursday always came. I'd go down to The Griddle and watch people read my paper like they were looking in a mirror. By God, that's what we do, kid. We hold up a mirror that doesn't lie and doesn't fade."

"What if they don't like what they see?"

"They'll blame it on the mirror, of course," Old Bell said. "Maybe we can change street maps, travel plans and a few politicians' minds, but we can't change human nature, kid. Plenty of good newspapermen have tried and they fizzle out, like some orphan chunk of a shooting star that flames out before the big show. Burn slow, kid, but keep the fire going. Here, this is yours."

Old Bell tossed him the missing back-door key and started to leave. As he brushed past Morgan, he gave his arm a fatherly squeeze.

"Wait," Morgan said. "There's something else I need to talk to you about."

Old Bell turned toward him, a concerned look on his face. He already knew. "Is it about the payment?" he asked.

Morgan said nothing, but looked surprised.

"Hell, it's a small town, kid. People talk and I still hear pretty damn good. You're having a little cash-flow problem, that's all. Don't sweat it."

"It's not so little, Bell," Morgan said. "The payment's overdue and I'm supposed to deliver the cash to the bank tomorrow. You've seen the paper. We're running low on ads and ... well, I'm just not sure what comes next."

Old Bell curled one rough hand in a fist and shook it in front of him, like a coach giving a halftime pep talk.

"Every little town has a sort of beat, a rhythm. You find the rhythm and everything will fall into place. It takes a little time. You'll see."

"It's more than that," Morgan said. "The bankers know I've been looking into the murder of Aimee Little Spotted Horse. I don't know why, but they're not happy about it. Without coming right out and saying it, I think they'd like to pull the rug out if I continue."

"Fuck 'em," he said. "Ham Tasker thinks he's a player, but he's nothing but an amateur clown in a three-piece suit. I wasn't gonna tell you, but he called me, too. He said the bank would foreclose if you stay on the story, and he wanted me to persuade you to drop it."

"Would they? Foreclose, I mean?" Morgan wondered.

"Maybe, but I don't think he has the balls. He's just try-ing to bluff you, make your life a little harder. But watch your ass anyway."

"Why would they care about this story so much?"

"Who the hell knows? Maybe they just don't want you to rock this fragile little canoe. Maybe a 'friend' of the bank would rather this can of worms stayed sealed up tighter'n a pickle jar. Maybe it's just a power thing, where they want to see if they can intimidate you."

"They're succeeding."

"My personal policy was: Never corner somthin' meaner than me. You gotta make the call yourself, kid."

"Sure, but—"

Old Bell sniffed disgustedly and cut Morgan off. "Look, kid, I still think that asshole Gilmartin killed that little girl, and you're probably licking up the wrong leg like some horny pup. But it's your story, not mine. And it damn sure isn't Ham Tasker's. If it's a good story, then follow it, goddam it. You got to have the courage of your convictions. You have to do what you know in your heart is right."

"So how do I handle it?"

Old Bell hitched up his khaki pants and headed toward the door, shaking his fuzzy white head.

"Christ Almighty, if you don't know, lock this son of a bitch up tonight and never come back."

Old Bell never looked back. He closed the door behind him and disappeared into the humid night.

CHAPTER TEN

The Friday morning rain was a melancholy, gray shroud. Morgan awoke in its mournful shadow, unsure of the time. Guttural thunder rumbled through his fitful dreams most of the night, and his digital clock-radio blinked perpetual midnight.

Now, the light in his bedroom was heavy, like transparent slate. With one sleepy eye, he looked at his watch. It was after eight, though it seemed much earlier because the light was barren and no birds were singing outside.

He reached across the cool sheet, but Claire was already up. Over the sound of whispering rain on the window pane, he heard her heaving in the bathroom. Wave after painful wave welled out of her, each followed by a visceral, reflexive groan as she caught her breath again.

Then she sobbed and Morgan went to her. She was slumped over the toilet in her panties and a Chicago Cubs T-shirt. He knelt on the cold tile beside her and held her sweaty forehead as her body convulsed again. All that came out was a glob of sticky, yellow bile that slung sinuously from her bloodless lips.

Claire wiped it away with a piece of toilet paper and slumped against her husband's chest, winded.

"Morning sickness sucks," she groaned as Morgan mopped her face with a damp washcloth.

"Maybe it would help to get something on your stomach," he said. "Can I fix you some breakfast? How about some eggs?"

Another violent retch shook Claire's body. After it passed, she pushed Morgan away and stormed back into the gray darkness of the bedroom.

"You're a son of a bitch," she said, her voice angry and weary.

"What did I do?" he asked.

His question echoed in the astringent, fluorescent loneliness of the bathroom.

That sepulchral Friday, August second, was the forty-eighth anniversary of Aimee Little Spotted Horse's disappearance and, in all likelihood, her murder.

Had she lived, she'd be fifty-seven, maybe a grandmother, Morgan thought. He wondered if children dreamed about growing old, if the life that flashed before their eyes when they died was the life ahead, not the brief life behind them. He wondered if a child knew how black and permanent death was.

The old Escort's wipers thumped back and forth against the inexorable rain in a struggle of rhythm against chaos. Chaos was winning. Morgan's breath condensed around the inside edges of the windshield, slowly choking his vision like frost on a winter pane.

Morgan couldn't see Aimee's face, although he tried. The newspaper hadn't printed any picture of her, and given her parents' circumstances, one might never have existed.

He'd seen dead faces, more than he'd ever been inclined to count, but he always tried to imagine them in life, before their soul had seeped out of them. Some had been children. He circumvented the sick feeling inside by picturing them playing and smiling.

Perhaps it was only a trick of the rain that he imagined Bridger's face as hers. For months after his son died, Morgan tried to shake the vision of his withered, white body in that hospital bed, tried to see him in the places where he'd been most alive. But the only place Bridger still lived was in Morgan's dreams and he was there night after night, talking about the fishing trip to Michigan, or his mother being too sad about his dying.

Pulling up in front of the newspaper office, he pulled his baseball cap lower and made a run for the front door. By the time he got inside, he was drenched.

"A good day for the grass," he said to Crystal Sandoval as he stood on the worn checkered tile of *The Bullet*'s foyer. He slapped his wet cap against his thigh. "The ranchers should be happy."

"Ranchers won't ever be happy," she replied. "If it doesn't rain, it's a drought. If it does rain, it's a flood. They love to suffer."

The newsroom was empty. The morning mail had a few checks, some letters to the editor, a few equipment catalogs and a couple dozen useless press releases. His calendar was empty, not because he had nothing to do, but because he'd never been diligent about writing appointments in his calendar. Still, he looked at it every morning, as if he expected some time-management fairy to make notations there every night.

But he knew he had two appointments. Lunch with Gilmartin's former lawyer, Simeon Fenwick, now retired. And a meeting with Hamilton Tasker at First Wyoming Bank, as late in the day as he could make it.

The brass bell on the front door jingled and he looked up.

Three people were bunched up at the door as Muriel Gumprecht, the director of the Winchester Chamber of Commerce, folded up an umbrella they'd been sharing. In her fifties, with her dyed black hair and beak-like nose, she looked like Margaret Hamilton in a power suit, Morgan thought, and she could be just as appealing when she opened her mouth. She'd had the Chamber job for almost twenty years. Morgan's late father, a normally unflappable hardware man who had dodged Main Street politics as skillfully as he matched nuts and bolts from their bins, was more blunt in his description: He called her the Wicked Witch of the West.

Behind her, checking his silk tie for water spots, was Dr. Jake Switzer, Winchester's only dentist. Known affectionately around town as "Jawbreaker Jake," his pomposity was only rivaled by his wealth, which, while it was considerable, wasn't nearly as much as he wanted people to believe. He was a bombastic ex-Marine who wore monogrammed shirts and silk sport coats, played golf four times a week and wintered in Tucson, leaving his dental practice to his salaried son-in-law for the cold months.

The last in the door was Sleepy Bill Garvis, his flaming red hair matted flat by the rain. His face was immediately familiar to Morgan because it still had a little-boy quality about it, an energetic look that probably helped him get elected to the Town Council. Most redheads he'd known looked younger than they were. Maybe it was the freckles.

Morgan met them at the swinging wooden gate that separated the newsroom from the entryway. He held out his hand to Muriel and smiled.

"Welcome, folks," he said. "To what do I owe the pleasure of your company this fine morning?"

Muriel tapped her umbrella on the floor, creating a muddy little puddle on the tile. She wasn't smiling, but that wasn't news.

"We'd like to discuss a small matter with you, Mr. Morgan," she said loftily. "I'm sure you know everyone. If you have a few minutes ..."

"Certainly," Morgan said. "Come into my office."

He held the gate open as they passed, then gathered a few rolling chairs around his cluttered desk in the middle of the newsroom. Muriel dispensed with small talk.

"We have some concerns about a story you are working on," she said. She sat erect in her chair, her sharp face looming toward Morgan, who rocked uneasily as he stroked an unsharpened pencil.

"On the Chamber of Commerce?" Morgan asked a little

disingenuously, knowing full well which story had the Chamber director's dudgeon up. If Ham Tasker knew about it, word must have gotten around by now. It was, indeed, a small town.

"No, Mr. Morgan, we are more concerned with your inquiries about the death of a little Indian girl a long, long time ago," Muriel said. "Perhaps you could explain to us why this would be news after such a terribly long time. It seems like old news to me."

"To begin with, I don't know if there's a story or not," he explained. "I was approached by someone who wanted me to look into it. It's possible—just possible, mind you—that the wrong man went to prison for that murder."

Dr. Switzer, who, uncharacteristically, hadn't said a word since he sauntered in, couldn't contain himself another second.

"That's just bullshit," he blurted out, his fleshy face flushing with anger. "And you're soft-headed if you believe it. That old man is a no-good, lying con-artist bastard. I was a teen-ager here when it happened, and there's no doubt in my mind, now or then, reasonable or otherwise, that he killed that girl. You're just trying to sell a few papers by dredging it all up again."

"Doctor Switzer, I'm merely looking into it. I don't know if there'll ever be a story ..."

"That's just a load of crap," the blustering dentist condescended. "How come we never see anything positive in the media? Always bad news, never anything good. You come back here to our quiet little town and all of a sudden you want to dig up the dead. What's wrong? The living aren't interesting enough?"

"I'm not digging up the dead," Morgan defended. "Right now, I'm just asking a few questions."

"We've heard about your investigation," Switzer said. "And we're going to do everything we can to make sure that killer is ridden out of town before he kills somebody else."

"He's an old man, and he's dying," Morgan said, defending Gilmartin at last. "He spent almost forty-eight years in prison, and there's a chance he didn't do it. He only wants to die. Believe me, you're all completely safe from Neeley Gilmartin."

"They should have fried his ass," Dr. Switzer fumed. "I'd have pulled the switch myself. And now I have to sit here and listen to some bleeding-heart liberal reporter defend the asshole. Pardon my French."

Morgan ignored Switzer, who was renowned for getting his way through intimidation. Morgan evaded his withering line of fire.

"What's your interest in this thing? Why are so many people so upset about me asking some questions?"

Sleepy Bill Garvis, who'd been sitting quietly with his hands in his lap, finally piped up. His unruly hair looked as if he'd combed it with a rake, and a cowlick sprouted on one side like orange crabgrass.

"It's just not good for the community to have this old wound opened up," he said, his calloused milkman's fingers still laced together primly. "We've seen some hard times and more are ahead. Why bring up bad memories? It's like re-victimizing the victim, only it's a whole town. Lots of people think this incident is better left forgotten. We simply wanted to come down and see if we could reach some kind of a ... well, an understanding."

The three visitors exchanged nervous glances. Sleepy Bill wasn't sure if he was supposed to say anything more, so after a moment, he settled back into his chair and, as if on some silent stage cue, Muriel spoke for all of them.

"Is there any chance you'll consider abandoning your so-called 'inquiry' today?" she asked.

Morgan weighed the question briefly. The combative tone of her question offended him.

"No," he said.

Muriel pinched her lips together, as if she were contem-plating a wicked witch's curse. "You leave us with little choice in this matter," she said as she handed Morgan the letter, creased lengthwise in three neat pleats. "We are prepared to suggest an advertising boycott of *The Bullet* to all our Chamber members. Given your current financial difficulties, a boycott could very well close your doors, and we really wouldn't want to see that happen. But it's better than letting you drag this town down with your yellow journalism."

Morgan read the boycott letter drafted to the merchants of Winchester. It spared no vitriol, asking merchants to "make a bold statement against big-city, tabloid-style sensationalism designed to arouse the public for the sole purpose of selling newspapers." A little farther down, it suggested businesses withhold advertising or subscriptions until "the attitude is changed."

Morgan re-folded the letter and tossed it on the edge of his desk closest to Muriel Gumprecht. It sat there in no-man's land, nobody touching it.

"I imagine this newspaper has been a good member of the Chamber since it began," he said. He felt the blood rise in his neck and his jaw begin to stiffen, but he kept his voice calm. "So I'm perplexed by this attempt to hijack our editorial responsibility with your blackmail."

"It's not blackmail," Dr. Switzer grumbled. "I resent the implication ..."

"It's not an implication, Doctor, I'm saying it right out," Morgan said. "I won't be blackmailed. I won't be bullied into ignoring any story just because you don't want to read it. And I damn sure won't run scared from you."

"So you'd risk losing your whole business just to sell a few papers?" Muriel sniped.

"You know, I've had it up to here with your half-witted insults," Morgan shot back. "I'm a newspaperman. Selling newspapers is what I do. It's the product on my shelf. There's nothing inherently wrong with selling newspapers. But if you're suggesting we fabricate, sensationalize, twist the truth, manipulate the facts or just plain lie in order to fool people into buying a twenty-five-cent newspaper, you're not just wrong. You're being absurd."

Dr. Switzer stood up to leave. His face was an angry crimson. "My father told me never to piss on a skunk, and now I know why," he seethed. He waggled his manicured finger at Morgan. "I won't sit here and be insulted by this ... this wretched hack."

Muriel Gumprecht hoisted her crooked nose a little higher and stood shoulder-to-shoulder with Switzer.

"This letter will go out today, Mr. Morgan," she said as she draped her business-like black handbag over her shoulder. "It's sad that you have no interest in compromising for the good of our neighbors here in Winchester. Perhaps the next editor will be more amenable to being part of the team."

They were both heading toward the door when Sleepy Bill Garvis, Morgan's old classmate who'd lived his life a little out of sync with everyone else, finally got out of his chair. He shrugged ineffectually and very nearly extended his right hand to Morgan before he thought better of it and left. He might as well have slept through the angry exchange that went on all around him.

As the door closed behind them, Crystal Sandoval, who'd eavesdropped on the conversation from the reception desk, managed a sweet, sympathetic smile for her beleaguered boss.

"You know," Morgan said, half-heartedly smiling back, "morning sickness sucks."

The persistent rain fell all morning. The overcast was so thick, streetlights glowed feebly at midday.

Morgan made some calls and wrote a few quick stories for the paper. He even made a few notes for next week's editorial. The primary election was just two weeks away and he hadn't decided whether to make any endorsements. If he was going to do it, next week's paper would be his last chance before Election Day.

His reporters had floated through the newsroom long enough to pick up the scribbled assignments he left on their chairs, because their desks were piled high with the old newspapers, books and loose paper that drift like snow within every reporter's reach. They approached Fridays with even less ardor than deadline days, and it rankled them to be expected to work, but they said nothing.

And he called Claire. After a few pieces of toast and some saltine crackers, the morning sickness had faded. She hadn't gotten much sleep the night before and planned to nap later in the day.

At lunchtime, Morgan drove over to The Griddle. An undisciplined rank of mud-splashed pickup trucks were parked at the curb. Ranchers couldn't work in the rain, so they came to town to run errands and trade the latest gossip over steak sandwiches—The Griddle's Friday special. In fact, the cafe's daily lunch specials always featured some form of beef, because it would be impolitic to serve chicken or fish in cow country. And ranchers weren't shy about saying so.

Morgan parked behind the restaurant, where the rain had collected in muddy lagoons and beaded up on the grease-coated back sidewalk beside the dumpsters. But even the acrid smell of rotting food and coagulating grease in 55-gallon drums outside the kitchen door couldn't dampen his appetite.

Simeon Fenwick sat alone in an oversized corner booth, a small man made smaller by the space he occupied. The booth itself was built into the angle of two windows, one looking onto the cafe's muddy driveway, the other onto the street.

Fenwick was pinched into the back of the enormous red Naugahyde seat. He was inspecting his spoon and wiping it with his napkin when Morgan approached the big table that almost hid him.

"Mr. Fenwick?" he inquired.

"Yes," the little man said. He scrupulously replaced the spoon beside his knife, careful to align their handles exactly.

Only then did he offer a flaccid handshake to his lunch companion. "You must be Jefferson Morgan. I'm so pleased to meet you. Please sit down."

Morgan slid around the table so he could face the old lawyer, but not so close that it was uncomfortable for either of them. Fenwick wore a tweed jacket over a white Oxford shirt, with a crisply knotted red bow tie tucked beneath his receding chin. His round, tortoise-shell spectacles, drooping shoulders and smooth, bald head made him look more like a priggish college professor than an attorney. His meticulous manner made him seem nervous.

"I'm sorry to be late, Mr. Fenwick," Morgan apologized. It was only a few minutes past noon, but Fenwick had a punctilious air about him. "I tried to call this morning, but you were apparently out."

"No matter," Fenwick said in his pinched little voice. "Perhaps I was a little early in arriving. An old habit from my courtroom days, I'm afraid."

"We've never met, but I knew you from when I was a kid here. I'm sure you don't remember me, but I recall seeing you at basketball games."

"Oh my, yes," Fenwick said. "I love basketball. Such a beautiful sport. You seem vaguely familiar to me. You played on the varsity here, did you?"

"Yeah, back in 'Seventy-five. I was a guard. We did okay that year. I played on the same team as Trey Kerrigan."

"Yes indeed, young Kelton was a magnificent player. He always seemed to be where the ball was. A beautiful jump shot, as I recall. He had the touch. All-State, was he not? And a fine sheriff he's been, as well."

It wasn't like that at all, Morgan wanted to say. It was the other way around: He'd always made sure the ball was always where Trey Kerrigan was. But it wasn't meant as an insult and he let it go, hiding behind The Griddle's familiar menu instead.

"Anything look good today?" Morgan asked politely while he scanned its gravy-stained pages, eager to change the subject.

"Oh, I'm afraid I wouldn't know. I always order the club sandwich. I don't believe I've ever had anything else here. They build a club quite nicely here, and they always let me order just half. I'm not a big eater, and the whole sandwich is so large, I can't possibly eat it all."

Fenwick sipped his tea timidly, his pinky extended, then refolded his napkin neatly across his lap as Suzie, the waitress, arrived at the table. Morgan noticed her hair was slightly redder since last week, as were her tired eyes beneath all that dark makeup.

"Long day?" Morgan asked her.

"Long enough," she said. She stood close enough that Morgan could smell her peach fragrance, mixed with the aroma of maple syrup, cigarette smoke and coffee. "I'm the only girl on the floor today. The other one called in sick. But I'm near done with this shift. Been too busy to notice. The rain really packs 'em in. You ready to order?"

Morgan gestured to Fenwick to order first.

"I'll have the usual," he said. "Light on the mayonnaise, please. Tomato on the side, no pickle. Remember, dear, whole wheat. Oh, and another Earl Grey, please, with hot water, but not boiling."

Suzie turned to Morgan, rolling her eyes so only he could see. She made no effort to be polite to the fussy old lawyer. In fact, Morgan noticed she never spoke directly to him.

"I'll have the special today, Suzie," he said. "Medium rare and an iced tea."

She gathered their menus and left. Fenwick brushed a few tiny crumbs into a folded napkin, which he pushed an arm's length to the far edge of the table for the waitress to take away, as if it were low-level hazardous waste.

"So, Mr. Morgan, you wished to talk to me about a case I handled a long time ago. Mr. Gilmartin's, wasn't it?"

"That's right. I just had a few questions you might be able to answer. You might know that Mr. Gilmartin recently was released from prison."

"I'd heard that, yes."

"Well, Mr. Gilmartin has asked me to look into his case. He's dying. To make a long story short, he says he didn't do it and he wants to die with a free conscience."

Fenwick's small eyes followed the fingers of his right hand as they re-adjusted the position of his silverware precisely on the paper placemat in front of him.

"Do you believe him?"

Morgan turned his palms upward and shrugged.

"I didn't at first, but I'm beginning to wonder about a few things."

"I'm certain you understand that the attorney-client privilege never expires, so I'm not quite clear on how I may help you. Besides, I wasn't on the case very long before Mr. Gilmartin confessed and pleaded guilty. A terrible crime."

Morgan leaned forward, his elbows spread wide on the table. Fenwick straightened slightly and maneuvered his tea cup between them like a breastwork.

"I guess the main thing I'd like to know from you is whether there was ever any evidence that would have helped him prove his innocence. Something that never came out. Anything."

Fenwick shook his head.

"The physical evidence linking him to the murder was non-existent and purely circumstantial, to be sure. But Mr. Gilmartin had no alibi and the prosecution had at least two witnesses who'd testify he had the motive and intent to harm the father of that little girl. We had nothing."

"In your mind, were there any other possible suspects?"

"Mr. Morgan, the law is about proof. And, I might add, we have some very fine slander laws in this state, so I am reluctant to suggest that some surviving suspect—other than Mr. Gilmartin—killed that little girl. Good Christian manners prevent me from suggesting that someone long-dead might have done it. It would be highly inappropriate and I suggest you show some decorum in such matters. I am aware that the press has a vital job, but too often you run rough-shod over good people's reputations."

Odd, coming from a lawyer, Morgan thought, but he had little doubt that the finicky Fenwick had no stomach for asking—nor answering—indelicate questions.

"What about the parents? The father beat her, didn't he? Could he have killed her, then conspired with or intimidated the mother to cover it up? That's not a far-fetched scenario, given what we now know about domestic violence."

"Many things are possible, Mr. Morgan, but not all things are probable," Fenwick said. He counted off defense arguments on his thin, delicate fingers: "The parents were away from the house when she disappeared. Their truck was parked at the Madigan ranch house all day. The body was found ten miles in the other direction. And in the Crow culture, murder is a far greater sin with far more dreadful consequences than under the white man's law. For the parents to have conspired in this killing, they would have had to plan it carefully, and child-beatings aren't premeditated."

"Unless it happened the night before," Morgan thought out loud. "Then they might conspire to protect themselves. They might have lied about the disappearance. Instead of riding fences, they might have gone back that day to dispose of Aimee's body."

Simeon Fenwick shook his small head.

"My, you've an active imagination."

"I was a cop reporter in Chicago long enough to know my imagination will never rival a desperate criminal's. The body was a problem and the killer was desperate to get rid of it."

"If the parents did it, why not bury her in a shallow grave somewhere out in that vast emptiness that surrounded them, then disappear?" Fenwick countered. "The body never would have been found, and who would care if an Indian family just disappeared? That was the killer's only real error, dumping the little girl where she'd be found. Maybe he wanted her to be found, or maybe he just panicked."

Morgan said nothing, but Fenwick continued.

"No, Mr. Morgan, if the circumstantial case against Neeley Gilmartin was thin, your hypothesis about the parents is even thinner. I'm sorry, but while it's possible, it seems highly improbable."

Morgan already knew his best alternative theory was full of holes. But as a reporter, he'd covered the murders of too many children who died at the hands of their parents to dismiss it too quickly. And it wasn't beyond reason: At least once, Aimee had been beaten by her father. Maybe, on a hot summer night in 1948, filled with anger and liquor, he'd beaten her again, with fatal consequences.

"So, in your mind, the parents are unlikely suspects?" Morgan asked.

"That's correct. To me, under the circumstances, they would have been implausible and improbable suspects."

"Was there anybody more plausible or probable in your mind?"

The corners of Fenwick's thin lips drooped as he rotated the handle of his tea cup neatly to three o'clock, but didn't pick it up. He spoke without looking at Morgan.

"In a case like this, where one has no direct physical evidence, no witnesses, no apparent motive, no single person with a clear opportunity, you may suspect anyone and no one. Mr. Gilmartin was as good a suspect as any, if I do say so myself."

"Did you ever ask him if he did it?"

"We're starting to get into privileged conversations now, Mr. Morgan, and that makes me terribly uncomfortable. But I can tell you I rarely asked my criminal clients if they were, in fact, guilty of their appointed crimes."

"Why?" Morgan asked.

"It matters very little," Fenwick replied in his supercilious manner. "My job was to provide the best defense, no matter whether my client was Jesus Christ or the Devil incarnate. I was always a bit frightened about knowing, to be quite frank. I never wanted it to influence what I might say in the courtroom. That's why, when I got a little more experience, I eschewed criminal cases and pursued a more sedate civil practice."

"So can I assume you didn't ask Gilmartin?"

Fenwick paused.

"I suppose that would be a safe assumption."

"Did he ever tell you he didn't kill Aimee?"

"Yes, he did. Repeatedly. I wanted to believe it, but he couldn't provide me with any evidence on his own behalf. He was a frightening man to me, with an alien lifestyle. I was quite young and inexperienced, and I certainly had very little contact with his ilk. Anyway, it was all over before I could conceive a proper defense."

"In the end, did you believe him when he said he didn't do it?"

"That's irrelevant."

Morgan scratched his chin. Lawyers never made interviews easy. Every conversation was a word game.

"Did you advise him to plead guilty to avoid the death penalty?"

"Once again, with all due respect, my advice to a client is none of your affair," Fenwick bristled in his finicky fashion, like a mouse shooed into a corner. "But it seems reasonable, does it not, that a man would do anything to save his own life? Wouldn't you?"

Suzie delivered their meals and slipped a greasy ticket under Morgan's saucer. Sim Fenwick tucked his napkin in his collar, smoothing it in a wrinkled diamond across his chest before dividing his half-sandwich into smaller, dainty pieces. He never touched it with his slender fingers, although it would have been much easier to eat that way.

The steak on Morgan's open-faced sandwich was tough and overcooked, so he slathered it in steak sauce to cover its flaws.

"When did you retire, Mr. Fenwick?" he asked as he chewed a gristly morsel of steak.

"Nineteen eighty-five," Fenwick said, cutting tidbits of his club sandwich with a knife and fork. "I'll be seventy-nine in December. Forty-three years at the bar. It was a fine career, for the most part. I still do a few minor things, wills, land deals and the like."

"Any regrets?"

"Very few, really," Fenwick said. Then, as an afterthought, he added: "Maybe one."

Fenwick unconsciously fingered the frilly end of one of the giant cocktail toothpicks that had pinned his triple-decker sandwich together. He spoke without looking up.

"As long as I can remember, I always wanted to become a judge. My grandmother always said I would be a good judge, but I never got the chance. I suppose she planted the idea in my mind long before I had any conscious memory of it."

"Your grandmother was probably just as proud that you became a lawyer, wasn't she?" Morgan asked.

"I suppose so," Fenwick said. "She raised me. She was a full-blooded Crow, a housemaid in Miles City, Montana, when she met a white drover from Texas. They never married, but she bore a child. Their half-breed daughter was my mother, who died when I was very young. I never knew my father, who I've been told was the son of an upstanding banker in Miles City and, of course, could never be allowed to marry a half-breed squaw. So my grandmother raised me and, as you can clearly see, dreamed for me."

Morgan was mildly surprised. Sim Fenwick had none of the noble, dark features of a Native American. His pale features were tender, his manner almost effeminate. The blood in his veins was at least one-quarter Crow Indian, but it was thin and blue, perhaps more like his promiscuous grandfather's.

"She did well," Morgan said. "Dreaming for you, that is. Did she put you through law school?"

"Yes, indeed. She worked all her life as a housemaid. She earned ten dollars a week, most of which she saved religiously to that very purpose. She gave me what she had never had, an education and freedom."

"That must have pleased her," Morgan said.

"Her father, my great-grandfather, had been a scout for General Phil Sheridan himself during the Indian Wars. There's a family story that he once watched white soldiers torture, then hang, some Lakota renegades. The experience crystallized, for him, what was happening to his people: The Indians were losing justice. Many years later, he told his daughter of a dream he'd had, in which a Crow brave carefully held a small, beating heart in his hand. When he lifts the pulsing organ to the sky, as if to seek the advice of the Great Spirit, it swiftly transforms into a hawk and flies away into the clouds. It sounds terribly grisly, unless you accept it as merely a symbol."

"How so?"

"The Indian man could have eaten the heart, or thrown it to the dogs. After what he saw, I suppose my great-grandfather believed that a white man would have done that."

"So what happened? To you, I mean. Why didn't you become a judge in the end?"

"I cannot say, Mr. Morgan. Perhaps my politics weren't right. And I suspect my involvement with the Gilmartin case did not improve my stature with my colleagues in the bar. I applied for all the court openings, but the governor always had a different notion. Nine governors, to be exact."

Morgan dumped two sugars into his sweating glass of tea and tossed the empty pink packets on the table. Fenwick intrigued him.

"Why a judge? What about the bench lured you?"

"It seemed to be the nexus of law's purpose and its practice. All my life, I saw incapable men holding court, toying with the livelihoods, and sometimes the lives of frightened people in trouble. One should be meticulous in such matters. Not all of them were fair men, nor were they even thoughtful

men. They didn't understand the gravity of their responsibility, and they wielded their power with no creativity. I believe
I would have been a very fine judge."

Fenwick picked up Morgan's empty sugar packets and
folded them neatly into tidy squares, which he deposited in
the ashtray.

"What about Judge Hand? I recall he was the judge here
for a long time, wasn't he?"

"Darby Hand was the law in Perry County for almost forty
years. He was a brilliant thinker, but the power rotted him
inside. I feared him. I still fear him, even though he's dead."

Morgan felt a little sorry for this obsessive, frightened
little man who sat across from him. Fenwick's only dream
had been beyond his power to control, so he compensated by
mastering the minutiae of his life. Unable to command order
in the court, he gave painstaking order only to what fell within
his reach.

The rain had stopped, although the sky was still obscured
by a sopping blanket of clouds. Morgan was watching tiny
concentric circles ripple across a puddle in the gutter when a
battered pickup, caked with equal parts of mud and rust,
splashed through it. The truck came to a stop just in front of
The Griddle's front door.

The driver was an elderly man with a long, white beard.
He wore a soiled gray-felt cowboy hat, its rain-warped brim
rolled tightly. His denim shirt was buttoned at the top, but
the collar hung loose around his neck. When he stepped out
of the truck into a wallow of run-off, Morgan saw he was
wearing knee-high irrigation boots.

The old man walked around to the passenger side, away
from Morgan's view, and opened the door for a younger
woman who was in the truck with him. She followed him, a
few awkward steps behind, her head cocked to one side. She
wasn't right.

"Who's the man who just came in?" he asked Fenwick.

The retired lawyer turned toward the front door, then just as quickly turned back.

"You don't know?" he asked incredulously. "That's Malachi Pierce."

Pierce stood by the cash register with a sheaf of papers in his hand, rain and mud puddling around his boots. He was looking for the cashier, who'd disappeared into the kitchen moments before. The young woman stood behind him, lolling her tongue and staring blankly at a cowboy sitting at the counter.

"Who's the woman with him?"

"That's his daughter, Hosanna. She's retarded, poor child. He takes her everywhere. Must be close to thirty years old. I've heard it said he considers her a punishment, sent by God."

"Punishment for what?"

"I wouldn't know. Perhaps you should inquire with him. However, I might suggest you accept it as an article of faith rather than try to communicate with him. He's a very angry man."

Pierce grew impatient. His dark, deep-set eyes crawled over the small dining room, looking for the cashier. He rapped the bell on the counter six or seven times as his daughter huddled behind him. She was watching Morgan.

Her sloping eyes were now fixed on him. She looked as if she had Down's Syndrome, her round face framed by closely cropped ash-blond hair, a kitchen-sink cut. She put her fingers in her mouth and watched him.

Pierce whacked the bell a few more times, then went around behind the cash register. That's when Hosanna Pierce saw Fenwick.

A tremor of recognition crackled across her face. She averted her eyes and soon began muttering incomprehensibly.

Suddenly, she wailed and fled toward the door. She thrust against it, unable to open it, flailing her arms and pounding the glass. She shrieked until her father grabbed her around the waist and hauled her out of the restaurant. She kicked violently as he wrestled her toward the truck and opened the door so she could curl up on the floorboard, weeping against the seat. His flyers littered the restaurant floor.

Pierce looked back through the window, glowering at Fenwick through the glass for a chillingly long moment, then they drove away.

The outburst had silenced the diners. Suzie squatted down to pick up the scattered papers Pierce had dropped on the muddy floor.

"Jesus, what was that all about?" a stunned Morgan asked Fenwick. "She saw you and just freaked out."

"She's a damaged child. I can't begin to know what dark delusions she harbors. Perhaps it was just an unfortunate spell. I'm an old country lawyer, not a doctor, Mr. Morgan. I hope you find whatever you are looking for. For the life of me, I cannot determine why it's so important to re-open this wound, but I suppose that is the habit of reporters."

Morgan smiled.

"Not just reporters. Don't lawyers seek justice, too?" he asked Fenwick, who shrugged him off.

"You said it yourself: Desperate criminals get very imaginative. Mr. Gilmartin is desperate."

Simeon Fenwick held out his soft hand to Morgan. His grip was still cool and damp.

"It was nice to meet you. I'm sorry I couldn't be of more assistance. Perhaps we can have lunch again sometime."

Fenwick snatched up the ticket and left it on the cashier's counter with a crisp ten dollar bill. He stooped to pick up one of Pierce's flyers, as if he were annoyed by the mess, then waved feebly at Morgan as he disappeared out the front door in a few fastidious steps.

Morgan sat alone in the big booth for a while, nursing his iced tea and trying to sort through what he'd seen. Although they were an unlikely pair, the radical militant Pierce and the prim Fenwick were connected, but how? Morgan's best guess: Fenwick had done legal work for the old man at some time. He fished a small notebook out of his breast pocket and made a note to himself to check for any court records on Pierce. His gut told him it was likely he'd find Fenwick's name somewhere in them.

Before he put his notebook away, he made another note: *Call Jerry Overton, ATF.* An agent in the Bureau of Alcohol, Tobacco and Firearms' Chicago office, Overton was the agency's top expert on radical religious extremists, white supremacists and dozens of underground militia groups. It was the perfect job for the former Methodist seminary student who quit school to serve two tours in the Marines in Vietnam. After he got back to the World, he eventually earned a master's degree in forensic psychology from the University of Illinois.

Now in his fifties and still fiercely competitive, he stayed fit by inviting a dwindling pool of hapless victims to his twice-a-week racquetball games; Morgan had lost more than his share to Overton's quick reflexes and withering kill shots. But he'd won a trusted friend whose word was always good, a friend who'd helped link the serial killer P.D. Comeaux to a little-known group of violent Christian fundamentalists known as the Fourth Sign. Overton would know if Malachi Pierce was on the bureau's watch list.

Suzie brought one of Pierce's flyers to Morgan. It was a mud-flecked copy of the letter he'd written to *The Bullet*, reproduced under a quote from the Book of Luke: *"For there is nothing covered that shall not be revealed; neither hid that shall not be known."*

"That man is crazy bad news," she said. "You watch yourself. Don't trust him."

Morgan spent the rest of his dark afternoon doing busywork, distracted by his impending meeting with the banker, Hamilton Tasker. He could do nothing more than beg for an extension. But he planned to put off the meeting as long as possible, and he glanced at the newsroom clock nervously every few minutes.

Morgan thumbed through his Rolodex and found Jerry Overton's number. It was after four o'clock on a Friday afternoon in Chicago, but Overton, who worked as hard as he played, answered his phone. Even with friends, he wasn't much for small talk, so the pleasantries were brief.

"So, what'll it be today, my investigative reporter friend: Alcohol, tobacco or firearms?" Overton jibed.

"Are those my only choices?" Morgan played along.

"We're specialists here, buddy. Beer, butts and bullets. You want amateurs, call the FBI."

"In that case, I'll take firearms for a thousand."

"Excellent choice. What's up?"

"This might be right up your alley, Jerry. I'm wondering what you can tell me about a guy out here who may be into some serious weaponry. He's one of those hardcore Christian Patriot types, heavy on the Armageddon and white supremacy. Sort of a malignant cross between Koresh, the Klan and the Oklahoma bomber. His name is Pierce, Malachi Pierce. He runs an isolated compound out here called Wormwood Camp."

"Nice touch."

"What?"

"From the Bible. Wormwood is from Revelations. If this guy's into Revelations, you're in for a lot of happy camping. The Revelation nuts are starting to see 'the signs' and they're breaking out the ammo."

"He is. But I need to know if he's worth watching. Can you help me on that, strictly off the record? No story, just background."

"You know I can't."

Sharing ATF intelligence wasn't just against policy, it was against the law. A felony. Overton's twenty-six-year career would be over in the blink of a cursor if he tapped into the Treasury

Enforcement Communication System for a civilian. TECS was a super-computer database shared by Customs, the Secret Service, the Internal Revenue Service and ATF, and if Pierce had ever run afoul of any of them, he'd be in The Box.

But as a matter of personal policy, Morgan never asked his sources in law enforcement to break the law and, in turn, they never asked him to break the ethical code of journalism. He wrote better with a clear conscience.

"I know, Jerry," Morgan said. "I've just got a feeling about this guy and I'm a little worried. He's made some veiled threats. Claire's home alone, we've got a baby on the way ..."

"Hey, congratulations. That's wonderful news. You were a great dad before, and you'll be a great dad again."

Overton knew more about the pain inside Morgan than anyone. His own teen-age son had died in a prom-night car accident and, after Bridger died, he'd take Morgan to Marley's Tavern on the most difficult afternoons and just listen as the grief poured from his heart. Somewhere inside Jerry Overton was still a clergyman with a gift for comfort.

"Thanks, Jerry. Maybe that's why I'm edgy. I don't normally take these guys seriously, but I got a funny feeling this time. I just thought maybe you'd be able to steer me in the right direction, that's all."

"Have you tried a Freedom of Information request?" Overton asked. No lawman ever casually suggested an FOI request to a newspaperman. Information was power, and most federal agents believed the bureaucrats who decided what data was public and what was private sometimes bent over too far for nosey reporters. But Overton clearly wanted to help his old friend—as long as it was legal.

"Yeah, right. I want to know in this lifetime, Jerry. An FOI request would take months, and you know it."

"Sorry, friend. You know the drill. Bad guys have all the rights. Wish I could help, but after all those leaks on the Unabomber and that Olympic security guard, ATF's determined to show we're a lot less talkative than our chatty brethren in the FBI. Management's got everybody spooked about talking to the press. You know, they're probably listening in on this call right now ... right boys?"

Morgan laughed.

"I understand, honest. But if you run across anything that might be public, let me know. I'd owe you one."

"One what?"

"Let's see. I'll owe you an Old Style at Wrigley. Good enough?"

Beer seemed to be Overton's one unwholesome habit. He preferred heady, imported ales, but he always said there was nothing like ballpark beer. Morgan knew it was a singular weakness in his otherwise flawless friend whose sense of honor now commanded that he keep his code. Morgan understood honor, and respected it.

"Yeah, Old Style. That's real good. The best thing I can say about the Cubbies is they got good beer. But, Jeff ... seriously, I don't think I can help. You know what's at stake. I'm really sorry."

Morgan said he did. It wasn't a lie.

They exchanged warm goodbyes and promises to drop in if they were ever in the neighborhood. But to Morgan, the old neighborhood never seemed so far away and he never felt so alone.

After Morgan hung up, Cal Nussbaum appeared from nowhere, his hang-dog face looming over the computer screen.

"Jesus, Cal, how long have you been standing there?"

"Not long. You got a minute?"

Morgan knew what was coming. The reticent printer had been unhappy for weeks and he wasn't one to chat up the editor about anything less than a crisis. He was too old a dog to learn new tricks, too near retirement to gut out the increasing difficulties. He was going to quit, and Morgan saw it coming.

"Sure, have a seat," he said. "What can I do for you, Cal?"

"There's something I want to say that ain't easy for me," Cal said in his slow manner, choosing to stand. "I been here since the Second World War. I was thirteen years old and my first week on the job, back in 'forty-three, Georgie Patton invaded Sicily. I was workin' here even before Old Bell, to give you an idea. So when Old Bell left, I started thinkin' about how long I'd been here at the paper."

"A long time, Cal," Morgan said.

Already, he was wondering where he'd find a new pressman. Morgan didn't know how to run a web press himself, so he hoped Cal would stay on until his replacement was hired.

"Yeah, a long time. Fifty-three years, just makin' a newspaper. A fella just sort of keeps his head down and does his work, and next thing he knows, he's an old man and he ain't done none of the stuff he promised hisself to do."

Morgan felt sorry for Cal, but he didn't want to lose him. Not while this house of cards was vulnerable to the slightest whisper.

"Cal, you've been a great help to me and to Old Bell. He told me there was only one person I could count on. You."

"That old fart lied. We was each other's biggest pain in the ass. Some days you'da swore we'd kill each other before we'd work side by side for fifty years. But I done my work the best I could, and so did he. I respected him for that."

Morgan imagined these two iron-willed men in epic deadline battles, firing off bursts of profanity in hand-to-hand combat over headline breaks and last-minute editing and all the balky machinery of small-town, weekly journalism.

"Anyhow," Cal continued, "a fella comes to a point in his life where he has to make some hard choices about his work. I guess I'm there. Damn arthritis gets worse every winter. I been savin' up for a long time, maybe for a little place down south where it's warm. I've always thought that would be how I'd like to spend the rest of my life. Warm."

Morgan was deflated, but he tried to be buoyant. Cal

Nussbaum had worked too long and too hard to go out on bad terms.

"Cal, that sounds like a fine retirement. We'll have a party. I'll miss you around here."

"What?"

"I'll miss you around here. *The Bullet* owes you a lot more than it can give. I haven't been here long, but you've been a great employee. Honestly, it'll be hard to get along without you."

"You firin' me?"

"I thought you were quitting."

"Jesus Christ, I'm too old to be moonin' around like some dumb-ass kid. I ain't goin' nowhere. I just wanted to give you this."

Cal Nussbaum dipped his inky fingers in his shirt pocket and handed Morgan a smudged check.

Ten thousand dollars.

"Cal, what ... I mean, why?"

"I been savin' up so's I could walk away from this goddam job someday. Then I figgered, what the hell, I don't want to walk away just yet. Not while they're laughin' at us. I been hearin' what they say about you, and Crystal tells me about the money problem with the bank. I worked too goddam hard to see this paper close down. This ain't much, and it's only a loan, but I ain't gonna let 'em shut this shop while I can still fight."

Morgan shoved the check toward his crusty pressman, barely able to speak.

"I can't accept this, Cal. I appreciate the sentiment more than you know, but I can't risk your retirement money."

Cal Nussbaum snarled resolutely at his boss.

"Goddammit, it ain't for you. It's for this place. You understand? I been workin' here all my goddam life. If this place closes down, it's like my life wasn't worth a shit. Anyhow, I got no place else to go."

Morgan laid Cal's check on top of his desk and stood up. He felt his eyes watering as he held out his hand.

"Thank you, Cal," he said. He gripped the old printer's stained hand, hoping some of it would rub off on him. "It means a lot to me. It buys us a little time. That's all we need. Let me know if there's anything you need. Anything."

Cal's long face remained stony.

"Try to make deadline. That'd help," he said, then turned and disappeared back into the backshop.

Morgan showed the check to Hamilton Tasker, who called up Cal Nussbaum's accounts on the computer behind his shiny cherrywood desk at the bank. He said nothing as columns of green digits scrolled up the screen.

"Will this cover the payment?" Morgan asked him after waiting patiently for a few moments.

Tasker tapped a few more keys, studied the numbers and slowly swiveled in his high-backed leather chair to face Morgan.

"It looks in order," he said. Morgan detected a curious note of disappointment in his voice. "Mr. Nussbaum has more than enough to cover his check."

"Then our little problem is solved," Morgan said.

"Not exactly," Tasker said. He leaned back in his elegant chair, pulling the cuff of his tailored silk coat over his gold wristwatch.

"What do you mean 'not exactly'?"

"A couple things. Your cash flow has almost evaporated and the next payment will be due in less than a month. I'm worried we'll be back in the same boat in a few weeks."

"We can fix that."

Tasker stroked his businesslike black mustache, which contrasted with his silvery, razor-cut hair. He wasn't yet sixty, but he cultivated his distinguished bearing and for good reason. To the citizens of Winchester, Wyoming, he was money made flesh.

"Are you aware of the Chamber's proposed boycott?"

"I am. We'll get through it. I grew up here, Ham, and I'm thinking my town is better off with a newspaper that has the guts to tell the truth when it would be easier to lie. Printing the truth was good enough for Old Bell and it's good enough for me. Will there be anything else?"

Tasker didn't look up. He trifled with spreadsheets on his desk.

"The 'truth' is overrated, Mr. Morgan. It seldom pays the bills. And it would be wise to remember that your particular version of the truth isn't necessarily the only version. We'll be watching with great interest. Good day."

The bank lobby was quiet. Morgan walked past the polished marble row of tellers' warrens, where a bow-legged cowboy was cashing his Friday paycheck, and through the massive glass doors onto Main Street. The sun had broken through the overcast and streamed down in bright columns. The air was still humid, but it smelled fresh.

Crystal Sandoval looked worried when Morgan returned to *The Bullet*.

"We've already gotten a few calls about the boycott," she said. "Word is getting around fast on the grapevine."

"Who called?"

Crystal's brown eyes focused somewhere beyond the ceiling fan as she tried to remember.

"Al, the one-eyed counter guy at the gun shop. Um, let's see ... Celine at the hairdresser's, a couple readers, the wife of the new guy at the Kwik Mart ..."

Morgan got the idea.

"What are they saying?"

"They're wondering what all the fuss is about, not even sure if they should be angry. But that's good. It's the ones that *don't* call we have to worry about."

"If we get any more, send them to me, would you?"

Crystal nodded and popped her gum.

"Oh, Jeff, just one message for you."

She handed Morgan one of her pink phone slips. Some-one named Kate Morning called after four-thirty. She left no message except the long-distance phone number where she could be reached.

"Another complaint?"

"Didn't say."

"Where's area code four-oh-six?" Morgan asked.

"Montana, I think."

"God help us if they're mad in Montana, too," he joked.

Morgan went back to his desk and called Claire. He'd inter-rupted her nap, but she was greatly relieved to hear about Cal's loan. He told her he loved her and let her go back to sleep.

He checked the local news queue in the Mac and saw that both of his reporters had filed stories before the weekend. A good sign. They were working ahead.

Kate Morning's message lay atop the stack of ad invoices and press releases. He checked his watch. It was after five and the rates were lower, so he dialed.

An older woman with an elegant voice answered.

"Hello, I'm calling for Kate Morning."

"This is she."

"Ms. Morning, this is Jeff Morgan at *The Bullet* in Win-chester, Wyoming. I had a message that you called."

The woman paused a few seconds before she spoke. Her voice had a faint, sweet cadence, foreign but familiar.

"Thank you for calling, Mr. Morgan. Please forgive this call, which might seem strange to you. I'm not sure how you can help me, but if you can, it will be clear."

"I'll try. What exactly is the problem?"

"I'd like to speak to you in person, if I may. Would that be possible?"

Morgan didn't relish the idea of a long drive.

"That depends. Where are you?"

"Hardin, Montana. Only a few hours from Winchester."

Western roads were long and empty, and distances were not measured in miles, but in time. By Western standards, a few hours wasn't far. Hardin was a small town on the edge of Montana's Crow Indian Reservation, a gas stop on the way to Billings, but it was well out of his coverage area.

Morgan wanted to know more before he embarked on a cross-country goose chase. What passed for dramatic news in the minds of his callers was often no more than minor social gossip. He couldn't justify making a six-hour round-trip for a three-graph story about a craft bazaar or a tea society fund-raiser.

"Can you give me some general idea what we'd talk about, Ms. Morning? I'm sure you understand ..."

She paused longer than before.

"Maybe you won't understand. I just need to know if you are the one."

"The one what?" Morgan asked.

"The one who can help me."

"I can try, Ms. Morning, but I'm afraid you have to be a little more specific."

The connection hummed and Morgan strained to hear. Then she spoke, almost too softly for him to understand.

"My daughter was Aimee Little Spotted Horse."

CHAPTER ELEVEN

Just across the Montana state line, where the tall grass prairie begins to fold into the badlands, Claire vomited beside the highway. The caustic smell of oil and browned grass on the sun-seared shoulder only made it worse for her.

Morgan rummaged in the Escort's glove box and found a fast-food wet-nap for his wife. She wiped her mouth as she rested her head against the open car door.

"Are you going to be okay? It's still a couple hours to Hardin. We can turn back, if you want," he said.

"It'll pass," she said without looking up. "Just be ready to pull over again. Fast."

An eighteen-wheel cattle truck hurtled past, going at least eighty. It sucked the air down the road with it, and the vacuum of its passing seemed to lift the compact Escort off the ground. A split-second later, a furious surge of dust and twigs enveloped them, then the nauseating aroma of hot cow shit.

Claire leaned out the door and vomited again.

While Claire was freshening up in the restroom, Morgan asked the Hardin Conoco's teen-aged Indian attendant how to find Kate Morning's house. The boy wore a long braid, a greasy green Boston Celtics cap, and wrap-around Oakley sunglasses that shimmered iridescently in the Saturday morning sunlight, like oil on the surface of a pond. The name "Ernie" was embroidered in script over his breast pocket.

"You mean the Morning *ranch*?" Ernie asked.

"I don't know. Maybe," Morgan said, a little confused. "I'm looking for *Kate* Morning. An older lady. Lives here in town. That's all I know."

The boy chuckled.

"Yeah, that's her, only she don't live here in town. Nice lady. The Morning Ranch is the biggest spread in the county, and she lives out there all by herself since Gabe died. Comes into town sometimes, but her hired men mostly run errands for her. You know her?"

In his mind, Morgan replayed the voice on the other end of the line. Somehow, he had imagined he'd find Kate Morning, once a runaway Indian girl who'd given birth to her child in a squalid homesteader's shack, living in less dignified circumstances. Now, he was a little ashamed to find out she'd apparently become a woman of considerable substance.

"Okay, then, is the Morning *ranch* hard to find?"

The Indian boy sauntered a few loose-jointed steps toward the road, his baggy jeans barely hitched to his thin hips. He pointed the way as far as he could see down Hardin's Main Street.

"No problem. You go down this road all the way through town, past the dump 'til the road turns to dirt. You keep on it all the way to the Medicine Sand coulee, but don't cross the water there. Follow the red bluff 'til you cross over the old wood bridge and the road forks. Don't matter which way you go, you end up at the same place. A big gray rock house. That's the Morning place. No problem."

"How far are we talking here?"

Ernie smiled. His grin was full of crooked teeth.

"All the way," he said.

Morgan paid for his gas and bought a 7-Up at the pop machine outside for Claire. She emerged from the restroom looking refreshed.

"Is it far?" she asked.

"It's all the way," he said.

"What?"

"All the way."

"Is that far?" Claire asked.

"Nope," Morgan answered playfully. "There's only two ways to go and they both end up at the same place. Just go all the way. No problem."

Claire's sense of humor was returning, and so was her color.

"Well, at least we won't get lost," she said.

To Morgan's surprise, the Indian boy's directions were impeccable. The paved road gave way to gravel, then to two rain-splashed ribbons of bare dirt a mile outside the town. At Medicine Sand coulee, some Indian children plunged into the cool reddish-green water from a tire lashed to an overhanging cottonwood branch. The road followed the base of brilliant red bluffs, carved by the ancient river and sanded smooth by the rain of millennia. Another mile, they came to a bridge of weathered timbers that lamented their passing with a low groan. A hundred yards beyond, where the bluffs parted, the muddy dirt road split in separate directions into the shallow valley, and neither looked more nor less inviting than the other.

"What did the boy say?"

"He said they both end up at the same place."

"A circle," she said.

"What do you mean?"

"The road is a circle. It doesn't matter which way you go, you'll eventually end up at the same spot. Many Indians saw circles as symbolic of life and the cycles around them."

Claire might have grown up in an affluent suburb of Chicago, but she was in her element where art intersected with history. Morgan grew up in a cattle town on the high plains and knew every ranch was a patchwork of pastures stitched together by roads forged more by convenience than culture.

They took the westerly fork, along the red bluffs. The road bounded irrigated fields of alfalfa like thick slabs of jade wrapped in rusty velvet.

"Up there," Claire said, pointing ahead.

A magnificent gray mansion rose before them, splendidly out of character with its surroundings. Morgan, once a reluctant student of architecture, recognized the style as Georgian Revival, a cross between an English country house and an American colonial estate popular around the turn of the century.

The house had three stories. No fewer than four stone chimneys sprouted from its tiled gambrel roof. Graceful, snow-white columns supported porticos on the front and western side. As they drew nearer, Morgan saw it was a stonemason's masterpiece: The massive granite blocks in the mansion's stone walls were shaped by hand, and the elegant quoins were fashioned of gray marble. Sweet honeysuckle vines scaled the stones toward the sky, reaching past the Palladian windows of the second floor.

A large black Labrador retriever, white-muzzled and heavy in the belly, barked unenthusiastically from the ivory-columned porch as the muddy Escort rolled to a stop in front of the house. Before its engine had quit sputtering and fuming, a woman came out the front door and shushed the big dog, which happily abandoned his tiresome grunting but kept his black eyes on the visitors.

The tall woman on the porch was dressed in a long denim skirt and plain white blouse, with an ornate silver and turquoise necklace tucked under her collar. Her long hair was the color of ash in a hearth, and it was pulled back with a simple blue ribbon.

Kate Morning, once Catherine Little Spotted Horse, was now in her early seventies, but she had a courtly bearing. Her chestnut-colored skin was smooth and translucent, her cheek-bones as stately as the red bluffs that surrounded her little valley. A certain sadness reflected in her eyes, as if she'd been crying not just all night, but for many years. Still, Morgan found her strikingly beautiful.

"Welcome," Kate said, extending her hand to him. It was the same exotic voice he'd heard on the phone. "You must be Jeff Morgan. I am pleased you could come on such short notice."

Morgan shook her hand. It was graceful but strong.

"Mrs. Morning, this is my wife, Claire," he said. The two women shook hands, too.

"You must call me Kate or I will feel very old. *Being* old is not as bad as *feeling* old," Kate said. "Come now. I have tea for you inside. My own recipe."

The fat dog sprawled dispassionately on the porch's top step and let them pass.

Behind its remarkable walls, the house was incongruously bleak. Plaster flaked from some of the walls and dust-encrusted cobwebs hung in the corners of the high, dark ceilings. The bare wooden floor was warped and water-stained. The few scattered antique furnishings weren't arranged in any apparent harmony. Old photographs in oval frames, a few mounted mule deer and elk heads, and unused gas lamps were hung almost randomly on the massive walls, but Morgan saw no mirrors.

So much dust stirred in the air, a ray of sunlight from a clerestory window high on the western wall appeared to be a sparkling liquid swirling in a transparent cylinder. The whole place reeked of burning grass, decay and neglect.

Despite the promise of the house's majestic facade, it was empty and dying inside.

A mist of dust floated around Morgan and his wife as they sat together on a threadbare loveseat. It faced a stone fireplace as tall as a man. Wisps of smoke rose from a thick layer of cooling cedar embers and charred sprigs of sage. A knitted afghan was thrown over the arm of an ancient rocking chair beside the hearth. Morgan imagined Kate had stayed up most of the night in front of her fire, alone and cold.

She served her tea made from huckleberries, sweetgrass and wild honey. An old Crow recipe, she told them. Chips of ice chimed in the tall glasses. Despite his addictive taste for it, Morgan thought better of asking for sugar.

"This is a wonderful house, Kate," Morgan remarked politely, sipping the fragrant tea.

Kate Morning looked up at her high, smoke-darkened ceilings. Her dulcet voice drifted upward and was nearly lost among whatever spirits moved in the emptiness above.

"It belonged to my late husband Gabe's family for almost one hundred years. His grandfather—John Morning was his name—struck gold in the Dakotas and settled this land. To build the house, he had all the stones shipped on the train from his boyhood hometown in Indiana."

"Was Gabe your second husband?" Morgan asked.

Kate's gaze shifted to the smoke curling in the fireplace.

"Yes," she said softly. "He was a good man, very generous. He had a big heart, but it was weak. He died last year."

"I'm sorry to hear that," Morgan said.

"Perhaps it is the only reason you are here," Kate said.

Morgan was puzzled. "Why's that?"

Kate Morning pulled a thick white envelope from a hidden pocket in her skirt and handed it to Morgan. It bore no marks and was still sealed.

"Open it," she instructed him.

Morgan used his finger like a letter opener, tearing a ragged opening across the top of the envelope. Claire looked over his shoulder with wide eyes.

"Jesus, there's easily more than ten thousand dollars here," Morgan said. He searched Kate's face for some sign of its meaning, but she just looked away. "What's this about?"

"It was left in a chair on the porch yesterday morning," Kate said. "Same as all the other times."

"Other times?"

"Many times. Always that same terrible day."

Just like Gilmartin, Morgan thought. *That day* ...

"The anniversary of your daughter's death," Morgan said bluntly.

Kate was surprised. "So you know?" she asked.

"I don't know where the money comes from or why. But I know someone else who has been getting money like this on the very same day for the past ten years. It's obviously not a coincidence, Kate."

"Who else?" she asked.

Morgan measured his words carefully.

"The man who went to prison for ... for Aimee's death," he said. "He is still alive, but he is dying. He doesn't know where the money comes from either."

"He's in prison, isn't he?"

"No, Kate. He's out of prison now, but you have nothing to fear. He is very sick. He will die soon."

"How do you know these things?"

"He came to me," Morgan said. "He claims he didn't commit the crime and he wants someone to prove it before he goes. He doesn't want to die with your daughter's murder in his heart."

Kate's hand trembled as she fingered the hand-made silver pendant around her neck, like a shiny rosary. She didn't speak, but her tired eyes looked frightened.

"Do you have any idea who would leave you so much money?" Morgan asked.

"I don't know who does it. I was told you would have answers for me."

"Who told you that?"

"One who has ghost medicine, *ahpaláaxe xáaplia*," Kate said. "Since my husband died last year, I am alone here. Always before, he was here to make me feel safe. Yesterday, when I found the envelope, I was frightened. So I took it to a woman in the tribe who sees with her heart. She looked at it in the Indian way and she told me a white storyteller would answer my questions."

Kate's enigmatic response frustrated Morgan. Clearly, she expected him to reveal some mystery almost as much as he had hoped she would reveal it to him.

"First, I'm a newspaperman, not a storyteller. Second, even if I were, there are many white storytellers besides me. Third, I don't believe in crystal balls, the psychic hotline or ghost medicine. And fourth, I have just as many questions as you do, and far fewer answers."

Composing herself, Kate turned to Claire.

"You are going to have a baby?" she asked.

Suddenly self-conscious, Claire touched her tummy. She wasn't even three months pregnant, so hadn't yet begun to show. She looked at her husband, who was clearly amazed.

"Yes," she said. "How could you know?"

"*Ahpaláaxe xáaplia.* She told me the white storyteller had lost a child, too, but that he would soon have another. She said he would know my anguish. Is it true that you have lost a child?"

Morgan breathed deeply. He looked at Claire and nodded.

"She said he would hear the *ilaáxe*, the ghosts. You have spoken my daughter's name before today?"

Morgan nodded again.

"Then you are the one who'll speak the answers," Kate said. Suddenly, her eyes were calm, hopeful.

"But, Kate, I told you: I don't know anything about your daughter's murder," Morgan said. "Your medicine woman was wrong about that. I'm sorry, but I have no answers."

It changed nothing. The spirits had spoken, perhaps from the lofty ceilings above them, and the spirits could not be wrong. Kate smiled patiently.

"Then I must wait until you do."

***

But there would be no answers without questions, and Morgan had many for Kate Morning.

She had prepared a lunch for them—a cold pasta salad of wild pheasant, chanterelle mushrooms from Medicine Sand coulee and rotelle noodles—and served it on the sun-porch. While he and Claire helped her set the outdoor table, Kate showed him the willow-cane chair where she'd found the money the morning before.

"It was right here. No note, no writing."

Morgan looked around. He could see at least a mile down the dirt road from Medicine Sand coulee to the Morning Ranch. A gravel driveway encircled the house, leading to a horse barn, some empty corrals and a winter woodpile in back. Otherwise, the house was isolated by the emptiness that surrounded it.

"An intruder would have to walk here in the dark, sneak up onto the porch, drop the envelope and walk out again. Maybe he came in with his headlights off and parked farther down the road where you wouldn't hear him."

Kate's fat Lab yawned and scratched his ear with a hind paw. He was no longer interested in the visitors.

"Did you hear the dog bark last night or early this morning?" Morgan asked.

"That overfed coyote sleeps inside with me. He's mostly deaf anyway."

"Any strange cars or trucks on the road that you recall?"

"I heard nothing."

"Do you have people who come and go? Ranch hands?"

"I have two men, but they both live in town. Nobody else comes out here, except the pure-gas truck and a few hunters in the fall."

They sat down to the pheasant salad lunch, with a pitcher of sweetgrass tea, a plate of warm sourdough bread, and fresh butter. Soon, Claire was feeling much better with food on her stomach. She touched her husband's hand under the table, as much a gesture of confidence as companionship.

"How many times have you gotten money like this?" Morgan asked Kate.

"Ten or eleven years in a row. My people would say it comes from an evil spirit because it is associated with death. I became so frightened by it, I wouldn't even look at it or touch it. Gabe always gave the envelopes to the Indian school to help children go to college."

"Didn't you come to expect it every year?" Morgan asked. "If it were me, I'd watch all night. Did you ever try to see who it was?"

"Sometimes Gabe would take his rifle and hide in the fields to see who came in the night, but he never saw anyone. And I was too frightened to see, like a little girl who hides her eyes when she imagines a ghost by her bed. The shadows know when we are watching. They see us, but we cannot see them."

Spirits.

Ghosts.

Shadows.

Morgan knew better. Someone had been making very large payments to both Kate Morning and Neeley Gilmartin for the past decade. He didn't know why, except that it was related to the murder of Aimee Little Spotted Horse. It might be some bleeding heart who felt sorry for both of them, or it might be the little girl's killer. It could be reparation or blood money. Either way, it came from someone who still cared deeply about the murder and who had access to large amounts of money, nearly two hundred thousand dollars over the past ten years.

"Whatever happened to Charlie?" Morgan asked abruptly.

"After our daughter died, we tried to stay together, but we fell apart," Kate said. "In 'forty-nine, he went to Oklahoma to look for construction work and I came back to Crow Agency. I was a woman on the outside, but still a little girl on the inside. A few years later, when I became a woman on the inside, too, I met Gabe Morning and became his wife. In time, I was happy again."

"You've done well."

"Gabe convinced me to make something of myself. He sent me to school to become a nurse. I worked for many years at the government hospital in town, taking care of the Indian babies. Touching them, it filled an empty place in me."

Kate Morning was neither a killer nor a conspirator. Morgan's gut told him that much.

"What do you remember of the time before Aimee died?" he asked her.

"That was another life. I wouldn't live it again, but I do not regret living it. Charlie and me, we were foolish children who thought they were in love, but after we found out I was pregnant, the only thing we shared was being scared. We ran away from the reservation. We lived in a shack in the middle of nowhere, barely enough to eat, hardly any money. But Aimee made us a family."

"I'm sorry I have to ask this," Morgan said, "but Charlie was in trouble once for hitting Aimee. He even went to jail for a short time. These things are very hard for families to deal with. Is there any chance ..."

Kate interrupted him, shaking her head.

"I know what you are thinking, but it isn't true. The sheriff believed it, too, for a while. Charlie was a good father, but when he drank, a devil took him. He struck me, and yes, he struck her, but all the pain was inside *him*. She was so small, so sweet. He feared that he would separate her soul from her body."

"How's that?" Morgan asked.

"The Crow believe a child's soul, *ilaáxe*, is inside the body, but it is not *bonded* to the flesh until they are grown. You have seen children play? When they are too rough, the soul can be separated from the body. A Crow mother will bring her children inside, then she will again call their names in the yard, in case a soul was knocked loose."

"And Charlie feared he might knock Aimee's soul loose?"

"In the year before she went away. He hit her so hard she was unconscious for many hours. That night, he fell to his knees under the stars and he called her name 'til dawn. A few days later, the sheriff came to arrest him."

"Did it ever happen again?" Morgan asked her.

"There was much anger in Charlie when he drank. He never stopped drinking."

"Did he ever stop hitting you and Aimee?"

Kate Morning shook her head. "But he didn't kill her. I would have known. A mother would know."

Morgan felt Claire tense beside him.

"Are you certain of that?"

"We both kissed her as she slept on the morning before we left. We were together all day up north, riding the fence. When we returned and found her gone, he cried all night in my arms. We cried together."

Morgan believed her. He didn't know why, exactly. Being a reporter was a vague science. Truth was, indeed, a matter of perception. Maybe Kate Morning was still hiding a terrible secret. Maybe she knew far more than she was telling. Maybe she watched Charlie do it, or maybe she did it herself.

But if Kate Morning concealed such a terrible secret, why would she risk it by coming forward now? She could have remained silent and forever anonymous to Morgan, but she didn't. She was alone and lonely, crying all night by the fire, afraid of ghosts.

"Kate, was there anyone besides Neeley Gilmartin who might have done this? Anyone who was angry with you or Charlie, or who knew Aimee was alone? Anybody who meant harm to your family?"

"Only him. They say he was a gambler and a drunkard who hated Charlie, that he made terrible threats. She was my baby, so innocent. And he confessed that he killed her. I believe he spoke the truth. His death comes too late and too easy. My heart is not heavy for him."

She was resolute, without forgiveness. No jury's verdict was so lasting as a mother's conviction. Neeley Gilmartin never had a jury, but Kate Morning's judgment was far more harsh. To her, Gilmartin had only one dimension: Evil.

"What became of Charlie after he left for Oklahoma?"

"I hear he was killed," Kate said. "I saw his brother in town one day and he told me that Charlie had been drunk and got hit by a train near a town called Pawhuska, and he was buried there in an Indian cemetery. I remember that was the year Kennedy was shot, because I was very sad for both of them for a long time. But I was happy that Charlie would see Aimee and tell her that we looked for her. I wanted her to know, because she might have thought we did not miss her. She might have thought we did not call for her."

Morgan glanced at Claire. Her eyes were filled with tears. They all sat silently, washed by a warm breeze that blew like a memory over each of them. They shared the loss of a child, an irrational loss none of them understood.

But time was an imperfect glass that distorted what it could not reflect. Some memories were too dark and too deep to catch the light. Morgan felt he was chasing old ghosts through a warped mirror.

Morgan thought about the weed-covered grave atop the lonely hill on the Sun-Seven Ranch.

"We've been to Aimee's grave in the Madigans' cemetery," he said to Kate. "There were flowers. Have you been there recently?"

Kate's hand floated momentarily above the white linen tablecloth, then caressed it delicately.

"It's too sad for me. Her spirit is not there anyway. Do you visit your child's grave?"

Beneath the table, Morgan reached for Claire's hand. They held tightly to each other.

"No," Morgan said. "He wasn't buried. He was cremated."

Kate nodded knowingly, comforting them.

"Perhaps they are caring for each other," she said.

It was late.

The afternoon sun was lowering upon the red bluffs around Kate Morning's little valley. It was three hours back to Winchester and Morgan was eager to get back on the road. While Claire helped Kate clear the lunch plates from the table, Morgan asked directions to the bathroom.

As he passed down a dark hallway toward the back of the house, he saw a fading photograph of two children on the wall. The old image had tapered to brown, blanched by sunlight that streamed through a window at the end of the hall.

In it, the children sat on the running board of an old Ford coupe, although the car was probably brand-new at the time the photograph was taken.

The little girl had wide, familiar eyes. She wore a fetching white dress that was too small and unlaced leather boots that were too big. Her thick, black hair was cut like Dutch boy's, her bangs trimmed straight across her forehead, framing her cherubic little face like a dark halo. Her smile was shy but beguiling.

A tiny oval locket hung over the frilly collar of her dress, a well-worn piece of little-girl jewelry that looked as if it were pulled from its usual hiding place around her neck to lend an air of elegance to the photograph. And in her small hand, she held three small, daisy-like flowers, their long stems drooping.

The tow-headed boy wore suspenders, a starched white shirt and dungarees and scuffed go-to-meeting shoes. A mutinous cowlick defied the butchwax in his hair, and his toothy grin was guileless.

"Wasn't she pretty?" Kate said.

She startled Morgan. He'd been studying the photo so intently, he hadn't seen her come up beside him in the narrow hall.

"Is this Aimee?" he asked.

"Yes. She was eight then. She had never made a photograph before. She wanted to be pretty."

"She *was* pretty."

"She made them wait while she put on the dress. It was the only dress she owned. She was buried in it."

Morgan put his finger on the little boy in the picture. "Who's this?"

"Her best friend, Bobby," Kate said. "She always said she would marry him, like all little girls dream, you know. On this day he came to visit with his father in their big, fancy car and she ran inside to put on her dress so they could make this picture. She was so shy."

"May I borrow this?" Morgan asked Kate. "I have wondered what she looked like. I'd like to make a copy of it and send it right back. I promise to take good care of it."

Kate hesitated, then took the dusty frame off the wall. She placed it in Morgan's hands delicately, as if she were handing him the wing of a butterfly. "It's the only one I have of my sweet baby. Bobby's father gave it to me after she went away."

"That was very kind. I'll take very good care of it," he said, studying the picture in his hands even more closely. "Did you know the boy's family very well?"

Kate smiled, one of those smiles that made Morgan think he hadn't heard something she said.

"Of course," she said. "Mr. Madigan was always very good to us."

CHAPTER TWELVE

The snow was not deep, but enough had fallen that two sets of small footprints could easily be seen in the blue moonlight. They led deeper into the dark trees, into the deadfall.

It was bitter cold. The runner's labored breath was frigid and thick, and his throat burned. Sweat trickled down his back like ice water. The air was reluctant, almost too thin to breathe. Frost crystals sparkled all around him, suspended like tiny stars in an airless infinity.

But he followed the footprints deeper into the trees, ghosts shrouded in hoarfrost. Their paths were parallel, never crossing as they meandered through the dark woodland. The air grew more shallow, until the runner's lungs ached.

Suddenly the forest surrendered to an immense meadow, where a luminous white mansion rose from the snow. The footprints led to it, up its wide steps and through the front door. The runner followed, though now his legs were too heavy to run.

The door was locked. The windows were dark and crusted with ice. He scraped away the rime and looked inside. Numb moonlight fell on the cold hardwood floor of an empty room.

Then he heard children's laughter, somewhere inside the house, a different room. He dragged his leaden legs to another window, where he scratched the ice with his bare fingers.

He heard the young voices, but all he saw were two black shapes in the center of the high-ceilinged room. Then, he was inside, through the icy glass, standing before the two shapes, which he now recognized: Two tiny coffins atop draped funeral biers, blue in the cold glow of the moon.

The runner lifted the heavy lid on the first coffin. There was his son, tubes and needles still dangling from him. But his face was sunny and supple, the way it had been before he got sick. The runner was not frightened, for he had not seen his son in a very long time, and when the boy smiled, he knew he had never died. It was all a mistake, the dying.

Then the runner opened the second coffin.

A white dress, lace frills at the collar, was wrapped around a homunculus, a glowing, bleeding mass of water-logged flesh. It squirmed on a block of ice, brown river water seeping from it and freezing in screaming tendrils.

A tiny hand rose from the gelatinous mess and reached for him.

The runner couldn't breathe and he couldn't run. He turned to his son, but the coffin contained only a pile of ashes. A deep, painful sob filled the burning void in his chest, and the last air rushed from him.

Somewhere, another child laughed.

Jefferson Morgan's clock radio clicked, but there was no music, just empty electric air.

The sun wasn't up. It was four-thirty in the morning. The FM station over in Blackwater, thirty miles away, didn't sign on until five on Monday mornings, later if the morning dee-jay was hungover. Of the four far-flung stations whose signals were potent enough to reach Winchester, it was the only one that played old rock, the music Morgan never really outgrew. It was also the only one without hourly livestock reports.

Morgan silenced the radio's breathy hum, then dressed in the dark, still haunted by his dream. He'd lost most of the weekend visiting Kate Morning in Montana and helping Claire move junk out of the workshed where she envisioned a paint-ing studio. He'd intended to go to the office for a few hours late Sunday night, but fell asleep after dinner. Too much wine.

He brushed back a strand of Claire's blond hair and kissed her, but she didn't wake up. He promised himself to call her later in the morning.

He left the long-suffering Escort in the driveway and walked to *The Bullet* in the indifferent, dewy shadow of morning. He smelled new-mown grass. Sprinklers pulsed, dogs barked somewhere in the distance, and a lumbering Garvis Creamery truck passed him, making its milk rounds. The driver saw him and raised two fingers from the steering wheel, more an acknowledgement than a wave.

Morgan slipped his key in the brass lock of the newspaper office door. As he opened the door, he caught the comforting smell of ink, an odor the color of night. He turned on the lights and started a pot of coffee before he booted up his computer. He looked forward to two or three hours to work unmolested before the workday started. He wanted to be at the court clerk's office when it opened, to satisfy his curiosity about the relationship between Malachi Pierce and Simeon Fenwick.

The phone rang a few minutes after seven.

It was Jerry Overton. The normally laconic ATF agent skipped saying hello altogether.

"The Cubs are playing at Wrigley today," he said. "It's a beautiful day and I got tickets. Field level, third base. Pick you up at O'Hare. We'll grab some burgers at Murphy's Bleachers. Man, I can almost taste an Old Style now. It's all on you. Whaddya say?"

"Yeah, sure. I'll just shut down the paper this week so I can watch the Cubs lose," Morgan said. "Actually, it doesn't sound like a bad idea. Who are they playing?"

Overton laughed.

"Does it matter?"

"I guess not," Morgan said. "But the way things are going here right now, I don't think I could get there before October. And what good Cub fan really expects to see baseball in Wrigley in October?"

There was more to this call than baseball, Morgan knew.

"Is that it? Just an invitation to see the Cubbies lose? Been there, done that. What's up?" he asked his old friend.

"You know I can't confirm or deny any open investigations," he said.

Overton's stiff-arm reply puzzled Morgan.

"I didn't ask ..."

The tone of Overton's voice turned abruptly official.

"But I have a few questions about the matter you reported to me last Friday."

"But I don't know anything."

"Just listen to my questions," Overton told him. "Sometimes you don't know what's important. Just listen carefully. It might help us help you. Do you understand?"

Morgan didn't.

"Whatever you say," Morgan acquiesced. "You're the cop. What do you need to know?"

Overton started his inquiry in left field.

"Do you have any information linking Malachi Pierce to the Fourth Sign?" he asked Morgan.

"The Fourth Sign? P.D. Comeaux's freaky militia buddies? How the hell would I know? No, I don't know anything about that. Is it true? Is he tied up with those crazies?"

"I'm sorry, but I just can't comment on that. I'm merely conducting an official inquiry here in response to your report of suspicious activity. If you'd just listen to my questions, then we might be able to help." Overton was more emphatic. "Do you *understand?*"

"But I didn't really make a report ..."

"Have you seen any evidence that would make you believe that Mr. Pierce is involved in illicit gun sales and explosives manufacturing?"

"Bombs? I told you what I know, Jerry. Some people hear explosions out on Pierce's land. Maybe he's just blowing out stumps. I just don't know."

"Any recent threats against government agencies or public officials?

"He seems the type that would, but, no, I haven't seen anything beyond the usual black-helicopter crap in his letter. The only real threat I saw was against me."

"Extortion by threat of violence?"

"No."

"Harboring fugitives?"

"No."

"Conspiracy to receive stolen military property like, say, automatic weapons, rocket launchers and explosives?"

"Jesus. No."

"Tax evasion by funneling income from gun sales through his church?"

"I wouldn't know anything about that. But, hey, how did you know about his church? I never mentioned it."

There was a long silence on the other end of the line.

"That much is in the public record, Jeff. You can look it up yourself. But at least you're listening. That's good."

At that moment, Morgan knew.

It was no slip of the tongue and this was no interview. Overton was telling him everything he wanted to know, the only way a straight-arrow federal agent could without dishonoring his code.

His questions were, in fact, answers.

"I understand now, Jerry."

"Good."

"Is there anything else you need to ask?"

"Yes. In regard to your fears about your family's safety, have you taken precautions?"

"Should I?"

"Generally speaking, it's always wise to be safe, Jeff. You've been around the block. You know how it is these days. And you know these guys."

Morgan nervously scribbled Comeaux's name on the back

of a blank ad invoice and retraced it unconsciously until the ink had soaked through to the desk blotter beneath it.

"Is the Fourth Sign somehow involved in this?"

"Jeff, c'mon. You know it's against the law for us to keep files on groups. Just individuals who are suspected or convicted of specific crimes. Sometimes these individuals have something in common, say, like membership in the same club. But if you asked about any one of them, I couldn't tell you one way or the other."

"You mean like P.D. Comeaux?"

"Yes. That's a good example," Overton said. He spoke deliberately. "If he or other members of the Fourth Sign were involved somehow, I wouldn't be able to tell you. Understand?"

"Are they?"

"Like I said, Jeff, if they were, I wouldn't be able to tell you. I just can't say."

"I understand," Morgan said.

Overton sounded a note of caution.

"You already know about the Fourth Sign from the Comeaux case and you know without me telling you that these aren't just bad dudes. They're *crazy* bad dudes. Don't turn your back on them."

By saying nothing, Jerry Overton revealed much.

At the time of P.D. Comeaux's arrest in 1993, the Fourth Sign wasn't even a blip on the FBI's radical-right radar screen, much less the ATF's. Mostly, it was just a small, secret society of angry Bible-Belt farmers on the verge of bankruptcy, seeking conspiracies that weren't there, rationalizing their plights irrationally and peddling a poor man's gospel. They believed the government was engaged in a global and domestic conspiracy to create a "New World Order" that would enslave ordinary citizens by taking away their means to revolt, namely their land and their guns. And when they searched their Bibles for answers, they came to believe even more fervently that one-world government was the last prophesied sign from God before Armageddon, the "fourth sign."

Nobody cared. The Christian Identity movement hadn't yet bubbled to the surface of the national consciousness. Its followers considered themselves soldiers in a war against the United States government, practicing an Aryan theology that saw racial minorities as sub-human "mud people," Jews as Satan's children and a New World Order as a precursor to tyranny.

At its core, the Fourth Sign was among scores of obscure and loosely organized Christian Identity bands mixing ultra-fundamentalist zealots and anti-government paranoiacs in a combustible, fuming frenzy that produced more smoke than fire.

But Comeaux was the spark that ignited a wildfire.

Before his arrest, he'd attended a few secret meetings at a small church near Dixon, Illinois, but mostly kept to the back pews. He put his faith in violence and fear, not talk. His heart burned with a savagery far more advanced than anyone had dreamed.

Once he was jailed, the word went out. He became a martyr. To the Fourth Sign's believers, he was no serial killer, but a casualty of a government conspiracy designed to uproot true patriots. Even if Comeaux were truly guilty, some said, he should be sainted for exterminating the vermin whores that dragged America toward Hell by its private parts. Offshoots of the Fourth Sign sprung up all across the forgotten interior, its demented gospel spread via the Internet and rallied by the whispered name of P.D. Comeaux.

The heart of the Fourth Sign beat somewhere in the Midwest, Morgan knew from his follow-up investigation on Comeaux, but its leadership was shadowy. It gathered money from its far-flung members through a series of drop-boxes rented by mysterious groups with names like The Millennium Institute and The Rapture Forum, most of the money going to an ever-expanding arsenal of legal and illegal weaponry. ATF intelligence suggested the organization's more militant factions—radicals for whom The Order and the Aryan Nations were not radical enough—financed themselves by declaring their own war on drugs, robbing and murdering dealers from Tulsa to Detroit.

On the day of closing arguments in Comeaux's South Dakota trial, a sophisticated pipe-bomb filled with roofing tacks, packed in a shoebox between two plastic bags of human feces, was mailed to the county prosecutor's office. When it exploded, it decapitated a legal secretary and badly mutilated a law-school intern, whose wounds became lethally infected by the excrement and dirty shrapnel blasted deep into him. The day before the student died in excruciating pain, an anonymous caller with a Western accent told a sheriff's dispatcher that the bomb had been sent by the Fourth Sign.

"And the shit inside came right out of the ass of Saint P.D. hisself. Consider yourself baptized," he cackled, then hung up.

Nobody was ever arrested, nor was it ever known if P.D. Comeaux had actually smuggled his own waste out of the county jail, but the Fourth Sign was quickly added to the feds' short list of America's most deadly domestic terror groups.

All this, Morgan already knew. It was frightening enough. But what he didn't know scared him most.

"Jeff, call me if anything comes up. You've got my number, here or at home," Jerry Overton said. His voice was gravely serious. "I mean it. Anything."

"Don't worry, I will," Morgan said. "And, hey, I'll take a raincheck on that Cubs game. I guess I owe you one for sure, huh?"

"Don't worry about it," his old friend said. "Right now, you just take care of yourself and Claire. I learned a long time ago there are two things not worth waiting for: The Cubs getting to the World Series, and you buying a round of beers."

Morgan laughed. "Dare to dream, Jerry," he said. "The Cubs might surprise you."

Morgan sat on a hard bench in the dark hallway outside

the district court clerk's office, leaning against the cool wall. It soothed him after the walk to the courthouse in the hot morning air. He heard women's voices inside the third-floor office, the lights were on, but the frosted-glass door was still locked.

He hadn't planned to spend much time checking on Malachi Pierce's court records, if they existed at all. He had a full day ahead, hoping against hope that he could finally get the paper out on time. He had too many stories to write, and so did his reporters. He wanted to finish four or five pages today, but that seemed increasingly unlikely without stories to fill them. He still hadn't decided whether to endorse candidates in the upcoming election, a task that hung like an albatross around his neck. And he expected more fallout from the Chamber's boycott as the week wore on. Later today, maybe tomorrow, he'd look in on Neeley Gilmartin.

Before it had started, the day seemed over.

Morgan checked his watch.

Eight-ten.

He had already decided to knock when the latch clacked noisily. The little bell on the other side of the door tinkled as a pretty, middle-aged woman poked her blond-streaked head out into the hall and looked around as if she were hiding from someone. The smell of morning coffee wafted out of the office into the sterile hallway.

Inside, some of the women were gathered around a desk, cooing over photographs of someone's new grandchild. The fluorescent blue light almost hurt his eyes after sitting in the darkened hall. A fresh pot was gurgling in a drip coffeemaker on top of some filing cabinets. Morgan could almost taste it.

"Can I help you?" the tall woman with frosted hair asked him as she propped the door open. Her face was younger and more friendly than her saucer-sized glasses and high-collared business suit made her look. Except for her bright red lipstick, she wore little makeup and didn't seem to miss it. Her hips were slender, her legs long. Morgan guessed she was, at best, only a few years older than him, maybe forty-two. And he felt as if he should know her.

"I just came to look at the card files," he told her, "but I could sure use a cup of that coffee."

The clerk smiled and touched his forearm.

"The cups are on the cabinet," she said warmly. "You help yourself, then I'll show you the case cards."

Morgan poured the strong black coffee into a Styrofoam cup, then emptied two pink packets of sweetener into it and stirred it with a plastic spoon. It was too hot to drink, so he pursed his lips and blew lightly across it, scattering tiny corkscrews of steam.

In the cool, dim vault, the clerk showed Morgan the familiar card files in their dented drawers. He slid open the drawer labeled "P-Q-R" and ran his fingers along the tops of the frayed, worn cards.

Peters. Pettit. Peyton. Phelps. Phillips. Pilcher.

Nothing.

Morgan thumbed through a few more cards, but none were out of place. Despite his suspicions, it appeared that Malachi Pierce had steered clear of serious legal problems in Perry County. He closed the drawer and slipped his notebook back in his shirt pocket. Dead end. Cross that one off the list.

"No luck?" the friendly clerk asked him. She'd busied herself with a stack of blue folders while he worked.

"I'm afraid not," Morgan said. "Sometimes it just isn't there."

"Tell me about it. We hunt for files around here every day and I swear there are some that just walk off," she said. "You look familiar to me. Have we met?"

"I'm Jeff Morgan," he said, not sure if he should offer his hand. "I'm the editor at *The Bullet*."

The clerk's lips formed a wet, red O.

"Good Lord," she said, astonished. "I heard you were back in town. You don't remember me, do you? That's okay, I mean, jeez, because I didn't recognize you right off either. My goodness, it's been more than twenty years. I was a year ahead of you in school, I think. I worked for your dad the summer before I went to college and I used to see you in the shop."

Morgan swept away the cobwebs of his memory.

"Cassie ... don't tell me ... your mother cleaned the hardware store on weekends. God, I'm so bad with names. Cassie ... Miller. Right?"

"Millen. Well, not anymore since I got married, but that's close enough," she said. "You were Class of 'seventy-five, right?"

"Exactly," Morgan said. "And you were ..."

"'Seventy-four. God, that was a year. That was the year we lost the football championship by one point and then lost the basketball championship by one point. You remember all that?"

Morgan laughed.

"How could I forget? That was the year I got up the guts for the first time to ask a girl on a date. She said yes, and I couldn't believe it. We had big plans to go to a Jim Croce concert in Rapid City, then the poor guy dies in a plane crash a week before. I was bummed. We just never got around to going out after that and it was another year before I felt brave enough to ask somebody else out. It was an unlucky year all around."

"Just think how Jim Croce felt."

They laughed together. Cassie's eyes sparkled and, for a moment, Morgan could imagine the fresh-faced teen-ager he'd surely have seen at his father's cashier counter that summer before his senior year, a lusty summer when almost no female escaped his notice.

Cassie brought him up to date on her life since high school: Her father had abandoned the family in her senior year, so her mother took cleaning jobs to support the family. As one of the top ten students in her class, she had been accepted at Stanford, but after her father left, her college plans changed like everything else in her life. She ended up at the University of Wyoming, majoring in marketing. She graduated, came back to Winchester, married a small-town Presbyterian preacher and quickly had two children, who were both now in junior high school.

"So you work here now?" he asked her.

"Sort of."

"Part-time?"

Cassie smiled demurely.

"No," she said. "I'm the clerk of district court. Duly elected and sworn to uphold the constitution of the State of Wyoming. And I make the coffee."

Morgan's eyes widened. He knew from the name on the door and in his own paper's election stories she was now Cassandra Gainsforth.

"*The* clerk? You're Cassandra Gainsforth?"

Cassie nodded.

"Twelve years now. As the clerk, that is. Fifteen years as Cassandra Gainsforth," she said, displaying a diamond ring on her left hand that was easily three times the size of the one Morgan gave to Claire.

"Well, Jeez ..." Morgan caught himself before he took the Lord's name in vain. "I mean, gosh, I am impressed. And a little embarrassed."

"Happens all the time. Everybody gets nervous around the preacher's wife. You should hear the language around here. I don't mind."

"No, I mean, I didn't recognize you and all. I've been away too long. Let me congratulate you, belatedly, on the election and the marriage."

"Hey, don't sweat it. It's a good job, but I'm not a very good campaigner. Good thing I'm usually running unopposed or I'd be a quivering blob of nerves right now. I'd be worse than Trey Kerrigan."

"I saw him the other day. He didn't seem too shaken about it."

Cassie smiled wryly. "He's a sly one. He makes like he's

got no care in the world, but he's got his little supporters out there clearing the way day and night. Trey campaigns hard, like he's a one-legged man in a three-legged race. Highlander Goldsmith's a nice guy, but he isn't gonna know what hit him a week from Tuesday."

Morgan conjured up an image of his childhood friend, puking his guts out in the locker room before every basketball game, scared to death he'd embarrass himself in front of the hometown crowd. Then he'd go out and sink almost every shot he attempted. He couldn't miss.

Once, Morgan knew Trey Kerrigan as well as anyone. Now he wasn't so sure he knew him at all.

"He hasn't changed much," Morgan said, leaving it at that.

"Oh, he's changed a lot," Cassie said, lowering her voice and glancing out the vault door to see who might be listening. "Politics is like an oven: You don't come out the same as you went in. Trey's harder now. It's like keeping that job is more important than doing it."

"He seemed fine when I saw him. Cocky as ever."

"He's a cool customer, I'll give him that. But I'm sure Trey's had his big supporters lobbying with you," Cassie said. "He calls them his 'homeboys.' You probably didn't know it, but I'm sure they've been working on you. They're slick."

Morgan shrugged. "Not really. Other than Trey himself, nobody has said anything."

Cassie looked surprised. "No kidding? You mean Jake Switzer and Ham Tasker haven't darkened your doorstep to ask for your vote and maybe a little campaign contribution? They must be slowing down."

Morgan, who had been blowing his hot coffee to cool it, held his breath for a long, uncomfortable moment. He hoped he didn't look as dumbfounded as he was. "They're working for Trey?" he asked. He felt his face turn hot and red. The walls of the vault seemed to close in on him. A nervous spurt of adrenaline coarsed through his body, making him feel slightly ill.

"Sure. They run his campaign. Fancy themselves to be real political movers and shakers, those two," Cassie said. "Whoever they haven't got in their pockets, they squeeze."

Then she leaned nearer, lowering her voice to a conspiratorial whisper. "A couple of stuffed shirts, if you ask me."

In that claustrophobic moment, a piece of the puzzle fell into place.

Gilmartin's case was a political liability for Trey Kerrigan, perhaps worse. He'd sent Tasker and Switzer to keep a lid on it, one way or another, and they'd nearly succeeded. His refusal to open forty-eight-year-old investigative records on Aimee Little Spotted Horse's murder was all too predictable for a small-town sheriff, but the heavy-handed political pressures on Morgan betrayed something darker and deeper.

"Well, enough about politics," Cassie said. "You probably get plenty of that stuff in your job. Did you find anything interesting in these old card files?"

Morgan shook his head. "Nothing."

"Must be looking for some really old case. These old index cards only go up to nineteen sixty-two. Ancient history. Everything else has been entered on the computer."

"Computer?"

"Yeah, you know, one of those machines with a little TV screen and a keyboard?"

Morgan looked sheepish. "I mean, there are more records? Why didn't you tell me?"

Cassie put her hands on her shapely hips and fixed him in a chastising glare. "You asked to see the card files, and here they are. You didn't ask to see the database. You only got what you asked for, but you didn't get what you wanted. Follow me."

She led him to a small desk in a corner of the front office where a sleek new IBM computer sat. She pressed a button and the machine came to life with a colorful whisper.

"This is Alyx. Two-hundred megahertz Pentium processor, thirty-two megs of RAM, a three-point-two gigabyte hard drive. One hundred percent pure techno-beefcake. It does the work of three people, never sleeps and never talks back," Cassie said proudly. "If it were a man, I'd marry it."

"And it contains every court file in Perry County since nineteen sixty-two?"

"They're all cross-indexed by date, criminal, civil, probate, judges' names, lawyers' names, defendant, plaintiff, even verdict. You name it. All the basic stuff."

"Not the bailiff's favorite ice cream?" Morgan joked.

Cassie rolled her eyes and continued. "You want to know Perry County's felony conviction rate? It's in here. Want to know who the toughest judges are? It's here. Want to know how many violent crimes we prosecuted in a given period? It's all right here, and lots more. All the original paperwork is still in hard copy and stored in the vault, but this computer helps us cross-reference and compile statistics. The governor is big on statistics these days. I hate politics."

A form appeared on the tartan-colored screen.

"Go ahead. Just tell Alyx what you want. And don't forget to say please."

Morgan sat down in front of the terminal. He scrolled through the blanks and under "Defendant," he typed "Pierce."

"Now click on the search button," Cassie told him. "Easy as pie, huh?"

A tiny digitized clock ticked off a few seconds, then a couple dozen listings appeared in chronological order on the screen. Morgan scrolled through them for the name "Malachi," but most were divorces and other civil cases, all unrelated to Malachi Pierce.

Then his eye caught a familiar name.

Not Malachi.

It was Case No. 76-368J.

In the Matter of *Hosanna* Pierce.

"What's this?" he asked Cassie, who stood over his shoulder. She leaned closer to the screen to see the case he'd highlighted with the cursor.

"That's a juvenile case. See the "J" in the number? All I can tell you from this is it's a juvie case from nineteen seventy-six, and it's not criminal. Other than that, it's a sealed record."

"Sealed?"

"The juvenile cases are all closed. Alyx has the case reference and all the usual index items, but it takes a special password to access family court and juvenile files, so the public can't stumble into them."

It didn't matter. Morgan already knew about this case. Old Bell told him: Years ago, Malachi Pierce had gone to court to commit his retarded daughter to the state hospital. In 1976, Hosanna Pierce would have been nine or ten years old, a hair's breadth away from spending the rest of her life in a mental institution.

"If I wanted to know who the lawyers were in this particular case, could I get that information?" Morgan asked.

"Not without the secret code," Cassie replied, leaving no doubt in Morgan's mind that the password would remain a secret. "Is that the case you were looking for?"

"No, but I'm not really sure what I was looking for," he said.

"Something related to that old murder case?"

Rumors flowed through small towns like electricity through a pure copper wire. There was no point in trying to keep secrets, which were bartered, sold and occasionally donated in the scandalous commerce of Winchester, Wyoming.

"No, not related to that. Something else," Morgan told her. "And if you can keep a secret, I'll tell you what I'm looking for."

Cassie smiled. "My job is keeping secrets."

Speaking softly, Morgan told her about Pierce's threatening letter, and Hosanna's frightened outburst when she saw Simeon Fenwick in the cafe. He explained that it caused him to wonder if Malachi Pierce had ever needed a lawyer, and why. And he told her what Old Bell had said about Hosanna's brush with oblivion. In the end, he said, he was only worried for his and his wife's safety.

Cassie listened intently. She seemed troubled by what she heard.

"I don't recall any cases with Malachi Pierce and, believe me, I'd remember if that scary old man had come through here. To him, we're the enemy, the government grandmas who're going to take away his guns. Thank the Lord, he pretty much keeps to himself out there on the ranch. He's in his own world, you know"—and she circled her finger around her ear.

"What about Fenwick?"

"I don't know. It's not likely he got involved if there were real fireworks. He retired shortly after I first got elected, but he was mostly doing civil work, wills and deeds and stuff like that. He begged for those little court appointments that other lawyers hated. The judges were only too happy to oblige. He took on so many guardian cases, they called him 'Uncle Sim.' He was a prissy old guy, you know, and I don't think he had the guts for the criminal cases."

"Or for Malachi Pierce?"

Cassie shook her head. "Fenwick and Pierce would definitely be strange bedfellows. I just don't see it. Two completely different characters."

"Was Fenwick any good?"

Cassie crossed her arms and leaned against the desk. She chose her words carefully. "As a lawyer? Let's just say the paperwork was always perfect. He was precise about it. Nothing out of place. Nothing late. Nothing missing. He was downright anal about his case files. A real pain in the gazoo."

One of Cassie's clerks brought a manila folder to her and whispered something Morgan couldn't hear, then left.

"Sorry. I have to deal with something right now, but it was sure good to see you after so long, Jeff," she said. "Maybe you and your wife could come over for a barbecue or something. I'd love to meet her."

"Sure, if you don't mind being seen with the newspaper editor," he said, only half joking. "My wife's a wonderful person, but I'm not the most popular guy in town right now."

Cassie touched his arm again and winked.

"Some of us think you're doing okay," she said. "If Old Bell thinks you're man enough to take over his paper, then I have nothing but respect for you. He's a great judge of character, trust me. Just hang in there."

The rest of the morning rushed by. Morgan laid out three pages and most of the opinion page, leaving a hole for his editorial. His reporters had filed a dozen stories and three takes of short items, obits and weddings.

But advertising had continued to dwindle. They'd sold less than four hundred inches, hardly enough to keep the doors open. Morgan kept the paper at twelve pages, even though the advertising lineage didn't justify it. He didn't want to surrender.

He worked through lunch, helping Cal Nussbaum typeset some classified ads and develop some photos from the weekend Little League games. It had been years since he'd souped film, but he got the hang of it after a few late-night practice sessions in the dark. He was spooling 35mm film on a processing reel in the pure blackness of the darkroom when somebody knocked.

"Don't open it," he warned.

It was Crystal. "There's a call for you," she said.

"Can you take a message?"

"The lady says it's urgent."

"Is it Claire?"

"I don't know. She's kind of freaking out."

Morgan looped the film loosely around the reel and sealed it in the light-tight stainless steel developing canister. To be safe, he stuck it in a cabinet before he turned on the overheard light and opened the darkroom door.

He picked up the phone on his desk. It was the whiskey-voiced clerk at the Teepee Motor Lodge and she was hysterical.

"That old man told me to call you if there was an emergency. Jeezus gawd, jeezus gawd. The maid took up some food and found him layin' there, all white and cold. Jeezus gawd. I coulda swore he was stone dead, but I wadn't gonna touch no dead corpse. No sir. I just called the nine-one-one, then I called you. You better come on over here. Jeezus gawd."

She let loose a bone-rattling cough and hung up.

Morgan sprinted out of the newspaper to his car, which would normally have been parked at the curb out front. He'd walked to work that morning.

He heard a faint siren in the distance. The ambulance was just leaving the hospital, a mile away, on the other end of town. He checked his watch. In less than three minutes, he could be home, if he ran.

He sprinted toward Rockwood Street, five long blocks away. A prickling, nervous sweat trickled down his back as he raced past the downtown storefronts, and he felt curious eyes watching him. The clinging midday heat sucked the breath from his lungs, suffocating him.

The old man can't die, Morgan thought. *Not yet.*

As he ran, he heard the siren coming closer, until it careened past him down Main Street. He cut across the bank parking lot and up the alley behind the post office, where mail carriers sat on the dock and hooted as he passed.

Hang on, old man.

The alley emptied onto Rockwood just four houses away. He covered the last fifty yards at a dead run. His lungs burned.

Morgan groped for the key he'd hidden under the driver's seat. He slammed it into the ignition and the Escort wheezed forlornly. He turned it again and again, pumping the accelerator hard, finally pressing it all the way to the floor, but the car wouldn't start. He cursed and pounded the steering wheel. He smelled gasoline and knew he'd flooded it.

He tried once more, and miraculously, the engine turned over. It belched blue-rimmed black smoke from the exhaust, barely clinging to life.

"C'mon, c'mon. Don't stop now," he pleaded with his car.

Morgan jammed the accelerator, jolting the groggy engine awake. It gasped twice, then growled back at him. In a moment, he was hurtling through the only stoplight in town, toward the western edge of Winchester, where Neeley Gilmartin lay dying, maybe already dead, among the flies and trash in his foul trailer.

The ambulance was already there, no siren. Its blue and red lights pulsed in a silent rhythm that always reminded Morgan of death. As a little boy, he remembered what his father said once, when an ambulance passed them on the highway, its emergency lights on, but not its siren: "Must be dead," he said. Morgan must have reminded himself of that day on a hundred murder scenes in Chicago, bathed in the surreal death beacons from silent ambulances, coroner vans and squad cars: *Must be dead.* They usually were.

Gilmartin's trailer door was open. A square-jawed deputy stood outside, sneaking peeks at several paramedics working inside. The motel clerk who called him lurked unsteadily at the edge of the weeds, smoking a cigarette and clasping the front of her shag housecoat to keep from baring her rheumy chest to the world. She looked drunk.

As soon as Morgan approached the trailer door, the deputy stopped him. The name on the brass bar above his pocket was "Bocek."

"You family?" the deputy asked him.

"No, he doesn't have any family. But I'm a friend."

"Then why don't you just wait over there so the medics can work, okay?"

"Is he alive?"

"I don't know."

"Will you ask? If he's alive, they should know, he's got

lung cancer, probably metastasized, and he doesn't want to go to a hospital."

Deputy Bocek hitched up his holster and his tight brown pants, and glared at Morgan.

"This guy have a name?" Bocek asked.

"Gilmartin. Neeley Gilmartin. Now please ask if he's alive," Morgan implored him. "It's important."

The deputy went inside the trailer. Morgan inched close enough to hear their voices, but not what they were saying.

Don't die, you son of a bitch. Not now. Hang on.

Deputy Bocek came to the door and motioned Morgan forward, but no farther than the front door, which swayed on its slack hinges.

"Your friend ain't dead, but he's bad off. Just stand here at the door and tell these guys what you told me," he said.

Morgan leaned inside. The TV set was on, some afternoon game show. The air conditioner must have finally given out, because the air inside was diseased and hot. The place smelled worse than before, as if death had been there.

Gilmartin lay on the floor. He was naked, his skin a pale, waxy yellow. Three paramedics worked feverishly over him. He was near death, but Morgan could see the skin of his bony chest being sucked in around his ribs and condensation in the oxygen mask. He was struggling for air, but he was breathing.

"Let's run an IV at a hundred an hour until we get the doc," one of the paramedics said. He was a clean-cut guy with wire-rimmed glasses and eagles tattooed on his thick, body-builder forearms, a little older than the other two, maybe in his thirties. Clearly, he was calling the shots. "Joey, check the pulse ox."

Despite the cramped quarters, they worked quickly. One of the younger paramedics unlooped a tube for the IV while the one called Joey clipped a small probe to Gilmartin's index finger and turned some dials on a small machine in a small, nylon pack. Red LED numbers flickered, sampling the oxygen in Gilmartin's tissues.

Their boss, positioning the oxygen tank between Gilmartin's legs, saw Morgan peering through the doorway.

"You know this guy?" he asked. He was emotionless, cold.

"Yes. His name is Neeley Gilmartin. He's seventy-three. Is he alive?"

Joey interrupted. "Bad news, Greg. Pulse ox is seventy-six and dropping."

Greg, the older paramedic who was in charge, turned his back to Morgan and muttered something Morgan couldn't hear. He adjusted a valve on the oxygen tank.

"You family?" Greg asked Morgan without looking at him.

"No. He's got no family."

"You know his problem?"

"Lung cancer. It might have spread. I don't know."

"AIDS?"

"I don't know," Morgan said. "I don't think so."

"He's yellow. Hepatitis?"

"I don't know," Morgan said.

Suddenly an alarm shrieked. One of the digital read-outs was flashing red. Morgan's heart was pounding.

"We're losing pulse ox. Jesus, it's going flat, seventy, sixty-nine," Joey said. He'd squeezed past Gilmartin's motionless body to reach for something in the crash box.

Greg scrambled to check Gilmartin's vitals. He checked for a pulse, then slumped.

Morgan couldn't breathe.

"What's happening, goddammit?" he said loudly. "Is he okay?"

The older paramedic reached beneath the old man's arm and held up a small clip.

"Dammit, Joey, you pulled off the fuckin' probe," he said angrily. "Tape it on and watch where you put your damned feet in this shit hole."

For the first time, Morgan felt a chill from the cold sweat that had been dribbling down his neck since he first heard the ambulance's siren.

Wasting no time, the older paramedic resumed his inquiry, his voice still flat and hopeless.

"I see pill bottles all over hell. You know this guy's meds?"

"Just painkillers."

Morgan breathed deeply and tried to visualize the pill bottles on Gilmartin's dirty countertop. "Uh, Tylox. Demerol. Mepergan. He might have been taking morphine, too."

"Nothing else?"

Morgan shook his head. "He was terminal." Morgan quickly corrected himself. "He *is* terminal. He doesn't want anything else. He hasn't got much time, maybe a couple weeks."

Greg had a funny, disdainful look on his face, like he might laugh if the situation were any less grave. But he didn't seem the type to laugh much.

"Maybe hours, more like. He's in real bad shape. His heart's barely beating, breathing's labored, BP is next to nothing. He's dehydrated and, judging by his color, he's probably already in liver failure. Right now, he's unresponsive. As soon as we get him stabilized for transport, we're gonna take him to the ER."

Morgan closed his eyes. The trailer's sticky, sour air clung to him. He had to say it, even if he didn't want to. "But he doesn't want to die in a hospital," Morgan said.

Greg lost his fragile cool. "Should we let him die right here? You want to stand here and watch this old guy croak, goddammit? Jesus fuckin' Christ ..."

"Go easy, Greg," Morgan heard one of the other paramedics say softly. It was Joey, the younger one.

"Shut up, Joey," Greg said. Then he faced Morgan. "Are you medically responsible for this guy?"

"What do you mean?" Morgan asked.

"Are you making his life and death decisions? If you don't, we do. He'll die right here if we don't get him to the hospital. Up there, at least he's got a slim shot at a few more days. If we get him working again and the doc says he can go home to die, that's the doc's call. What's it gonna be? Are you gonna make the call?"

There was no one else, Morgan knew. He certainly didn't want to be the one who pulled the plug on Neeley Gilmartin by walking away. And he knew Gilmartin couldn't die. Not yet.

"For now, I will," he said reluctantly.

"Okay, just how far do you want us to go here?"

There was only one answer. "Save him," Morgan said. "Keep him alive, please."

He saw the young paramedic, Joey, smile.

"Good enough. Is he packaged?" Greg asked his crew. "Are we ready to roll?"

"Yeah, Oh-two and IV are going, and pulse ox is up to ninety-one," Joey said. "And we need to get on the road. I didn't have time to check the oxygen bottle this morning and we're running low. You want the monitor? We left the damn thing outside."

Greg shook his head. "Let's roll. We'll plug him in once we're get him in the rig." Greg stripped off his rubber gloves and looked at Morgan with tired, empty eyes. "You coming to the hospital? You need to talk to the doc. Like it or not, you're this guy's only angel."

Morgan nodded.

They covered Gilmartin's nakedness with a white sheet and loaded him onto a scoop stretcher, a two-piece contraption that was better than a conventional stretcher in close quarters. In a few seconds, they were out the door.

Morgan ducked into the rancid bathroom and pulled Gilmartin's wad of cash from behind the toilet. He stuffed it in his pocket, where it would be safe.

While Greg and the other paramedic loaded Gilmartin onto a waiting gurney and rolled him across the weeds to the ambulance's open doors, Joey hung back. He reached in his pocket and held out his hand to Morgan.

"He'll want you to take care of this for him," he said. "When I cut off his T-shirt, it was around his neck on a chain. We had to take it off, but I didn't want it to get lost."

Morgan opened his palm. Joey gave him a thin silver chain and a medallion.

"I recognized it right off," Joey said. "I was in the Navy before all this. He must have been somebody once."

Morgan looked closely at the emblem in his trembling hand.

The Navy Cross.

Before Morgan looked up, Joey was gone. The ambulance rolled around the side of the decaying Teepee Motor Lodge toward the highway.

When it hit the asphalt, the siren wailed. Morgan said a prayer, relieved to hear it scream.

It meant there was still life inside.

CHAPTER THIRTEEN

Perry County Memorial Hospital's emergency room was cold as death.

Jefferson Morgan was alone in the waiting room for more than an hour, except for a janitor who was scrubbing fresh blood stains out of the carpet. He'd choked down two cups of bitter vending-machine coffee, unsweetened, but he was still chilled. The muscles in his gut shivered.

And the smell. Ever since Bridger died, maybe longer, Morgan hated the antiseptic odor of hospitals. Whatever chemicals they used to strip away the blood and disease and death also sterilized hope.

Neeley Gilmartin clung to life, however tenuously, but that's all the nurse would say when Morgan first arrived, breathless from his run across the parking lot. He phoned Claire from a pay phone in the waiting room to tell her about Gilmartin's collapse, and he called *The Bullet* to say he'd be back late in the afternoon, maybe after dinner. Then he settled into a thinly padded steel chair, and tried to read a week-old edition of *USA Today* someone had left on the seat.

Morgan couldn't focus. If Gilmartin died now, there could be no redemption, if he deserved it at all. And although the original case against the old man had been air-thin, Morgan had uncovered no shred of real evidence pointing specifically toward anyone else.

The only evidence in Gilmartin's favor was in Morgan's gut. He had a visceral feeling about the old man, and on the mean streets of Chicago, he'd learned to respect his intuition. He knew fear drove men through rage to insanity. He believed that much of Gilmartin's story: that a streetwise punk in the hungry maw of the justice system would do anything to save his life. *Anything* ... even confess to a crime he didn't commit to avoid a searing, agonizing death.

But even if Gilmartin didn't kill Aimee Little Spotted Horse, after fifty years, her real killer might be dead now, and it was hard enough proving live killers guilty without chasing after murderous corpses. The old man had given him an impossible task and too little time to accomplish it. Morgan was dead in the water.

Except for the money.

He touched the lump of cash in his pocket. He could almost smell the blood being washed from someone's guilty hands. If he could find its source, he knew a big piece of this puzzle would fall into place. He might even find Aimee Little Spotted Horse's killer.

A stainless-steel water fountain vibrated and hummed on the wall nearest the nurses' station, scattering his thoughts. Morgan stood up and checked his watch. It was after three o'clock, still no word. He paced toward the water fountain, just to keep moving, and to rinse the acidic taste of guilt and bad coffee from his mouth.

"Are you here with Mr. Gilmartin?" asked a woman's voice behind him.

Morgan turned, wiping cool, metallic water from his lips with the back of his hand. A blond woman in her late twenties, wearing blue surgical scrubs, was standing at the nurses' station. Even for a young woman, she looked tired and serious.

"Yes," Morgan replied. "Is he okay?"

"I'm Doctor Gail Snyder. Are you a relative of Mr. Gilmartin's?"

"No. He doesn't have anybody else. I guess I'm it."

The doctor managed a brief, disappointed smile. "Well, he's in serious shape. His lungs are full of small-cell tumors. It's likely he fell unconscious from anoxia, too little oxygen getting to his brain. Near as we can tell by looking, the cancer in his lungs has probably spread to his liver and other organs, maybe his brain. We can't be sure without the test results."

"Is he in pain?"

The doctor paused. She studied Morgan's face to be sure he really wanted to hear what she was about to say. "He must have been in very great pain before this episode," she said gravely. "He probably felt claustrophobic, as if he were suffocating very slowly. Progressive cancer at this stage is quite excruciating. The tumors in his lungs alone are putting enough pressure on the nerves in his shoulders and arms to torment him day and night. If it's in his liver and bowels, well, there's not much we can do except try to make him comfortable."

Morgan looked at the gray carpet beneath him, expecting it to fall away at any second. "Is he going to die? I mean, you know, tonight?"

Dr. Snyder offered little hope and less of a prognosis. "Time will tell. I don't really know."

Morgan pressed her. "Best-case scenario, doctor. How long?"

"God knows how he's fought off the pain this far. If he maintains his extraordinary will to stay alive, maybe a few more days. Not much longer."

"Will he wake up again?"

"I'm sorry, but I just don't know right now. We've got some fluids back in him and he's starting to breathe easier. He's responding but he's still in a stuporous state, so we've got him restrained. In a few minutes, we'll be moving him up to ICU. What I need to know right now is whether he has any medical directives, to your knowledge."

"Like what?"

"Does he have a living will, or any specific orders should we face a life-or-death choice?"

"Only one. He doesn't want to die here. That's all I know. And, please, unless it's absolutely necessary, could you take off the restraints? I don't want him to wake up and be shackled. It'd scare him to death."

"The restraints are for his protection. He was flailing around semi-conscious, trying to pull off the oxygen mask and his IV lines. It's natural. If he comes around, we'll take them off."

Morgan only heard the *if.* His jaw clenched. The sterile, hopeless smell of the place came back to him. He wanted to cry. "Don't let him die, doctor. Please."

The young doctor smiled and touched Morgan's arm supportively. "We'll do our best. Now, there's no need for you to wait around here. It'll be a few hours before we know anything more. Just leave your name and phone number with the clerk and we'll call if his condition changes appreciably."

"Can I see him before I go?"

Dr. Snyder considered the request, then nodded. She led Morgan through the nurses' station down a narrow hallway past three empty trauma rooms. Neeley Gilmartin's bed was parked in a narrow alcove on the other side of the hospital linen closet.

He was a living corpse, withered and yellow against the bleached white sheets. His skin was translucent, as if coated in a thin layer of wax; his eyelids parted slightly as death peered into him. Only the rhythmic, reassuring beeps of the monitors around him told Morgan he was alive.

He stood at Gilmartin's bedside, holding the rail. A deathly odor rose from him, overpowering even the disinfected air of the hospital. Padded restraints were looped around his emaciated wrists, and the tobacco-stained fingers of his right hand fluttered as oxygen whispered through his mask.

Morgan reached down and touched Gilmartin's twitching hand. His skin was papery and cold. He wondered if the old man was dreaming, if he'd ever dreamed.

"Don't go," he leaned close and whispered softly. "It's not time."

Gilmartin's fingers closed weakly around Morgan's, then relaxed.

A package was waiting for Morgan when he got back to *The Bullet*.

"Who left it?" he asked Crystal, inspecting the sealed bubble-pack envelope for clues to its origin. It was unmarked except for three words handwritten neatly in blue ink on its front: *Jeff Morgan, Confidential.*

"I don't know. I took some classified ads to the backshop and when I came back, it was on the front desk," she said. "I didn't see anybody come in or leave."

Morgan carried the envelope back to his desk, where he fished an X-acto knife from the clutter in his top drawer. He slit a neat incision across the top.

Inside were twelve floppy disks, all numbered in sequence, and another smaller envelope. It contained a short, typewritten note.

Dear Jeff,

These disks contain the complete database of the state court in Perry County, from 1962 to present. After you left here today, I called Bell Cockins, who told me the difficulties you've been facing. He said you were a good man and I should help you in any way I could. It is not known to anyone but me (and now you) that Old Bell paid for my college education after my father left. I can never repay what I owe him, but consider this a "down payment." Please be discreet, since it is a felony to disclose these records. Let me know if I can help further. I hope you find what you're looking for, whatever it may be.

Cassie Gainsforth

Morgan tore up Cassie's note, the only evidence that connected her to the disks. With his handkerchief, he wiped the disks clean of any fingerprints except his. He would keep Cassie's secret forever.

He knew what to do. The data could be downloaded to his laptop at home, then he could browse through it with Paradox, the same database software that had helped him discover P.D. Comeaux's serial-murder spree.

He'd start with the secret case of Hosanna Pierce. Morgan couldn't shake Simeon Fenwick's offhand remark that Malachi Pierce's retarded daughter was a "punishment" sent by God. Punishment for what? What guilt gnawed at the old fanatic's black heart? Morgan knew these disks were unlikely to answer those questions, but maybe he'd find some key, some tiny clue to the fearsome character of Malachi Pierce.

Then again, maybe not. He didn't know what he'd find, if anything. No reporter ever did. But he wouldn't be guessing anymore.

He dialed Cassie's number at the court clerk's office, to thank her, but it was almost five and she'd already left for the day. So he stuffed the disks in a fresh envelope and tucked them safely in his briefcase.

Cal Nussbaum stood in the backshop doorway, saying nothing. It unnerved Morgan that the old printer always seemed to be watching him.

"Everything okay, Cal?" he asked.

Cal said nothing for a moment, then spoke.

"Got some pages for you to check," he said.

All twelve pages of this week's *Bullet* were spread out along a bank of the backshop's slanted composing tables. Seven were finished; the other five waited for unsold ads, unprinted photos and unwritten stories to fill ominous blank spaces. Morgan suddenly remembered the film he'd stashed in the darkroom cabinet.

"Looks like we're in good shape," Morgan said as he scanned the headlines and ad copy on the completed pages.

"Let's see, we've only got the front and back pages, sports and the last classified pages to go, right?"

Cal huffed. "And the edit page."

Morgan grimaced and glanced up at the ink-smudged backshop clock. Time was running out on his indecision. He ran his finger over the hole on the page where his editorial should be. It not only remained unwritten: At this moment, it remained unimagined.

"Don't worry," he told his impatient printer. "It'll be there before deadline. I've got a few other stories to write and I'll soup the photos tonight. Anyway, we're ahead of the game at this point, thanks to you."

Ironically, Cal Nussbaum's long face drooped even more.

"I ain't takin' no chances this time," he said in his slow-burning drawl. "I'm gonna work on these later tonight. We ain't gonna miss no more deadlines if I have to write the goddam stories myself."

"We'll put her to bed right this time," he assured Cal, patting his shoulder. "I think we're finally getting the hang of it. Now, if we could only sell a few more ads ..."

Half of Cal's face crinkled in a tepid smile. He was the kind of guy who found most forms of hope delusive.

"I'm goin' to dinner," he said. "I'll come back later and work on these pages."

After Cal left, Morgan sat before his blank computer screen in the empty newsroom for two hours. He again weighed an endorsement in the sheriff's race, but his mind drifted to Neeley Gilmartin and Malachi Pierce, and to the photograph of little Aimee still stashed safely in his briefcase, proud in her Sunday best. He sharpened his pencils, shuffled papers on his desk, rocked in his uncomfortable chair. His reporters had drifted in, filed a few stories and left to see a movie together, but he still had not written a single word. The time got away from him.

The street outside was dark when the phone rang. It was Claire.

"Can I interest you in some dinner?" she asked.

"Can you give me an hour? I have a couple things to do."

"Is that sixty-minute hour, or is it one of those 'I'll-tell-you-an-hour-and-be-home-at-midnight' kind of hours?"

"Sixty minutes," Morgan said. "Give or take a day."

"I'll be waiting," she promised him, and hung up.

Claire never scolded him. She knew a newspaperman's time was measured not in minutes and hours, but in irregular moments. To her husband, no two hours elapsed at the same rate and, for as long as she'd known him, his days rarely ended at exactly the same moment, although they all tended to end very late.

Morgan locked the darkroom door behind him and flipped off the dim, red bulb that hung overhead. The complete blackness unbalanced him; he spread his invisible feet on the damp wooden floor to regain his equilibrium. He fumbled with the undeveloped rolls and wondered why he bothered to close his eyes in the darkness.

His mind projected the faded picture of Aimee, only it wasn't a still photograph as it flickered in the dark theater of his brain. Now it was a movie, tinted the brown of memory, unreeling in the slow motion of a dream. Yellow clouds scudded across a buckskin sky, and the earth was dusty mahogany. The light in her cinnamon eyes was like the chinook winds that seeped from the eastern slope of the mountains into the basin, ethereal, warm and soft. She turned toward him, toward the camera in his mind, and smiled innocently. Then she looked away, off to the empty west, behind the camera where a rusty shadow spilled across the margin of Morgan's imagination. She wasn't afraid as she held out one of her flowers to the specter. Suddenly, the wind rose and ochre dust swallowed her.

Then the screen went blank.

Morgan looped the movie in his head again and again, but the swirling wind always swept her away before he saw the shadowy figure lurking at the edge of his consciousness.

Was it Aimee's allegedly dead father, who still had not quite shaken Morgan's suspicion? Or had it been Kate herself haunting his imagination? Or was it simply a blank, evil space for which he had no face, no name?

Morgan didn't know who it was, but he now knew who it *wasn't*: Neeley Gilmartin. The old man hadn't killed Aimee Little Spotted Horse, he was certain. If Gilmartin's claim of innocence was just an elaborate con, he'd have long ago surrendered to the agony of his cancer. But another pain burned more intensely in him, and the promise of deliverance had kept him alive. There was enough room in one man's heart for guilt or for hope, but not both.

Lukewarm water trickled into the darkroom sink, the only sound in the humid blackness that engulfed Morgan. When he turned on the red darkroom light, there was no more movie. He finished the film and clothes-pinned the strips to a wire strung overhead in the mildewy space.

The newsroom's fluorescent lights stung his tired eyes. It was after nine o'clock and for the first time today, Morgan was hungry. He'd promised Claire he'd be home thirty minutes ago, although plenty of work remained to be done tonight. He thought about calling Claire and telling her to put a plate in the refrigerator for him, a request he'd made more times than he cared to remember.

But his stomach groused. He decided to take a break and come back later. He retrieved the leather briefcase he'd hidden under his desk, turned off the lights and locked the front door behind him.

The recalcitrant Escort sat forlornly on the empty street. It wheezed and snorted and belched, but it refused to start. Morgan slammed the driver's door as he got out, then kicked it. He plotted a painful, rusty death as he walked home in the dark summer night.

While Claire warmed a plate of roasted chicken and rice

for him, Morgan telephoned the hospital. A tired Dr. Snyder, at the end of a long shift, told him Gilmartin had not yet regained consciousness but his vital signs had improved slightly after he was moved to the intensive care unit. She promised to call if the old man's condition changed, for better or worse, but she didn't expect any news before morning, a sentiment that encouraged Morgan.

"How is he?" Claire asked as he hung up.

"He's better," Morgan said, rubbing his fatigued eyes. The pungent smell of Dektol developer lingered on his hands, reminding him that his night wasn't finished. "I think he's going to make it. He's one tough son of a bitch, and I don't think he survived a world war and half a century in prison to die quietly in the night. God, I hope not."

Claire kneaded his shoulders. The tautness in his muscles melted away. The buoyant T.J., swinging his bushy tail in a wide swath beneath the kitchen table, nudged his hand for an affectionate pat. The Doors' morose anthem, "The End," pulsed low and endless on the stereo in the darkened den, on a fading cassette tape that had survived a thousand replays since Morgan's college days.

"Can you put something else on?" he asked. His mood was somber enough. "Anything."

Claire disappeared into the next room. From the dark, he heard the distant, delicate harmony of Crosby, Stills and Nash. Claire resumed her massage. "Better?"

"Much."

"Will you make deadline this week?" she asked, running her fingers along the taut cords of his neck into his hair. He felt the tingle of blood spilling into the stress-pinched capillaries of his scalp as she rubbed.

"I don't know. There's still a lot to do, but maybe ... right there, yeah ... I have to go back tonight."

"I suspected you would. I'll make a Thermos of coffee for you. Just the way you like it: Extra sweet."

"Thanks. If they find me dead on the newsroom floor tomorrow morning, it was the saccharin."

The oven timer buzzed. Morgan opened the screen door to let the dog out, and stood to watch midges dancing madly around the backyard porch light while Claire served his late dinner. She sat beside him as he ate in silence, still consumed by a difficult day that wasn't yet over.

"What if he dies?" she asked.

Morgan tried to respond, but he couldn't. He had no answer. Crickets paused in the backyard, and his iced tea glass sweated quietly into a wet ring on the table, but he couldn't speak.

"Right now, right at this moment, do you think he did it?" she pressed him.

The hot night embraced him. The pleated linen curtains over the sink hung limp, waiting for a refreshing wind to change the subject.

"No," he said after a moment. "I don't think he killed her."

Claire touched his hand and leaned close to him. Her fingers were cool on his.

"Then he needs you more than ever right now," she said, comforting him. "I'll pray, but you've got to be his angel. You've done more with less, and right now, nothing else matters. Not this freak-show militia thing, not the greedy little bean-counters at the bank, not your egotistical sheriff buddy, not even the damn newspaper. Nothing. If you really believe this old man is innocent, then you've got to prove it."

Morgan sipped his tea and traced his finger through the perfect circle of water where his glass sat. His own circle was broken. He felt lost.

"Time has run out," he said. "I feel sorry for the guy, I really do. If he's innocent and he spent his life in prison ... Jesus, I don't even want to think about it. But there isn't time to finish this thing his way. He only gave me two weeks to solve a crime that was committed before I was born. Two weeks. It's his own goddam fault. He let time run out on me."

"Don't talk as if he's dead. He's still alive."

"Barely," Morgan said, his voice rising in frustration. "I keep thinking the phone's going to ring and they're going to tell me he's gone. I used to think that would be it. I'd be released from this thing. Now I've got this knot in my stomach, like I'm letting him down."

"For God's sake, Jeff," Claire snapped at him. "This is why you do it. Remember that night, that first night we were together, when you told me you wanted to tell stories that changed lives? Remember that?"

"Jesus, Claire ..."

"I know you wanted to make lives better, and you did, but now you can change a life that's already been lived. This old man doesn't want to live it again. He came to you for one thing: Absolution."

"I'm not God. I'm not even sure there is a god, but it ain't me, Claire. I don't perform miracles. I can't raise the dead. And I can't just wipe the dirty slate of Neeley Gilmartin's life clean."

It seemed an eternity before Claire spoke again. She sat silently, her hands in her lap, not looking at him. There were only the sounds of a summer night—children playing somewhere down the block, the random ticking of moths against the porch light, crickets in the grass—until she looked directly into his eyes and spoke.

"You said you wanted to dip your finger in ink and touch hearts. Something burned inside you, some passion, and the light came through your eyes. I saw it. I fell completely in love with you that first night. Because you really believed you could touch people with your words, and you made me believe. In you."

Morgan tenderly touched his wife's cheek. If anything had changed since his first night with her, it wasn't Claire. She remained, as always, tougher than he was.

"Do you still believe?"

"I never stopped," she said.

He kissed her, his fingers gliding across her tummy under the loose bottom of her tee-shirt. A soft breeze had come up, rustling the curtains over the sink. Claire pulled him closer and he tasted the saltiness of her neck. Then she stood up from the table and led him by the hand to the dark den, where they hid from the light and made love on the couch.

When they finished, Claire lay against her husband, the slow rhythm of old music and a warm breeze washing over their naked bodies in the dark.

"Aren't you glad we kept the couch?" she asked.

Morgan smiled in the dark. "Hey, you were the one who wanted to sell it," he reminded her. "Fifty bucks. Remember?"

"Do you really have to go back tonight?" she asked him, brushing her hand lightly through the hair on his chest and knowing he did.

Before he could answer, the night erupted.

A thundering explosion split the air, close. A flash of light pierced the darkness a split-second ahead of the sound. The blast shrieked like the collected voices of Hell itself. The windows facing the street strained and rattled against their casements, but didn't break.

Instantly, Morgan rolled Claire off the couch onto the floor and covered her with his body, feeling the floor rumble beneath them. A mournful keening rose as dogs began to howl throughout the neighborhood.

He could feel Claire's nude body shaking against him.

"Are you okay?" he asked. He felt her nod.

"What was that?" she whispered, barely able to speak.

Morgan didn't know. He reached across the rug for his pants, which he hurriedly pulled on. He crawled across the floor toward the front window.

"Don't leave me, Jeff," Claire begged.

"Stay there," he told her. "Don't move until I tell you."

Crouching in the dark hall near the door, Morgan reached up and turned off the front porch light. Then he opened the door slightly. Neighbors were already gathering on the street in front of the house, but they were looking and pointing toward the downtown.

A glimmering orange light reflected on billowing smoke just a few blocks away. Then he heard the fire department's siren wail, desperately calling volunteers out of their homes all over town.

He hurried back to Claire, feeling for his shirt and shoes in the dark. The hair on his neck felt like needles as he wrapped his shirt around him without buttoning it.

"Stay here, Claire," he commanded her. "There's a fire downtown someplace. Get the dog inside, lock the doors, and stay put. I'll call."

Morgan grabbed a fresh notebook and sprinted out the front door toward the roaring light that glowed like a tarnished sunset just a few blocks away. Over his pounding heart and his electrified breathing, he could hear smaller, secondary explosions in the fire.

Still two blocks away, cinders drifted to earth and smoke surged through the trees, stinging his lungs. One block away, he felt ripples of heat on his face and shattered glass from broken windows sparkled like diamonds at his feet.

As Morgan ran across the bank parking lot, around the corner that separated the neighborhoods from Main Street, he saw flames rising high into the night sky. Sparks curled toward heaven in blistering zephyrs. The first firefighters were just arriving, shielding their faces against the growling inferno.

His stomach clenched and he wanted to vomit.

The Bullet was fully engulfed.

CHAPTER FOURTEEN

By morning's first light, only the charred bones of the printing press stood above the smoldering remains of *The Bullet*. The old newspaper's skin had been cremated and ripped away, exposing the steel spine that had always given it strength. Pools of ash-choked water from the fire engines' hoses seeped like black blood from the debris.

The bomb had exploded inside the building, probably in the pressroom. A firefighter had already found a shallow crater, filled with black water, in the concrete floor beneath the back window. The blast had blown out the entire back wall of the building, igniting the stock of paper and ink in the pressroom. The damage wasn't confined to the newspaper office: Buildings on both sides of *The Bullet* suffered the shock of the blast, their walls disfigured, their broken windows gaping like black wounds.

Rod Dombeck, a lantern-jawed sheriff's investigator who'd sped away from his teen-age son's American Legion baseball game in extra innings when he heard the explosion the night before, had already blocked the alley with yellow crime-scene tape and he was scouring the brick-strewn parking area for evidence.

A little after five AM, as soon as they could see in the dim light, firefighters fanned out from the hulk of the press, probing in the mess with pikes and pry bars. Half-ton rolls of tightly rolled newsprint, once stacked four high, were reduced to feathery embers. Ink barrels had burst in the intense heat, feeding the fire with their flammable contents.

Morgan coughed up gray-flecked phlegm as he wandered through the incinerated newsroom. The fire chief wouldn't let him go any farther into the wreckage, which was now a crime scene. He saw nothing familiar, except a few orphaned pieces of common office hardware that hadn't been vaporized in the intense heat: Blackened steel parts from chairs, desks and light fixtures, crushed filing cabinets, and the small safe where Crystal kept petty cash and receipts. The rest—phones, computers, desks, wooden chairs, books, even the old newspaper pages and the clock on the wall—were burned beyond recognition.

Morgan was numb. The lingering smoke nauseated him. The smudged light of morning stung his eyes as the soul of his newspaper, his dream, rose in smoky tendrils to the sky and drifted slowly to the east in a sinuous cloud.

The Bullet was gone.

Somewhere in the ashes, or somewhere in the clouds above, was the last edition. Morgan tasted it in the air, a mordant bitterness that cloyed his tongue and churned in his belly. The week's paper was certainly lost, and he didn't know how or where he could make next week's.

"Over here!" a young volunteer firefighter yelled from the pile of rubble near the press.

The boy sagged to his knees, pinching his blackened mouth and nose with his left hand. Morgan recognized him from the Conoco station, where he pumped gas after school. He'd helped Morgan push the Escort across Main Street the night before, safely away from the fire. Now, he looked ill as a half dozen other firefighters and deputies scrambled across the wreckage to his side. Morgan followed them and nobody stopped him.

The corpse had been hidden under a collapsed wall. The boy had uncovered it when he yanked on a deformed piece of sheet-metal, and was immediately enveloped by the caustic stench of charred human flesh.

In the half light of the new morning, the body lay on its back, its empty eye sockets staring up at the smoky sky. In the intense heat, the eyeballs had split open and shriveled like grapes on a griddle. The soft tissues of the face had been stripped off by the fire, revealing grayish white bone beneath. Pieces of its skull had peeled away in thin, flat layers. Its jaw was frozen in a savage, silent scream at the sky.

The corpse had no hands, but the stumps of its forearms were thrust out in front of its body like a fistless boxer protecting his seared viscera, which were exposed to the air. Skin and fat were broiled away, laying bare a hash of scorched muscles that had ruptured.

Morgan had seen and smelled burned bodies before, but nobody he'd known in life. He tried to envision Cal Nussbaum's long, rumpled face on the skeletal countenance in the hole. Vomit rose in his esophagus and he choked it down.

"Get him outta here," Dombeck barked, pointing at Morgan. "We got a murder scene now. Call the sheriff and tell him we got a ten-seventy-nine, well done. And for God's sake, watch where you step. We might have more crispy critters under all this shit."

A uniformed deputy escorted Morgan away from the corpse's shadowy hole, back to the front sidewalk where they ducked beneath the freshly strung yellow police line. Shattered glass was everywhere. A small crowd of gawkers had gathered across the street. All night, he'd seen them, standing on distant corners, parked along side streets, feeling the heat on their empty faces, watching his life collapse in flame. Now, Morgan stood with his back to them, feeling embarrassed and angry. He wanted to take them, one by one, to stare into what remained of Cal Nussbaum's face. If they were still curious, they could trace the cracks in his bare skull where Cal's boiling brain had seeped out.

Morgan walked across Main Street to examine his car. Some plastic piping had melted off the front bumper and the paint on the hood had blistered before he and the young firefighter had pushed it out of harm's way. He sagged against the front fender and peeled off some of the scorched blue paint, letting it flutter down the street.

Sheriff Trey Kerrigan parked his white Blazer in the middle of Main Street, behind a fire truck. He wore his election-year Stetson and a short-sleeved brown uniform blouse, with his silver sheriff's star on the breast and razor-sharp creases. His father's gun was on his hip in a polished black leather holster. Trey's face was drawn and serious.

The sheriff spoke briefly to one of his deputies before climbing up to view Cal's body in the smoky debris. A few minutes later, he clambered down, the cuffs of his brown uniform trousers black with soot.

"I'm sorry about all this, Jeff," he said, wiping the smell of death away from his nose. "Looks like a bomb. We got the state arson team and the ATF on the way from Cheyenne. I'm fair certain they're gonna want to ask you some questions."

Morgan nodded but said nothing. He was eager to tell them about Pierce's threats, and to begin rebuilding his newspaper, starting with the next edition.

Trey Kerrigan swept his boot through the glass that covered the sidewalk.

"You don't happen to know who the body is up there, do you?"

"I think it's Cal Nussbaum. The place was empty when I left for dinner, but Cal was going to come back to the office last night to finish some pages," Morgan said. Then he realized the dark task before him. "I have to tell his wife."

"Don't worry," the sheriff said, "I'll send somebody over to his place as soon as we get the coroner up here. Shouldn't be long."

"No," Morgan insisted. "It should be me. I owe him that.

They have a place up on Nightcap Creek, ten miles out. They
don't have a phone. She won't know about the fire."

"I'm sorry, Jeff. I can't let you go."

"What?"

"I can't let you go."

"What, am I a suspect now?"

Kerrigan looked away, down the street. "Maybe."

Morgan was stunned. "You must be shitting me. You think
I'd blow up my own newspaper? Give me a fuckin' break,
Trey."

The sheriff glared at his old friend. "No, you give *me* a
break. Don't play me for some dumb-ass tinhorn cop. I ain't
sayin' you done it, but everybody knows you're havin' major-
league financial problems. It raises questions. Big-city cop reporter, you been around these investigations. You know the
routine."

"You think I torched the paper for the insurance money?"

"I didn't say that."

"You don't have to, Trey. I know the routine, remember?
Well, goddammit, I didn't do it. We'd just turned the corner
and I always had other options for money. But not this. No
way. You know me."

"That was once upon a time. You went away and I don't
know who you are now, Jeff."

Anger welled in Morgan. "I didn't change. You did. You're
too goddamned worried about keeping your job. That badge
is weighing you down, my friend."

Morgan nearly spit the last word. He saw Trey Kerrigan's
right hand curl into a fist at his side and he stepped back to
give himself plenty of time to fend off the blow. It never
came.

Instead, Kerrigan leaned toward his old friend and spoke
in an angry whisper: "Fuck you, Jeff. I'll take you down in a
minute and don't think I won't."

A nervous sweat trickled down Morgan's sides. For the

first time in his conscious memory, he faced Trey Kerrigan as an enemy. He felt as if he were fighting for his life. Even if he understood his suspicions, it frightened him to be a suspect. He fought through it.

"Trey, if you're arresting me, then take me back to the jail so I can call my lawyer. If you aren't, get out of my face. I have to go home and tell my wife what happened here," he said, trying to hold himself together. "Then I need to go out and see Betty Nussbaum. She needs to know. What's it going to be?"

Momentarily outmaneuvered, Kerrigan scowled. "The feds and the state fire boys will be here by lunchtime." The sheriff thumped Morgan in the chest with his thick index finger. "You'd better be where I can find you or I'll hunt down your ass myself. I swear to God I will."

Morgan said nothing and walked away. Kerrigan watched him get into the wounded Escort and attempt to start it. By the third gasping try, the sheriff was shaking his head, a mocking smile on his lips.

Just as Morgan was about to abandon the heap and walk, the engine turned over. Kerrigan himself pointed the way through the emergency vehicles still parked in the street, across several unfurled fire hoses toward home.

As he passed, the sheriff cocked his thumb and forefinger like a pistol and, from his hip, aimed it at Morgan. Through the windshield, Morgan watched the hammer fall.

Claire was waiting for him. Already dressed in her baggy painting pants and a gray Northwestern University T-shirt, she rocked nervously on the top step of the front porch. When she saw his car, she ran out to the end of the driveway to meet him. Before he spoke, she lost it, her shoulders heaving as she wept in his arms.

"It was the paper, Claire," he told her as she held him tight. He clung to her as if she were the last thing in his world. "It's gone."

"They killed him," she sobbed, unable to catch her breath. "They were here and they killed him. I went out to make room in the shed for my painting stuff and I found ... him that way. Oh, God."

Claire's face was buried in his chest, but she swept her arm toward the house.

She couldn't have known about Cal. Not so soon. Morgan wrapped his arms more tightly around her and guided her across the lawn toward the front door. Safely inside, he sat her on the sofa and searched her tear-streaked face. Her eyes were frightened and red.

"Killed who? Tell me," he said, wiping tears from her cheeks. "Please tell me."

Claire just pointed toward the back door. "Out there," she said.

Morgan touched her cold hands and went into the kitchen alone. Last night's dinner dishes were still on the table, but nothing looked awry. The back door was open. Outside, the porch light still glowed as morning blossomed.

He walked across the backyard. The thick lawn was dewy and he felt the cool wetness seep through the soles of his shoes. It was still before six and the neighborhood was quiet. No children playing, no dogs barking.

No dogs.

He called for T.J.

Nothing.

Morgan called again, but the dog didn't answer.

As he turned toward the house, he found T.J. The pup had been skinned and hanged by a chain from the porch eave, dangling from a railroad spike driven through his neatly sliced neck. His belly had been slit and blood dripped onto a small, sad pile of guts that cooled in the morning air beneath the carcass.

Morgan ran inside to Claire. She had composed herself, but was still trembling and cold. He wrapped a hand-knitted afghan across her shoulders.

"He called," she murmured as her husband held her close, trying to share his body heat. "He called after ... I was afraid to answer the phone, so I let the machine pick it up. I heard him."

She pointed toward the answering machine on a curio table in the hallway. It blinked ominously.

Morgan left her on the couch and pushed the button. The machine beeped once and rewound. The message was brief and chilling, the voice unfamiliar.

"You make it too easy, Jew-lover. We got your paper and your fuckin' dog, easy. We're comin' for your pretty Jew wife next if you keep askin' questions. We don't need your kind here. You ain't gonna do to us what you done to P.D. Comeaux. You know us and you know we don't care nuthin' about killin' prairie niggers or Jews, which ain't even good as dogs. That Indian-trash kid wasn't worth comin' home and findin' your wife gutted like a dog, was she? So don't go pokin' your fuckin' nose where it ain't supposed to be."

The message ended abruptly. Morgan removed the tape from the machine and dropped it in his pocket. His hand was shaking and his head throbbed. He was exhausted and afraid.

But now he knew.

He couldn't know exactly who called, but he knew in his heart who'd sent the message.

He knew who'd bombed *The Bullet*, killing Cal Nussbaum.

He knew who slaughtered Claire's puppy.

And, for the first time since Neeley Gilmartin had come to him, he knew who'd probably killed Aimee Little Spotted Horse and thrown her tiny body into the Black Thunder River gorge. Even if he didn't know why or how, he knew there was a connection.

Malachi Pierce.

Morgan didn't want to leave Claire alone at the house, even though she had progressed from shock to seething anger. Now she was mad. But he wasn't sure she was safe by herself, so he took her with him to deliver the answering-machine tape to Sheriff Trey Kerrigan. Not only would it exonerate him, it offered a new lead in the arson-murder at *The Bullet.*

Downtown at the fire scene, Morgan found Trey Kerrigan in a grim conversation with the county coroner about the dead man, whose remains lay heaped in a black plastic body bag on a gurney between them, part of the discussion but past caring. He hung back, watching and listening.

The verbose Carter McWayne had followed his father and his grandfather in the funeral business and the distasteful corollary job of Perry County coroner. In his mid-forties, his fleshy face and enormous belly might have belonged to any devotee of The Griddle's fatback-gravy specials, but his bulging eyes marked him as a McWayne.

Now the coroner waggled his sausage-like fingers as he explained it would be a day or two before he could positively identify the body with dental records and medical X-rays, if they existed at all.

"We got your basic full-thickness, fourth-degree burns here," he said with all the passion of his craft. That is to say, none.

Carter McWayne had always fancied himself a medical professional, even though he was no more qualified to the privilege than a hospital janitor. He was an undertaker, not a doctor. But his sepulchral voice rose from the blubbery tomb of his chest and spilled out fifty-cent anatomical words with unimpeachable authority, albeit with a fat man's breathy punctuation. The corpulent coroner's heavy breathing seemed to be a conscious process.

"There is coagulation necrosis of the epidermis and dermis, with destruction of the dermal appendages. Soft-tissue facial structures are mutilated, muscle is exposed and ruptured, no fingers for prints, cranial vault shows heat fractures. We got significant epidural hematomas, frontal and parietal, probably postmortem."

"Goddammit, Carter, try to say it in English," the sheriff bristled.

"That *is* English," McWayne growled in his deep voice. "But it means this fella's a big mess."

"Will you be able to make an ID?"

"Not me. I'll have to get the forensic pathologist down in Cheyenne to come up here. If he can't get comparative X-rays, he'll probably do DNA. But don't count your chickens, Trey. There's a chance we'll never know."

"That's it?" the sheriff asked incredulously.

"I don't have X-ray vision."

"Could it be Cal Nussbaum?"

McWayne shrugged his massive shoulders. "I can only tell you it was a male."

"How's that?"

"That's a funny thing about fire victims. Where he was laying on the flat, concrete floor, the skin of his back was perfectly preserved, along with some clothing and glass. No obvious mortal wounds, but there's too much hair on his back for all but a few of the women around here."

"Did he die before the fire started?"

The short-winded McWayne shook his head, the mushy bag of fat under his chin quavering out of sync. "Sorry, sheriff. Too friggin' much damage."

"Best guess, Carter."

"That's your job, Trey. But the floor under him wasn't scorched, and there was lots of unburned debris. It's a better-than-even bet he was rendered unconscious, maybe killed, by the concussion of the bomb. Don't quote me."

Kerrigan twisted one end of his prodigious mustache as he listened, his forehead creased with impatience. He wanted more and he wanted it faster than he was getting it.

Morgan couldn't wait any longer. He stepped forward and pressed the cassette tape into the sheriff's hand. Trey Kerrigan seemed startled to learn that he'd been standing near enough to hear. Suspects, he knew, should be kept at a comfortable, uninformed distance.

"This should help your investigation," he said brusquely. "It's from my answering machine. The caller makes threats against my wife. And if you send a deputy over to my house, he'll find my dog butchered on the back porch. They made their point."

Kerrigan turned the cassette over and studied it. Then he squinted at Morgan.

"What am I gonna hear on this?"

"Threats."

"Who?"

"I don't know. But it looks like this explosion is related to the Gilmartin case. Listen to the tape and decide for yourself. But, personally, I think you're going to want to have a little talk with Malachi Pierce."

"Pierce? Christ, you think this was a militia hit?"

"It's more than that. It might be a murder cover-up. But right now, you don't want to take my word for it anyway. I'm still a suspect, remember? Listen to the tape yourself."

Kerrigan unbuttoned his shirt pocket and put the cassette inside. "Any other surprises?"

"No, but I need a big favor. Can you have a deputy take Claire to the airport in Blackwater and put her on the next flight to Chicago? I need to know she's safe. The tape will tell you why. I'll take her back to the house and pack some things and make the arrangements, if you'll have somebody pick her up in, let's say, an hour?"

Kerrigan pondered his request, but not long. "I ain't no taxi service," he bristled. "Damned if I'm gonna help a suspect's wife flee the state."

"In that case, Trey," Morgan said. He scribbled Jerry Overton's name and the phone number for the Chicago ATF bureau in his pocket notebook, then tore the page out. He handed the scrap of paper to the sheriff. "Call this guy. Tell him everything. He can help. And if something happens to me or to Claire, make sure he knows."

Morgan turned and started back to his car, where Claire was anxiously rolling the radio dial up and down the FM band, searching for distraction. He'd left the motor running.

"Not so fast. We got things to settle, damn you."

Morgan kept walking. "Go to hell, Trey."

Nightcap Creek was a place of legend.

Before the turn of the century, a mad French trapper claimed the stream was visited by a ghostly brigantine that sailed up its rocky channel at midnight on a certain night each year. Nobody ever saw the supernatural sailing ship, although in Morgan's day the secluded stream became a favorite haunt of horny teen-agers who stole away in their fathers' cars to watch for it through the carnal fog on their windshields. Many stories were told on the banks of the Nightcap.

A few families—Cal and Betty Nussbaum among them—bought land in the Nightcap drainage and hauled their shabby trailers up there. Most of them were set back from the dirt road among the lodgepole pines, close enough to pump water from the creek in the warmer months.

Cal's mobile home was sun-washed green and dirty white, surrounded by a buckrail fence. A rough-hewn cedar shingle hung from the top rail, with the name NUSSBAUM spelled out in three-inch-high block letters. Morgan turned through the open gate, rolled the Escort to stop in front of the trailer and set the emergency brake so he wouldn't have to turn off the engine.

"Want to come in with me?" he asked Claire.

She shook her head. "I couldn't take it right now," she said.

Claire turned up the radio and pushed the buttons huffily. On the way to Nightcap Creek, her husband had explained why he wanted her to go to her parents' home in Chicago for a week, maybe two, until he could find his equilibrium again. She didn't want to go. She resisted, saying she was a big girl who learned more about prejudice before she was ten than he ever had. The more Morgan deflected her arguments, the more frustrated she got. By the time they reached Nightcap Creek, she had nothing left to say and no new way to say it.

"I won't be long," Morgan said.

The mountain forest around him smelled fresh and clean, although smoke still adhered to his clothes. The air was cool under the cover of the trees, the soil soft. Old pine needles crackled under his feet as he climbed the three steps to the trailer's front door. Morgan breathed deeply and knocked. He checked his watch: it was six-fifteen in the morning and the sun cut long, sharp shafts through the pines. He hoped he would not be waking Betty to a nightmare.

Someone moved inside. The trailer rocked gently as someone walked across the floor. The latch clicked and he steeled himself to deliver the grim news of Cal's death. He prayed she didn't ask if he'd seen the body.

Betty Nussbaum was tall, like Cal, but with a pleasant face and faded strawberry-blond hair sugared with white. She wore thick glasses that made her green eyes as big as shimmering pools on the Nightcap. As she opened the door, Morgan smelled fresh coffee and biscuits wafting from the trailer. She'd been making breakfast.

"Good morning, Jeff," she greeted him. "You're up early."

Morgan cleared his throat and looked down at his shoes. "Betty, it's about Cal."

"Cal's not here. He was gone when I got up."

"I know. That's why I came up."

Betty saw Claire waiting in the car and waved. "Oh, your wife is with you. Don't be such a fuddy-dud. Tell her to come on in and have some coffee."

He focused on his grave task. "I know Cal isn't here. I'm just ..."

"Was he supposed to wait for you? That man, I swear. He gets an itch and he's gotta scratch. The good Lord put fish in the stream with more patience than my husband."

"Betty, I'm afraid there's bad news."

Oddly, Betty Nussbaum's pretty face brightened at that very moment. Morgan was puzzled, speechless as she looked past his shoulder.

"Then you might as well deliver it yourself," she said. "Cal, haul your butt up here and apologize to Jeff for goin' fishin' without him, you impatient old fart."

Morgan swiveled to see Cal Nussbaum, very much alive, stowing his fishing pole and old-fashioned basket creel in a lean-to shed beside the trailer. He carried a proud stringer of eight pan-sized browns, fresh from the Nightcap. Breakfast.

Morgan felt the blood drain from his head and, for a moment, believed he might pass out. He reached for the two-by-four handrail that encircled the small porch.

"You're alive!" he blurted out.

"Hell, yes, I'm alive," Cal said, irritated. "Fly-fishin's almost as good for a man as gettin' up before the chickens. You come all the way up here to tell me that?"

Morgan was dumfounded at the sight of Cal. The scowling old printer suddenly felt self-conscious.

"Christ, you smell like a jerky fart," Cal said. "You been smokin' them cow-pie ceegars again?"

"It's from the fire," Morgan said lamely.

"What fire? What the hell are you talking about?"

"Cal, *The Bullet* burned down last night. It was a bomb. They found a burned body in the rubble and I thought it was ..."

Morgan felt light-headed. Cal grabbed his elbow and led him inside, seating him in an easy chair near the door. Betty brought him a glass of water, then hovered nearby like a tall mother hen. Before he knew what was happening, Claire was beside him.

"I went back down there last night to pick up some work and bring it home," Cal explained to them both. "Godawmighty, no wonder you look like you seen the ghost ship."

Now Cal's hands were shaking, too. He sat on a steamer trunk beside the couch.

"Are you okay, Jeff?" Claire asked.

"I'll be fine," he said, holding her hand tightly. After a long, deep silence, he began to question Cal. "Was anybody there when you left? One of the reporters? Anybody?"

"Nope. I turned off all the lights, locked her up and came home. It was nine-thirty, quarter to ten."

Morgan wondered if the charred corpse in *The Bullet's* rubble was the bomber himself, caught in a violent trap of his own making. He was angry. He wanted desperately to know who destroyed his newspaper and the body in the wreckage might hold the key.

"Did you see anybody suspicious out back? Anybody hanging around?"

Cal flexed his fingers, trying to remember. His memory was blank. He shook his head.

"Wasn't there more'n fifteen minutes. Just loaded up the pages, set some type and hauled my ass outta there. I came home and worked on 'em for an hour, then went to bed."

"You've got the pages *here?*" Morgan asked.

"Right over there," he said, pointing toward the trailer's breakfast nook. All the page flats for the week's edition were spread out on the table. "Just missing a couple stories and a few pictures. Pretty much ready to go."

Morgan leaned forward in the easy chair, his eyes suddenly full of life again. "Who could print it for us if we fill the holes?"

Cal thought a moment. "*The Trib* over in Blackwater, maybe the *News-Letter* down in Newcastle. They're good people. They'd make sure we had a paper."

Morgan stood up and rattled off instructions. He made a few notes for Cal. "Get to town and find Crystal and the reporters. Leave me forty inches across the top of the front page for a fire story and picture, and a hole on the edit page.

Fill up everything else the best you can. Have one of the reporters take photos of the fire scene and soup the film at the high school newspaper's darkroom. Then call around and find somebody who'll print *The Bullet* for the next few weeks. Tell them we'll have one before the end of the day tomorrow."

"What the hell are we gonna write these stories on?"

"If you can't beg or borrow a computer and printer downtown, go to the library and type them to fit the holes, the old-fashioned way. It won't be pretty but it'll be a paper."

"No problem."

"Cal, I'm sorry to put this in your lap, but you can do it better than anybody else. Keep me in the loop. I'll have my stories done when the time comes."

Cal nodded.

"One more thing. Betty, can you take Claire to the airport in Blackwater this morning? I'd sure appreciate anything you could do."

"Certainly, dear. When?"

"Come to the house in, say, an hour. Is that good for you?"

"I'll be there."

"What are you gonna be doin'?" Cal asked.

"You think I'm going to leave this one to the cops? This is personal now," he said.

Cal smiled broadly and poked his ink-stained thumb in the air. "Old Bell brung you up right," he said. "He's sure gonna get a kick outta this one."

CHAPTER FIFTEEN

Morgan changed out of his smoky clothes and packed two suitcases while Claire showered and fixed her hair for the trip to Blackwater, the only commercial airport within a hundred miles. In a futile, last-ditch effort, she had begged him to let her stay, arguing bravely. But she made no headway and had no choice.

Over the phone, the United ticket clerk reserved the last seat on the eleven AM puddle-jumper to Denver, with a two p.m. connection to O'Hare. Morgan left the return ticket open. He arranged for Claire's mother to pick her up at the airport and drive her home to Winnetka. He told her about the fire, but he said nothing about the butchery of their dog or the sinister threats against her daughter. Some things could wait.

Finally, he called the dispatcher and asked to be patched through to Trey Kerrigan. He told the sheriff that Cal Nussbaum was indeed alive and the burned body belonged to someone else, probably nobody employed by *The Bullet*. Maybe it was the bomber himself, Morgan surmised. Kerrigan exhaled a frustrated sigh and hung up without engaging in any further conversation, much less speculation, with an erstwhile suspect.

Betty Nussbaum came to the door just before eight, gussied up in a flowery print dress for the hour-long drive to Blackwater. Morgan begged her indulgence for a last few minutes alone

with his wife. Betty winked at him and hovered over the mari-
gold bed, pretending to be enthralled by the wizened blossoms and the controlled tragedy of a city flower garden.

Claire sat on the edge of the rumpled bed upstairs. Everything was packed. Morgan sat beside her and rested his head
on her shoulder. She wore no perfume but he smelled the
sweet fragrance of her long, soft hair.

"I'll miss you," he said, "but at least I'll know you're safe.
You need to take care of our baby."

Claire didn't look at him. She began searching in her
purse for something, maybe she didn't even know what.

"But what about you? Will *you* be safe? I should be here."

"I'll be perfectly fine. There's nothing more that can happen."

He knew it wasn't so. Much more—and much worse—could
happen. The idea of it crawled around inside him, scraping to
get out. Morgan closed his eyes and wished it away.

She kissed him and made him promise to call every night.
Morgan carried his wife's bags downstairs to Betty's bruised
'seventy-eight Chevy pickup and kissed her one last time before she crawled into the front seat. As the truck rumbled
casually away down shady Rockwood Street and disappeared
around the corner onto Main, Morgan already felt alone.

Nobody answered the phone at Old Bell Cockins' house.
Morgan let it ring more than a dozen times.

By now, he reasoned, the old editor probably knew about
the fire anyway. He'd spent fifty years with his finger on the
town's pulse. He didn't just stop caring about what happened.
Somebody in town would call him. He'd hear it on his police
scanner. He'd see the smoke from his majestic cupola. Hell,
maybe he'd just *know*. Old Bell was probably down there right
now, taking notes.

Morgan tried to fight off his fatigue. He'd been up more
than twenty-four hours. He went upstairs and took some aspi-

rin to tranquilize the drumming in his head. He lay back on the unmade bed, one foot on the floor to fool his body, if not his mind.

The morning sun streamed through the bedroom's skylight, its elongated symmetry sliding across the floor imperceptibly toward the bed. Morgan closed his eyes, still raw from smoke and dulled by exhaustion. Ghostly designs in the shape of reflected light drifted in the blackness behind his eyelids. He nestled his face in the cool pillows and smelled Claire's body beside him again.

Sleep took him without a fight.

And except for dark shapes that flew across his subconscious like the shadows of frightened birds, he didn't dream.

Morgan heard the thumping even before he awoke. It echoed in his empty sleep.

When he opened his eyes, the sunlight had filled the bedroom and he was sweating. His mouth was dry and his left arm, folded beneath his chest, was numb and bloodless.

Someone was pounding on the front door downstairs. Morgan glanced at the clock as he rolled out of bed. Two thirty-nine. He'd slept more than six hours, though it seemed only minutes to him.

He made his way stiffly down the stairs and opened the front door. Trey Kerrigan stood on the porch with two companions: a balding, moon-faced man in a yellow golf shirt embroidered with the State Fire Marshal's logo, and a cleancut Hispanic man in a dark suit and tie. Neither smiled.

The sheriff introduced them. The yellow golf shirt was Ray Forney, a state arson investigator from Cheyenne. The suit was Bruce Montoya, the sole ATF agent in Wyoming. Morgan shook their hands and invited them inside. He offered cold drinks, but they declined.

Trey Kerrigan sat on the edge of the long sofa, uncomfortable and grim. The two investigators sat on either side of him.

"Jeff, we've got a tentative ID on the body."

"Was it somebody from around here?"

The two investigators looked at their shoes. The sheriff cleared his throat.

"Jeff, it was Old Bell. I'm very sorry."

"What?"

"His wallet was still in his back pocket, underneath him. It was protected by his body and it didn't burn. Carter McWayne found it among the remains."

"Are you sure?"

"He's comparing dental records from Jake Switzer's office right now, but we're pretty sure. I'm really sorry, Jeff. I know what he meant to you."

"Jesus Christ ..." Morgan swallowed hard.

Old Bell must have been inside when the bomb exploded, just like the night Morgan found him there, lonely and alone. Morgan covered his eyes. He didn't want them to see him cry for his old friend and mentor.

"Can you tell me what happened?" he asked without looking at them.

"Are we off the record here?" asked Forney, the state arson investigator. Morgan noticed his unusually small hands were smudged black.

"Where the hell would I print the story if we weren't?"

Nonetheless, the dweebish Forney looked to his colleagues for assurance. Kerrigan consented with a patronizing nod.

"Looks to me like a fertilizer and fuel-oil bomb," he said. "It was a high-order blast and my gut tells me it was ammonium nitrate, some diesel and a simple fuse. Common ingredients, untraceable, big boom in a little package."

"Like Oklahoma City?"

"Same stuff," Forney said, his head bobbing comically. "In this case, small enough to carry, but big enough to bring down half a brick building. It detonated inside and ignited some flammable materials in the printing area, probably ink or solvents."

"Was it already there?" Morgan asked. "Did we just not see it?"

"There's a remote chance it was planted earlier and wired to a timing device, but I don't think so. You got a nice sized crater in a fairly open and conspicuous area of the floor, just a few feet from the back window of your building," Forney said. "Assuming your bomber had any brains at all, if he'd planted it deliberately, he'd have placed it more strategically, to do more immediate damage. Plus, two or three people came and went without seeing it. Personally, I think the bomb came in through the window and exploded right where it fell."

"A toss and run thing?" Morgan asked.

"Probably. We found a fairly large fragment of a five-gallon gas can in the debris."

Forney rubbed his tiny fingers together nervously. He was intimate with volatility, blast physics, chemistry and burn patterns; he wasn't so comfortable with soft tissue.

"And, uh, there was some shrapnel, um, some pieces of the same material we found imbedded in the, uh, body."

"Will you be able to trace this thing?" Morgan asked.

Forney's round face rumpled. "Maybe we'll get lucky and a witness or a feed-store clerk will come forward. We're sending the gas-can remnants to the ATF lab in Glynco, Georgia. Don't quote me on this, but it has all the markings of a militia-style bombing."

Morgan stared at his own hands. Like Forney, he couldn't wash off all the sooty stains, almost as indelible as printer's ink. Or a memory. Still, he tried to rub it away.

"And Old Bell was inside. A fluke. He wasn't supposed to be there," he told them.

Trey Kerrigan began to question him. "Do you have any idea why he was at the newspaper at that time of night?"

"He'd come down at night sometimes, after everybody left, just because he missed the place."

"Did you know he was there last night?"

"No. He'd never tell anybody. He was too proud. Christ, he was just in the wrong place at the wrong time."

"When did you leave last night?"

"After nine. I came home for dinner and was planning to go back to print some photos when I heard the explosion."

"Was anyone else around?"

"Nobody. Cal Nussbaum came back to pick up some pages after I left. He said he was there maybe fifteen minutes around nine-thirty, then went home. You can ask him, but he told me he didn't see anybody or anything unusual."

"And you ran downtown when you heard the explosion, a little after ten, right?"

Morgan thought about it. "Yeah, about then."

"Stayed all night?"

"The whole time. The firefighters will tell you. When I got back, I found the dog out back and the phone message on the machine."

"A deputy should have been here already to pick up the dog and examine the scene. Was there anything else you think we should know?"

"The tape. Did you listen to it?"

Montoya, the ATF agent, spoke. He was less animated than Forney, professional and concise. "We have it now, Mr. Morgan. The ATF will be very involved in this investigation. We'll analyze the tape in the next few days for voice characteristics and so forth."

"Have you contacted Jerry Overton in Chicago?"

"Yes," Montoya said. "He vouches for you. He said you reported some threats against you and, rest assured, we're investigating those. We've already had some intelligence on those individuals."

"You've talked to Malachi Pierce already?"

"Not yet. We'd wanted to round up a few more details before we went out to Wormwood," Kerrigan said.

"So am I still a suspect?" Morgan asked.

"Everybody's a suspect," the sheriff said. "But let's just say you're looking less and less likely."

After the investigators left, Morgan rummaged through unpacked boxes in his little room at the top of the stairs, the place he dreamed of putting all his books and someday writing his own. His laptop computer would come in handy until *The Bullet* could be rebuilt, but he needed it for something more pressing now.

Cassie's disks were still in his briefcase, rescued almost accidentally from the inferno. So was Kate Morning's only photograph of her dead daughter.

Morgan cleared the dirty dishes from the breakfast table and propped Aimee's picture against the sugar bowl. He plugged in the wall adapter for his IBM 760ED and began downloading all of Perry County's court data since 1962 into his laptop's ample hard drive, where once he'd pieced together the puzzle of P.D. Comeaux.

It took only an hour. Within another thirty minutes, he'd adapted his database software to the court records and was ready to search for the key to Malachi Pierce's demons.

First, he queried for the name "Pierce," just as he had asked Cassie Gainsforth's computer, Alyx, the day before. And again, his search produced nothing more than twenty-two unrelated hits, plus the locked case of Hosanna Pierce.

Morgan scrolled down and highlighted Hosanna's filename, then asked the computer to retrieve it. He expected his request to be rejected, but the computer whirred softly, ticking occasionally. Cassie might have unlocked all the sensitive data when she transferred it to disk. He got no lock-out message, no high-tech rebuff. A good sign.

Within half a minute, a screenful of data appeared. The once-secret case of Hosanna Pierce proved to be brief and undramatic, except for one detail:

On April 24, 1976, Malachi Pierce sought the court's per-

mission to commit his nine-year-old daughter, Hosanna, to
the state mental hospital. District Judge Harold Biggerstaff
scheduled hearings on Case No. 76-368J within the month
and appointed a lawyer to represent young Hosanna's interests in the matter.

Within ninety days, in midsummer, Judge Biggerstaff agreed
with a state psychologist's finding that the girl was moderately
disabled by Down's Syndrome, but exhibited no threat to herself, her family or the community. Neither the state's nor her
interests would be served by locking her up in a public asylum,
he wrote in his brief order. He denied her father's attempt to
warehouse her and ordered indefinite supervision at the request
of her court-appointed *guardian ad litem*.

That supervision ended an astounding nine years later, in
1985.

In that year, Hosanna Pierce turned eighteen ... and the
lawyer who'd successfully argued to keep her out of the insane
asylum retired. Simeon Fenwick.

Morgan now understood a small part of the hatred boiling in Malachi Pierce. If he believed Hosanna had been sent
by God as his punishment for some mysterious sin—and maybe
it was the murder of Aimee Little Spotted Horse—the courts
and Simeon Fenwick had ensured she would rise every morning in his house to remind him of it.

For two hours, Morgan queried the computer with dozens
of other relevant keywords, such as "Wormwood," "Fourth
Sign," "church," "arson," even "bomb," and found nothing
remotely related to Malachi Pierce. The digitized paper trail
was cold.

Fenwick would be no help. His lips were sealed as tight as
his ass. He wouldn't even admit his role in Hosanna's case,
and Morgan couldn't broach the subject without betraying
Cassie's confidence. Still, Morgan had found what he was
looking for: Fenwick's legal connection to Pierce. It just wasn't
all he'd hoped for, and it solved no mysteries.

It was an ironic legacy for a lawyer who'd had no children

of his own, but Morgan had never been able to divine the spark that burned inside most attorneys he'd known. For the moment, he was happy that Fenwick had stood up for Hosanna Pierce, who might still be moldering in the state asylum without his help. No matter what daily wretchedness she might endure at Wormwood Camp, Morgan was certain her life was better than if she were shut away and forgotten in a mental institution.

Aimee Little Spotted Horse, for one, hadn't been so lucky. Morgan looked at her photograph and traced his finger across her smile. In the end, nobody took her side, nobody stepped between her and death. Somebody should have been there for her, somebody ...

"Oh, Jesus," he whispered.

Morgan stood up so quickly his chair fell over. He glanced at his watch. It was almost five. He went to the phone table in the front hallway and fanned through Winchester's thin phone book, then hurriedly dialed a number.

It rang several times. Finally, a woman answered.

"ICU, please," he told her.

A nurse picked up.

"This is Jefferson Morgan. I'm calling about a patient, Neeley Gilmartin. Can I get an update on his condition?"

"Are you family?" the nurse quizzed him.

"No, but I am ... shit, I don't know what I am, I just need to know if he's okay."

He heard the nurse shuffling papers on the other end of the line. After a painfully long time, she came back.

"The doctor will have to contact you, Mr. Jefferson. We can't release any information."

"My name is Morgan. Jefferson Morgan. Is the doctor there?"

"She's been paged. If you'll give me your number, I'll have her call as soon as she can."

Morgan gave her his phone number and hung up. Then

he found Cassie Gainsforth's home number. A man answered. It was the Rev. Gainsforth.

"Hello, is Cassie there?"

"Who may I say is calling?"

"Jeff Morgan with *The Bullet.*"

"Good Lord, we're sorry to hear about your paper. We're praying for you, Jeff."

"Thanks, I need all the help I can get. But we'll be back better than ever. Really. Anyway, I just had a quick question for Cassie."

"Of course. Here she is."

Cassie got on the phone. "Hello?"

"Cassie, this is Jeff Morgan. I really hate to call you at home, but I need your help with a file."

"No problem, Jeff. Come in tomorrow and we'll dig it out."

"No, Cassie. It's urgent. I need to see something right away. I don't know what I'll find, but I need to know tonight."

"Are you sure you don't already have access to it?" she asked. He knew she was referring to the disks she'd made for him.

"No, it's older than that. Can you help?"

There was silence on the other end.

"Cassie?"

"I don't know."

"Cassie, they think Old Bell was killed in the fire. He meant a lot to me, and I know he meant a lot to you. Now I need your help to find out who killed him."

Morgan waited a long time before she spoke again.

"Later tonight," she said, her voice barely above a whisper. "Meet me at the back door of the courthouse at nine. Don't park nearby."

He agreed and they hung up.

As Morgan put the receiver back in its cradle, the phone rang, startling him. It was Dr. Snyder at the hospital.

"Mr. Gilmartin has stabilized, but he's still borderline," she said in a serious tone. "He's asked for you."

"He's awake?"

"From time to time. He's in severe pain and when he's conscious, he's in a kind of stupor."

"Have you taken off the restraints?"

"Yes, he's unstrapped. But it might not be long that he's conversant. Could be minutes. You might want to get down here pretty quick. He's drifting in and out."

"I'll be right there," Morgan promised. He was out the front door before the doctor heard the dial tone.

He had backed his Escort into the sloped driveway so he could push-start it, if he had to. He turned the key. When the car convulsed and gasped, he rolled it down the concrete drive into the street, put it in gear and popped the clutch. The engine grabbed and sputtered, but it kept running.

At the hospital, the receptionist at the front desk directed him to the intensive care unit, a suite of four rooms in the rural hospital's west wing. Past two pairs of swinging doors, Dr. Gail Snyder met him at the nurses' station and led him into one of the chaste cubicles where Neeley Gilmartin balanced unsteadily between life and death.

Gilmartin seemed even smaller now. Against the pure white pillow, his withered head looked like a rotting fruit under a transparent green oxygen mask. His eyes were closed, but Morgan could see his eyelids fluttering slightly, as if Gilmartin wanted to be awake, to cuss him for not being here, for not fulfilling his last request.

"Can he talk?" Morgan asked Dr. Snyder.

"Not too much."

Gilmartin's eyes opened slightly, then rolled back in their sockets until all Morgan could see was their undersides, which were not white but chicken-fat yellow. He raised his right arm toward his face, but it moved only a few inches and fell lifelessly across his chest. Beneath the mask, Morgan saw Gilmartin's lips moving.

"He's trying to talk," Morgan said. "Can you take off the mask for a second?"

Dr. Snyder removed Gilmartin's oxygen mask and Morgan leaned close. The old man smelled of decay, his breath like rotten meat.

"I'm here, Neeley," Morgan said.

The old man opened his eyes and tried to keep them focused on Morgan, but they floated behind their lids like bubbles on a drug-induced tide. He pursed his cracked lips in a dry circle, but nothing came out except his putrid breath.

"I don't understand," Morgan said, leaning closer.

Gilmartin strained. "Ho ... home," he said, his voice choked to a raspy hiss. His body shook with a convulsive cough as he used up what little air remained in his cancer-choked lungs.

Morgan looked beseechingly at the doctor for an answer, but she just as quickly looked away, shaking her head.

"You can't go home right now," Morgan said. "You have to get better. Then I'll take you home."

Gilmartin turned his face to the far wall, then rolled it back again in contempt. With death at hand, he was still fighting for something he could hardly remember. Freedom.

"I'm sorry, Neeley," Morgan said. "They won't let you go home yet."

The old man turned his head away and raised his feeble right hand. Its bony middle finger was extended defiantly at Morgan.

"I'll keep my promise," Morgan told him. "Do you hear me, Neeley? I'll keep my promise."

Gilmartin didn't respond. Morgan waited for a long time, hoping for forgiveness, but Gilmartin had lapsed again into unconsciousness. The doctor replaced his mask and led Morgan back into the hallway. They waited for the door to close behind them.

"How long?" he asked her.

"Two or three days max. We've got him heavily medicated right now, for pain. The cancer has spread, but it isn't in his brain, so as long as he's conscious, he should be more or less communicative."

"Will you let him go home with me to die?"

"Absolutely not."

"He doesn't want to die here. I promised I wouldn't let him die in a hospital."

"I'm sorry, Mr. Morgan. Under the circumstances, I can't authorize his release."

"What circumstances?"

"No family, no real home, no indication he'd get professional care. The paramedics told me he was living in a pig sty."

"It was a shit-hole, but to him, it was freedom. He spent most of his life under the control of other people and he doesn't want to die boxed in. He can stay with me until he goes. I'll hire somebody to help. I don't care. I'm the only family he's got. Please don't do this to him."

The doctor stood firm. "I'm sorry, but I can't."

"Is there anyone else I can talk to?"

Dr. Snyder's face turned an angry red. "So you want to go over my head?"

"If I have to."

"It won't make any difference, you know."

Morgan erupted. "You don't give a shit for that man in there. To you, he's a dead man right now. And as long as you keep him here, he might as well be dead."

"I resent that," Dr. Snyder said.

"Well, I'm sorry about that," Morgan said sarcastically. "Sorry all to hell. But you don't know anything about him that you don't get from a test tube or a machine."

"That's not fair. Our first job here is to prolong a life. I can't compromise that, and I can't allow him to be put in more pain than he's already suffering."

"Bullshit. You don't know his pain."

"No, I don't. But maybe you don't either."

"How do you want to die, Doctor Snyder? Did you ever ask yourself that? Do you want it to be on your terms or somebody else's?"

Dr. Snyder raised her hands in surrender, shaking her head. "Chief of staff. John Garner. He can overrule me."

She made a note on Gilmartin's chart and shoved it angrily in a steel cubicle on the nursing desk. She didn't look up.

"Where can I find him?" Morgan asked.

She delivered her answer to Morgan's question as she retreated down the hall, never bothering to turn around.

"Oh, somewhere on the Middle Fork of the Powder River, I think. He's one helluva fly-fisherman. He should be back here next week. I'll tell him you're looking for him."

Neeley Gilmartin would be dead before that and she knew it.

Defeated, Morgan went home. He called Claire in Winnetka and she begged him to let her come home in a few days so she could help him rebuild *The Bullet*. He promised to think about it and urged her to get some rest.

After they hung up, he dialed Bell Cockins' number again, as if the old man might answer the phone and prove them all wrong. It was like a bad dream. The old man couldn't be dead. To Morgan, he was immortal.

He let the phone ring twenty or thirty times, unanswered.

Time had lost its rhythm. Soon, the sun was going down and the empty house was a melancholy place. Morgan sat for a while on the porch, then walked downtown. Halogen floodlights illuminated the wreckage of *The Bullet* as workers dismantled the confusion of twisted metal and charred lumber, heaving it into dump trucks to be buried without ceremony at the county landfill. The yellow police tape fluttered in the evening breeze. Only the press was left standing, brazenly defiant against the setting sun.

Morgan picked up a brick and felt the weight of it. He mourned the loss of the old newspapers stored upstairs, all the machinery of community journalism, the place itself. He remembered what Old Bell told him: *A newspaper is printed here*. But no more.

Like *The Bullet* itself, Old Bell was gone. Morgan couldn't separate the two and, in the end, neither could fate. They died together.

Morgan tossed the scorched brick back onto the rubble. In a few minutes, it would be nine o'clock.

"This better be good," Cassie Gainsforth whispered as she let Morgan in the back door where the district court bailiff generally brought prisoners from the jail. Her hair was pulled back under a long-billed aviator's cap. She wasn't wearing her glasses, and her jeans hugged her long legs.

The dark, empty hallways of the courthouse reflected every sound. Morgan heard his shoes squeak on the polished floors.

Cassie's office was already unlocked but the lights were off. Inside the massive records vault, she closed the door behind them and turned on just one of the fluorescent overheads near the center of the room. The dim air was close, uncooled, as the light hummed and flickered.

"Damn janitors only replace these things when they go black," she complained. "Okay, so what do you need?"

"I want to see a file on Charlie Little Spotted Horse. A domestic abuse in nineteen forty-seven."

Cassie pulled out one of the ancient file drawers and flipped through the index cards. She stopped and studied one. "Didn't call it domestic abuse back then. Case number four-seven-dash-six-oh-one. Assault with a deadly weapon. Should be over there on the wall, about halfway up."

Morgan scanned the ratty manila folders, in chronological order with their tabs all color-coded by the type of case, until he found Case No. 47-601: the State of Wyoming vs. Charles Little Spotted Horse.

Morgan took down the folder and fanned the court papers across a wooden table.

According to the sheriff's affidavit, Charlie came home drunk and demanded that his wife give him money from the craft items she sold in town. When she refused, he hit her with a skillet, opening a bloody gash in her scalp. Eight-year-old Aimee rushed to help her mother and was also knocked unconscious when her father beat her with a broken broom handle. His choice of weapons elevated his crime to assault with a deadly weapon, a felony.

The crime would have gone unreported if one of Jack Madigan's ranch hands hadn't been camped nearby. He rode back to the big house the next day. Madigan himself called Deuce Kerrigan, who arrested Charlie three days later.

After three weeks in the Perry County Jail awaiting trial, Charlie pleaded guilty and was sentenced to a year in stir. But after only a month, Jack Madigan himself asked Judge Darby Hand to release Charlie into his custody, with a lengthy probation. Morgan knew that without Madigan's intercession, the court would have shown no mercy to a drunken Indian who nearly beat his family to death.

"What are you looking for?" Cassie asked him.

"I'm not sure," Morgan replied. "Anything and nothing."

He leafed through the sentencing order, hand-copied probation reports, even a contrite letter from Charlie himself, swearing off the booze that poisoned his mind and promising never to touch his child in anger again.

The last document in the file was a carbon copy of the judge's order releasing Aimee Little Spotted Horse from a court-supervised guardianship. It was hand-stamped, 2 August 1948, a year after the beating.

"What's this?" Morgan asked as he read the single sheet of carbon-smudged notice. Cassie read over his shoulder.

"It's the end of the little girl's guardianship," she said. "You don't see many of those in these old files."

"Why?"

"You kidding? Fifty years ago, we weren't as enlightened about such things."

"Child abuse?"

"The laws weren't so sophisticated in Wyoming back in those days. Most domestic violence was considered a private thing. Even when there was an arrest, family violence didn't get the kind of attention we give it today."

"So why would a judge appoint a guardian in this case?"

"I don't know for sure. If the judge were convinced there was an extraordinary reason to ensure the safety of the child, he might."

"Why this case, do you think?"

"I haven't got a clue. But it would take a pretty passionate argument. It would be awfully rare, from what I hear about old Darby Hand. The girls in the office say he raised a hand to his wife from time to time."

"Where would the original be?"

"The girl's parents would have been served with it. It should have been delivered the same day this copy went into the file."

"By whom?"

"It was a civil paper, like a subpoena. The sheriff, most likely."

Morgan looked around the stacks of files, some dating back nearly a hundred years.

"Would there be another file in this case?"

"What kind of file?"

"I don't know. A guardian file or something?"

Cassie looked closer at the judge's order dissolving Aimee's guardianship. "Yeah, there's a separate case number here, but it's probably sealed, like a juvenile case."

"Where?"

Cassie waved him off. "Oh no, Jeff. It's bad enough we're here doing this. God, it's bad enough I gave you the database. But if we break the seal on a closed file ..."

Morgan touched his finger to his lips to quiet Cassie. He spoke calmly. "I won't ask you to break the law, Cassie. But you should know that file might free an innocent man."

"You already owe me big time. No way."

"Okay," he said. "I'm sorry. We can go now."

He closed the file on Charlie's crime and started to walk out of the main vault.

"Wait," Cassie stopped him. "Would you do it if you were me?"

"For you personally, probably not. But would I do it to save a man's life?" Morgan asked her. "In a heartbeat."

She closed her eyes and wrestled with the conflict inside her. The balky fluorescent tube oscillated audibly over them for a long time before she spoke. "Give me the number again."

Morgan recited the number written on the order while Cassie wrote it down on a paper scrap.

"And the name?"

"Aimee Little Spotted Horse."

"Same year, right?"

"Right. 'Forty-seven."

"Wait here."

Cassie went to a second, smaller vault. She rotated its combination lock in a deliberate sequence, heaved open the heavy door and disappeared inside. Less than a minute later, she emerged, holding a thin yellow envelope in front of her. It was closed with a wax seal.

Morgan reached for it, but she pulled it away from him. "You have to swear you won't tell a soul you saw this," she said, a frightened look on her face. "I mean *ever*."

"Cassie, nobody will ever know."

A man's voice from the shadows startled both of them. "I'll know."

Trey Kerrigan leaned against the main vault's doorway. In one hand, he held a long, black flashlight. In the other, his father's black-handled revolver.

Cassie cursed under her breath and began to hyperventilate. A cold sweat beaded on the back of Morgan's neck and his heart pounded like thunder. He raised his hands in front of his chest, not in surrender, but in submission.

"Trey, hear me out before you get the wrong idea here," Morgan pleaded.

"This don't look good, friend," the sheriff said gravely.

"No, it doesn't," Morgan admitted, "but I can explain."

"You bet your ass you'll explain. You might want to start by explaining how breaking and entering is covered by the First Amendment."

"It's not that way, Trey."

"Oh no? In that case, maybe you'd like to show me the judge's order that says you can sneak in here after hours and unseal that file, huh?"

Morgan said nothing. Cassie began to tremble so badly she grabbed the back of a chair to steady herself.

"Goddammit, Jeff. You come back here from the big city and start stirring up shit," Kerrigan fumed. "You had to know you'd get splashed. You go on a fuckin' crusade to save some lying convict son-of-a-bitch and sell some newspapers. Now you're up to your brassy balls in deep shit. Why couldn't you just let sleeping dogs lie?"

The sheriff's gun was still pointed at Morgan's gut.

"Neeley Gilmartin didn't kill that little girl. I think I can prove it. That's why we're here. He didn't do it."

"So now my daddy's a Keystone Kop who couldn't collar a dog?" Kerrigan said angrily. His face was red. "Is that what you're saying, old buddy?"

Morgan shook his head. His tongue cleaved to the roof of his dry mouth. "No, Trey. Your dad was the best cop I ever knew. But maybe he got caught up in something that wasn't right."

Trey Kerrigan lurched toward them, his eyes infuriated. "You son of a bitch."

Cassie whimpered. Her knees buckled, but she held herself up by leaning against the table. She was praying silently. Morgan reached under her arm to hold her up.

"Trey, please," Morgan begged. "Put the gun away and let me show you something. We're no threat to you. Please."

"I'm not interested in more of your bullshit, Jeff," Trey snarled, angrier than before. "I want you to lie down on the floor and put your hands on the back of your head. Move."

"Trey ..."

"Now! Get down!"

Morgan sank to his knees, then lay flat on the cold tiles. He laced his fingers behind his head and watched the sheriff's shiny brown cowboy boots walk around behind him, out of his field of vision. "Look at the file, Trey," he said. "Just look at the file."

"Shut up!" Kerrigan barked at him. "You have the right to remain silent, you have the right ..."

"The file, goddammit! Open it!"

He felt the sharp steel of Kerrigan's gun crash against the back of his head, crushing his knuckles and smashing his face hard against the floor. A gash in his scalp welled with blood, but his skull would have been split wide open if his hands hadn't shielded the blow.

Blood trickled between his fingers into his hair. His nose was broken and his left cheekbone throbbed where it was driven into the tiles. His left eye quickly began to swell shut and he tasted blood from a deep cut in his mouth. Cassie was crying now.

"Keep your mouth shut for once and put your right hand behind your back," Kerrigan threatened, continuing to read Morgan's rights. "Anything you say can and will be used against you in a court of law ..."

Morgan was dazed. The metallic rattle of handcuffs seemed to echo from the distance. Muddled words piled up in his bloody mouth. "Trey, the file. Somebody ... somebody was there ... the day she disappeared. The file. Not Gilmar ... somebody ... else."

"Put your right hand behind your back. Now."

Morgan's tongue thickened and his voice trailed off.

"The paper. There was a paper ... in the file ... not delivered. Somebody took it. Didn't come forward. Maybe the last one ... to see her alive."

Except for the buzzing light above them, silence.

Kerrigan's boots walked away, where he couldn't see them.

Morgan heard papers shuffling. Blood was now dribbling across his temple and dripping onto the floor. The crimson puddle spread, congealing at the edge. He tried to flex his left hand, still behind his head, but it was numb and three of his fingers were broken. His hair was sticky.

"Who was it?" Kerrigan asked.

The edges of the room grew gray. Morgan felt dizzy. He swallowed the bloody spit in his mouth and closed his eyes.

Faces swirled on the movie screen in his head, faces he'd never seen and faces he'd never forget. The shadows behind the camera eddied like ghosts in a dark stream. Faces in all the violent colors of death. Faces from dusty folders and old newspapers. Faces from the fire. All of them, laughing at him.

"Who was it, damn you?" Kerrigan yelled. He was miles away now, his voice distant and unapproachable.

Morgan whispered a name, so softly no one could hear. So softly, he wasn't sure the sound got past his slack lips.

"Deuce," he murmured.

Then blackness fell over him.

CHAPTER SIXTEEN

Gray, painful dawn seeped through a small window high up on the jailhouse wall. Morgan's left eye was swollen shut, but the right one allowed in enough of the dim light to ignite an excruciating spasm deep in his brain.

His tongue was parched and shriveled because he couldn't breathe through his nose. It stuck to his flypaper lips and the inside of his cheek until it found enough saliva to wet itself. The old blood in his mouth tasted like brass.

He clamped his good eye shut until the throbbing in his head subsided. When he opened it again, he saw Trey Kerrigan sitting on the bed across the jail cell, watching him.

"Morning, sunshine," the sheriff said. His tie was draped across a chair and his bloodied uniform shirt was unbuttoned at the collar, a tuft of dark hair showing at his neck. "You alive?"

"What time?" Morgan whispered hoarsely.

"Six."

Morgan groaned and closed his eyes. A sparkling filament of light danced behind his eyelids, as if he were watching a bad memory glimmer across an airless synapse.

"I brought you down here and cleaned you up," Kerrigan said. "Jail nurse come down and put a couple stitches in the back of your head, no extra charge."

Morgan covered his face with his arm and said nothing. A long finger of pain scraped his neck as he tried to turn his head toward the wall.

"You were in and out all night, talkin' to yourself. A couple times, I thought you were awake and you'd drift off again. Nurse says you got a few busted fingers and probably a mild concussion."

Morgan's throat was dusty. His voice sounded like two flat rocks being scraped across each other. "You stayed?"

"Yeah. I stayed here with you."

"Cassie?"

"She went straight home last night. Don't worry. She's a little shook up but she'll be okay."

Somewhere down the corridor, another prisoner grunted, then vomited forcefully. The sickening sound reverberated in the hot closeness of the basement jail.

"Well, Arly's up," Kerrigan said. "That boozer will be wantin' breakfast, soon as he finds his teeth in the bottom of the crapper."

Morgan squinted and looked at the man who'd once been his best friend. In the past day, he realized just how long ago it had been. "Why?"

"'Cause he upchucked 'em."

"Why did you hit me?"

Kerrigan paused but made no effort at apology or explanation. "Can I get you some eggs and bacon? A roll? Coffee? We got a regular all-you-can-eat buffet, as long as you like eggs and doughnuts."

"You lost it."

The sheriff rubbed his tired eyes. He didn't look up. He just spoke toward the floor. "You remember how when we were kids, we'd ride our bikes out Wilkerson Road in the summer and hunt for dust devils?"

"For Christ's sake, Trey ..." Morgan mumbled.

"You always told me that if I jumped in the eye of a dust

devil, it'd just blow itself out. Remember that? Like its life came from the center. Like any little boy had the power to snuff out a prairie cyclone if he just knew where to stand. Remember?"

"What's your point?"

"I always thought I knew where to stand. I never thought I'd get sucked up in this whirlwind. It was like things were swirlin' too fast all around me and I got scared. The election, you comin' back to town, this little girl's murder, and now the bomb. There I was, right in the eye of it, and the dust devil didn't blow itself out, goddammit. It sucked me dry."

"The election?"

"Yeah, mostly. This job is the only thing I ever dreamed of. When you brung up this old case, I got all defensive about my dad. I felt betrayed by you. I just sort of dug in my heels until I was in over my head."

"You sicced Switzer and Tasker on me, didn't you?"

"I only wanted to put the fear of God in you. That's all. I needed time. I didn't want this old murder case fuckin' everything up."

"But you should have wanted justice done. You forget about that?"

Kerrigan couldn't look up. "I guess I did."

"Why?"

"Part of me couldn't believe my father might have been wrong about this guy. The other part of me didn't want anyone else to think it, either. It got so dark, I lost my way, Jeff."

Morgan's old friend had betrayed him. That hurt worse than any physical wound he'd inflicted. "The paper. Was that part of the plan, too?"

"No, that wasn't me. Swear to God. You gotta believe me. No rough stuff, just mind games."

"Then what was last night? A tea party? You held a gun on me, for Christ's sake. You scared the shit out of me."

"You scared me, too. I thought maybe I killed you there for a minute. But I was wrong. I wasn't myself."

"No, you were a total asshole."

The sheriff chuckled self-consciously. "You always had a way with words, my friend. But you're right. I was an asshole."

"A total asshole."

"Total. I'm sorry."

"What the hell were you thinking?"

"I wasn't thinking at all, Jeff. I was just outta my head. I wouldn't blame you if you didn't forgive me, but I'm sorry from the bottom of my heart. I'm ashamed of what I did. My dad would whup my ass good if he was here."

There was a long silence between them. A steel door opened down the corridor and Morgan heard unintelligible voices before it closed again.

"What are the charges?"

"What charges?"

"Against me."

"You're not under arrest."

Morgan was astonished. His last conscious memory before waking up in jail was being pistol-whipped and handcuffed in the courthouse vault. "I can go? Just walk right out of here?"

"Not yet."

"What the hell do you mean?"

Kerrigan stood up and tossed a manila folder on Morgan's belly. "Read this and clean up a little bit, then I'll take you home."

"What is it?"

"The investigative file on Gilmartin. There's an autopsy report in there, some interview notes, affidavits, photos, stuff that was never made public."

"Deuce kept this?"

"You're probably the only other person who ever saw it, besides me. The defense never even got this material."

Morgan rolled onto his side and fumbled with the folder, but his broken fingers were splinted in rigid plastic tubes and wrapped in sterile tape. He had trouble opening it. "Like what?"

"Well, the girl had a little locket that was never found. Could be at the bottom of the Black Thunder River, but in case her killer kept a souvenir, it was kept quiet."

"Anything else?"

"Her body was in bad shape, but the doc said she was probably raped. Her vagina was badly ripped, deep inside. Serious injury, but not likely from the river. If there was semen, it had decomposed."

The possibility Aimee had been raped had always haunted Morgan. He was not surprised. He tried to put her little face out of his mind.

He couldn't turn the pages in the folder, so he spread them across the blanket. He caught a glimpse of grisly, black-and-white autopsy photos, now faded brown and crisp to the touch. But even if they'd been more sharply focused and in color, he couldn't have recognized the bloated mass of water-logged flesh as Aimee.

"Just give me the quick summary," he stated. He was flustered by his painful disability, sickened by the pictures in the file.

Kerrigan walked out the open cell door and stood in the corridor outside, buttoning the collar of his uniform blouse. The dried blood on it was Morgan's.

"Bottom line? Your guy probably didn't do it."

Morgan bolted upright on the jail bed. "What?"

"Almost thirty years ago, my dad sent a letter to the judge, saying he'd uncovered new evidence in the case that, at the very least, should mean a new trial for Gilmartin."

"What evidence?"

"Those two witnesses who said they heard Gilmartin threaten the girl's father in a bar fight? They lied."

"Why?"

"Gilmartin had been stealing cows for months and selling them at the South Dakota feedlots. The big ranchers had their suspicions. Of course, one of them decided he didn't need the law to punish a cow thief. These two boys worked for him. It was all a set-up."

"Who was it?"

"Jack Madigan."

Morgan was stunned.

"I'll be damned. Jack Madigan? Are you sure?"

"My dad busted one of those cowboys on a statutory rape charge in the late 'sixties. He cut a deal by spillin' his guts on the Gilmartin frame-up. A couple weeks after the girl was killed, he and Madigan come up with this story. Pretty damn cold-blooded, but there wasn't gonna be no more rustlin' on the Sun-Seven."

Aimee's photograph flashed through Morgan's mind. He saw her in her pretty white Sunday dress, the one she was buried in. He saw Bobby Madigan, the lonely boy who grew up to be known as Buck. But the face behind the camera, the face he couldn't see, was Jack Madigan's.

"How'd they know Gilmartin wouldn't have an alibi?"

"Turns out they'd been at the same bar on the day of the murder. He was drunk on his ass the whole time, passed out in the corner."

"They could have just beat the shit out of him as a warning."

"What they did was worse than any beating. They took away his life without ever layin' a finger on him."

The cowboy's hand-written affidavit, dated eleven-four-'sixty-nine, was in the file. Morgan read it quickly as his grim astonishment transformed to anger.

"Jesus Christ, why didn't the judge order a new trial?"

"The second worst kind of politics: Friendship. Darby Hand served in the state legislature with Adhamh Madigan back in the Thirties, before he was a judge. They were real close and he wasn't about to put a Madigan in jail for suborning perjury. They had nothin' else. He tore up my dad's letter."

"But Gilmartin's threat against Charlie was their whole case. Without it, Gilmartin goes free."

"You can see how the old man was satisfied a certain twisted justice had been served: Gilmartin had already confessed his crime, and his accuser, an admitted liar, was going to prison, too. From where the judge sat, all the bad guys got what was comin' to them. But it didn't make any difference."

"Why's that?" Morgan asked.

"Jack Madigan died a month later and his cowboy got shanked his first week in prison. Seems he wasn't in a romantic mood. Dead men make bad witnesses."

"If Gilmartin didn't do it, who did?"

"I don't know."

Morgan's suspicion took a sharp new turn. "Could Madigan have been covering up a murder?"

"We'll never know. Maybe. Then again, maybe he was just an opportunist, looking to plug a varmint predator. Either way, he was a damn smart fella."

"How long have you known all this?"

"Since you asked me for the file. It was in my dad's private papers, stuck in a box in my cellar."

"Why the hell didn't you do something?"

"By the time I knew, Gilmartin was already out of prison. He wasn't gonna live long enough for the county attorney to file a motion, much less for another trial. Wasn't much more I could have done for the guy."

"You could have cleared the man's name in two minutes. No fucking press releases or legal briefs. Clean. Why didn't you?"

The sheriff pursed his lips and stared at the floor, like a little boy caught in a big lie. "The worst kind of politics," he demurred. "Money. If it wasn't for Buck Madigan, my campaign wouldn't have two nickels to rub together. Gilmartin was gonna die and the whole goddamned whirlwind was goin' to disappear if I just stood my ground. I only needed to stall you until the old man died and the whole thing would go away."

Morgan's gut was twisted in a knot. Gilmartin came to him seeking redemption, but found doubt. He'd been offered the uncommon chance to change one man's life—the only thing he'd ever really yearned to do as a newspaperman—and he'd walked away from it. Now, Gilmartin might die never knowing. Hell, Morgan wasn't even sure if the old man had survived the night. He wanted to vomit.

"So why are you telling me now?"

"Because I got a scoop for you. I'm finished. I'm pullin' out of the sheriff's race."

"Oh, shit."

"When I was a kid, I only wanted to be like my dad. He happened to be the sheriff, so I wanted to be the sheriff, too. But last night, while I laid there in that bed and prayed to God I hadn't killed my best friend, I knew I wasn't like my dad at all."

Morgan swung his legs to the side of the bed and looked for his shoes. "Trey, listen to me. This thing isn't over. I think the killer is still alive."

"Alive? Here? How do you know?"

"There's no time to explain. I need your help now, more than ever."

"Sure. What do you need?"

"I need you to take me home, then you've got to find out who delivered that judge's order in the file we were looking at last night. Check the number. It was issued on the same day Aimee disappeared: August second, nineteen forty-eight."

"Who the hell you think I am? Barney Fife?" the sheriff asked indignantly. "I already looked."

"And?"

"Our logs say the paper was delivered by Wes Crockett, a deputy back then."

"The old guy who used to bust up the beer parties with the dogs? What do you know about him?"

"Boy Marine, straight arrow. Enlisted in the Corps when he was fifteen and saw action all over Hell. Never got a scratch. By the time my dad hired him as a deputy right after the

Second World War, they say he was already an old man, all of twenty-one."

"Could he be involved?"

"Wes Crockett? No way. Real quiet and soft-spoken for a grunt. Never talked about the war. He was the one that convinced my dad we needed a canine unit, so they called him Deputy Dawg. Forty years he worked here, then just decided that was enough."

"Is he still alive?"

Kerrigan huffed. "Christ, Jeff. Give me some credit, will ya? Yeah, he's still alive. Retired back in 'eighty-five. He took his dogs and bought himself a cabin somewhere on the Oregon coast. No phone. I got the local county mounties tryin' to contact him right now."

"Do your logs say who got the paper? If Kate and Charlie were out riding fence, your deputy sure didn't give it to them."

"The logs don't say. If Wes Crockett can't remember, we're screwed. I expect to hear back any time now."

Morgan stood up. Blood pulsed against the fresh gash in his scalp. Suddenly, he was light-headed, unsteady.

"Whoa, you better sit down 'til you get your sea-legs," Kerrigan said, taking a step toward him.

"I'm okay," Morgan reassured him, taking a deep breath and shaking the cobwebs out of his brain. "I have to get moving."

"Where are you gonna be if I hear from Crockett?"

"I'll be at the hospital," Morgan said. "Do yourself a favor: Pray that Gilmartin is still alive."

The sheriff dropped him at the curb in front of his house and sped away. Morgan went inside, changed his blood-stained clothes and called the hospital. A nurse in ICU told him Gilmartin was indeed still alive, but failing fast.

He searched frantically for his car keys and remembered, finally, he'd left them in the Escort.

The car sputtered churlishly, refusing to turn over. Morgan held his breath and gritted his teeth as he pumped the accelerator, hard. It defied him openly. His broken fingers ached as he wrestled with the key. He pressed the entire weight of his animosity on the pedal before the engine finally caught.

"Fuck you," he cursed, and wished it had been parked only a few feet closer to the explosion at The Bullet. It would have been a delightful casualty.

He found a parking place on a downhill slope in the hospital's near-empty lot and backed in, in case he needed a helping hand from gravity to push-start the sinister little shitbox.

The receptionist stared at Morgan as he hurried through the door, headed determinedly toward the intensive care wing. An ICU nurse stopped him briefly in the corridor, but Dr. Snyder came out of Neeley Gilmartin's room before Morgan could push his way past her.

"What the hell happened to you?" she asked, surveying his damaged face under the bright lights of the hallway.

"You should see the other guy," he said.

"Your eye needs some attention."

Morgan brushed her off. "Is he conscious?"

"He's floating."

"Can he hear me?"

"Maybe."

"I need to tell him something and I need to know he heard."

Dr. Snyder glanced at the large clock on the nurses' station wall. It was not yet eight AM. "He's heavily medicated right now. The pain is getting worse. We've got him on a morphine drip," She glanced at his chart. "He is awake less and less now."

"Can he still talk?"

"He's been unresponsive. He hasn't tried to communicate since you were here yesterday. His brain is diverting all its energy and resources to keeping his body alive. And, without the morphine, he'll be in great pain."

"I want to see him."

Morgan went in. The air in the room was repulsive. Gilmartin's face, shriveled beneath his oxygen mask, was turned away from the door. But Morgan could hear his unnatural breathing.

Morgan sat down beside the bed and touched the old man's frail hand. It was cold. "Neeley. It's Jeff. Can you hear me?"

Gilmartin didn't move. Morgan looked at the doctor, then spoke again, squeezing the old man's hand a little harder, until his own wounded hand hurt.

"Neeley, I have news. Please ..."

Nothing.

"Maybe later," Dr. Snyder said.

"There's no time," Morgan said. "He's waited too long already."

The old man's chest jerked involuntarily with each breath, starved for air. Morgan recognized its face. Death was at hand.

"Maybe in a few hours. We can reduce the morphine drip and maybe he'll rise back to the surface. I'm sorry."

Morgan buried his head in his arms against Gilmartin's bedrail. For a long time, there was only the invariable pulse of the machines that kept him alive.

"Is he dreaming?"

"I don't know. Maybe, if he's in a dream sleep."

"The morphine doesn't kill his dreams?"

"No, not necessarily."

"Do you dream?"

The personal question caught Dr. Snyder by surprise. She crossed her arms across her breasts as an unconscious sign of her uneasiness. "How do you mean?"

"When you sleep."

"Of course. Why?"

"What if you didn't? What if sleep was just another form of death, all black?"

"Sleep is also an escape from pain. It's not death, but life without all the hurt."

Dr. Snyder's beeper interrupted them. "I have to go," she said.

"Can I wait?"

"Certainly," she said as she left. Her voice had softened.

For twenty minutes, he held Gilmartin's hand. He wasn't particularly religious, but he prayed briefly to a God he had lost faith in. He thought about his son, Bridger, and wept. But Gilmartin never stirred.

"Mr. Morgan?" a voice whispered from the door. A nurse had stuck her head inside.

"Yes?"

"There's a call at the desk for you."

He followed her across the corridor and she pointed to an unhooked receiver on the counter. It was Trey Kerrigan.

"How's the old guy?"

"He's alive. Barely. What do you have?"

"Not a hell of a lot. A Coos County deputy found Wes Crockett walkin' his dogs on the beach and patched him through on the car phone."

"He remember anything?"

"At first, he just laughed. The old fart said he couldn't recall what he had for lunch yesterday, much less fifty years back."

"Shit."

"But just talkin' about the murder must have jiggered his memory. He said the first time he ever saw that shack was when he went out to help look for the girl after she disappeared. He never met the parents until that night. He never took the paper out to the ranch."

"He's sure about that?"

"Wes Crockett was born sure."

"So who got the paper?"

"Hold on," Kerrigan said, cupping his hand over the mouthpiece. When he came back, there was frustrated urgency in his voice. "Goddammit, I gotta take this call. Long distance. Hang around there a few minutes. Don't move. I'll call right back."

The phone clicked, its dial tone a monotonous flatline.

The red second hand on the hospital clock swept smoothly and inexorably around its face, too slow for Morgan, too fast for Gilmartin. He couldn't stop it, and he couldn't speed it up. He watched it circle more than three times, an eternity and an instant, before the phone pulsed softly again.

The nurse pushed a blinking button to answer the call, then handed him the receiver.

Kerrigan was on the line again. He spoke deliberately, as if he were sorting it out himself as he talked. "That was Crockett calling back. Damned if he didn't make that deputy get me back on the line."

"What's going on?"

"Somethin' funny. He told me he always put the recipient's initials in the log. I looked and, sure as hell, there's two little letters under that entry on August second, nineteen forty-eight. But neither one of us could match 'em up with anybody in the case."

"What are they?" Morgan asked.

"Looks like ST," the sheriff said. "Maybe SF. Wes woulda flunked penmanship for sure. Anyway, it could be somebody long gone."

There was a prolonged silence. Morgan closed his eyes and tried to see a name he recognized. His lips formed silently around each one. "Oh, God," he said, his eyes popping wide.

"What is it?" Kerrigan said.

"SF," he said. "It's Simeon Fenwick."

"Fenwick?"

"He must have been Aimee's guardian ad litem. Oh, Jesus. He was there that day. His name would have been in that sealed file."

Kerrigan was still confused. "Fenwick?"

"Trey, I don't have time to tell you everything I know, but you need to get a favor from your buddy Ham Tasker down at the bank."

"What?"

"Find out if Fenwick has made any big cash transactions, more or less regularly, just before August second every year. Check for wires, withdrawals, transfers of any kind. Go back ten years or so."

"What the hell for?"

"I'll explain later. Just do it! Then wait for me to call."

"Where the hell are you going?"

"I'm coming back into town," he said. "I have to pick up something at my house. Just go."

Morgan lied. He wasn't going home.

Simeon Fenwick's modest house was on the southern edge of town. A veil of meticulously groomed poplars obscured his life from anyone who might pass.

The driveway was a narrow gravel path between two dense lilac hedges, and Morgan didn't see it until he'd already passed. He hit the brakes and shifted into reverse, but popped the clutch too soon. The Escort died in the middle of the street and refused to start again. Cursing, Morgan left it and walked up to the house.

Fenwick's new, champagne-beige Buick Century was parked in the morning shade on the west side of the house and the garage door was open. A small sprinkler sputtered in one corner of the freshly mowed lawn.

Morgan rang the doorbell. A moment passed before Simeon Fenwick opened the door, long enough for him to start the micro-cassette recorder in his shirt pocket. The old lawyer was wearing a crisp white shirt, natty red suspenders and a tartan-plaid bow tie. He seemed surprised to see Morgan on his sunny porch.

"Well, good morning, Mr. Morgan," he said. "I was expecting the lawn boy. He was here this morning, and did a dreadful job of gathering the clippings. Children today seem to have little regard for quality work. However, it's a pleasant surprise to see you again."

Morgan glanced at the broad expanse of grass behind him and saw nothing unusual.

"I am very sorry to hear about your newspaper," Fenwick continued. "I will miss it."

"I need to speak with you, Mr. Fenwick."

"Please come in."

Fenwick's house was painstakingly neat, uncluttered by the things that might define him. There were no magazines on the coffee table, no family pictures on the wall, no rumpled rugs, worn rockers or fading flowers in Mason jar vases. There were no telltale odors of breakfast or even oil soap on the polished hardwood floors, no sounds other than the wooden tapping of a magnificent grandfather clock in the hallway. The space was as sterile as the man.

"Coffee?" Fenwick offered first, but then apologized. "Forgive me. As I recall you drink tea, but I'm afraid I have none of the artificial sugar you favor."

"Nothing, thanks."

"Please sit," Fenwick said, staring at Morgan's bandaged hands. "It looks as though you've had an awful accident."

"Oh, I just got my fingers caught where they didn't belong."

"That can be painful. At any rate, what can I do for you this morning?"

Fenwick sat on a princely wingback chair without seeming too comfortable in it. Morgan sat on the edge of the couch.

"Mr. Fenwick, I just have a few questions about the murder of Aimee Little Spotted Horse."

"As I said at our luncheon, there's not much I can talk about. I'm sorry, but I hope you understand."

Morgan laced his splinted fingers together. His palms were sweating. "You see, I need to understand something about the day she disappeared."

"Then you should consult with your friend, the sheriff, about such investigatory details."

"I've done that and I was surprised to discover that you were Aimee's court-appointed guardian in an unrelated case. How is it possible that you also could represent her alleged killer?"

The old lawyer took off his round glasses and cleaned them nervously with a white handkerchief. His hands trembled. "It's a very small town, Mr. Morgan, as you know. Very simply, the judge had few choices. No other attorney wanted Mr. Gilmartin for a client. His was a futile case."

"But you did, even though you had the best reason of all to walk away from it. A potential conflict."

"Through no fault of my own, I assure you, my previous history with the girl was apparently overlooked. And at the time of her death, I was not her guardian."

"How's that?"

"The guardianship had ended."

"When exactly?"

Fenwick face was drawn, beginning to pale. It wasn't the question he expected. "I don't know."

"A month before? A week before? Give me a ballpark estimate."

"It was a very long time ago. I don't remember."

It was Morgan's only ace and he feared he was playing it too early. "I know. Shall I tell you?" Fenwick nodded. "The judge issued the order the same day Aimee disappeared. The same day."

"What a tragic coincidence. I wasn't aware of that."

"Really? Now that's interesting. A deputy says he handed you the order to deliver to her parents."

"That's simply not true."

Morgan looked around the immaculate room. "That's what sticks in my craw. That little piece of paper. That wouldn't be like you, Mr. Fenwick. Not like you at all. It would be highly irregular to leave such an important thing unresolved, wouldn't it? Very messy."

Fenwick's breathing quickened. "You can prove none of this poppycock."

"I'm not a lawyer, Mr. Fenwick. I'm not even a cop. I'm just a reporter asking some questions. I don't even have a paper where I can print a story. So we're just talking here. What is it I can't prove?"

"I'd like you to leave now."

Morgan pushed ahead. "See, I'm just wondering what happened out there. I thought maybe you could help."

"Nothing happened."

"Something happened. A little girl was raped and murdered."

Fenwick nestled deeper into his chair. His whole body seemed smaller, as if he were moving farther and farther away from Morgan. "It wasn't like that," he said.

"What was it like?"

"Please go!"

"Did she cry?"

"Get out!"

"She was pretty, wasn't she?"

"She was a little girl, for God's sake."

"But you liked little girls, didn't you? You asked the judge to give you all those cases. Poor, sad little girls who wanted to believe in somebody. They wanted to be loved by somebody, anybody. You were their only friend."

"I was their attorney."

"You made them believe you were going to help them. To make all the hurt go away. That they were loved."

"I did help them."

"I understand."

"You don't understand at all."

"I understand how we all need to feel close to someone. I understand how it feels to be pushed away. I understand how easy it would be to just care a little too much, to touch them ..."

"Absolutely not!"

"You didn't care for these poor kids? You didn't hug them when they cried? Maybe they misunderstood your affection."

"Sometimes," Fenwick said, but he quickly caught himself. "But there was nothing to misunderstand. They were confused."

The grandfather clock chimed once. Eight-thirty.

"Confused about what, Mr. Fenwick? Help me understand."

"They were troubled children. Some of them entertained fantasies. They were wild, uncontrollable children who needed discipline."

"Like Aimee?"

"Yes, for one."

"You went out there to the ranch, didn't you? Aimee was alone. And something happened."

Beads of sweat glistened on the thin skin of Fenwick's bald head. The blood had gone out of his face.

"What happened out there? Did you touch her? Was she confused?"

"You're wrong."

"I don't think so," Morgan said calmly.

"You weren't there."

"But you were, weren't you?"

Something inside Fenwick gave way. He put a shaky hand over his chest. His shoulders collapsed and Morgan believed for a moment that he was having a heart attack. Then he saw tears in the old lawyer's pained eyes. "Yes," Fenwick said.

Morgan breathed out and hung his head. It took a few seconds to sink in.

"What happened?" he asked.

Fenwick began to weep in low, keening sobs. He could barely speak. "It shouldn't have been me."

"What do you mean?"

"The deputy should have delivered the document. It shouldn't have been me."

"But it was you."

"I didn't mean to harm her."

"What happened?" Morgan pressed him gently.

"She was there alone. She was making something with flowers on the porch when I drove up. She ran to me and hugged me around the legs, and her face ..." A frightened sob seeped from him. His hand circled over his groin area. "I had never touched her. Never. Not like the others. You must believe that."

"I do."

"She aroused me. I was losing control. I asked after her parents, but she told me they weren't there and she took me into her little house to show me her little things. That little girl wanted to sit on my lap."

He won't say her name, Morgan thought. He looked away as Fenwick forced himself to retell the story.

"I touched her soft brown skin and I was overpowered by it. I began to undress her. She struggled and I pushed her down on the bed. She began to scream. Oh, my God, why did she have to scream?" Fenwick covered his mouth as if to hold the horror back, but he couldn't. "She was so small. It must have been excruciating, but I couldn't stop myself. I was out of my head. She kept screaming, even more as I forced myself into her. I held a pillow over her face until I was finished."

"You smothered her?"

"I didn't mean it. I didn't know she was hurt until ... I saw blood on myself as I pulled out of her and I knew I had hurt her badly inside."

He stared at his wizened hands, now shaking uncontrollably. "She wasn't breathing. I tried to wake her up, but she wouldn't. I was frightened out of my mind. I didn't know what to do. I dressed her again and put her in my car to take her to the hospital, but I came to the turn-off back to town and I stopped. I crawled into the back seat to try once more to revive the little girl, but I was sure she was dead. She wouldn't wake up. Her lips were blue. Blood had soaked her pants."

Say her name, goddamn you, Morgan wanted to shout.

"I panicked. I didn't want anyone to know about ... what I had done. I wanted to take her back to town, if I could save her, but she was dead already. So I turned the other way, toward the Iron Mountain Bridge."

"And you threw her off."

"The water was high. When I was certain nobody was nearby, I carried the body to the rail and pushed it over. I couldn't bear to watch it fall."

"The coroner said Aimee was probably alive when she went into the water. She wasn't dead, was she?"

"I thought she was, you must believe me. I have lived a nightmare for almost fifty years, knowing that I made the wrong turn at that crossroad. I might have saved her life, but lost my own."

"Didn't you think somebody would find her eventually?"

Fenwick shook his head feebly. "When they did, I was mortified. I was ready to surrender and throw myself on the mercy of the court. But when they arrested Gilmartin, the whole plan came to me. It seemed so perfect."

"You volunteered to represent him."

"Yes. Nobody else would. If I had to, I would lose his case and let him pay the price. But he made it unnecessary by pleading guilty to avoid an execution. In the end, I did nothing before the bar to betray him. I could have, but I didn't."

Morgan choked back his anger. "You betrayed him by not doing everything you could to save his life. You let him spend his life paying for a crime you committed. You didn't just kill Aimee, you killed Neeley Gilmartin, too. He just hasn't hit the water yet."

"He did nothing to save himself. A man must take responsibility for his own actions."

"How about you? Will you stand up and take responsibility for the murder of Aimee Little Spotted Horse?"

Fenwick managed a relieved little smile as he wiped his

eyes. He was unburdened. "I already have. I have made my compensation under the customs of my ancestors."

"How's that?"

"The Crows believe an accidental death can be atoned by requital. Simple payments. Under blood law, I have given my money, nearly all of it, to the girl's mother and to Gilmartin to redress my sin."

"You're a lawyer, not a Crow Indian," Morgan corrected him. He was aghast. "You know the customs of our culture, and you know you can't make it go away with money."

"Don't be naive, Mr. Morgan. Especially in this culture, money makes many things go away."

"Not this. Not guilt."

Fenwick arched his eyebrows, then slumped in defeat. "Indeed. You have won. If you will call your friend, the sheriff, I will tell him everything I have just told you, and much more."

"More?"

"Oh my, yes. The other children through the years. After the accident, I was frightened, but I couldn't stop myself. There have been so many, although none suffered the same tragic fate. Rest assured, they all survived and they're all grown women now. I am certain they would confirm what I tell you: I did not force them to do anything."

"Hosanna Pierce, too?"

Fenwick's dead eyes closed. He nodded.

It all made sense now, but it turned Morgan's stomach. No wonder Fenwick had so aggressively sought the role of court-appointed guardian. It had given him extraordinarily secret access to his young victims, most of them in troubled homes and chaotic family situations. They were the easiest victims for sexual predators, most of whom used their authority to befriend and establish trust with the child before stealing their innocence.

"I'm sure he'll want to hear about those," Morgan said.

"And the explosion at your newspaper."

"That was you?"

"I saw Malachi Pierce's flyer in the diner. I knew with a little help, you would suspect him immediately. And if it worked as a scare tactic, you'd drop this inquiry. Clearly, you're a man on a passionate mission."

"You blew up *The Bullet?*" Morgan asked incredulously.

"Oh no, not I. It was a terrible little man who will do anything for money. He owed me a favor. I didn't have the stomach for such violence myself. And I am very sorry about your dog. That wasn't part of the plan. My 'employee' was improvising and got carried away. Now, if you'd be so kind to call the sheriff, the phone is on the desk in the library, just down the hall to the right."

Morgan stood up and walked slowly down the hall to a small office lined with law books. An old-fashioned rotary phone sat atop the polished desk, with only a banker's lamp and a fresh green blotter. He reached inside his pocket and turned off his tape recorder.

Using his unbroken left index finger, he awkwardly dialed Trey Kerrigan's number and waited as he was transferred by the receptionist. The sheriff came on the line.

"Trey, this is Jeff."

"Hey, you were right about the money. Fenwick has made several big wire transfers from a New York brokerage in the last week of July every year for about ten years. Sometimes twenty thousand bucks. This year, it was ten thousand."

"It's blood money. The son of a bitch has been paying Gilmartin and the girl's mother for years, just to salve his conscience. It was always on the day of Aimee's murder, August second."

"Well, he must have forgot to check his calendar. He closed out his personal account yesterday, the sixth. Fifteen thousand bucks. He picked it up himself in cash."

"That would be what he paid to blow up *The Bullet*."

"How the hell ... ?"

"I'm already here, Trey. He confessed. I've got it on tape. Get over here quick."

Morgan hung up. He went back to the living room to wait with Fenwick.

But the old man was gone.

Before Morgan realized what was happening, he heard Fenwick's Buick peeling down the driveway, fishtailing on the loose gravel. By the time he was out the front door, the car had hit the street and sped away.

Morgan sprinted across the lawn and plunged through the protective hedgerows. He leaped into the Escort and turned the key.

The ignition clicked a few times, then went dead. He horsed the gear shift and tried again.

Nothing.

"You motherfucker!" he screamed at it, pounding the steering wheel. He stomped the accelerator pedal and tried the key again, but the car showed no life.

Frustrated and seething, Morgan stripped off the plastic splints on his fingers. Shifting to neutral, he jumped out of the car and heaved his body against the door frame. His legs burned as the car inched forward, picking up speed gradually. He pushed for one long, flat block, finally leaping inside and shifting into second gear while he popped the clutch, and praying Fenwick had not gotten away.

The engine rolled over and, after a few erratic spurts, roared to life.

He spun the little car around in the street and squealed across the black asphalt in search of Fenwick, who now enjoyed a headstart of several minutes.

As he passed through town, Morgan heard sirens. He knew Trey Kerrigan would find Fenwick's house empty and scramble his deputies to search for both of them.

Where would he go?

Morgan raced up the hill past the hospital, but as the highway crested, he could see ten miles down the straight road.

Fenwick hadn't run south. Cursing, Morgan screeched to a dusty stop on the shoulder and turned back toward town.

As he passed the hospital, he thought of Gilmartin. He looked at his watch. Over the stressed whine of the Escort's puny engine, he heard himself say: "Hold on just a little longer."

Suddenly, he was struck by something Fenwick had said, something about the choice he'd made at the crossroads. To the hospital ... or to the bridge.

The Iron Mountain Bridge was a good fifteen miles east of Winchester. He could take Highway 57 to Wilkerson Road, an unpaved county road that cut across the prairie and crossed the Black Thunder River on the way to Iron Mountain. The old railroad bridge, long ago converted to a one-lane car crossing, still stood almost seventy feet above the raging river, a grim marker for the spot where the frightened Simeon Fenwick had dumped Aimee's body into the raging water below.

He was there, Morgan knew.

Once he hit Wilkerson Road, Morgan could see a wedge of dust rising behind a car six or seven miles away. He stepped harder on the gas, but the car slipped sideways, nearly rolling across the shoulder into a mossy irrigation ditch. He was already going more than sixty; the car ahead was traveling even faster.

Within a few minutes, he reached the Black Thunder overlook, a few hundred yards from the bridge. As he rolled slowly toward it, he could see the dusty Buick in the center of the span. Its door was open but he couldn't see Fenwick. When he reached the southern end of the old steel bridge, he stopped.

"Fenwick!" he yelled.

There was no answer.

Morgan looked back down the road and saw nothing but buckskin-colored dust settling on the empty prairie. No deputies. Then he faced the Buick twenty yards away. His fingers ached. He couldn't wait.

He walked down the center of the narrow roadway. He could hear the river growling far below, now almost directly under him. Old boyhood fears about the place surged in him, and he felt almost unbalanced as he drew nearer the car.

It was still running. He heard a tiny electronic bell ringing because the door was open. As he moved carefully closer, he peered through the rear passenger-side window, but the back seat was empty.

Morgan cupped his hand against the window and looked inside. The front seat, too, was empty, except for a small wooden box.

As he walked around the front of the car, he heard Fenwick, speaking softly from somewhere above him.

"Don't come any closer," he said.

The old lawyer was standing on the guardrail, four feet above the road, hiding himself tightly against a steel beam. With one small step, he would plunge to his death. His tie remained neatly knotted beneath his weak chin.

"Don't move!" Morgan said.

"It was about here I threw her in," Fenwick said.

"Just don't move."

"I have had nightmares about it. Wondering if she knew she was falling."

Urine trickled down Fenwick's shoes and dribbled off the steel railing as a dark stain spilled across the front of his pants.

"Don't do this," Morgan begged him.

"I didn't mean to kill her. I *only* wanted her to like me."

"I know."

"Will you tell her mother for me? And Gilmartin?"

"You can tell her. I'll go with you to see them both."

"I thought the money would make this guilt go away. I have given them everything I had. It's all gone. How can they ever forgive me?"

"They will. But they'll want you to tell them. Please come down."

"You must tell them for me. I cannot face them. Not now."

"They only want to know. They have no more hate in them."

"That's good."

Fenwick teetered. Morgan took two anxious steps toward him.

"Stop!" Fenwick ordered. "I'll jump if you come closer."

"I won't," Morgan said, holding up his hands.

"There's a box on the seat. Get it."

Morgan walked slowly to the passenger side of Fenwick's Buick and got the wooden box he'd seen there.

"Open it."

He unlatched a tiny brass hasp and lifted the hinged lid. Inside was a piece of folded paper, stained watery brown.

"What is it?"

"Just open it."

As Morgan unfolded the delicate paper, a locket and chain fell out. It was the same one Morgan had seen around Aimee's neck in the photograph. The paper itself was the undelivered court order dissolving Fenwick's guardianship, dated 8/2/48. The ruddy discoloration on it was blood.

"I found the necklace in my car much later. I couldn't destroy it, though I often thought I should. Her mother should have it."

"Come with me and we'll give it to her."

"I made my peace with her daughter, you know. I took flowers to her grave and I told her how sorry I was. She understood."

"Her name was Aimee," Morgan said.

Fenwick whimpered. "They all had names, but it was easier not to know."

Morgan inched closer to the rail. If he could grab Fenwick's leg, he could wrestle him away from the brink. He didn't want Fenwick to die; his death now would serve no purpose except to frustrate the process of sorting out his crimes.

"Go back!" Fenwick screamed.

Morgan took a few steps backward, but was still close enough to lunge for the old man at the right moment.

"Listen to me," he said calmly to Fenwick. "You need to do the right thing. You need to be wise, like a judge. You must help us all understand. Judges do that. They help us understand what is right. We need you to help us understand."

Fenwick looked confused. "You need me?"

"Will you come down here, where we can talk?"

"A judge would do the right thing," Fenwick repeated aloud to himself.

"Yes. He would do the right thing."

Grasping the rigid beam with white knuckles, Fenwick leaned out to see the river below.

"The right thing," he murmured.

Then he simply stepped off the rail, into oblivion.

EPILOGUE

A ripe August moon lolled like a fat peach on the eastern edge of the prairie.

Morgan watched it rise from Neeley Gilmartin's hospital window. In a few hours, it would pour its light down the Black Thunder's steep canyon walls, illuminating the boiling whitewater and the foamy pools where a dozen men were still searching in the dark for Simeon Fenwick's corpse. It might be days before the angry river spit him up.

Neeley Gilmartin had not awakened. His breathing was shallower than before. He hovered near death in the soothing embrace of morphine, dripping into his veins like whispered words of comfort.

Morgan knew there could be no life without pain, any more than there could be dreaming in death. When his son died, a look of calm passed over him, like a soft shadow across the moon, even though Bridger had been comatose for several days before the end. His sleep had been full of pain.

"Mr. Morgan?"

Dr. Snyder stuck her head in Gilmartin's door. Her blond hair was pulled back in a ponytail and she was wearing jeans and a denim shirt.

"They paged me at home and told me you were here. I wanted to talk to you."

Morgan nodded. "I thought I'd stay with him. Is that okay?"

"Certainly," she said. She came inside and leaned against the door as it closed silently behind her. "Can we talk off the record?"

"Sure. What's up?"

Dr. Snyder spoke quietly. "The news you had for Mr. Gilmartin this morning, how important is it?"

Morgan searched Dr. Snyder's eyes for some glint of hope. She had stood in the way before and he wasn't sure he could trust her. "It would remove a great burden from his heart."

He told her Gilmartin's story. When he finished, her eyes were full of tears.

"There's something we can do, but it's got a downside," the doctor said.

"What could be worse than this?" He pointed at Gilmartin's wasted body.

A sterile silence settled between them. Dr. Snyder crossed her arms protectively in front of her before she spoke.

"There's a drug called Narcan. It's fast-acting and can counteract the morphine in his system, very briefly. It's mostly used in treating drug overdoses, and I am pushing the limits of medical ethics to suggest it in a case like this. But we can bring him around for two to three minutes. Long enough for you to tell him."

"What's the downside?"

Dr. Snyder touched Gilmartin's hand. "The morphine in his veins will be neutralized. He'll be in excruciating pain. It might kill him."

Morgan turned his back to her and watched the moonrise.

No life without pain, no death with dreaming.

"Do it," he said.

Dr. Snyder immediately called the attending nurse to the room. "Annie, bring me an amp of Narcan," she said.

The nurse looked confused. "Are you sure, doctor?"

"Just do it."

The nurse left the room, but was back within a minute with a small vial and a syringe.

"Draw point-four milligrams IV," Dr. Snyder ordered her. "Are you ready, Mr. Morgan?"

Morgan pulled a chair close to one side of Gilmartin's bed and held his hand. Dr. Snyder turned off the morphine drip and injected the Narcan in the old man's left arm. She pulled back her sleeve and looked at her watch for several seconds.

Almost a minute passed before Gilmartin stirred. Morgan leaned close.

"Neeley, it's Jeff Morgan. I have news."

"Wait," Dr. Snyder told him. "Just a few more seconds."

Gilmartin arched his neck, struggling for air. He tore at his oxygen mask and groaned, a deep and mournful cry that never passed his lips but rattled deep inside him. Finally, he opened his glassy eyes. They were unfocused and dilated.

"Now," Dr. Snyder said.

Morgan spoke quickly. "Neeley, it's Jeff Morgan. We have proof you didn't kill Aimee Little Spotted Horse. You've been cleared. Do you understand me?"

Gilmartin's eyes rolled back in his head as his body was wracked by a jolt of pain. Air gusted from his tumorous lungs as he tried in vain to fight it off.

"Neeley, did you hear me? It wasn't you. I'm sorry for everything, but it wasn't you. We cleared your name. Oh God, I'm sorry."

Gilmartin began to convulse. Monitors beeped frantically as his heart raced. Morgan held his hand tightly. Dr. Snyder re-opened the morphine drip.

"We'll keep it wide open for a few minutes to give him a bolus of morphine," she said, keeping a close eye on her wristwatch. "You've got less than a minute."

"Neeley, please hear me. You're free forever. You didn't do it. I know now. Everybody knows. You're innocent."

Gilmartin's body relaxed. He turned his head toward Morgan and opened his mouth. Nothing came out.

"Neeley, can you hear me? Show me."

He felt the old man's fingers tighten. His lips moved but made no sound.

"You've got to hear me! It wasn't you! It was Fenwick. Fenwick killed Aimee. He confessed. He's gone now. It wasn't you."

Suddenly, there was no more pain in the old man's face. His dry mouth curled in a fragile smile. With one hand, he touched his chest, at the top of his ribs just below his neck. His fingers searched for something beneath his hospital gown.

The Navy Cross. Morgan stood up and fished the medal out of his pants pocket, where he'd carried it since the young paramedic had given it to him. He pressed it into Gilmartin's hand.

But the old man pushed him away, and pointed weakly at him. Morgan knew what he meant.

"I will take care of it," Morgan promised him.

Gilmartin nodded. His eyelids began to flutter.

"Neeley, don't go!" Morgan said. He held the old man's hand tighter, the medal clasped between their hands.

The old man floated away, like a leaf on a cool stream. Morgan watched the muscles in his neck and shoulders slacken. He was nearly gone when his eyes opened again, a glimmer of life still there.

He mustered all the wind in his festering body to whisper. He strained to speak. Morgan put his ear next to Gilmartin's chapped lips. "Remember me," he said.

The morphine filled him again and he sank beneath the surface once more, drifting downstream, out of their reach.

That night, Morgan went home and called Kate Morning. He told her almost everything. He couldn't bring himself to say, over the phone, that her daughter had been brutally raped.

When she learned Gilmartin was near death, she wept on the phone. Not knowing what else he could say, Morgan said he was sorry for all her pain, promised to return her daughter's photograph soon, and hung up.

Old Bell Cockins was buried beside his wife, mother and father, beneath the sweet woodruff in Mount Eden's hidden pleasance.

More than three hundred townspeople paid their respects, many of them—like Cassie Gainsforth, who dropped one red rose on the casket—the secret beneficiaries of Old Bell's many kindnesses. Some came because they read Jefferson Morgan's touching story about Old Bell's life in *The Bullet*; others came because a small town cannot bury its dead the way it buries its secrets.

The Bullet had missed its weekly deadline and came out two days late, but devoted three full pages to the forever-entwined stories of Aimee Little Spotted Horse, Neeley Gilmartin, Old Bell Cockins and Simeon Fenwick. It overshadowed the second biggest story in town: Trey Kerrigan's withdrawal from the sheriff's race. Within a day, every copy was sold and advertisers were calling to reserve space in the next week's edition.

After a brief graveside ceremony, Morgan lingered behind. He poured some ashes from *The Bullet* in Old Bell's grave. A new building was already being planned on the site of the old one. Cal Nussbaum had even sketched a new backshop for himself, complete with computer ports and a long wall for his collection of nudie calendars. With any luck, *The Bullet* would be printed again in Winchester before the leaves changed.

After the mourners left, an unfamiliar man in a double-breasted charcoal suit sat beside Morgan on a garden bench overlooking Old Bell's fresh grave. The silver-haired man had a refined bearing, but Morgan saw a red rim around his eyes. He'd been crying.

"Are you Jefferson Morgan?" the man asked.

"Yes."

The man held out his right hand to Morgan. "My name is

Ty Clancy. From Cheyenne. I was Old Bell's lawyer. He was one of a kind, he was."

"He sure was."

"I grew up here and he put me through law school back in the late 'sixties. When he called me to do some legal work for him, I offered to do it for free, but do you think that crusty old fart would accept it? No way."

They sat for a moment in uncomfortable silence. The sun was bright and hot. The fragrance of roses wafted through the garden.

"You related to Hug Clancy?" Morgan asked, recalling Old Bell's special compassion for the old ballplayer.

"My grandfather. My dad named me after Ty Cobb, which really pissed off my granddad. He hated Cobb."

"Well, look on the bright side. He could have named you Rube," Morgan said, and they both laughed.

Ty Clancy cleared his throat and got down to business. "Look, Mr. Morgan, I'm here to wrap up Old Bell's estate," Ty Clancy said, pulling some documents out of his briefcase. "If you'd just sign off on some of these papers, I can get the probate started today."

"What papers?"

"The will and so forth."

Morgan was puzzled. "Why me?"

"Didn't Old Bell tell you?"

The lawyer looked for some hint of recognition in Morgan's wide eyes, then he just laughed. "Jesus Christ! He didn't tell you."

"Tell me what?"

"That son of a bitch."

"What?"

"Old Bell called me three days before he died and changed his will. He doesn't have any heirs so, pretty much, you get it all. This whole place is yours free and clear. And minus taxes, the loan pay-off and a couple of small endowments, you get most of, let's see ..." Clancy flipped through several legal-sized papers. "You get most of one-point-eight million bucks in trust, and half a million in life insurance. That part's tax-free, you know."

Morgan felt unsteady, but Clancy continued.

"Old Bell also provided that in the event of his death, the estate would pay the balance of your loan on the newspaper. He was very specific about this when I talked to him last week. He said he didn't want you to be—let's see if I can remember his exact words—'at the mercy of peckerheads.'"

Morgan couldn't speak. He just shook his head as he tried to read the documents Clancy shoved before him. It was a blur.

"One more thing," the lawyer said, handing Morgan a sealed envelope as he stood to leave. "He wanted me to give this to you. Hell if I know what it is. I'll file these papers up at the courthouse today and we'll be in touch."

Morgan waited until he was alone again in Old Bell's magnificent garden, then opened the envelope. Inside was a short, handwritten note.

> "If you're reading this, then you've probably already written my obituary and you know I'm dead. If you got scooped, I'll haunt you forever.
>
> "Please tend my mother's garden and take care of my newspaper. Both require a heart that knows how the seasons change, an eye that sees beauty where there is only barrenness, and a mind that accepts only the possibility we are utterly wrong about everything.
>
> "That said, I cannot resist a few last instructions to the new editor: Meet your deadlines. Have the courage of your convictions. Always put your money where your heart is. And if your mother says she loves you, check it out."
>
> Belleau Wood Cockins

***

Claire returned to Winchester the next day on the afternoon flight into Blackwater. Morgan embraced her as she emerged from the jetway, never wanting to let her go again.

On the way home, she cried when he told her about Old Bell's bequest, happy and sad at the same time. And after a long silence, she asked Morgan if there might be a place in Old Bell's garden for Bridger's ashes. Then he cried, too.

When they arrived, they were astonished to find Kate Morning sitting on their front porch. She'd come to visit Gilmartin, to cleanse her own heart of the misplaced hatred she'd felt for him for most of her life.

Together, the three of them went to the hospital to see him.

Gilmartin had wasted away. He was a living skeleton, suspended between life and death by tubes and electronics, unaware that he even existed.

Kate hung a small dream-catcher over his bed. Aimee had made it long ago, and Kate had saved it. For what was left of Gilmartin's life, it would capture the good in his dreams.

Before they left, Kate spoke privately to Dr. Snyder. When they were finished, the doctor came to Morgan and Claire with tears in her eyes.

"If you still wish to take him home, you can," she said.

"What's changed?" a startled Morgan asked her.

"Mrs. Morning is a nurse and she says she will stay with him until the end, if you approve."

Morgan looked at Claire, who agreed immediately.

The ambulance brought Gilmartin to the bungalow on Rockwood Avenue later that night. The paramedics made him as comfortable as they could on a rented bed in the living room, delivered a few final instructions from Dr. Snyder, and left.

Morgan stayed beside him until dawn, dozing off occasionally. In one of his dreams, Gilmartin was a young man again, walking off across the prairie toward the edge of the earth, free. Several times, he'd wake up and listen for the sound of Gilmartin's arduous breath, the only sign that he still clung to life.

Morgan balanced between waking and sleep until the morning sun came through the front window and warmed them both. It was the sound of sparrows in the trees outside that woke him. A dog barked somewhere. But he heard nothing else.

He touched Gilmartin's cold hand.

He was gone.

Neeley Gilmartin died on a Wednesday, having never awakened again.

That afternoon, Morgan took the old man's money and paid his hospital bill. What was left, a little more than seventeen thousand dollars, he put in an envelope for Celestina and her fatherless children.

Morgan had arranged for a military burial at the Black Hills National Cemetery, not far from the long-gone railroad town where Gilmartin had been born seventy-three years before. A Navy honor guard escorted the old man to his grave among the orderly ranks of white headstones, and fired a salute while a bugler sounded taps. A Navy captain gave Claire the freshly folded flag and she hugged it tightly.

Kate Morning wiped away her tears and put a garland of yellow tickseed on Gilmartin's casket.

High above them, a red-tailed hawk circled against the azure sky, riding a column of rising warm air.

Free.

TO THE READER

The *USS Terror* (CM-5) was an authentic American warship in the Pacific Theater during World War II. In the smoky dawn hours of May 1, 1945, off Kerama Retto, a Japanese kamikaze slipped through the minelayer's defenses and crashed into the communications deck. Its two bombs exploded after impact, killing 41 and wounding 123. To this day, seven sailors are missing in action from the May Day attack, according to the Dictionary of American Naval Fighting Ships (*Navy Department*). In 1971, the *USS Terror*, winner of four battle stars in World War II, was sold for scrap.

A writer might sit alone, night after night, in his dark office, tapping out a story, but few stories would find their way to your hands without the help of many others.

The author wishes to thank **Deb Michaels**, one of the good lawyers, and Sheriff's Lt. **Rod Warne**, who knew how to make this crime pay. Also, **Tim McCleary** of Crow Agency, Mt., a delightful spokesman for Crow Indian culture; **Dr. George McMurtrey** and **Warren "Stretch" Bohnet**, healers who could imagine as well as I; and my friend, **Larry Smith**, who works at a ranch. And, of course, to my editor, **Dorrie O'Brien** at Write Way Publishing, who put this book on the shelf where you found it.

Three people made sacrifices bigger than all the rest: My wife **Ann** and my children, **Ashley** and **Matthew**. They graciously allowed me the time and the space to tell this story, and seldom complained.